The Crystal

By

Sandra Cox

The Crystal by Sandra Cox

Formerly published by Ellora's Cave

The Crystal by Sandra Cox

Dedicated To:
Randy and Janet Blanchard

To you, the reader, thank you.
Your support is appreciated.

Prologue

The stone was the size of a large man's fist.

Tamarilla, princess of the fairies, touched the fiery emerald in passing as she fluttered back and forth, her feet not touching the floor. Incandescent sparks of light flashed from her wings as they twitched in agitation.

"The Future Stone has belonged to the women of my family for generations to prophesy and to foretell their lover," the princess told a wizened old woman sitting against a masonry wall.

"Zan, the prince of elves, is only marrying me to get his hands on my stone. To unite the kingdoms, my father is going along with it."

Tamarilla stopped pacing and stared wistfully at the flawless emerald, yearning for a vision of a young and handsome leman. With a heavy sigh, she straightened her shoulders and put away the dreams of youth. Her lips, likened by many to rose petals, thinned into a straight line.

"Zan will not use it for good, can't my father see this?"

Her heart thudded against the wispy confines of the gown she wore, as if it would tear free of her body and fly away from the restrictions of royalty. She sighed at the fanciful thought then turned to the old woman. "I know my destiny is to marry Zan, that I will never have true love. I have foreseen it in the stone. I accept it. With royalty comes responsibility. But how do I protect the stone for the women of my family who are to come? Hundreds of years from now my descendants will be mortal. The fairy line will die out. I have seen this too in the stone. Somehow, I must keep it safe for them, safe from Zan."

She knelt beside the woman who, in Tamarilla's seventeen years of life, had been her nurse, teacher and wisewoman and put her head in the old woman's lap. *"What shall I do, Nimue?"*

Nimue touched the glittering strands of hair that fell like sheaths of gold over her faded purple skirt. *"Be brave little one and embrace your destiny with dignity. Zan is not a bad elf. But he is a male. And they all have their failings."*

The old woman stood and raised the princess to her feet. *"Get up child. I will protect the stone for your line."*

"How?"

"Watch," the nurse commanded, in a voice she had never used before. Electricity crackled around her. She stretched out her arms, pointed her long bony fingers at the stone and began to chant:

"Stone of light, stone of wealth,
May the seed of this child's future dwell.
Only Women of her line
May see their true love in their time
Exception of the spell is this
The Chosen's mate shall know stone's bliss."

As Nimue chanted a mist began to form in the room, purple and blue swirls of smoke danced through the chamber. The haze thickened. It formed and reformed, swirling faster and faster, until it settled around the stone.

Outside, the sky grew dark as a wild green and black storm rolled in. Loud booms of thunder shook the room. A brilliant bolt of lightning shot through the open window. Like a thrown spear, it cut through the purple-blue mist, straight to the emerald.

Then all became still.

Tamarilla blinked and crossed her arms to control the trembling that shook her body.

From outdoors, she heard the tentative chirp of a wren. She glanced at the window, surprised to see sunlight once more pouring through. The black and green fury of the storm *magically dissipated, being replaced by fluffy white clouds and a soft blue sky.*

The purple and blue mist blanketing the room dissolved.

The princess looked at the table and froze as fear and shock coursed through her. The Future Stone gone!

In its place sat a green crystal ball.

"What have you done? Where is my emerald?" she cried.

"I was once the lover of the great Merlin himself. He taught me much magic," the old nurse explained. "Your Future Stone is safe. Look closely at the crystal."

Frightened, the princess forced herself to approach it. She reached her hand out stopping just inches from the beautiful orb.

"Go ahead," Nimue urged her. "It knows your touch like a lover's."

Tamarilla leaned forward and traced its surface with her index finger. Her eyes widened and she smiled then encircled it with both hands, throwing her head back, arching her neck and closing her eyes in ecstasy. As she held the stone, colors inside it began to swirl with a life of their own.

Feeling the globe pulsing in her hands, the princess opened her eyes and gazed in wonder as the swirls formed a pattern and the pattern became a child, a child that looked exactly like her.

Nimue's voice was gentle. "You will never know the wild excitement that comes from carnal knowledge of your one true love, but you will know contentment and love of a child that is purer than the love of a man. Your life will not be a maelstrom of passion but you will know quiet fulfillment. You and your king will reign in peace for many years. And that is a better legacy than many are given."

The princess studied her offspring. "And my beautiful

child?"

Nimue smiled. "She will know love and passion. She will have a good life."

Tamarilla tapped her shell-pink fingertips against the crystal. In its center lodged the emerald known as the Future Stone. "And this?"

"It shall be as you wished. Passed down from generation to generation to the women in your family, who will see their true love in the stone."

"And if it's stolen?"

"It will find its way home."

"What if the globe is broken and the stone stolen?"

"No one, not even a family member, can break through the protective orb."

Tamarilla stared fascinated. "What about women outside my family?"

Nimue laughed. "Oh, child you were always one for questions. Only those of your direct line, those that mingle their blood with that of your direct line, or the children added by love to your line—the chosen ones—or their mates will ever be able to see the magic contained in the globe. Now come, it is time for the engagement ball."

Chapter One

Springfield, IL

The wind keened and rain blew down in liquid sheets. Gabriella Bell clapped her hands over her ears and blinked as thunder boomed and lightning lit the sky.

She had forgotten her umbrella, again. Head down, she turned the corner and ran full tilt into the arms of a stranger.

"I'm sorry," Gabby mumbled into an expensive, camel-colored raincoat, her nose pressed against a hard chest.

Long arms wrap around her, steadying her. For a moment the clean smell of rain mingled with the scent of expensive aftershave and crisp cotton, before the man gripped Gabby's upper arms and thrust her away, holding her at arm's length.

Icy green eyes, colder than the wind stinging her skin, stared into her own. His rain-darkened hair was drawn back in a ponytail and beads of water glistened on his coat.

"May I suggest you watch where you're going?" The stranger stared down his nose at her, his voice brusque, his manner arrogant. Letting her go, he walked away.

She stared after him, as he wove through the throng of pedestrians with the lithe grace of a cat. Still feeling the heat of his hands, she rubbed her forearms as she watched him disappear into a sea of umbrellas.

Determined to forget the whole unsettling encounter, she wiped the rain from her eyes and made a dash for a small store, with a purple awning, a few yards away.

Reaching the awning, she pressed past a couple standing under it and stepped inside.

Her sandals squished and puddles formed at her feet. She'd stepped into one of the popular little novelty shops that lined Main Street. Crystals glittered and winked. Pewter moons hung from the ceiling on silver chains.

Bags of dried plants and herbs lined one wall. She picked up a little plastic bag and sniffed…lavender. She put it back and glanced at the jewelry counter. Stars and pentagrams gleamed against black velvet.

Starting toward the counter to get a closer look at the jewelry, she paused as she caught a glint of color out of the corner of her eye. Shifting, she craned her neck to see, but the tinted shimmer disappeared. Curious, she walked in the direction the flash of green came from.

A row of black capes blocked her view. She pushed them aside and stared into the shadowy corner. Hidden in the gloom, was a sea-green crystal ball. It stood in solitary splendor on an antique claw-footed stand.

She took a step forward and ran her index finger along its smooth surface, the globe toasty warm against her damp skin.

Drawn, she splayed her fingers until her palms nestled around it. A delicious wave of heat ran through her, like sitting in front of a crackling fire on a cold winter day.

Ecstasy coursed through her body.

Transfixed, she watched glowing green change to blue, its hues dancing and sparking like moonbeams on the water.

The crystal pulsed beneath her hand.

By degrees, the feeling of warmth disappeared and fear crept in. Her breath hitched as the color in the crystal fell away and a face formed. Its blurred outline moved back and forth, wraithlike and then sprang into sharp focus.

The blood drained from her face, as her nerveless fingers dropped from the ball. The face in the globe belonged to the hard-eyed stranger she'd bumped into outside the shop only moments before.

Taking a hasty step back, she jostled against the row of hooded capes, knocking them over. One of her heels caught in the slippery velvet. As she threw out an arm to catch herself, she hit one of the pewter moons hanging from the ceiling. The momentum of her hand sent it clanging in a cacophony against another, setting off a chain reaction as she sat down abruptly in a pile of black velvet.

Her breath came out in a sharp gasp, as she tried to disengage herself from the pile of capes.

"Here, miss, what are you doing?" A myopic young man hurried toward her, his glasses down on his nose.

"I err, tripped." Her teeth chattered like castanets. She wasn't about to admit she'd just had the hallucination of a lifetime.

With a surprisingly strong grip, the clerk yanked her up. As soon as she was on her feet, he dropped her clinging hands and began picking up the capes.

A long shudder ran down her spine. She cut her eyes toward the crystal, once more a calm sea green.

She rubbed her eyes. Had she imagined it?

With a hand that had a decided tendency to shake, she pointed toward the crystal.

"How do you do it? How does that thing work?"

The clerk gave her an odd look, before going into his spiel.

"When the lunar pull of the moon hits the emerald ball," he intoned, "it comes together pulling the stress of the day from its beholders."

"Hogwash."

"You asked."

"I'm not talking about your rehearsed stress relieving thing. I'm talking about the other thing."

"What other thing?"

"You know." She narrowed her eyes and jerked her head in the direction of the crystal like a bad actor in an espionage film.

"Oh, the other thing," he nodded. He looked around and said in a low voice, "I'm not at liberty to discuss it."

She frowned, impatient. Mr. Myopic had no clue what she was talking about. It was pretty obvious no one had leered at him from the crystal. "How much?" she heard herself say.

"Sorry, we're holding it for someone." He pushed his glasses up to the bridge of his nose with his index finger.

No. No one else can have that globe! A wave of panic swamped her. She swallowed it down then batted her baby blues at the clerk and gave him what she hoped was an ingratiating smile. "I'm sure you can get him another one. How much?"

The clerk's expression turned crafty. "Five hundred."

"Five hundred dollars! Why I've seen the very same thing in catalogues for $39.95." *Well, maybe not exactly the same.*

The clerk crossed his arms and curled his thin lip. "Then order one."

Her shoulders sagged in defeat. The clerk had her and he knew it. "Do you take credit cards?" *What the hell am I doing?*

But even if she'd been hallucinating, she had to have that globe. Regardless of what had caused the phenomena, regardless of the cost, she wanted that crystal.

She couldn't even explain it to herself. For one brief moment, when she held it, the globe had been a part of her, had flooded her brain and coursed through her blood with more intensity than a sexual climax. And then she'd seen the stranger...

The young man's smile of triumph jerked Gabby out of her reverie.

He took the globe and carried it carefully to the front, where he wrapped it in tissue paper covered with silver stars and placed it in a silver box.

Gabby fumbled in her purse then handed him her credit card, praying to the gods that watched over fools and angels—and there was no doubt which category she fell in—that it didn't exceed her meager credit line.

He ran her card through then gave her a slip to sign.

She signed it in a fever of impatience.

The clerk placed the boxed crystal ball in a shopping bag, marked in purple lettering "Earth Religions" and handed it to her.

Clutching the bag, she rushed out of the store. The deluge had slowed to a misting rain. Oblivious to the damp, she hurried along the sidewalk gripping her prize.

The clerk whistled out of tune as the proprietor, a heavyset, balding man, came out of the backroom.

"Did I hear someone, Albert?" The proprietor reached over and straightened the row of perfectly arranged jewelry.

"I just sold that old globe your friend brought in for five hundred dollars, Uncle Nigel." He held up his hand, his manner smug. "I know. You said we were just holding it for him and that was why you put it in the corner where it wouldn't be noticed. But five hundred bucks! We'll just give him one of those $19.95 crystals we've got in the back and he'll never know the difference."

The man's color turned ashen. "You did what?"

* * * * *

Christopher Saint turned his coat collar up and burrowed into it, blinking against the sharp pricks of rain hitting his face and running down the front of his three-quarter length raincoat. He'd found the green crystal.

Standing on the sidewalk, he stared into Earth Religions, the store name emblazoned in gold across the large, front windowpane.

As he watched, the proprietor, one Nigel Robey, walked

to the window and glanced up at the overcast sky. Robey wiped the glass, peered through and frowned as the rain ran in rivulets down the street gutters.

As the big man's head swung in his direction, Christopher turned and walked away, blending with the other pedestrians in a sea of raincoats and multicolored umbrellas. It had been over a year since that little altercation between him and Robey over a yellow diamond.

Maybe Robey would recognize him maybe he wouldn't. But why take a chance?

His brow wrinkled. What or who was the equating factor that put Robey and Leaky in the same formula? Leaky, a small-time thief based out of New Orleans, had stolen the crystal and shipped it to Robey, who sold illegal antiquities from all over the country, his front, a shop that catered to mystics.

Quite ingenious really, who would think to look for a crystal ball stolen in New Orleans in an occult shop in Springfield, Illinois? A shadow of a smile crossed his face.

Who, that is, besides himself.

He had been about to retrace his steps and watch the shop—Robey had to leave sometime—when a statuesque blonde came barreling into him. It would have been a pleasurable experience if he didn't have more important things on his mind. The supple, wet body that slammed against him fit his length like a tailored suit. He plucked her off, with a directive to watch where she was walking and kept going.

Glancing over his shoulder, Christopher saw the blonde enter Earth Religions.

He cursed under his breath. She was the kind of woman one automatically noticed and, if Christopher was any judge of human nature, and he was, one with a temper. He hadn't missed the spark in her eye or the upward thrust of her chin at his curt demeanor. He didn't need her calling attention to him by accosting him in public for his rudeness.

But he was nothing if not patient. He would come back tomorrow and take a careful look around the shop, check out the number of exits and the alarm system. Christopher clenched his jaw and thrust his fists into his coat pockets. No one would keep him from getting the crystal.

The crystal had been in his family for several generations. And in some quarters, particularly among those folks who believed in mysticism and magic, considered priceless.

He didn't personally believe all the malarkey about seeing your lover's face in the ball, but his Aunt Tam did. She insisted that she'd seen her beloved Edward's face in it.

The thought of his fey relative loosened his clenched jaw. His Aunt Tam, a birdlike creature many would have termed crazy, if she hadn't come out of her perpetual preoccupied state long enough to fall in love with a very rich man when she was young. And since the young man completely reciprocated her feelings they had married.

So Aunt Tam went from being that crazy Werner girl to the eccentric Mrs. James.

There was only one person in the world Christopher cared about and that was Aunt Tam. And now Leaky had stolen her crystal. The man was either incredibly desperate or incredibly stupid. Whichever, Christopher intended to point out the error of his ways.

His mind roamed back to the first time he'd met Tamara James. The meeting had become a bedtime story she had told him over and over again while he was growing up. Out of all the children in the world, she would say, they had chosen him to be their little boy and that made him special, the chosen one. His hands deep in his pockets, he fingered the ring on his right hand with his thumb, remembering the story.

The James were traveling in Calcutta, when a half-starved Anglo-Saxon child cut Tamara's purse strings and took off down a side alley. If Uncle Edward hadn't been in top physical form and the boy weak from hunger, he would have never been caught.

There was something about the boy's tough demeanor that appealed to Edward James. Even though the man was in his prime and the boy malnourished and small, he'd still been ready to fight.

But it was Aunt Tam who'd seen the scared little boy beneath the exterior of the scrapper. And since she and Edward had been married for over ten years and their union had never been blessed with a child, they took the young boy in.

They questioned him extensively. But all he remembered was a dark-haired woman who disappeared a long time ago. They made discreet inquiries at the embassy, but turned up nothing. It was only too clear he was a street brat.

A charm in the shape of a tiger had hung from a thin silver chain around his neck. The cat's eyes were simple green peridots. The charm's origins, like his, were a mystery.

The blast of a car horn brought him back to the present. He shook his head to clear it of old memories. That life had ended and a new one begun twenty-odd years ago. Edward had since died, so now it was just Christopher and his aunt.

She had explained when she took him in, she had no intention of supplanting a woman she was sure loved him and so became Aunt Tam instead of his mother.

Pulling his right hand out of his pocket, he glanced at it. The cat on his finger stared back at him, its eyes glittering in the gloom. On his twenty-first birthday, Aunt Tamara had the charm made into a ring. The peridots had long since fallen out and had been replaced with emeralds.

Christopher grinned sardonically, the ring actually quite

symbolic. Polite society knew Christopher Saint as an extremely eligible bachelor and an indolent playboy.

The Tiger, as he was known to the underworld, was a master cat burglar. Ah well. You could take the boy out of the slums. But you couldn't take the thief out of the boy.

Chapter Two

Clutching the handle of her Earth Religions bag in one hand, Gabby fished inside her jacket pocket for her key with the other, anxious to see if the globe phenomena would repeat itself.

On the other side of the door, she heard barking overshadowed by the high-pitched yowl of a cat.

"I hear you." She unlocked the steel screen security door then braced herself and pushed open the interior door.

She wasn't a small woman, but the combined greeting of a sixteen-pound Siamese and seventy-pound brown Chow-Sheepdog mix was enough to stagger her.

"Yes, I'm aware you're starving," she told the complaining Siamese, weaving between her ankles.

"And that you have an urgent need to go outside." She patted the large brown head of the dog butting against her, his tongue hanging out, his bushy tail waving hard enough to stir a small breeze.

She set her prized possession on her secondhand coffee table then let Ned out into the small backyard, enclosed with chain-link fencing, and fed the cat.

When peace once more reigned, she sat down on the living room floor. Leaning back against the faded blue sofa, that Jericho considered his personal scratching post, she rolled her hips from left to right trying to get comfortable on the thin, frayed carpet.

She plucked brown hairs off her capris then picked up her package. Tissue paper rustled as she pulled out the ball.

Closing her eyes, she let the tingling warmth of the crystal seep through her fingertips and up her arms. When she opened them, the color inside the ball had once again begun to swirl and churn, turning a beautiful aquamarine.

18

She stared fascinated. It was like watching the pitching waves of the ocean during a storm. As she watched, the stranger's face began to materialize. The face in the globe seemed to sneer at her.

"GAAABBYY." The voice from the hall sent her heart thumping in her throat as she fumbled the globe.

"In here. Don't you ever knock?"

Her friend Amy tossed a set of keys onto the couch. "Not when you leave your keys in the door." She brushed halfheartedly at the cat hair in a cushioned, white wicker chair, and settled into it.

"Whatcha got?" Amy, dressed in a black silk shirt that set off her flaming red hair and designer black pants that couldn't have been larger than a size two, held out her hands.

Reluctant to let go of her treasure, she was also curious. Would Amy see the stranger in the globe? Curiosity won out. With a firm grip, she handed the ball to her friend. "Be careful with it."

"Cool." Amy studied the globe. "Are you throwing a party and going to have parlor games?"

Gabby ignored the question. "What do you see in it?"

Amy hunched over the crystal. "I see a tall, dark stranger," she intoned.

Deep in thought, Gabby closed her eyes. Dark, she really hadn't thought of him as dark. Tanned, yes, and wet hair that reminded her of a lion's mane. "And with a definite sneer about his mouth," she supplied, opening her eyes.

"Hey, if you want to be original, it's okay with me. 'And with a definite sneer about his mouth'," her friend parroted. "I'll tell the fortunes all right?" Amy pursed her glossy, coral-colored lips. "I'll call myself Madame Sasha. I'll wear a veil and a long flowing dress."

She tapped her chin with a coral-tipped manicured nail. "No, on second thought you can tell the fortunes. I know just

19

the costume to set off your, shall we say, attributes." Amy grinned at her best friend.

Gabby gave an inelegant snort. "Not in this lifetime. Don't you see anyone in the crystal?" She gave an involuntary glance at the globe. It looked like an ordinary green crystal ball. No churning colors. No stranger's face sneering at her

Amy winked at her. "I just told you. I saw a tall, dark stranger, with attitude.

"When's the party?"

She reached over and took the globe, relieved that her best friend hadn't seen the bad-tempered stranger in the crystal, though, why she wasn't sure.

Unease followed on the heels of relief. Why was she the only one seeing him? She was certain the store clerk hadn't seen anything. If he had thought the globe was a paranormal phenomenon he would have tacked a few more zeroes onto the asking price.

"I'm not having a party and I'm sure as hell not using my crystal to tell fortunes." Gabby hugged it to her as if it were her firstborn.

"Then why did you buy it?" Amy gave her a knowing look. "You hit a sale."

"Not exactly."

Amy tilted her head to one side, studying her. "How much?"

Gabby swallowed. Phenomenon or not for her it was a lot of money. "Five hundred."

Amy's eyes widened. "You paid five hundred for a crystal ball? Honey, you got took. You could have ordered one on line for $39.95."

Amy snapped her fingers. "You're working on a story, aren't you?" She nodded sagely. "Tax write-off, very wise."

Gabby was a freelance reporter, a struggling freelance

reporter. So far she'd sold a total of three stories. But they had been good ones she consoled herself.

She chewed on her lower lip, thinking. Amy was right. There just might be a story here. Probably, "Reporter goes mad and sees man of her dreams in crystal ball."

Though, he was hardly the man of her dreams, she corrected herself.

"Am I right?"

Amy's question brought her back to the present.

Gabby arched her brows and leaned toward Amy. "Can't fool you for a minute."

Ned, scratching at the door, howled to be let back in.

Amy pushed out of the chair. "I'll let the mutt in."

"Just a minute!" Gabby grabbed the discarded tissue paper, nested it in a sandstone bowl sitting on the coffee table and placed the crystal inside it. Picking the bowl up, she carried it to her battered bookcase and sat it down.

She stared at the globe, tapping her finger against her lips. *I'm going to learn your secret. Contrary to gypsy fortune tellers, faces do not appear in crystal balls.*

"Okay?" Amy asked, breaking into her thoughts.

"Okay."

Amy went to the kitchen and opened the back door then nimbly stepped back as Ned galloped in. His tongue hanging out the side of his mouth, he made a beeline for his beloved mistress then went to play with his pal Amy.

Amy complied for a few minutes then headed for the door. "Got to go. Let me know when the party is."

"Umm," Gabby responded in an absent manner, her friend already forgotten. As she stared at the globe nestled in the bowl, she fought the urge to touch it. "What hold do you have on me?"

As if it mocked her, the globe remained silent, an inanimate object devoid of brilliance or changing color.

* * * * *

The bell overhead jingled as the old man pushed open the door of Earth Religions. With an irritable gesture, he pushed stringy gray hair out of his face. Hunching his shoulders, he leaned on his cane and shuffled across the floor. *Tap. Tap. Tap.*

The clerk glanced up from behind the counter then turned his attention, back to his paperwork.

The newcomer leaned heavily on his cane causing the tapping to increase in volume. "Young man."

He received no response.

"Young man." The newcomer let a peevish note slip into his voice.

Not looking up, the clerk said, "I'll be with you in a minute."

The old man raised his cane. "I bet a sharp rap alongside your noggin will get your attention you young whippersnapper." He smiled in satisfaction as the clerk's head jerked up and his eyes widened behind the thick lens of his glasses. The salesman jumped backward bumping into the wall.

"Now that I have your attention, the green globe I saw in the corner yesterday, it's gone."

The young man frowned, his back and the palms of his hands still pressed against the wall. "I don't remember you being in the store yesterday."

"That's probably because you were too busy ogling that long-legged blonde." The old gentleman wiggled bushy gray eyebrows and winked, his manner switching from threatening to conciliatory.

"Oh that one, not my type." He brushed his fingers through mousy-brown locks and tossed his head.

I bet she's not, you little toad. "She had a little too much of everything, too leggy, too much bosom," he agreed.

"Like a milk cow," the clerk muttered under his breath, propping his chin up as he leaned on the counter.

Milk cow. A surprising spurt of anger ricocheted through Christopher. His eyes, hidden behind the horn-rimmed glasses, narrowed before he forced himself to relax and shrug it off. So the obnoxious paper shuffler didn't care for the knockout blonde, so what? "Personally, I prefer someone with a more boyish figure," Christopher lied and placed his fingers over the clerk's.

The clerk pulled his hand away, but showed no signs of embarrassment.

Christopher's quirky sense of humor surfaced. *Prefer them younger and not so stringy do you?* "But that's neither here nor there, where's the ball?" His chin quivered with the tremors of old age as he pounded the floor with his cane.

The clerk winced, but put his elbows on the counter and leaned forward in a familiar manner. He jerked his chin in the air and sneered, "The heifer bought it."

Christopher stiffened as shock shot through him at the sale of the crystal, quickly followed by anger on the blonde's behalf. *Heifer now is it?* He rolled the cane between his hands in a considering manner. *The man, and that word was questionable, really needed a lesson in manners. No,* he thought with more than a tinge of regret, *he had more important things to do and it would hardly be a fair fight.*

In keeping with his role, his bushy eyebrows drew downward and he pursed his lips in disappointment.

The clerk hurried on, "There's plenty in the back that haven't been unloaded, if you'd like to see one."

Behind the querulous expression, Christopher's mind clicked rapidly. He tapped his lips with his index finger. "Yes. Yes. I believe I would."

The clerk nodded and disappeared behind the curtain separating the stockroom from the display area. The heavy black fabric dividing the two rooms made a soft swishing sound as it swayed then settled back into place.

Christopher looked around. The only other person in the store was looking at the herbs. He leaned over and thumbed through the papers on the counter. Yesterday's credit slips, perfect.

He glanced back over his shoulder. The woman still had her nose buried in the neatly little packaged bags of dried aromatic plants.

The papers rustled between Christopher's fingers. Ah. He smiled in satisfaction as he glanced at the ninth slip, *Gabriella Bell—Green Crystal Ball—Five hundred dollars.*

He snorted. *Five hundred dollars! The girl had practically stolen it herself. Robey must be beside himself.*

Minutes later, the curtain rustled as the clerk pushed aside the heavy black material. "This actually has more aesthetic appeal than that old antique that was sold yesterday."

He looked up. The old man was gone.

The doorbell tinkled and a young couple came in.

From the street, Christopher watched the clerk shrug and put a crystal ball in the same spot the original had been in. The clerk then fussed with a cape, straightening it, his head turned away from the window.

While the salesman busied himself with the cape, Christopher flagged down a taxi with his cane and hopped in the backseat. With a whine of the motor and a belch of exhaust fumes, the vehicle pulled away from the curb.

Fifteen minutes later, he shuffled into Springfield's most prestigious hotel, his head down, his shoulders bowed.

Reaching his room, he ran his key card through the lock. A green light flashed and he pushed open the door.

Stepping inside, he pulled off the wig and tossed it on the bed. Carefully, he pulled off the eyebrows and placed them in a brown calfskin attaché case.

He glanced at the colorful guidebook lying beside it, compliments of the hotel. Featured prominently on the cover was Abe Lincoln's tomb. In a smaller picture, near the top, was a depiction of endless rows of cornstalks.

He shook his head. *Only for his aunt would he have ventured into corn country. Not that there was anything wrong with living in the middle of a prairie, if you were a farmer.*

He peeled off his clothes and lowered himself into the Jacuzzi. Leaning his head back against the edge of the tub, he closed his eyes and let the steaming eddies of water, lapping against him, wash away his tension. He had his laptop in his attaché case. It would be the work of a moment to find out where Gabriella Bell lived.

He would need to make his move before Leaky or his pals did. The girl was irritating but he didn't want her roughed up.

A pair of long tanned legs danced tantalizingly through his mind. The effeminate clerk was a fool.

Chapter Three

Dusk gave way to dark. Streetlights softened the night casting a misty yellow glow on the gray sidewalks. Down the block a dog barked and another answered. No lights shone from the front of Gabriella Bell's small house.

She sat at her desk in her study, a converted walk-in closet, located off of her bedroom. She bent over her keyboard tapping at the keys. Pausing, she pushed her reading glasses up the bridge of her nose with her index finger.

Ned lay at her feet, his large woolly head resting on his paws, his tail thumping against the worn tan carpet. Jericho sat on the bookcase staring at her. It was time for his supper.

"Rrf." The Chow-mix gave a sharp bark and ran to the front of the house. A moment later, the doorbell rang.

"Damn." The brilliant idea for an article about illegal dog fights might not be so brilliant if she had to leave it and come back.

She ignored the bell and concentrated on the story. "Two gentle family pets were stolen from their backyard in broad daylight." The bell rang again. Clenching her teeth, she continued to type. "A brokenhearted child mourns…"

She closed her eyes trying to focus. She typed another couple of sentences then paused frowning, her fingers splayed on the keyboard. The doorbell had quit ringing, but Ned continued to bark. Someone was outside.

Hitting the save button, she grabbed her purse—spilling the contents onto the desk—snatched her mace and crept through the living room to the entryway.

Ned stood at the door, growling.

Waiting a heartbeat, she took a deep breath then drew back the chain and turned the lock on the interior door. The mace clenched in her left hand, she flipped on the porch light

26

then opened the door a crack. The security screen door was still locked. Feeling safer, she opened the interior door a bit wider.

On the other side of the security screen, a stranger stood blinking in the light, leaning toward the doorknob. As the man straightened, he slid a thin metal object into his pocket.

Ned stood beside her, his lips drawn back in a silent snarl.

The man jumped backward, his eyes on the dog.

Gabby tensed. At times like this, she appreciated every one of her seventy-two inches.

The man was as tall as she and big, with a large, crooked nose as if it had been broken at one time. Despite the chill in the air, beads of perspiration stood out on his forehead.

She raised her mace. "Breaking and entering is against the law. You've got two minutes to tell me what you want then I'm calling the cops."

He widened his eyes. "I have no idea what you mean."

She snorted. "You're down to a minute and a half. What do you want?"

He ran a hand across his balding head. "We got off to a bad start. I'm Nigel Robey and I'm looking for Ms. Gabriella Bell."

"You've found her." She glanced at her watch then into his eyes.

The stranger gave her a nervous smile, as he shifted from foot to foot. "Well, Miss, I'm the proprietor of Earth Religions. I believe my nephew sold you a green crystal ball."

Gabby nodded. "He did."

"Well you see, Miss, I'm afraid he sold it in error."

Gabby raised her left eyebrow, a trick she'd learned from her father when he was skeptical—usually at of one of her more inventive childhood deceptions. "In error?"

The man gave an artificial laugh. "Sounds silly, I know." The wind raised his thinning hair and he patted it back down. "Do you mind if I come in? I'll explain everything."

"Yes, I mind."

He shrugged. "Well, the thing is, my nephew was unaware I was holding it for a customer, a very important customer."

Her eyes narrowed at the bubble of panic in his voice. Whoever his customer was, this big brute of a fellow was afraid of him.

"I'll pay you what you bought it for."

She blinked in surprise. "It's not for sale."

"I believe you paid five hundred for it?"

"Yes. But as I told you it's not for sale."

"I'll give you a thousand." She blinked. A thousand dollars was a lot of money for an unknown journalist.

Rubbing her lip with her index finger, she rested her shoulder against the door.

There was a story here. She could smell it.

"It's not for sale," she repeated.

"All right, two thousand. But that's my last offer."

Two thousand? For one brief, wonderful moment, she thought about her charge card being paid off and having a small down payment on a new used car.

Staring at several moths circling the porch light, she let the image fade. There was a story here, she repeated to herself. And even if there wasn't, the globe held her in thrall.

"It's not for sale, at any price."

She knew what the man saw as his gaze traveled around the house's unpretentious exterior, white paint, fading to a dirty gray, peeling in several spots on the porch. His lips curled in a sneer. Then he looked her in the eye. "All right, miss."

She couldn't help it, she shivered. She could only hope

he would blame it on the wind.

Robey laughed, a raw unpleasant sound.

Reading the menace in his eyes, she straightened, her hand tightening on the doorjamb. Why did all these strangers have to have such cold eyes? But the message was clear. He intended to have that globe.

Robey looked at the mace, then the dog, his expression considering, as if weighing his odds. Just then a car door slammed and her neighbor came walking up his sidewalk.

"Lo, Gabby," he called.

"Hello, Bobby."

Gabby turned to the stranger. "I believe you were leaving."

"Another time."

She took a quick step back and shut the interior door, leaving him standing on the porch.

For several heartbeats, she stared at the door. Finally, a loose board creaked. She'd always meant to fix that board. Now, she was glad she hadn't.

The fur on Ned's ruff returned to normal, which meant it only stood up about eight inches instead of a foot.

She walked to the window and looked up and down the street, then gave a sigh of relief. The stranger gone.

Running to the phone, she picked it up and dialed, then with a sigh cradled the receiver. Unless it was a matter of life and death she had no intentions of involving the police. The last thing she needed was the boys in blue complicating her life.

Chapter Four

Exactly five days after her encounter with Nigel Robey, the fortunetelling party was in full swing. Amy had been so insistent about throwing it that Gabby, as usual, had given in. Since both Gabby and Amy had a wide circle of friends, Gabby's little house overflowed with enthusiastic revelers.

Her mind drifted from her guests back to Robey. For several nights, she'd started at any unusual sound, but as the days passed and she saw nothing further of the owner of Earth Religions, she began to relax. The proprietor must surely know if the globe disappeared, he would be the first person she'd blame.

The downside to this line of reasoning was that as long as he wasn't caught in the act he could always claim innocence, just an honest businessman trying to purchase an item that had been sold by mistake.

Though she'd bet her next paycheck that Nigel Robey had no idea how the Springfield police would frown on her home being broken into.

A crash from the living room brought her back to the present.

"Don't worry, I'll clean up the broken glass," someone yelled.

Standing at her tiny kitchen counter, she eyed another empty cheese tray while tugging at the plunging neckline on her gypsy getup.

She was going to murder Amy for sticking her with this bimbo outfit. Amy had picked it out, picked it up and dropped it off...when Gabby wasn't at home, of course. It had even come with a brunette wig.

With a sigh, that swelled her overly exposed bosom, Gabby filled the cheese tray, paper crackling as she ripped open the cracker pack.

She sprinkled wheat wafers around the little blocks of white and yellow cheese in the center of the plate, then spearing one of the yellow squares, popped it in her mouth, savoring the tangy taste of Wisconsin cheddar.

Feeling ill-used, Gabby plunked another handful of cheese squares in the center of the tray. The party was Amy's idea and she wasn't even here. Amy had promised to help, but at the last minute had backed out because she had a date with a divine stranger. So instead of doing prep work for the party, Gabby's best and most irritating friend had opted for getting a facial and her nails done at a pricey little salon that wooed its customers with new age music and glasses of white wine.

"Princess Amy," she muttered under her breath, then threw a couple more crackers on the tray, hoisted it over her shoulder and headed for the living room.

The smell of spilled beer permeated the air, causing her to wrinkle her nose. She snaked her way through the crowd, balancing the tray on the palm of her hand with the efficiency born of moonlighting as a waitress.

As she wound her way through the room, the doorbell pealed, rising above the noise of the revelers.

Ned barked and pushed his way through the crowd. Gabby shrugged. He stood a better chance of getting there than she did.

Reaching a little round table she'd picked up in a secondhand shop, she set down the tray. As she straightened, the door opened.

It was a good thing she'd put the tray down, because she would have dropped it.

Amy walked in, on the arm of the stranger she had bumped into in the rain...the stranger who kept sneering at her from her globe.

A stocky-built young man jostled her. "Sorry."

"No problem," she murmured never taking her eyes off Amy's date.

The man in her crystal ball was gravely listening to Amy, who was batting her eyelashes and flirting for all she was worth.

As if feeling the pull of her stare, he looked up.

Their eyes locked. The people and noise receded into the background. It was the weirdest thing she'd ever experienced. It was like the two of them were alone in the universe. She had read about this peculiar phenomenon, of course. When she wasn't reading murder mysteries, she was devouring romances. But she had always thought the phenomena greatly exaggerated. Boy, was she wrong!

"Gabby. Gabby." She heard a voice droning her name, but ignored it. She started walking toward the door.

As she watched, Amy tugged at his arm to pull him forward, but he stood his ground, waiting.

His obvious expectancy that she would come to him snapped her out of her trancelike state. "You! What the hell are you doing here?" She stopped in front of him, bound and determined not to acknowledge that strange magnetic pull that surged through her a moment ago.

"Oh, you've met." Amy smiled brightly, showing exquisite white teeth, whose orthodontia had cost her parents a bundle during her teen years.

"I don't believe so." The stranger's low, hypnotic voice drew Gabby like the pull of the moon.

Ignoring the tightening in the pit of her stomach, she gave him a brittle smile. "In front of Earth Religions. You nearly knocked me down. And you keep appearing in my damn crystal ball." She hadn't meant to add that, but she was glad she did. His eyes widened and color washed and receded from his face, before he quickly regained his composure.

"I beg your pardon?" He gazed down his nose at her as his left eyebrow rose. As it settled back to normal, he looked her over.

Much as one assessing a horse one planned to buy, Gabby thought with disgust.

His gaze lowered to her cleavage, skimmed her short skirt, wended down her tanned legs and red-tipped toes, then traveled back up and rested on her brunette wig and large hoop earrings. He grinned nastily.

Her face heated. No self-respecting gypsy would be caught dead in this getup. Damn it, this was all Amy's doing. She'd worn this goofy costume because she was supposed to tell fortunes. And there stood her best friend in a clinging turquoise jersey and white designer slacks, while she looked like an escapee from the circus.

The damn man wasn't helping much either, with his look of amused condescension.

His hair pulled back in a ponytail, he wore an expensive sports jacket over a green silk shirt that matched his cool eyes. Her gaze lowered to tight faded jeans and soft leather loafers. She'd always had a weakness for faded jeans on a well-built male.

She let her eyes travel back up his lean frame, looking at him as insolently as he'd eyed her.

With an almost imperceptible nod, he acknowledged the exchange.

"Are you telling fortunes?"

"How did you know?" her flighty friend asked, putting her tiny well-manicured hands around his hard biceps.

At least, if Gabby remembered correctly, they were hard. Hard arms, hard chest, flat stomach, she fanned herself with her hand. She was beginning to feel uncomfortably warm.

"Call it a hunch." His gaze remained on Gabby. "So where's the crystal ball?"

A prickling sensation at the base of her spine traveled straight up to Gabby's cranium. She'd had it three other times, all three times had turned into paying stories.

"And why would you be interested in my ball?" She watched him closely, her eyes narrowed.

He waved a languid hand around the room. He fit in with the rest of her friends about as much as a tiger did with housecats.

"I thought that's what this, err, party was about. We were to get our fortunes told. Or maybe I misunderstood. You read palms, perhaps?"

"How did you meet, Amy?" she countered.

Before he could respond, Amy burst out, "Darling, it was the wildest thing. We literally bumped into one another. And you know," she twitched her shoulders and tossed back her hair, smiling. "One thing led to another."

"Oh, really. All I got was 'a watch where you're going'"

"I'm afraid you have me confused with someone else," the stranger said.

Heat sparked behind her eyes. She didn't believe for one moment that he didn't remember her.

Amy looked from one to the other then said skeptically, "It's not like Gabby to forget a handsome face. But since there seems to be some confusion let me introduce you. Christopher Saint, meet my friend Gabriella Bell."

He took her hand and bowed over it in a European manner, then dropped it as a charge of electricity ran up her arm. "Charmed," he said in a bored voice.

"Likewise," Gabby replied flatly.

Either unaware of the antagonistic sparks flying around her or deciding to ignore them, Amy clapped her hands. "Gather round everybody. Gabby bought a new crystal ball and is going to tell our fortunes."

A mass of bodies surged forward, crowding eagerly

around the party's fortune teller.

Gabby held up her hands, laughing. "Just a minute, I have to get it."

His gaze bore into her back, making her shoulders twitch, as she walked through the open door into her bedroom. She'd bought a $24.95 crystal ball specifically for the party. But she knew in her bones he'd come to see her crystal and she wanted to know why.

Walking to the bookcase, she plucked it out of the sandstone bowl. Holding it protectively, like a mother cradling a child, she headed for the living room.

"Me first." Amy clapped her hands.

"Of course." Gabby heaved a resigned sigh.

She glanced at Christopher.Saint. He stood with his arms crossed, a sneer of distaste on his face.

She wasn't particularly excited about using her precious crystal to do parlor tricks either, but it angered her that this stranger stood there looking down his nose at her and her friends. Especially when it was at his instigation she'd brought the ball out. She felt certain he'd wanted to see it not play parlor games.

"Bring in a couple of the kitchen chairs," she called.

A couple of men, who'd been high school jocks, swaggered into the kitchen and returned stiff-arming the chairs over their heads. "For The Norse Queen and Princess Amy," Joe, the shorter one with freckles and red spiked hair said.

Gabby smiled. They had been dubbed that in high school and it had stuck through college.

Making a show of sitting down in her rickety pine chair, Gabby placed the ball on the coffee table in front of her. She gestured toward the other chair with a flourish.

"Princess Amy."

Amy nodded her head, gave a regal wave to her loyal

subjects and sat down then spoiled the effect by giggling and winking at Joe.

Gabby placed her hands on the ball. Heat and comfort surged through her.

"Well?" Amy demanded.

"I see a tall dark stranger. With a ponytail," she added.

Amy looked at her date flirtatiously.

He still stood with his arms crossed, his expression bored, his gaze on the ball.

"Go on," her friend urged.

Gabby complied, staring into the globe. "I see a marriage ring and six, no wait, seven children."

"Good God!" Christopher started out of his studied indifference. Someone standing nearby snickered.

Gabby bit back a giggle. He looked positively appalled.

Amy threw him a hurt look then brightened. She pulled on his sleeve. "Your turn."

He started to protest, but the people standing around laughed and pushed him forward.

Gingerly, Gabby put her hands back on the crystal. Her fingers began to tingle and the colors in the ball rushed together like waves. She closed her eyes and when she opened them, he was staring back at her from the crystal, his eyes cool.

"Well, Norse Queen, what is my future?"

The voice shattered her communion with the ball. Reluctant, she tore her gaze from the globe and studied the stranger. Even though his expression was bland and his voice light, Gabby could sense the tension running through him like lightning bolts.

When she glanced back down the spell was broken and the crystal was once more clear.

"Alimony payments."

A ripple of laughter broke out around them.

Christopher rose from his seat. He could not quite hide his relief at the dire prediction.

Gabby watched him through narrowed eyes. Just what had he expected her to say?

"It's been quite educational. Are you ready, Princess?"

"But we just got here," Amy protested.

"Ah, I thought you wanted to see my etchings or something equally quaint."

Amy brightened. She winked at Gabby.

Gabby pursed her lips and glowered at Amy, but her best friend appeared not to notice.

"Or something." Amy wrapped her hand around that hard arm.

Gabby looked at Christopher. "I'm sure you can see yourselves out."

Christopher smiled back nastily. "It's been a memorable experience, but I wouldn't give up your day job."

Amy giggled. "Of course not, darling, Gabby's a reporter."

Gabby could have sworn he paled.

"A reporter," he echoed in a hollow voice.

Chapter Five

A reporter, well wasn't that just dandy. Christopher sat on the side of his bed and yanked off his shoes, sending first one then the other hurling across the room. Reaching up, he pulled off his wig. His hair was the same tawny color of the hairpiece but much shorter. Without the wig, the hard planes and angles of his face appeared even sharper. He ran his hand through the thick tufts, sending them on end.

He'd known that woman was trouble the moment she cannonballed into him. He moved restlessly on the bed. Just thinking about the few moments her long supple body pressed against his made him tense and edgy.

Cursing, he jumped off the bed and stalked across the room.

Picking up the remote he sank into the plush couch cushions, pushed the button, and as the TV flashed into life grinned. Ms. Bell hadn't liked the idea of him having a *tête-à-tête* with her flaky friend one little bit.

Amy had clung like a barnacle. After they left the party, he'd had to plead a headache, like a damned debutante, to get rid of her.

But she had served her purpose. It had been almost laughably easy. He'd needed access to the Norse Queen's house. He smiled. The moniker fit. With that long blonde hair, statuesque build and haughty carriage she did resemble a queen of old.

Once he'd discovered Ms. Bell's name, it had been the work of a moment to track down her address.

He frowned. Unfortunately, there had been no mention of her reporting career when he traced her background. Some waitress work in nightclubs had been about all he'd dug up. She obviously wasn't a big name or he'd have heard of her.

He'd watched her house for a couple of days, seen her friend pop in and out and arranged an accidental meeting.

It would have been easy enough to just break in, but he preferred as few surprises as possible.

He now knew every room in her home and, most importantly of all, where she kept the globe. How ironic that it was in the bedroom. His brow wrinkled like corrugated cardboard. Why had the troublesome woman said she'd seen his face in the globe? Surely, she didn't know about the legend.

Restless, he stalked the length of his room then glanced at the clock on the desk. *Midnight.* Was the Norse Queen asleep yet or should he wait another hour before paying her a visit?

Well there was only one way to find out. He walked to his closet and pulled out a pair of black jeans and a black pullover.

He left the hotel, slipped into a rental car and turned on the ignition. With a purr of the engine, the automobile glided onto the quiet, dark street.

Fifteen minutes later, he parked the car on a darkened street a block away from Ms. Bell's house.

Turning off the car lights, he killed the motor and got out, the slam of the door unnaturally loud on the quiet street.

He heard a rustling in the shadows and whipped around.

"Mrrow."

He relaxed and his lips curved up as a big yellow tomcat strolled into the light.

"Headed for a midnight rendezvous are you?"

The cat gave him a disdainful look then disappeared into the dark.

Stealing down the street, he kept to the shadows. In a matter of minutes, he reached Ms. Bell's house. The curtains silhouetted her as she walked through the living room. Not in bed yet.

He grinned. She was still in her gypsy getup. That outfit was enough to turn a clergyman lustful.

At the sound of a car engine, he straightened. Beams flashed at the end of the block. The last thing he needed was to be caught loitering about after midnight. He walked quickly to the backyard fence. Ignoring the locked gate, he placed his palm on the cool aluminum rail, stuck his toe in the six-foot fencing and vaulted over.

He could hear the dog barking inside as he drifted into the shadows. The back door opened. Ms. Bell stuck her head out and looked around. Seeing no one, she shrugged and went back inside.

He watched the door close then leaned up against the old oak prepared to wait. The car that had turned onto the street slowed down in front of Ms. Bell's house then went on by. As Christopher listened, someone cut the motor. Two car doors   slammed. He slipped to the side of the house, waiting.

Minutes later, the gate rattled. A voice hissed, "What are you doing you idiot? You're making enough noise to wake the whole neighborhood. Go back to the car and wait for me."

Stretching, Christopher peered around the side of the house. "But, Mr. Leaky," a large man protested, "how are we supposed to get in? The gate's locked." He rattled it again.

"Go back to the car," a small wiry man hissed again.

Christopher nearly purred. Well, well, well, Leaky. Leaky was the son of a bitch who'd stolen the crystal to begin with. He smiled grimly. Apparently, word had gotten back to Leaky that one of his minions had screwed up…badly.

He shook his head. Thanks to him someone had sold Gabriella Bell a priceless crystal for five hundred dollars. He wondered if she had any possible idea of its worth.

Not likely since she was using it to tell fortunes.

His conscience had briefly bothered him about the intended theft, until he'd seen her using it like a gypsy with a crystal ball for God sakes!

The idiot, whom Christopher recognized as the shopkeeper, slunk back into the darkness.

Leaky pulled a small tool from his back pocket and picked the lock. He slipped through the gate and closed it behind him then crept toward the back of the house.

Christopher flexed his fingers and stepped out of the shadows. He was going to enjoy this. "Are you lost, Leaky? You seem a bit far from home."

The small man gave a violent start. Even in the darkness, Christopher could see him blanch. But then he had the eyes of a cat.

Leaky tried to bolt, but Christopher was too quick. With a panther-like leap, he reached out and wrapped his arm around Leaky's neck. "We have to talk." He drew his quarry into the shadows.

Sliding both hands up, he squeezed the jugular. "Now tell me, my little rodent, why you had the audacity to steal from me?"

Leaky gasped for air. "I didn't know it was yours, Saint, honest."

Christopher's fingers tightened.

Leaky pried at them to no avail. "A customer offered me a fortune for it, but I wouldn't have touched it if I'd known it was yours. You got to believe me."

Christopher shook him.

Leaky's head snapped back so sharply, that for a brief moment, he thought he'd broken the man's neck.

"Who?"

"Don't know," Leaky gasped out. "You know how the business works. Never any names. Just telephone calls and manila envelopes exchanged."

Christopher pressed him up against the house and smiled a wolfish smile. "Too bad for you, you didn't bother with a little more information."

His ring glittered like arcing green fireworks in the dark, as the back of his hand made contact with Leaky's face. The slap echoed through the night.

Leaky tasted blood before it trickled down his chin.

Even though a chill March wind blew, beads of sweat stood out on his forehead. The rest of his body cold and clammy, frozen with fear.

In the circle Leaky moved in, Saint was called The Tiger, though never to his face. It was said he once ripped out a man's heart while it still beat.

Leaky liked to think the story exaggerated, but regardless of whether it was true or fictionalized, The Tiger was not a man to cross.

Saint moved an arm against Leaky's throat and pressed him hard against the house.

A splinter dug through Leaky's shirt and lodged in his back.

Something silver glittered in the moonlight. A thin stiletto appeared in Saint's right hand.

The spit dried in Leaky's mouth as the knife hovered along his neck.

Before Leaky knew what was happening, the knife arched downward and Saint made a short slice on his arm then crossed it. Droplets in the form of an x beaded up on Leaky's arm.

Leaky forgot caution. "You cut me," he screamed.

The dog began to bark. Another dog down the street followed suit. The light on the porch stoop flashed on, creating a circular yellow glow in the dark.

Christopher grabbed him by the collar and drew him deeper into the darkness. He brought his face up against Leaky's. "Don't ever mess with me or mine again. Stay away from the crystal and the girl. Or next time I'll cut your heart out." Then he was gone, disappearing into the shadows. Moments later, the soft purr of an engine sounded down the block.

"Who's there?" Gabby called from the porch.

The dog went racing past her.

Leaky stood like a statue, frozen with fear—except for his galloping heart—the dog between him and the gate. His sense of self-preservation kicked in and he raced toward the fence that Saint had disappeared over moments before.

He jumped for the fence. *Rip*. His hindquarters stung as he vaulted over it. Inside the enclosure, a huge fuzzy mutt stood snarling at him, a piece of dark blue cloth dangling from his jaws.

He took off holding the flapping material covering his posterior. "Let's get out of here!" he hollered at Robey as he opened the car door and jumped in.

As the automobile raced away from the curb, he rubbed his stinging butt. "I hope you know a discreet doctor in this benighted burg because I'm going to need a tetanus shot for sure."

* * * * *

Gabby clapped her hands then whistled, a sharp, piercing sound that her neighbors wouldn't appreciate. "Ned. Come here, Neddy boy."

Ned came trotting out from the backyard, with something dangling between his teeth.

She squatted down and he came to her, wagging his tail and dropped his treasure into her lap. She held up the cloth. It was dark and coarse, material pants were made from. She began to shake. Someone had been lurking around her house.

43

"Good dog. Good, Neddy." She hugged the Chow-mix then straightened and looked around. In a voice that she hoped was firm, Gabby called out, "I'm going into the house, to call the police. If you are still out there I strongly suggest you get the hell out of Dodge."

Get the hell out of Dodge? Jeez oh Pete! Where had that come from? As if she didn't know! The colloquialisms that escaped her lips when she was under extreme stress could be laid directly at her father's door. Her dad was an old westerns buff and fascinated by the ten-foot tall sheriffs, who proudly wore their tin stars and stood unafraid in the middle of the streets, their legs splayed, ready to mete out justice to the bad guys.

Besides, if someone was still out there, Neddy wouldn't be standing next to her with his tongue hanging out, he'd be out in the dark, chasing the bad guys.

Ole Ned must be a bit of a sheriff fancier himself. She gave his fuzzy head a final pat. "Let's go in now."

One step inside and she nearly tripped over Jericho, sitting smack-dab in front of the kitchen door, complaining as only a Siamese can about being left out of all the excitement.

As soon as both animals were out from under her feet, Gabby locked and bolted the door, then ran through the house to the bedroom. She stopped in the doorway her eyes instinctively drawn to the bookcase where the globe rested in its bowl.

The crystal lay quiet. No churning waves of color swam about inside the circular orb. She walked over, picked it up and clasped it to her bosom. No one, but no one was getting her green crystal. The analytical portion of her mind knew she was becoming obsessed with the globe and knew as well there wasn't a damn thing she could do about it.

Holding her precious orb, she walked into the living room, stopped and sniffed. The faint scent of a man's cologne hung in the air. It had since the party.

She sniffed again. *Expensive and spicy.* She knew exactly who had been wearing it. For some reason she found the idea of Saint's scent in her home almost as disturbing as having an intruder in her backyard only in a much more elemental manner.

She gave a small humorless laugh, causing Jericho to stop in the act of cleaning the hind leg he'd hoisted in the air and look at her inquiringly.

"You could just tell by the condescending way he looked at all the poor fools at the party that he thought he was better than everyone else." She paced the floor. "He probably considers himself the greatest lover since Casanova. And if Amy tells me about her exploits and his prowess, I'll kill her."

"Meow. Meow."

"I am not being catty. No offense," Gabby told the cat.

To make matters worse, the globe chose that moment to reveal Christopher Saint's face smiling nastily at her.

She said a word her sainted mother, God rest her soul, would have considered highly improper. Holding it at arm's length, she marched back to the bedroom, put the globe in the bowl and threw her gypsy shawl over it.

Muttering to herself she undressed. Leaving her clothes in a heap on the floor, she pulled a worn cotton nightshirt, with a picture of a Siamese, over her head.

Ned trotted to the window, stood on his hind legs with his front paws on the sill and began to whine.

"What's the matter, Neddy boy?"

He barked and wagged his large plumy tail, still looking out the window.

Gabby walked to the window. Leaning over she opened it and peered through the screen at her dark backyard.

* * * * *

Christopher swore quietly, his side pressed against the house. Did the woman have no sense of self-preservation or just no sense?

In fact, he'd been swearing monotonously since she'd begun to undress. Just how much privacy did she think those little lace curtains provided? Why didn't she have blinds?

He'd come back almost immediately after having left. He parked on a different block then resumed his vigil, taking no chances on Leaky returning.

He leaned deeper into the shadows and away from the window as she gave a last look around, her face pressed against the screen. "Must be a squirrel, Neddy."

"You should call the police, you idiot," he whispered under his breath.

Stunned, he watched her slam down the window, a strange expression on her face.

His voice had barely been a whisper on the wind. Unless she had the hearing of a cat, there was no way she could have heard him. Nonetheless, he was sure she had.

The lights went out. He frowned, pensive. She was probably at this very moment convincing herself she'd imagined the whole thing. He sure as hell intended to blot it from his mind along with that comment about staying out of her ball. What the hell had she meant by that? Surely, she couldn't actually see him in the damn thing. No. It wasn't possible.

He moved restlessly then stopped, listening. His senses were particularly acute. They'd been developed as a child living on the streets of Calcutta. And the rattrap she lived in apparently wasn't insulated.

But whether it was his own acute hearing or the paper-thin walls, he could hear the bedsprings groan as she sat down on the bed. They groaned again as she lay down and rolled over looking for a comfortable sleeping spot.

Blessed or damned with the healthy sexual appetite of a young animal, he could picture her vividly as she would look without the wearisome nightshirt, the perfectly-formed breasts, the long, long legs and slender rib cage.

Beads of sweat popped out on his forehead. He cursed savagely. He should have taken her ditzy friend up on her blatant invitation.

He pushed away from the house and stole through the shadows toward his car. To hell with it, he couldn't get to the crystal with the dog there. And the dog could certainly take care of Leaky, if the man was stupid enough to disregard his warning.

* * * * *

In the downtown district, a light was burning in the back of one of the small shops. "I don't care. I'm telling you it was The Tiger that threatened me tonight. I saw the ring just before he lashed it across my face." Leaky dabbed at his oozing lip with a dirty handkerchief then swearing, dabbed at his arm.

"Get yourself another boy." He slammed down the phone.

Chapter Six

Bright sunlight streaming through the window woke Gabby up. That and Ned whining to go out and Jericho howling for his breakfast.

She stretched and glanced at her alarm clock. The large glowing-red numbers read ten o'clock. She jumped out of bed. She hadn't meant to sleep so late!

Last night came flooding back, the party, Christopher Saint, the man outside her house and the bodiless voice telling her to call the police prefaced by the term *idiot*.

She glanced at the piece of dark blue cloth sitting on her dresser and sighed. There was no way around it. She would have to call, but not before a good strong cup of coffee.

Throwing on her clothes, she ran a brush through her hair, took care of her pets and made coffee. The smell of fresh ground beans filled the air.

It wasn't until her second cup that she built up enough courage to call the police. Plopping down on the couch, she dialed. An impersonal voice came on the line.

"I'd like to speak to Sergeant Bell."

"Gabby, is that you?"

"Yes, Agnes," Gabby responded in a resigned voice.

"Are you working on anything?"

"Err, yes, I've got a story going." Which was almost true.

"Just a minute, I'll get Jimmy. It was good talking to you."

"You too, Agnes." *Liar, liar pants on fire*. Talking to Agnes was like, well, being interrogated by the police.

A gruff, familiar voice came over the phone. "Gabby?"

"Hi, Daddy."

The Tiger, who'd managed to elude his clinging date

long enough to slip a listening device on Ms. Bell's phone before they left the party, went reeling. Daddy! He put his head in his hands and groaned. Could things get any worse?

"Gabriella, what's wrong?" Sergeant Bell demanded.

Gabby stalled. "Why, Daddy, what makes you think anything is wrong?"

"You never call me at work, unless something is wrong. Now quit stalling and spill it."

"Uh, there was a man lurking about last night." She forestalled her parent's explosion, adding hastily, "Not to worry, Neddy ran him off." Then to her horror, she heard herself say, "And I heard this voice outside telling me to call the police."

Christopher clutched his hair and wanted to howl.

She heard a muffled sound on the other end of the phone. Long experience told her it was her father breathing heavily through his nose. He did that when he was really, really upset.

The sergeant's voice was suspiciously soft. "How much did you drink at that party of yours, Gabriella?"

Gabby held the phone away from her ear and looked at it, then put it back against her ear. "How did you know about the party?"

"Mr. Edison called and complained."

Mr. Edison, a short balding seventy-year-old curmudgeon, lived at the end of the block and called the police regularly with some complaint or another.

"Why you had to move into that crummy little house, on that crummy street instead of living at home is beyond me. I'll be right over."

Before she could respond, the phone clicked. She sighed and looked at her watch. She had about five minutes before her father came roaring down the street, sirens blaring. It was another reason some of her neighbors didn't like her. She was sure the thirty-thousand-plus car parked next door hadn't come from working at the local department store. People were in and out of that house at all hours. Oh well, live and let live was her motto.

Gabby got up and tripped over a beer bottle. "Damn!" She rushed around plucking it, and its dozen or so companions, up and headed for the kitchen, the bottles clanging against each other as they hit the trash.

She was just spraying disinfectant in the air, making wide loops with her arm, when her dad walked in.

Ned jumped up barking enthusiastically.

Jimmy made a face as he inhaled chemical fumes, grabbed his daughter and hugged her. She got her height from her dad. Her dad stood well over six foot, while her mother had barely topped five foot.

The years had been kind to Jimmy Bell. Other than a bit of paunch around the middle and his blond hair a bit grayer, he was still a fine figure of a man as her mother used to say. He held her at arm's length and studied her.

She fought a desire to squirm as she stared back. He threw a ham-like arm around her, led her to the couch and pulled her down beside him. The worn sofa creaked as they settled into it. "So how about telling me what's been going on, my girl."

"There's really not that much to tell."

He waited.

"Oh all right. It all started when I bought this green crystal ball."

Jimmy listened without interruption as she told him about the shop owner offering to buy it back for twice its worth and Ned running off a stranger lurking in the backyard. Then she handed him the torn cloth.

Her father studied it, placed it in a plastic bag and put it in his pocket. "And what about this voice telling you to call the police?"

"I probably imagined it." She sighed, winding her hair into a ponytail and knotting it.

Her dad stood up. "Well, let's see the blamed thing."

"You, you want to see it?" she stuttered, looking at him in dismay.

"Something wrong with your hearing, girl? Yes, I want to see it."

Dragging herself into the bedroom, she prayed Saint didn't pick that moment to materialize in her ball. Her father stopped in the middle of the room. "What the hell kind of getup is that?" he roared.

Gabby mentally kicked herself. She'd forgotten to pick up her gypsy outfit from the floor where it had landed in a heap.

"Chill, Dad. I was telling fortunes last night."

"Hope one of them wasn't 'You're going to get lucky tonight'."

"Dad!"

"Sorry. Let's see that globe."

Reluctantly, she pulled off the shiny, multicolored shawl. To her relief, the globe sat quietly. No glowing colors. No hard-edged face staring back at her.

Her father rubbed his chin. She grinned at the raspy sound. For a blond, her father had a heavy beard.

"It's pretty enough, but I don't see anything special about it."

She took his arm and led him out of the room before he did. "Dad, would you do something for me?"

He stopped and fixed an eagle eye on her. "Gabriella Josephine Bell."

Gabby winced. Josephine was her mother's name.

"You aren't going to ask me to run a make on someone are you? That's taking advantage of my position you know."

"I know, Dad."

"You got a wild hair about a story don't you?" His face fell in disapproving lines. Her father had no problem with her work as a reporter, just the fact that she wasn't working on a regular basis.

"Sort of."

"What do you mean sort of?"

"I'd like you to find out what you can about a man named Christopher Saint. I think he's tied up somehow with the globe. And there's so much interest in my crystal ball that I think I'll do an exposé on it, could be my big break, Dad."

"So why do you think this Christopher Saint is tied up with your globe?"

As much as she loved her father, she had no intention of telling him about seeing Christopher's face in the crystal. Her father's flat feet were planted firmly on *terra firma*.

"Just a feeling."

"A feeling?" Her father's left eyebrow rose, his expression skeptical.

"He showed up about the same time the globe did."

"Ah." Her father looked happier. "Now that's something that makes sense."

He kissed her forehead. "Okay, honey, I'll check on it for you. In the meantime, I'll have a squad car patrol the area."

"Thanks, Dad." It was just as well, she didn't have a love life. Even if she was twenty-six, her father still frowned on that sort of thing.

She watched as he let himself out then went and poured herself another cup of coffee.

As she drank her coffee and read the Sunday paper, her conversation with her cop-parent played about in her mind. Why not do a story on the globe? See if she could dig up its history.

Giving in to impulse, she set aside her paper, grabbed her purse and car keys, and headed for the door.

She spent the rest of the morning at the library where she poured over books related to crystal balls and their history.

Finally, she got up, stretched and rubbed her neck. She'd become interested in spite of herself. Apparently, the Curie brothers had discovered that if a slice of quartz was mechanically compressed it became electrically charged. Piezoelectricity she believed they called it.

She thought her ball was probably either green quartz or green tourmaline.

Tourmaline would certainly explain the color changes. Known as the crystallized kaleidoscope, tourmaline provided an overwhelming abundance of color. Green was supposedly connected with the fourth chakra, which pertained to matters of the heart. It also represented constant love. She shrugged her shoulders unsure what that had to do with the crystal or its history.

Picking up one of the books, she went to the counter to check out. It was a book on legends and she was hoping it would shed some light on her ball.

"You owe $4.20 in overdue fines, Ms. Bell." The young lady behind the counter pursed prim lips.

She rolled her eyes, but dug through her purse 'til she found four ones and two dimes.

"It's due in two weeks."

She nodded, grabbed her book and hurried out.

The phone was ringing when she got home. "Hello."

"You stay away from that ne'er-do-well."

"Dad?" She took the phone away from her ear and looked at it.

"Who else would it be?" His irritation radiated right through the phone line.

"What did you find out?"

53

"That he's a dilettante hand in glove with a cat burglar that goes by the name of The Tiger."

Gabby narrowed her eyes . *Hand in glove with a thief? I knew that man was up to no good.* "The Tiger?"

"I don't want you…"

Years of experience had taught her she wouldn't get any more information out of her father. Better to nip the lecture in the bud now, before he worked up a real head of steam. She interrupted. "He steals cats?"

"Of course not, he steals jewels."

"Then why did you say cats?"

Her father gave a long-suffering sigh. "Just stay away from him."

The dial tone sounded in Gabby's ear as her father cut the connection.

Chapter Seven

Christopher watched from the television cable van as Ms. Bell pulled out of her driveway. It had taken a hefty bribe to borrow the truck for a few hours. But the driver had been young and he'd fallen for the tale about Christopher having a bet with some frat buddies that he could pass himself off as a cable repairman.

As soon as Gabby turned the corner he picked up a navy duffel bag lying on the seat and got out of the van. He looked up and down the street then strode to the porch. If anyone saw him, they'd just think the owner of the house was having cable problems. Taking a lock pick out of his pocket, he opened the door.

The dog stood in front of him, his fur on end, his teeth drawn back in a silent snarl.

He'd been expecting just such a greeting. When no one was looking, he'd filched one of Ms. Bell's tops at the party. Earlier today he'd rubbed it over his clothes so he'd have her scent on them.

The animal sniffed, confused then sniffed again.

"Good boy." Christopher slipped cautiously inside, reached in his pocket and drew out a plastic baggie filled with strips of steak he'd brought as an added inducement.

He opened the bag and held one out. The dog's tail began to wag. "So you can be bought huh, guy?"

The cat came running into the room. He didn't bother saying hello, just grabbed the strip from Christopher's hand and ran off, the meat dangling from his jaws.

He handed the dog the rest, scratched him behind the ears then ruffled his fur. It was like patting a giant cotton ball.

The animal was completely won over.

Christopher walked into the bedroom. The room smelled of raspberries or some other fruity scent, overladen with a strong smell of dog. He found the globe on the bookcase, sitting in a bowl lined with tissue paper, Ms. Bell's gypsy shawl thrown over it. He grinned, how appropriate.

Pulling off the brightly colored cloth, he studied the ball. For the life of him, he couldn't figure out what all the fuss was about. He'd never really paid any attention to it when his aunt had it. These things were a dime a dozen and certainly not in Leaky or his associate's line. And then there was the added puzzle of who hired Leaky.

Picking it up, he walked to the window and opened the curtains for a bit more light.

For a moment the sun shone full on the globe. He squinted as he studied it. For the first time, he noticed its core. It was similar to the rest of the crystal, but had more fire and brilliance.

He pulled out the loupe he always carried in his pants pocket and examined it.

He gave a low whistle. "Good God. This certainly gives new meaning to the term fortune telling." He grinned. "All these years, Aunt Tam, and you never said a word. I wonder if you know, and if you know, if you care."

He put down the globe and reached for his wallet. Opening it, he pulled out twenty hundred dollar bills. The new bills rustled crisply between his fingertips. He tossed them on the bedside table. That should compensate the tiresome woman for her loss.

As he stared down at the money lying carelessly on the table, an unfamiliar twinge tweaked his conscience. The girl had bought the green stone in good faith, an innocent victim of the dark currents swirling in the underworld.

He gave himself a mental shake and picked the globe back up. It was cold as ice. The chill of it seeped through to his bones.

Quickly, he stuffed it in the duffel bag then blew on his hands to warm them. The globe was Aunt Tam's, he reminded himself. He was merely returning it to its rightful owner.

He zipped up the bag and carried it out of the room. The Chow-mix followed him to the door, his tail wagging. He patted him and glanced at the cat. The Siamese gave him an enigmatic stare, his blue eyes glowing, his tail twitching. When no more food was forthcoming, the cat stalked away.

After a quick, encompassing glance around the house, he slipped out the door. Reaching the van, he tossed the duffel bag in and threw the vehicle in gear. As he pulled away from the curb, Ms. Bell pulled in. In the rearview mirror, he watched her expression go from curious to disbelief.

"Damn it." A baseball cap was jammed on his head. He wore a dark blue repairman's jacket with the initials AT&B monogrammed in white across the pocket and dark glasses covered his eyes. The woman should have never recognized him. But she had. He was certain of it.

He leaned closer to the rearview mirror and cursed. The blasted female was pulling out of her drive, intent on following him. He knew it! He knew that woman was trouble from the day she'd run full tilt into him in the rain.

He increased his speed then swerved as a dog ran out in front of him.

Glancing in his mirror, he grinned. "Good doggie." The woman, a look of intense frustration on her face, screeched to a stop. She sat waiting for the stupid animal to decide which side of the road it was headed for.

Up ahead the yellow light blinked to red. He stomped on the pedal and shot forward.

He glanced in his rearview mirror. Ms. Bell had tried to follow, but she'd had to throw on her brakes at the last minute as the traffic came whizzing across South Grand.

Sticking his arm out the window he waved as he pulled away then picked up his cell phone and punched numbers. "Bring my car to the intersection at North Grand and Davy Jones Parkway. Be here in five minutes and I'll give you an extra two hundred." He punched the off button then swung the van onto the shoulder and quickly removed his jacket and cap.

Four minutes later his rented car came screaming into view. Holding the duffel bag, he jumped out of the van, handed the young man two bills, climbed into his car and headed for the airport.

Grinning as he pocketed his money, the driver returned to his van. He was still smiling ten minutes later, when a lovely blonde in an old red clunker pulled up alongside him and motioned him over.

While the young man tried to strike up a conversation with the pretty but infuriated blonde, several miles away Christopher settled into the pilot's seat of his plane.

His hand on the throttle, he nosed it off the runway.

He'd left the rental car at the airport. Both the car and his hotel bill had been paid in advance and his luggage stowed on his plane. All the loose ends had been tied up except perhaps the blonde. A twinge of regret nudged him. Under different circumstances he would have enjoyed getting to know her better. His grin widened, much better. Oh, well, it just wasn't to be.

He circled once. Then like a large silver bird, the plane glided upward toward wispy white clouds. Capitol Airport grew smaller and smaller, until finally it disappeared from view.

Soon the green crystal would be in the hands of its rightful owner. He glanced at the duffel bag sitting in the seat beside him then jerked the wheel as a luminous green glow radiated through the canvas.

Icy fingers trailed his spine as the blood drained from his face. He blinked then stared. There was no phosphoric glow, just an ordinary canvas bag set on the seat beside him.

White-knuckling the wheel, his teeth clenched, he straightened out the plane as he flew it through the clouds. "It was just my imagination."

* * * * *

While Christopher winged his way toward New Orleans, Gabby wailed into the phone, "But, Daddy, he stole my crystal."

As soon as Gabby realized she had really and truly lost Saint, she'd turned around and headed for home, a hollow feeling in the pit of her stomach. She knew before she'd walked in the door that the crystal was gone.

"Gabriella," her father's bull-like voice bellowed over the phone, "we've had one murder, three rapes and five break-ins. And that has been in the last four hours. I don't have time to be chasing down a nineteen-dollar crystal ball."

The receiver clicked in her ear.

"Make that six break-ins," she said into the phone, but the only response was a dial tone. She cradled the phone then stared at it, her expression pensive.

Flopping down on the bed, she picked up the crisp, green hundred dollar bills. "Probably counterfeit."

Jericho and Ned sat side by side watching her. Ned's head cocked to the side as if trying to figure out her mood. Jericho, a bored expression on his narrow face, obviously didn't care about her mood one way or the other.

She tapped the bills against the palm of her hand, an idea forming. "Christopher Saint, you are going to rue the day you took my ball."

She picked up the phone and tried again. The dispatcher came on. "Agnes," Gabby began.

"He won't talk to you, Gabby. He said specifically not to put you through."

Gabby sat on the edge of the bed, curling the phone cord around her finger. "As a matter of fact I don't want to talk to him. I want to talk to you."

"Uh-oh."

Gabby had known Agnes as long as she could remember. The dispatcher was a feisty sixty-year-old black woman with a tough exterior that hid a heart of gold.

"Agnes, would you get me Christopher Saint's address?"

Heavy suspicion laced the voice on the other end of the phone. "Girl, what you want it for? And why ain't you askin' your daddy?"

"Duh, Agnes, he won't talk to me. I'm working on a story." Which was true as far as it went.

That was all it took. Gabby's father might grumble constantly about her not having a real job and living off the trust fund an aunt left her, but Agnes was a true fan. Every story, no matter how insignificant or how far back in the paper, was praised and admired.

"Give me ten minutes, I'll call you back. What are you working on anyway?" she added in a conspiratorial whisper.

"Crystal balls."

"Oh."

Gabby grinned, knowing Agnes was struggling to keep the disappointment out of her voice. "I know, Agnes. I was a skeptic too. But there's something to all this mumbo jumbo. Did you know that if you compress quartz it creates a positive and negative charge? Isn't that wild?" Not as wild as seeing that hateful man's face in her green crystal, but she wasn't going into that right now.

"But that's not really what I'm working on." This time it was Gabby who lowered her voice. "Agnes, you knew someone stole my crystal didn't you?"

"The whole department knows. We all heard your dad's less-than-melodious voice telling you not to bother him about a nineteen-dollar toy. The sergeant's a good man, Gabby, and a good father, just overworked."

Gabby strove for patience. "I know that, Agnes. But someone offered me a thousand dollars for the crystal. Now why would someone do that for a *toy* as Dad calls it?"

Why, indeed?

Before she could mention the two thousand that had been left on her nightstand and if that didn't have implications she didn't know what did, Agnes interrupted, "Gabby, maybe you're getting in over your head. Something doesn't smell right."

His timing impeccable, Ned chose that moment to pass gas.

"You got that right." Gabby wrinkled her nose. Nope, she definitely better not mention the two thousand to Agnes. Maybe it was just as well that Daddy had hung up on her before she could tell him that little gem.

She took another tack. "What if this is it, Agnes? I know it's a long shot, but what if this is my big break? From what my dad said, Christopher Saint is news. Maybe we peons in the Midwest have never heard of him, but I bet if you checked the society columns in the rest of the country, you'd find his name."

"You really think he stole your ball?"

"I'm sure of it. I saw him."

"Gotta go, got an incoming. I'll call you back with that address."

"You're a babe, Agnes."

"That's what the men tell me, honey. Hee. Hee." The phone clicked.

Ten minutes later Agnes called back. "He lives in New Orleans. And you were right, honey. His family is as rich as

Croesus."

Gabby nodded to herself. "Do you have an address?"

"Do I have an address? Of course, I do."

"And it is?"

"1010 St. Charles Street. He lives with his aunt Tamara James."

"You're the best. I'll bring you back some beads."

"Girl, don't you go exposing yourself!"

Gabby grinned. "It's not Mardi Gras and I promise I will purchase them."

"Gabby."

"Yes, Agnes?"

"You be careful, hear."

"I'll be as safe as houses, whatever that means."

"Houses tend to get blown away in a hurricane."

"I'll be careful. Bye, Agnes."

"Bye, honey."

"And Agnes."

"Yes?"

"Thanks."

Agnes whispered conspiratorially, "You're welcome, baby. Sarge just walked by got to go."

Gabby redialed. "Amy, I'm going to be out of town for a few days, will you take care of Jericho and Ned?"

Chapter Eight

Gabby stood on St. Charles Avenue in front of a house that looked right out of the pages of *Gone With the Wind*.

Before she left Springfield, she'd sat down and whipped out a piece on energy derived from crystals and sent it to the newspaper. It was the first in a series on crystal balls and the people that used them. Hopefully, the paper would like it enough to buy it and the subsequent series.

She had then gone to the library and done more research. It had taken her two days, but she'd finally found what she'd been looking for. It had been in a tattered copy of a private work donated to the library in 1980 titled *Crystal Balls*.

Tamara James, Christopher Saint's aunt, had a crystal ball that had been in her family for generations. It was said to possess unearthly power. Disbelievers scoffed, but believers considered it a holy relic.

Gabby had also found a microfiche copy of a more current weekly magazine that catered to the occult. In it, a gossipy little piece suggested the ball had recently been stolen.

It hadn't taken a rocket scientist to put two and two together. Her crystal and Mrs. James' stolen crystal were one in the same.

Gabby straightened her shoulders and walked briskly up the brick walkway. She didn't quite have all the pieces yet, but she soon would.

Her sandals clicked against the wood as she walked across the wide verandah then stopped at the door, took a deep breath and rang the bell.

A heavyset black woman wearing a black dress and crisp white apron answered the door. She looked at Gabby inquiringly.

63

"I'm here to see Tamara James."

"Do you have an appointment?"

"Yes."

The woman gave her a look she'd seen on her mother's face whenever she had been caught out in a lie.

She backpedaled. "No. But I must speak to her. I believe she has something of mine."

"And what might that be?" The woman's raised eyebrows expressed her skepticism.

She jutted out her chin. "My green crystal ball."

The woman gave a long-suffering sigh. "Lord save us," she muttered under her breath. Then in normal tones, "Won't you come in?"

Gabby stepped into the hall and looked around. A large chandelier hung from the ceiling and tinkled with the wind from the opened door. For the second time in less than a month, she was in love. Or lust. Her crystal ball belonged here. *She* belonged here.

The maid broke into her reverie. "This way please."

As they walked through the house, Gabby gawked like a tourist. After what seemed like miles, they came to a courtyard.

She stared in wonder. "Oh, this is beautiful." The courtyard was bricked in to keep the world out. At its center was a fountain, with a fish spouting water. The water cascaded in a soothing continuous flow, the sound soft and hypnotic.

The knot in her stomach eased.

The scent of jasmine tickled her senses and made her smile. White orchids and red hibiscus bloomed profusely. Ivy covered the walls.

She was still smiling dreamily when an intrusive voice asked, "Young lady, who might you be?"

Gabby snapped back to reality. She straightened and

before the maid could introduce her, marched forward. "Gabriella Bell and I believe you have my crystal."

The two women eyed each other. Gabby had never felt more like an Amazon, an underdressed Amazon at that. She wore a peach-colored denim jumper that stopped two inches short of her knees, with a white tee underneath. Her legs were bare, her feet shod in white sandals.

Over the years she'd found that she could wear a tent and still draw admiring glances. Unfortunately, that wasn't the case today. Next to her hostess, she resembled a bag lady.

The diminutive woman in front of her looked more like an aging fairy, than she did a flesh and blood mortal. She couldn't have been more than five foot tall, which made her nearly a foot shorter than Gabby. She wore a purple, wispy something that seemed to billow out like wings with each movement. The deep color accentuated her snow white hair.

"Young lady have you lost your senses?" the diminutive woman asked, her tones crisp.

Gabby fought down the feeling of intimidation and straightened her shoulders. "No, ma'am, I bought a green crystal for five hundred dollars. I believe your nephew Christopher Saint stole it from me."

"Good heavens," the woman said faintly. "And what makes you think it was Christopher or my crystal?"

"Research. I'm an independent reporter." She lifted her chin. "It's what I do."

The small woman held out her hand. "I'm Tamara James."

Gabby took it, her own paw engulfing the tiny woman's. "I know."

"Beatrice, would you be so kind as to fetch us some tea?"

Beatrice nodded and disappeared into the house.

Tamara, her head tipped to one side, studied Gabby

The Crystal by Sandra Cox

much like she would an exotic bird that had mistakenly flown into her courtyard. She motioned toward a wrought iron bench. "Won't you set down, child."

Gabby sat down, exposing bare skin halfway up her thighs. She pulled at her skirt, but there was no way she could get the fabric to her knees. Giving up, she straightened her shoulders and put her feet together flat on the floor, her hands folded in her lap. A reflex from her mother's etiquette lessons, drummed into her head since she was six years old.

With a swish of airy fabric, Tamara sat down next to her. "So you think I've stolen your ball?"

"Not you, ma'am, your nephew. I won't press charges. I just want it back."

Tamara laughed.

It reminded her of bells tinkling.

"Can you show me proof?"

Gabby dug into her tiny white clutch and handed her the receipt.

Tamara took it and squinted at it. She handed it back. "Young woman I respect your tenacity. I will freely give you the five hundred you paid for it, but under no circumstances will I give you my ball."

Gabby's eyes narrowed. "Why would you do that if you didn't think you had my globe?"

"Because I admire your grit. Coming here took a lot of courage."

Gabby glanced at her out of the corner of her eye. The word grit seemed out of place in this woman's vocabulary. She was too otherworldly. She should be discussing fairies and magicians and sprites.

At that moment, Beatrice came out carrying tall crystal glasses of iced tea with sprigs of mint floating in them. The cubes clicked as she handed a glass first to Mrs. James, then one to Gabby.

The drink dampened Gabby's hand with condensation that had already formed along its surface. Idly, she drew a ring around the glass with her forefinger.

"Beatrice will you get me my checkbook?"

"No," Gabby said firmly, causing both older women to look at her. She turned to Tamara. "You can't buy me off. I want my crystal. Besides, someone left two thousand dollars beside my bed when they took it. I have no doubt it was your nephew."

Beatrice glanced from one to the other uneasily.

Tamara motioned her back. "It's all right, Beatrice. You can go about your duties."

Beatrice gave Gabby a dark look. "I'll be watching you. If I come out here and find you gone, and Miz. James' cold, lifeless body lyin' on the ground, I'll personally come after you."

Gabby blinked in disbelief. "Good Gad," she exclaimed in much the same tones as her father.

Tamara shrugged and smiled as her maid strode off, throwing obstinate glances over her shoulders. "She reads murder mysteries. And why would my nephew leave money by your bed?" She lifted her perfectly-formed silver eyebrows.

"That question is unnecessary and in extremely bad taste."

"Then let me try again. Why do you want my globe, child? To resell for unimaginable dollars?" Tamara prodded gently.

"No! It's mine I tell you. Mine." She sounded more like a spoiled child than a reasonable adult. But damn it, she wanted her globe back, had to have it back, much like a druggie wanting a fix.

She squirmed a bit under Tamara's thoughtful gaze. Her eyes were a pretty violet shade that matched her costume.

She wondered fleetingly if that was their true color or if Tamara wore tinted contacts.

"Have you ever seen anything in the ball?"

Gabby straightened. "Why, er, yes. That's what crystals are for, to see and tell fortunes, right?" She notched her chin again, her tone flippant.

"Who have you seen in the ball, Ms. Bell?"

She blinked at the intensity of the older woman's gaze. She managed to bite back "your nephew". "No one, I just made that up."

"What do you think of Christopher?" Tamara probed.

Gabby threw her a startled look. Could the old woman read her mind?

"I think he's a common thief. And," she added, "he has cold eyes."

Tamara smiled. A smile that softened her features and made Gabby realize she must have been a beauty without peer in her day. "There is nothing common about my nephew." Then she said briskly, "Well, young lady, we seem to be at an impasse."

"I want my crystal." The globe was here, pulling at her like a magnet.

"You can't have it." Tamara took a sip of her iced tea, completely unperturbed.

Gabby stood up. "Then I will go to the police."

"You do what you must, my dear, but I feel it only fair to warn you everyone in New Orleans, including the police, know that ball has been in my family since the beginning of time. The only way it will leave my possession is on my death.

"Now that's a thought." She cocked her head as if thinking then shook her head. "No Beatrice would be onto you."

Gabby rolled her eyes.

"Actually, there is one other way. When my nephew marries, I will give the ball to his bride. Do you want the ball enough to marry my nephew?"

Gabby shuddered. "Not for your ball, your wonderful estate and all your money."

"My, you do have strong feelings for my nephew."

Gabby tried to clear her head. The conversation was getting out of hand. And then she opened her mouth and made it even worse. "And no society tart he might marry is going to have it either. I'll steal it back," she threatened.

Tamara tapped her index finger against her chin, thinking. "What an excellent solution to our dilemma. My nephew, of course, would have to come after you."

She stood up, the interview at an end. "I'll send Beatrice to show you out." As she walked away, she said over her shoulder. "I keep it in the solarium. And child to be a good thief, you really shouldn't warn your victims."

Gabby stood stunned, her mouth hanging open.

* * * * *

The driver of the dark sedan, parked across the street, lowered his paper as Gabby came out of the house. He picked up a phone and dialed quickly. "It's the same woman, madam. I'm sure of it. Somehow Saint must have gotten back the globe. Do you want me to stay here or follow her?

"Very good."

He started the engine and pulled out into traffic keeping a safe distance between him and the cab Gabriella Bell had hailed.

Chapter Nine

It was nearing dinnertime.

Christopher walked into the sunroom where Tamara sat in a comfortable looking, white wicker chair. A ceiling fan moved the air, its blades reflected in the high glossed oak floor. His aunt lifted her cheek for his kiss.

A paper tucked under his arm, he eased down in the chair beside her. Unfolding the paper, he glanced at the headlines then turned to the sports page, the chair creaking as he settled in.

Tamara leaned forward and picked up her glass of iced tea, sitting on the white wicker table between them. "Are you going out tonight dear?"

"Um hmm," Christopher mumbled from behind the paper.

"Anyone, I know?"

"Sherry."

"Oh." His aunt's voice spoke volumes.

With a sigh, he put down his paper. "I know you don't like her, but it's not like she's going to become a member of the family. I promised I'd stop by this evening."

"You may not be intending to marry her, but she intends to marry you by fair means or foul."

He arched his brows. "If you are insinuating what I think you are, you don't need to worry about that." Rustling his papers he stuck his nose back in them.

"You're a man," she said darkly. "Of course, I have to worry."

Christopher could feel her silent stare. He lowered his paper an inch. She tapped a frosted pink nail against her lip and her violet eyes held a glint of speculation.

"I had a visitor today."

"Oh?" There was something in his aunt's voice he didn't quite trust.

"A young lady."

"Mm," he grunted.

"Your vaunted appeal with the opposite sex has certainly slipped with this one. In fact, she thinks you are quite common."

He sighed and put down the paper. "All right, Auntie. Spit it out. Who was your visitor that thinks I'm quite common?"

Tamara smiled, a Cheshire cat smile, as if she were savoring the moment.

His apprehension grew, though, why he had no idea.

Finally, she said, "Gabriella Bell."

"What! How did she find...? I mean," Even to his own ears he sounded like a fish out of water, gasping for air and flopping on a sandbar. He shook his head. "Never mind."

"So you do know the young woman?" Tamara took a delicate sip of tea then sat her glass down.

He scowled. He had the most uncomfortable feeling in the pit of his stomach, a feeling he was getting on a regular basis since meeting Ms. Bell. "Yes, I know her. What in sweet hell was she doing here?" *As if he didn't know.*

"Tsk, tsk. Language, Christopher."

He mumbled an apology.

Tamara cupped her ear. "What?"

He started to speak but she waved him to silence. "She wanted her crystal ball. She is laboring under some misguided notion that my ball is hers."

"It got stolen, Aunt Tam. She found it in a specialty shop and bought it. She was well recompensed."

"Hmm. I believe the young lady did mention something about two thousand dollars. Though, when she referred to you as common, she attached the word thief. But don't worry, dear, I told her there was nothing common about you."

"Thank you. I think. What else did she say?" Neurons shot a sensory reaction from his brain and had his muscles tightening.

Tamara picked up her needlepoint sitting on the table and ran a bright scarlet thread through the net. "She informed me she intended to get it back even if she had to steal it."

"And what did you say to that?" The sinking feeling in the pit of his stomach congealed into a hard knot.

"I told her I keep it in the solarium." She studied the effect of the bright red against the silver.

The paper slipped from Christopher's nerveless fingers. He stood up and walked out of the room hardly aware of where he was going. His voice drifted back as he left the room. "You told her you keep it in the solarium." And then he began to laugh, the sound rising to a hysterical note.

"If I didn't know better, I'd say the boy was coming down with something," Tamara murmured to the maid, who'd just brought her a fresh glass of iced tea.

While Tamara chatted with Beatrice, Christopher ran up the honey-colored suspended staircase and strode to his suite.

His bedroom was large and filled with the paraphernalia of boyhood. Sports trophies, from grade school through college, lined the walls. An old baseball bat leaned against a battered bookcase. A football sat beside a state-conference ring. There was no indication here of the hard-edged man he'd become.

He'd left the room as it was when Edward James died. His uncle had been so proud of every award, every home run and every touchdown. It was his only way of saying thank you. That and taking care of Aunt Tam.

He walked through the bedroom and into the den. No symbols of youth were present in this room. It was a man's room, mahogany wood gleaming everywhere.

Reaching the desk, he picked up the phone, pushed the digits with his index finger then held the shiny black instrument to his ear.

The line was busy. He disconnected and tried again. It was still busy. Murmuring a curse, he cradled the phone.

Grabbing a set of car keys off his desk, he strode out of his rooms and down the stairs.

* * * * *

Christopher pulled up in front of a modern brick condo. He killed the engine then jumped lightly out of his black convertible, whose license plates read SAINT.

When he rang the doorbell, a middle-aged woman, dressed in black with a white apron, opened the door.

"Hello, Mr. Saint. I don't think Miss Davis is expecting you this early. I'll tell her you're here."

"I'll announce myself. Where is she?"

"The bedroom." Her face expressionless, something flashed in her eyes then disappeared.

With a curt nod, he walked past her.

He had no problem finding Sherry's bedroom, he'd been there many times before. With a shove, he pushed the door open.

Sherry sat at a delicate cherry dressing table applying a pencil to her eyebrows. She wore expensive black underwear and her red hair cascaded down her back, the image extremely erotic.

It left Christopher cold. He knew now he hadn't just been coming over to break their date for the evening. He had come to say goodbye. It had been a good ride, but the time had come to end it. Sherry had become a tad bit possessive of late. He wondered uneasily if Aunt Tamara was right. Sherry had always claimed to be sterile. 'Til tonight, he'd never doubted her.

Her lovely green eyes met his in the mirror. She gave a start then smiled provocatively.

She got up from the table and approached him slowly, an invitation in her eyes. "Darling, you startled me. You look like a large tiger ready to eat a poor little gazelle."

Her eyebrows arched. "A redheaded gazelle maybe?"

Earlier in their relationship he would have found her conversation titillating; now he just found it trite.

She reached him and placed well-manicured hands on his chest. Throwing back her head, she smiled up at him. She was petite and very firmly put together. Aerobics no doubt, he thought cynically.

He wondered fleetingly what it would be like to kiss someone and not get a crick in one's neck, someone with heavy blonde hair and flashing blue eyes. The Nordic Queen was nearly as tall as he.

"Christopher?" Sherry questioned, when he did not respond.

"I've got to break our date tonight. Someone came into town unexpectedly."

Her eyes narrowed. She removed her hands from his chest and walked back to the dressing table and sat down. "Then why not bring him along, darling."

He gave a sardonic grin. Sherry was on a fishing expedition.

"He's from the country. Wouldn't fit in at all."

She powdered her nose as they talked. "I'd love to meet him. I'm sure it would be quite entertaining."

"Quite."

She gave him a sultry look. "Darling, this is very awkward. I had special plans for tonight."

"I'm sorry. It can't be helped."

He watched her in the mirror, her face hard and calculating.

74

Catching his gaze on her, her face immediately softened. She pouted, sticking out an unnaturally full lower lip. "Please."

He gave an impatient sigh and ran his fingers through his hair. He had known she wouldn't make this easy. "I wish there was a better way to say this, but it's over, Sherry. It's been fun. I wish you well."

Her face went white before the blood came rushing back into it.

She stood abruptly. The elegant little stool she had been sitting on went tumbling to the floor, the crash muffled by the thick white carpet.

"Fun? Why you arrogant bastard. Is that what you call what we have?"

He still stood in the doorway, his posture relaxed lounging against the doorframe but heat burned behind his eyes. "And what would you call it?"

Sherry flinched but recovered. "Why love, of course."

He snorted inelegantly. "Miss Davis, you are in love with only one person and that's yourself."

"Why you..." She raced toward him, her arm drawn back. But before she could slap his face, he grabbed her wrist.

"Now, now," he admonished. "Let's try to behave maturely."

"Why, you bastard," she hissed.

He dropped her hand. "Your vocabulary is quite limited. Frankly, you are beginning to bore me."

Thinking furiously, she played her trump card. "What if I'm pregnant?"

He arched a brow. Damn Tamara anyhow. "Immaculate conception? I do recall, between moans of passion, your assurance that you were sterile."

"Maybe they got the charts mixed."

He grabbed her arm and drew her close, his voice deceptively soft. "Understand me and understand me well. If you are pregnant and if it's my baby…"

Her breath caught. "How dare you insinuate I might be pregnant by someone else!"

He continued as if she hadn't spoken. "I would support it emotionally and financially, but I would not marry you."

"But I love you." Her breasts heaved, her breathing labored.

He let go of her, his voice bored. "Give it a rest, Sherry. You may be in love with my money and you may enjoy yourself in my bed, but that hardly means you're in love with me."

"And how would you know you heartless bastard?"

He sighed. At least she'd switched from arrogant. Maybe her vocabulary was more extensive than he'd given her credit for.

"You have no idea what love is."

For a moment, he could see Aunt Tamara's beloved face twinkling up at Uncle Edward, then a dim picture of a dark-haired woman holding a toddler. "Perhaps, you're right. Goodbye, Sherry."

She clung to him, refusing to let him go. "No. No. You can't leave me."

He pulled her hands away, compressing his lips in distaste. He hated scenes. Sherry had always seemed so cool and controlled, except in the bedroom. It was one of the reasons he'd taken her for his lover.

"May I suggest you pull yourself together and try for some dignity."

She straightened, her eyes flashing. "You're right, of course, Christopher. One must maintain one's dignity at all costs."

She turned her back on him and undulated toward her

dressing table. Quick as a cat, she picked up a delicate bottle filled with perfume and flung it at him.

He ducked.

The bottled smashed against the entryway, spraying him with her heavy, cloying scent.

He flicked a piece of broken glass off his shoulder. "Goodbye, Sherry."

"Wait, darling!"

He curled his lip as he watched the look of cunning that flitted across her lovely, cold face.

"Maybe, you are right. Maybe it's time we saw other people. Will you at least attend the charity ball with me, the one that my parents are hosting? It's less than a week away. They are planning on our appearance you know," she wheedled. "Please, for old time's sake."

It was a mistake and he knew it, but he'd told her over a month ago that he'd take her. And a man was only as good as his word.

"If that's what you want," he said curtly. "But it's over Sherry, spending an evening together isn't going to change that."

As he closed the door, he heard a scream of pure rage and a dull thud against the door.

He nodded to the maid as he left. He didn't particularly care for the woman, but he couldn't help feeling sorry for her. Her evening wasn't going to be pleasant.

Chapter Ten

Restless, Christopher stirred on the hard bench. He had spent the last three nights waiting in the solarium. After his little *tête-à-tête* with Sherry, he'd come back to begin his vigil. He knew Ms. Bell would come, the question—when.

He glowered. The damn globe belonged in a steel-lined vault, not left out in a room filled with plants, begging to be stolen. He sighed and wondered if Aunt Tam had any notion of its true worth. Knowing his aunt, even if she did, it would make no difference.

He straightened as he heard a rustling at the far end of the solarium. A tiny pinpoint of light flickered in the dark.

"Damn," came a low whisper.

Christopher grinned. The Nordic Queen had just encountered some of his aunt's more prickly specimens.

He waited, his hand resting on the globe.

The stealthy footsteps drew closer.

He blinked as she waved the penlight in his face.

"You!"

He stood and gave her an abbreviated bow. "Ms. Bell."

"What are you doing here?"

"I live here. More to the point, what are you doing here?"

"I came for my globe."

He grinned. The woman was a pit bull. Once she had an idea firmly fixed in her head neither reason nor commonsense would dissuade her.

"It belongs to my aunt."

"It's mine!"

He stepped closer. "Are you always this obstinate? Don't you realize some might term this breaking and entering?"

"Well, you should certainly know about that."

He'd been fighting an uncontrollable urge ever since she'd plastered her body against him in the rain. He was very much afraid he was about to give in to it.

"I suppose I should." He drew her into his arms and lowered his head.

"Don't even think about it."

Her body stiffened against him.

"Darling, it takes no thought at all." He tilted her chin up and placed his lips on hers.

She remained rigid as his lips moved persuasively over her mouth. Finally, her muscles loosened, and her arms crept around his neck and clung. She returned the kiss with enough heat to send his blood ricocheting to his toes.

Reality fled. In his arms, he held loaded dynamite that would either blow up in his face or send him careening toward the celestial heavens.

A calm voice shattered the crystalline moment. "That's right, Christopher dear. Hold her until the authorities arrive."

He jerked his head up and looked around, his breath coming in short sharp gasps.

Gabriella's head was thrown back as if her neck muscles were too weak to hold it up. Her parted lips were wet and swollen from his kiss, her eyes unfocused.

He shook his head to clear it. When had Aunt Tam come in? And what the hell was she talking about?

"What the hell are you talking about?"

"Language, dear," she chided. "You caught her in the act. She was trying to steal my crystal."

"She hasn't even touched the damn globe." He raked his fingers through his hair.

This was way too bizarre.

"Young woman what were your intentions?" Tamara asked calmly.

He watched Ms. Bell squint wild-eyed at the shadowy

figure. But when she replied her voice was almost as calm as Tamara's. "To recover my property."

Tamara put her palms in the air as if to say, "You see." The gesture was barely discernible in the moonlight.

She walked to the wall, flipped on the light, looked at her nephew and put her fingers over her mouth as if hiding a smile.

He returned his aunt's regard. Instead of the usual flowing robes, she wore black jeans and a black turtleneck, not too dissimilar from his work clothes.

Tamara pulled a cell phone out of her pants pocket.

He dragged his mind away from his aunt's strange attire as she began to dial. "Who are you calling?" Then he glanced at Ms. Bell and rolled his eyes.

Not only was the woman dressed in dark colors, she'd blackened her face. He wiped his chin and glanced at his fingers. Black, no wonder Aunt Tam had been grinning. It served him right for making up to a thief.

"Freddie, of course."

"For God sakes why?" Christopher exploded. Frederick Hermodson III was a judge and not a particularly young judge at that. To make matters worse, he was dotty about Aunt Tamara, or maybe just plain dotty. He'd been trying to get her to marry him for years.

"He's the law."

Gabby looked from nephew to aunt, her glance uneasy and muttered under her breath, "The nephew's ruthless and the aunt's crazy. I should make a break for it while I still can."

Tamara pointed a finger and said crisply, "Young woman, stay." Then she tipped her chin to talk into the phone. "Freddie darling," she gushed.

Christopher tugged at Ms. Bell's arm. "We may as well sit down," he said wearily.

Following his own advice, he sat.

Ms. Bell flopped down beside him.

"Yes, I know it's one in the morning, but I've had an intruder."

A squawking could be heard on the other end of the phone as Tamara held it away from her ear.

"No, darling, that won't be necessary." Tamara glanced in Gabby's direction. "I'm sure she wouldn't hurt a fly, though she is a very formidable young woman. What I want you to do, Freddie darling, is…"

God he wished she'd quit calling that clown Freddie darling.

"I want you to turn her over to my custody."

"What!" echoed through the room. One voice deep, the other husky, but Christopher's and Gabby's faces wore the same indignant expression.

"Yes, I know it's a bit irregular, but I really think it's the right thing to do, don't you? She was trying to steal my crystal ball you see.

"No. No. I'm sure she won't murder me in my bed. Besides, I have my big strong nephew to protect me."

Tamara smiled. "You're on to me. What do you say? Three months? That will be fine."

Tamara clicked the phone shut. "Christopher dear, show Ms. Bell to the daffodilly room. All my guest rooms are named for flowers," she explained.

Gabby closed her eyes, counted to ten then opened them. Two faces stared back at her. Next, she pinched herself then rubbed her stinging arm. Dang! She was awake and this wasn't a dream.

"Are you all right, dear?" Tamara asked, her expression concerned.

Gabby ignored her. She craned her neck looking for a

video camera. Maybe she had stumbled into a weird reality show. Nope. None was visible.

With a resigned sigh, she stood up. Apparently the old saw about truth being stranger than fiction had some validity, at least in this crazy household.

Christopher rose too.

Gabby's chin jutted out, her hands firmly planted on her hips. "You can't keep me here."

"Oh, yes, dear, I can. Shall I have Christopher run over and get your things?"

Gabby watched Christopher close his eyes and move his lips. He took a deep breath and said, "Aunt Tamara, even for you this is incomprehensible. What the hell are you doing?"

She gave him a hurt look. "Well, dear, I thought that was obvious. The young woman has no intention of giving up what she believes to be her globe, even though it's mine. The only way to keep an eye on her and the globe is to keep her here."

Gabby threw up her hands. "I have a job. A career," she corrected herself.

"I know, dear. You are an independent reporter. You can write here as long as you give me your promise not to run away."

"The heck I will."

"It will give you an opportunity to convince me the globe truly does belong to you.

If you can do that, the globe is yours."

"Aunt Tamara, you can't just give that damn, er the globe away to a perfect stranger."

"Of course, I can, dear, it's mine." She turned to Gabby. "But that's not to say I will."

"I have responsibilities. I have a dog and a cat."

She glanced at the globe and weakened. She wanted it back.

"I'll have them flown here." Tamara stuck out her hand. "Deal?"

"Aunt Tamara, I absolutely forbid it."

Tamara only smiled. Giving Christopher a defiant look, Ms. Bell stuck out her hand. Tamara took it.

"You've got yourself a deal. By the way have you ever heard of Sergeant Bell of the Springfield Police Department?"

"Why no, dear, I haven't."

"You will," Cassandra, a.k.a. Gabriella, prophesied darkly. "And I guarantee you won't have him eating out of your hand like darling Freddie."

"We'll see," Tamara said calmly. "Christopher, take Ms. Bell to the hotel to get her things."

Christopher put his head in his hands and groaned.

* * * * *

Gabby awoke to a familiar complaining sound. She opened one eye. A blue one stared back at her from a mere inch away, while a paw swatted her face.

She sat straight up in bed, sending Jericho sprawling. "Rrrow."

"Woof."

"Oh, no." Gabby tried to move but she was too late. The Chow-mix landed with a plop in the middle of the bed. She gave him an absent pat then pushed him away and looked around.

She frowned, perplexed. Where was she?

Memory came rushing back. *Tamara James...Christopher Saint...the green crystal...the kiss. Oh no.* She closed her eyes mortified as she remembered her brief, but enthusiastic response. Her chest heaved, as she took a deep cleansing breath. *Forget the kiss. Even if it had been one of the most memorable, earthshaking...*

"Give it up, Gabby, those lips come attached to an

arrogant, rich—okay rich is not so bad—thief."

Tamara had kept her word, was her next thought. Her animals were here. She shook her head, amazed.

She looked around her room, determined to think of something besides last night's lip lock. The daffodilly room Tamara had called it.

One would be hard put to have a fit of the doldrums in this cheery yellow room.

Someone, Tamara she would guess, had painted a garden on the far wall, with tiny fairies flitting among the flowers. Sprays of fresh daffodils and bright red tulips sat around the room in crystal bowls.

The satin sheets slid against her flesh as she sat up. She threw her legs over the side of the bed and scrunched thick luxurious carpet with her toes.

But while her body soaked up her sumptuous surroundings her mind ticked like a time bomb. *What was she doing here? What was Tamara James up to? And why had she blatantly taunted her into trying to steal the globe then put her under house arrest?*

A thought struck her. She addressed her audience of two. "Surely, she's not trying to match make between me and the arrogant, kissable nephew?" *Forget the kiss.*

She burst out laughing, as she pushed herself off the bed and headed for the shower. *Of course not. How crazy would that be?* She stopped in mid-stride. *She wasn't completely certain Tamara wasn't just a little, well, she hated to use the term crazy, but crazy.*

Then shrugged, who was she to talk? She saw Christopher Saint in a crystal ball.

Maybe a shower would clear her head. She stepped out of her tee shirt and undies then opened the shower door and turned the gold handle. Warm water spurted out of the faucet. Holding out her hand, she tested the water then stepped in.

As the warm spray washed over her, she sighed with pleasure. It was very nice not to have to trot down the hall to a bathroom where the fixtures were rusty and the pipes leaked.

A bath tray held shampoos and gels of every variety. After a judicious study, she reached for a loofa and a golden liquid called Wild Poppy. A gentle fragrance rose with the steam.

Twenty minutes later she stepped into the bedroom wearing a large fluffy yellow towel, with another one wrapped around her head, and walked to the dresser.

Opening a satiny oak drawer she grabbed a tee shirt that read, "Be Responsible. Spay or Neuter Your Pet" and a pair of jean shorts.

She dressed quickly, ran a comb through her wet hair and headed downstairs, the animals following closely behind.

Her first stop was the kitchen where Beatrice was loading the dishwasher. The room filled with gleaming, state-of-the-art appliances.

The maid turned her attention to the animals. "They've both been fed."

"Thank you."

Beatrice continued her loading. "Breakfast is in the breakfast room, through the swinging doors."

Well that made perfect sense.

"And do you have a luncheon and dinner room?"

Beatrice took so long in responding, Gabby thought her poor attempt at a joke was going to be ignored.

"There's a dining room for formal occasions."

I just bet there is. Following Beatrice's pointing finger, she walked through white swinging doors that looked like large shutters.

"My, isn't this cozy." Actually it was in spite of being rather large for a "breakfast room". A buffet lined one wall.

A large butcher-block table, topped with a bouquet of pink tulips, stood in the center of the room surrounded by leather chairs on wheels that could glide easily away from the table.

Gabby raised her head and sniffed. Coffee. She followed her nose to the buffet table and poured the dark, steaming liquid into a large black cup covered with tiny Swiss-size white polka dots.

She set her cup on the table then went back to the buffet and began opening silver covers. *Umm, more wonderful smells.* Scrambled eggs. The lid made a clanging sound as she sat it back down and picked up the next. Toast. This one she sat down more gently.

Bacon and sausage. Since she was a vegetarian that wouldn't work. Hot cinnamon rolls. *Now this was more like it.*

Gabby picked up a black octagon-shaped plate and began to fill it like she hadn't eaten in years. She carried her plate over to the table and sat down.

She took a long sip of coffee, then a bite of browned butter toast. She closed her eyes, "Umm. Heaven."

A nasty male voice interrupted her ambrosial state.

"My, my we do enjoy our food don't we? But then I'm sure it takes quite a bit to fill up a big strapping girl like you."

She opened her eyes, so much for ambrosia. Raising her chin, she gave Christopher a haughty stare, at least as haughty as she could with her mouth full.

Then, in spite of her cheeks puffed out like a chipmunk's eating nuts, she grinned. If the circles under his eyes were anything to go by, the boy was definitely suffering from sleep deprivation. Well, well, well. At least she knew who was responsible for getting Ned and Jericho.

She swallowed. "And a good morning to you too." She gave an exaggerated yawn then stretched. She watched

Christopher's eyes narrow as the tee shirt pulled across her chest.

"I slept like a baby." She looked up at him, one eyebrow arched as she inquired, "And you?"

"Like a log." He strolled to the buffet.

Forking up eggs, she watched as he passed the espresso machine and poured a cup of coffee from the coffeemaker. She raised her eyebrows. She would have sworn Mr. International Playboy would have been an espresso man.

Carrying his coffee, he sat down across from her and picked up the paper.

"Thanks for getting the animals," she mumbled around her mouthful of eggs.

"What makes you think I got them?" he asked from behind the newspaper.

She reached over. The paper rustled as she pulled it down.

His left eyebrow shot up. He gave her a look that reminded her of a phrase she'd read in one of her Regency romances. It was a "lord to the peasant look".

She reached up and placed the long nail of her index finger on a frown line between his eyes. "This." She moved the nail and gently touched the smudge marks under each eye. "And this."

At her first tap, he'd blinked and stilled, as if stunned, but when she'd moved her finger from one shadowed eye to the other, he'd jerked his head like a nervous stallion.

She dropped her hand.

"I'm not the touchy-feely type. A fact I'd appreciate you remember in future, if you insist on moving in bag and baggage."

She smiled sweetly and drawled in a honeyed voice, "But, sugar, I believe you moved in the bags."

"That's right," he shot back. "The baggage was already

here."

"Not much of a morning person are you?" She reached for the butter and spread it over her cinnamon roll.

Christopher shuddered. "How can you eat so much and stay so, so…"

"Big and strapping?" she supplied. "You should eat yourself. Breakfast is the most important meal of the day. Besides it would do you good. You're a bit on the scrawny side." It was a blatant lie. While he didn't look like a body builder he was hardly thin, but she believed in getting as good as she got and then some.

He gave her an astonished look.

As his eyes narrowed, she decided to change the subject. "How did you get the animals so quickly?"

He winced as she took a huge bite of the cinnamon roll. "I have a plane."

Doesn't everyone?

"Did you tell Amy?"

"That flighty redhead. Good God no!" He promptly buried his head back into the newspaper.

So Christopher was not destined to become one of Amy's conquests. She didn't know why she should feel such overwhelming relief, but she did.

"Poor Amy, she'll be worried sick. She'll think somebody broke in and stole the animals." She ignored the inelegant snort that came from behind the newspaper. "It won't be the first time I've had a break-in you know." Her heart hitched as a thought struck her. "She'll think someone broke in and call my father."

Christopher heard the timbre of her voice change, in it a note of pure terror. He put down the paper and looked at her curiously.

She jumped up, nearly knocking over her chair and

looked around wildly. "Where's a phone?"

"In the kitchen."

He watched appreciatively as she dashed to the kitchen. Her hair, now dry, flew behind her in silken strands. And she certainly filled out her jean shorts to a nicety.

He pulled his wandering thoughts up short. "Don't even go there," he muttered. The woman was trouble. He'd known it from the first moment she'd crashed into him in the rain. And best not to think about those full lush lips.

He turned back to his papers and rustled them determinedly then grinned as Beatrice's voice came floating through the door. "Girl, will you slow down? You nearly knocked me off my feet."

"I'm sorry, but I really need to use the phone and my cell's upstairs. It's an emergency."

The Siamese came stalking majestically out of the kitchen, his tail waving high in the air. He sat down in front of Christopher and stared unblinkingly.

Finally, Christopher threw down his newspaper. "Oh, all right." He got up, went to the buffet and grabbed a piece of sausage.

The cat followed.

Squatting, he held it out. "I've created a monster."

Jericho took it delicately between his teeth and walked off, his tail still straight in the air.

Christopher filled his cup while he was up. The buffet was next to the kitchen door. It was impossible not to overhear Ms. Bell's conversation.

"Amy, did I wake you? Well, sorry but it's important. Who's that in the background? Oh, well tell Georgio hello." A pause ensued. "Well isn't that sweet. Amy, by the way, you don't have to feed the animals. They're with me. Well, it's a long story." Caution crept into Ms. Bell's voice. "Uh, yes as a matter of fact I have. Uh, yes, I'll be sure and tell him. Now listen, Amy, do you have pen and paper? I want you to write down this number in case you need to get hold of me and my cell's dead. Well I'm no longer staying there. If you must know, I'm staying with Mr. Saint's aunt."

Christopher grinned. He could almost hear the featherbrained redhead quacking.

"Yes. Yes. I'll be sure and tell him. Did you get the number? And, Amy under no circumstances are you to tell my father where I am! Yes, Amy. Goodbye, Amy."

The syllable on *bye* was emphasized as she finally broke the connection.

He poured himself another cup of coffee and began to whistle. The restorative powers of caffeine were truly amazing. Maybe he'd eat breakfast after all.

Immolating their statuesque houseguest, he heaped his plate and sat down. He looked up as Tamara walked into the room, a long flowing dress billowing around her. "Hello, dear."

He dutifully raised his cheek for her kiss as she bent over him.

"You're eating breakfast?"

He shrugged and bit into a sausage.

Ms. Bell came back in through the kitchen door. She saw Christopher's plate and began to smirk.

"Don't say a word, chipmunk cheeks."

"Why Christopher," Tamara admonished as she sat down with a cup of hot tea and a bowl of fresh fruit, "how can you possibly say that after looking at those lovely cheekbones?"

"You'll soon see." He speared another sausage and bit it in half.

Tamara turned to her guest. "It will probably come as a shock to you, Ms. Bell, but most young ladies find my nephew quite attractive."

90

Gabby shrugged her shoulders and sat down. "Money talks." She folded her napkin in her lap, adding, "Please call me Gabby." Before Tamara could respond, Gabby looked over at Christopher. "You may continue to call me Ms. Bell."

Christopher said nothing, but his eyes narrowed. Then he grinned reluctantly. She had moxie. He'd give her that. In fact, she was like no woman he'd ever known. The women he knew fell into two categories: spoiled rich debutantes and hard, fast women looking for a good time.

Normally, outside of the bedroom, the opposite sex bored him. This one didn't. What she did was irritate him past all bearing.

Beatrice came trudging into the breakfast room, interrupting his cogitations. "Miss Davis is on the phone, Master Christopher." She looked at him hopefully. "Shall I tell her you're not available?"

For a moment he hesitated, it was tempting. Then he shook his head, "I'll take it in the study." He got up and excused himself.

Tamara sighed as he left the room.

Gabby gave her a questioning look. Really, it was none of her business, but a good reporter needed to be awake on all suits she reminded herself. "Is something wrong?"

"Sherry Davis is a spoiled little socialite that has every intention of becoming Mrs. Saint."

"Is she a redhead?" Gabby heard herself ask. *Geez, Gabby,* she groaned internally.

"Why yes, dear, how did you know?"

"Just a guess." She changed the subject. "Why do you call my room the daffodilly room instead of daffodil room. Is it a Southern thing?"

Tamara smiled gently.

Really, Gabby thought, even though she has my globe,

91

she's a likable old soul.

"I miscarried. It was a girl. I named her Daffodil and planned to call her Dilly for short."

"I'm sorry," she said quietly, determined that for once in her life she wasn't going to place both size nine feet in her mouth.

"Don't be. Those days are long past. Would you like to see my globe?"

"I would like to see my globe." It was quite disturbing how desperately she wanted to see it.

Tamara laughed. "Then come along, my dear."

Chapter Eleven

Stepping into the conservatory was like stepping into a damp, lush rainforest. Tropical plants abounded. Two bright colored parrots sat in a banana tree and a macaw sat on a rubber plant.

As they walked along the pathway, wide green leaves brushed them. Gabby pointed toward an exotic, spotted flower. "What is that?"

"Spider orchid." Tamara grazed it with her fingertips. "Do you like it?"

"No."

Tamara laughed, unoffended.

In the center of the conservatory was a shrine-like structure made of smooth gray stones.

Gabby's pace quickened. She didn't need to be told what she would find at its center. She could feel it. It drew her, like the smell of baking bread would draw a starving child.

"I'll leave you alone."

It's almost as if she understands the hold the globe has over me. Then all coherent thought fled as Gabby approached the globe, the pull growing stronger, more demanding.

Tamara turned and went back in the house.

As if in a trance, she moved forward. The globe, beginning to glow, beckoned her like a lover. She leaned toward it and reached out her hands. Warm to the touch, it comforted.

She closed her eyes, her thoughts centered inward, as she immersed herself in the feel of it. She threw back her head and arched her neck as warmth crept over her like ocean waves lapping at her feet.

Time had no meaning.

In a dreamlike state, she turned as hands on her arms moved her, strong, gentle hands that pressed her against a hard body, a body that molded to hers as if it were made for her. She could smell the clean scent of shampoo and freshly laundered clothes, mingled with the expensive fragrance of a man's cologne.

"My love," she breathed, just before firm warm lips closed over hers, causing awareness of everything else to sift to the back of her mind like smoke. Conscious only of the mindless pleasure filling her as his mouth moved across her own.

She heard his breath catch, before he murmured, "My darling, my darling," over and over against her lips, her closed eyelids, her arched neck.

She mewed in protest as his lips drew away, reluctantly, she'd swear it.

He shook her gently. "Gabriella, open your eyes," her lover's voice commanded, hoarsely. The lover she had waited for all her life. No man had ever measured up and now she knew why.

"Open your eyes."

Her eyes fluttered open. A smile trembled on her lips. She blinked a few times and the hawk-like face staring into hers came sharply into focus.

She stiffened. "You!" she squeaked, her voice high with disbelief.

She watched his nostrils flare and his head jerk back as if he'd been slapped before his habitual expression of *ennui* settled over his features.

"And who were you expecting? Prince Charming? Now that we are both aware of the parties involved shall we try it again, *love*?" he added hatefully.

Blood drained from her face. How dare he! Head in the air she brushed past him, hurrying from the conservatory. His eyes bore into her back as she rushed away. She heard him mutter, "Smooth, Saint, very smooth."

She raced up the long winding white and honeyed staircase, nearly knocking Beatrice over as she came down them with her arms full of towels.

"Sorry," she choked out over the lump in her throat as she pounded up the steps.

The maid's voice floated after her, "I sure would like to know what Master Christopher did to discomfit that long-legged Northerner."

Racing to her room, Gabby slammed the door behind her. She glared in frustration at the closed portal. Well-oiled, it shut silently, allowing no venting of her tumultuous emotions.

Flopping on the bed, she put her head in her hands and groaned. "How dare he come along pretending to be my Prince Charming?"

A long, wet tongue licked her face trying to comfort her. Ned had been napping at the foot of the bed.

She patted him absently. "Would you listen to me. I'm starting to sound like a heroine in a sappy romance. Prince Charming indeed! What is wrong with me?"

Ned whined and wagged his tail.

She got up and moved around the room. It had to be the globe. She was beginning to comprehend drug and alcohol addiction. She'd always had a supercilious attitude about people stupid enough to get hooked on artificial highs. But she'd become every bit as bad with the crystal, obsessed with it.

The carpet nap darkened into perfect footsteps where she strode, restless, back and forth. Ned's head tilted first one way and then the other as he followed her with his eyes his tongue hanging out as he panted.

"What is happening to me? Why did I ever let that

arrogant man kiss me?" She took a deep breath. "And why did it feel so right?"

It was as if she were in a trance or dreaming a dream so beautiful that being brought back to reality was devastating. Christopher Saint, rich dilettante, was not her idea of the perfect man.

And just why in Hades had he kissed her? She was hardly his preferred style. A petite redhead she was not. And whether he cared to admit it or not that kiss affected him every bit as much as it did her. His voice had been hoarse and ragged when he told her to open her eyes.

If she had any sense at all, she'd get the hell out of Dodge, with or without the globe. And with that sensible thought she pulled her suitcase out of the closet and began throwing her clothes into it.

She didn't bother with everything, just the essentials, makeup from the bathroom, underwear and a change of clothes. She could send for the rest. She must go now before she weakened, before the globe wove its insidious web around her resolve.

Gabby clicked her fingers. "Come, Neddy. We'll round up Jericho and be on our way."

As she reached the foot of the stairs, she glanced toward the open door of the sitting room. Tamara looked up from the magazine she had been idly thumbing through. Drat!

Tamara rose gracefully to her feet. Reminding Gabby once again what a fairylike creature she was.

"Where are you going, dear?"

Gabby straightened and squared her shoulders, bringing her height to nearly six feet. But Tamara didn't seem the least intimidated.

She felt like such an Amazon around this tiny lady.

"Back to the hotel and you can't stop me."

Tamara gave her an astonished look. "My dear, I

wouldn't begin to try. It's really very sporting of you, leaving the globe with its rightful owner. I can but thank you."

Gabby sensed a trap. She began to weaken. She still wanted the globe. Damn it.

"It's my nephew isn't it?" Tamara gave her a commiserating look. "We are just frail vessels where the stronger sex is concerned aren't we? I don't blame you. I'd run too. Christopher can be frightfully appealing when he chooses."

"Run?" Gabby stiffened. "You think I'm running away from your nephew?"

Tamara tipped her head to one side like a small bird. "It's the only explanation. I know how badly you want that globe. Obviously, you're more concerned about falling under my nephew's spell." She put her hand on Gabby's resting on the newel post.

"Truly, I understand. I'm sure under normal circumstances no one could turn you from your chosen course."

Gabby ground her teeth as she bit out the words. "I am not under your nephew's spell."

Tamara looked her in the eye. "Prove it."

Gabby gave the older woman a look of intense dislike. She'd been checked and checkmated. Wordlessly, she heaved her suitcase under her arm, turned around and headed back upstairs. She could have sworn she heard Tamara's soft laugh echoing behind her.

Once again, she tried without success to slam her door. It glided smoothly shut with a muted thump. With a resigned sigh, she dropped her suitcase and went to the window seat in her room. She plopped down on the soft peach pillow and stared down at the courtyard.

Christopher came strolling out, his hands in his pockets. He looked around then back at the house. She pulled back and flattened herself behind the window embrasure. He stared at her room for a long moment. She could almost feel his eyes raking her. Finally, he turned and headed toward the back of the courtyard.

Her breath quickened as a man stepped out of the shadows. Christopher put a hand on his arm and drew him behind the large sprays of jasmine that effectively hid both men from her sight. Where had the man come from? There must be a hidden gate in the courtyard.

The scent of a story grew stronger. "What are you up to Christopher Saint?"

Twitching with impatience, she hurried toward the door and threw it open. Tamara went stumbling back.

Gabby reached out and caught her before she went sprawling. "Oh dear, are you all right?"

Tamara laughed, patting her silver hair back in place. "You are an impetuous young thing, aren't you? I was coming to ask if you'd like to attend the masked ball tonight with my nephew, myself and Miss Davis."

Gabby's first reaction was to refuse. Then she remembered the meeting in the courtyard. If she wanted to discover if anything fishy was going on, she would need to stick to Saint like glue. And was completely disgusted to realize just how much the idea appealed.

"I have nothing to wear."

"Not to worry, dear, I have just the thing."

"I refuse to go as a gypsy."

"With that blonde hair, I should say not."

Gabby smiled, satisfied.

* * * * *

The two men stood motionless at the back of the courtyard. A huge spray of jasmine blocked them from the view of anyone coming into the walled garden. "What did you find out?" Christopher asked a middle-aged, wirily built man.

The man looked around almost fearfully.

"I can assure you. You are perfectly safe here."

"Like the globe?" he sneered.

Christopher's eyes narrowed. He said in a low, silky voice. "Did you come here just to waste my time?"

The man cringed. He had been a fool. No amount of money was worth placing himself between two such powerful adversaries. But the bottom line was that one stood in front of him and was willing to pay and pay well. The Tiger had a reputation for paying those who delivered—and those who didn't.

The man's glance darted from side to side, he lowered his voice.

Christopher had to bend forward to hear him. "The word on the streets is a woman wants that ball of yours, a foreign woman."

Chapter Twelve

"You invited Ms. Bell to the masked ball tonight?" Christopher tried without noticeable success to rein in his temper. "I didn't think you were going."

He glanced around the study. A picture of Edward James hung over the fireplace, another of Christopher on the wall behind the desk. And an eight-by-ten of the three of them, the year before Edward died, sat in a silver frame on the desktop.

"Of course, I'm going, darling. And why shouldn't I invite Ms. Bell? She's a guest you know."

Other than the fact this evening is going to be trying enough, no reason at all. "Trying to tweak Ms. Davis's nose, are you?"

"Why, Christopher, what an unkind thing to say," his aunt replied placidly.

"You can drop that sweet, absentminded little old lady act with me, Auntie. I know beneath that mild expression is a razor-sharp mind plotting who knows what devilment."

"And to think I actually encouraged you to speak your mind when you were young. I should have been pounding respect for your elders into your head, plotting devilment indeed." Tamara sighed, shaking her head.

Christopher's muscles relaxed and he gave Tamara a smile reserved for her and her alone. He pulled her to him and kissed the top of her head.

"You're an old fraud, my girl, but I love you dearly."

She buried her head against his chest. A sniff escaped her. After a moment, she stepped back and said in her usual calm voice, "I know you do, dear boy."

He walked to the desk and picked up the picture of the three of them. They had been vacationing in San Francisco. It was a happy memory. "It's really not necessary, you know.

100

Sherry and I are through."

"Then why are you taking her?" she asked, her hands folded primly together in front of her.

"In between the broken shards of glass raining down on my hapless head, Sherry reminded me that I had already committed to it."

He shrugged. "One evening, it's not that big a deal."

His aunt bit back a smile. "I see. Well, as you said, it's not that big a deal. Now, shall we go find our lovely young guest?" They left the room arm in arm.

The lovely young guest was at that moment looking at herself in the mirror, turning this way, then that. She had to hand it to Tamara the old girl certainly had a sense of style. A tiara gleamed atop Gabby's hair. She sincerely hoped the glittering stones were paste but she had serious doubts that zirconium could possibly gleam with this much fire and brilliance.

She tilted her head and studied the dress. It was exquisite, made of a gossamer-like material, shot through with silver threads, done in a medieval style that fit her like it had been made for her. She picked up her scepter, a long silver rod with a crystal ball on the end of it.

Gabby wondered for the thousandth time where Tamara had ever found it. What had Tamara called her, The Lady of the Lake and Guardian of King Arthur's Sword? She rather liked that.

She tapped the scepter thoughtfully, remembering the afternoon. By the time she'd reached the courtyard it was empty. But something was going on, she was sure of it.

And she, Gabriella Josephine Bell, intended to find out what. She straightened her shoulders heading for the door.

She walked to the head of the stairs. With a hopeful feeling, she looked down, but no Rhett Butler stood staring up at her. *Oh well*. She shrugged and started her descent.

Her foot on the last rung, she paused as Tamara came into the hall.

"Don't you look lovely."

"And might I return the compliment. You look ageless." And it was true. Tamara was garbed as Mab, sometimes called Titania, the fairy queen. She wore a gauzy lavender gown, with delicate wings attached to her back.

"I'll be the envy of every man there tonight, with two lovely ladies on my arms." Christopher stepped out of the shadows and executed a gallant bow.

Gabby jumped. The man moved like a cat. She turned slowly and looked at him, speaking of cats. She couldn't quite hide her consternation.

Christopher laughed.

"You're going as a thief?" She raised her eyebrows. He wore a black turtleneck, black slacks and a pair of black canvas shoes. "Isn't that a bit close to home?"

"I prefer the term cat burglar, so much more elegant. Don't you agree?"

"A rose by any other name."

He grinned then turned toward Tamara. "Want me to order a limo?"

"That won't be necessary. You take Gabriella in the Jag. I'll ride with the judge."

"And where is Miss Davis to sit?" he asked dryly.

"The judge and I will pick her up."

Christopher's eyebrows shot up as he tilted his chin down and looked at her.

"It will give Miss Davis and me a chance to get better acquainted."

"That's certainly how Sherry will see it."

Tamara's placid features tightened and her violet eyes snapped. "If she views this as a stamp of approval as my daughter-in-law she will be sadly mistaken."

Christopher bit down on his lips, though they had a tendency to twitch. He straightened his features. "Yes, ma'am."

Tamara reached over and pinched his cheek, her good humor restored. "You're a rascal but I love you."

"And I you, ole girl."

The smile he gave Tamara took Gabby's breath away. Who would have thought those hard planes and angles could soften or those cold green eyes glow with such warmth? And who would have thought she could be so drawn to that smile?

He turned to Gabby his expression once more polite but distant, "Shall we go, Ms. Bell?" Then he arched an eyebrow as he studied her expression. "Is something wrong?"

How can he turn on and off his emotions like a water spigot? She ordered herself to stop gawking and gave a high-voltage smile of her own. "No, of course not."

"Oh here, dear, your mask." Tamara picked up the mask setting on a nearby marble-top table and handed it to Gabby.

Gabby gasped. "It's beautiful." It was a silver half-mask inset with tiny blue rhinestones. At least, she hoped they were rhinestones.

"If I were a gentleman, I'd say the blue of the gems pales in comparison to your eyes." And mighty fine eyes they were too, Christopher thought appreciatively, studying her.

"And since you're not?"

He shrugged. "Then I would just suggest we go."

Christopher kissed his aunt's cheek. It was as soft as rose petals and as thin as parchment. He felt a fleeting regret for her mortality. The old girl wasn't going to live forever.

Tamara broke into his thoughts. It was uncanny, the way she always sensed his moods.

"We still have plenty of memories to make. Now," Tamara said more briskly, "Don't forget your domino." She reached toward the table and picked up a plain black mask that covered only his eyes.

"Thank you, dear."

He could sense Ms. Bell watching the interplay between him and his aunt.

Determined not to let her get too close, he schooled his features into his perpetual façade of *ennui* as he turned toward her. "Shall we go?" He held out his arm and she took it.

As they walked to the black sleek car parked under the streetlight, she glanced at the license plate that said SAINT in bold letters.

"Well that's certainly low profile."

He grinned and opened the door.

Silk rustled as Ms. Bell sank into the gray leather upholstery.

He slid into the car, closed the door with a muffled thud and inhaled. He never tired of the smell of expensive leather. As he started the engine, it purred to life. "So what do you think?" He patted the dash like a proud papa.

"It's all right. Nothing out of the ordinary."

He snorted. "Good try, Ms. Bell, but I've seen your mode of transportation. Don't you think it's time to put the poor thing out to pasture?"

His passenger twisted to face him. "Clara is a fine car. She's reliable and sporty in an economy sort of way. She's hardly in the league of this, this," she waved her hand around wildly, "car," she finished. "But then neither am I."

Shame coursed through him. Who knew better than a ragged orphan boy about life's challenges if you weren't one of the rich and powerful? But there was just something about this woman that brought out the worst in him. She was pigheaded and opinionated, though, some might call those same traits proud and independent. And she carried such a lethal dose of sex appeal it was downright scary.

Gabriella Bell was beautiful in a sultry Swedish sort of way, but the world was full of beautiful women. He'd had them ever since puberty. What attracted him to her was her inner fire and the recognition of a kindred spirit.

He drew himself up short. This would never do. He had chosen his path long ago. He had neither the time nor inclination for involvement of any kind. They were messy, time consuming and eventually boring. And this girl was no one's one-night stand.

He broke the lengthening silence. "Well, you are right about one thing at least. We are leagues apart."

He gunned the car and tore off into the night.

* * * * *

The twenty-minute drive passed in stony silence. Christopher had no idea that Ms. Bell might take his remark to mean her lack of social status, when that had never entered his mind. What had, his cynical outlook on life and shadowy background.

He was a creature of the night, at home both on the Riviera and in the back city streets where million dollar deals went down without the sanctity of law or taxation. Ms. Bell was a shoot from the hip personality, a middle-class girl with middle-class values. A policeman's daughter, things were right or wrong, black or white. There were no shades of murky gray. And his dealings were very murky indeed.

Lost in thought, he nearly missed the drive of the Davis's country home. He turned sharply to the right throwing his passenger against the door, pulled the car in front of a white pillared mansion and shut off the engine.

Lights glittered from every window. "What are you sulking about?" He came out of his preoccupation and noticed her stony silence.

"I never sulk."

"Good. Then let's get this over with shall we?" Getting out, he slammed the door. At least in any other car it would have been a slam. In his pricey sports car, it was a muffled thud. A handsome young man, dressed in white livery, opened the passenger door.

Christopher tossed him the keys then pulled Ms. Bell out of the car and walked her up the red-carpeted outdoor steps, her arm stiff as a board.

"I'll be watching you," she warned.

"I'm flattered and may I return the compliment."

She frowned at him. "It wasn't a compliment. I saw you in the courtyard this afternoon."

"Oh, dear, a spy in our midst." He schooled his expression to boredom.

"You better put on your mask. You don't want to be recognized when you lift the crown jewels," she shot back.

He threw back his head and laughed, a rich throaty sound that had a smile tugging at the corners of Gabby's mouth, then did as instructed.

His eyes twinkled down at her. "I can see the headlines now. 'Cub reporter nabs cat burglar'. Or 'Society stunned to learn Christopher Saint is famous cat burglar'. Hmm, I think I like that one better don't you?" He bent his head close to hers.

"Oh, do be quiet."

They approached the receiving line behind two other couples. Luxurious red carpeting ornamented the wide hallway and a crystal chandelier glittered overhead.

Mrs. Davis was talking to the couple in front of her, her hand extended. While speaking, her hostess's gaze darted about the receiving line. She saw Christopher and smiled. Then she noticed Gabby and the smile was, quite literally, wiped off her face.

Hurriedly, she ushered her next guests through, 'til

Christopher and Gabby stood in front of her.

Gabby examined Mrs. Davis every bit as intently as Mrs. Davis did her. Dressed as a Southern belle from a bygone era, their hostess had a flawless complexion with eyelids drawn a shade too tight and red hair just a little too lush to be natural.

Gabby smiled at her hostess.

Mrs. Davis smiled back, though her eyes remained cold. "Christopher, dear, how good to see you." She held up her cheek for a kiss. "I thought you were bringing Sherry."

Christopher dutifully brushed Mrs. Davis' cheek with his lips. "My aunt and Judge Hermodson are picking her up."

"Oh, really." Mrs. Davis almost purred.

He could hear the wheels turning in the woman's head. *The aunt was reclusive and hard to pin down. It would be the first time she had made any effort to speak to Sherry. She must have finally decided to give the match her blessings. Yada,yada,yada.*

"Judge Hermodson? It's like that is it?"

"I sincerely hope not," Christopher said in bored tones.

Mrs. Davis protested, "The judge is from a very old and distinguished Southern family. He would be an asset to any family tree."

He looked her in the eye, his jaw tightening, not bothering to hide his distaste of the subject.

Mrs. Davis glanced at him and hastily changed the subject. "And who is this enchanting creature?"

Christopher bit back a grin. The woman looked like she had just bitten into a particularly sour persimmon.

"A friend of the family." His facial muscles relaxed, as he gave her a knowing look.

Taking Ms. Bell's elbow, Christopher directed her attention to Mr. Davis, a thin balding man who eyed her lecherously.

Christopher deftly inserted himself between them. Mr. Davis was a pincher. He wasn't as concerned about Ms. Bell getting pinched as he was about Ms. Bell slugging Mr. Davis. He always tried to avoid scenes. They were so tiresome.

Gabby and Christopher followed several others down a long hallway that ended in a vast room with a white marble dance floor. A tango was playing.

"Shall we?" he asked.

If he'd hoped she'd have to cry off because she didn't know ballroom dancing, or dancesport as it was called these days, Christopher Saint was in for a surprise, Gabby thought with mean satisfaction. Dancing was one of the few things she excelled at.

"If you like." She knew the sparkle in her eyes belied any lack of enthusiasm.

As they passed a small table with a spotless white linen tablecloth, she paused.

"Excuse me," she said politely to the older couple sitting at the table.

They watched in astonishment as she plucked up the red rose sitting in the middle of it.

She turned to Christopher. "I'm ready." She placed the rose between her teeth.

He quirked an eyebrow then gathered her into his arms and moved across the floor.

Her movements were flawless and Christopher was no slouch. They moved as one with sultry grace. Neither took their eyes off the other as the music beat out its sensual tempo. One by one the other couples stopped to watch, clearing a path for the Lady of the Lake and her cat burglar. Completely lost in the moment neither was aware of the crowd gathering around them.

The music stopped. Christopher dipped her low then

brought her up to where their lips were mere inches apart. A spontaneous round of applause broke the spell.

Gabby blinked disoriented. Reality came rushing back. Pulling her upright, he gave her a mocking bow, though his eyes seemed as unfocused as hers.

The band began to play a foxtrot.

As Gabby took the rose out of her mouth, she caught a flash of movement out of the corner of her eye and grinned. The judge and his party had arrived. A short, pudgy man was whirling Tamara around the floor like a demented dervish.

She moved her head this way and that trying to watch them, but they were lost to sight as several men came hurrying to claim her for the next dance.

Christopher was reaching for her hand, when an aging Romeo shoved his way through the male throng surrounding her and whisked her away before she knew what had happened.

Out of the corner of her eye she saw Christopher watch them then shrug and walk away.

She stared over the shoulder of her partner, as Christopher wended his way through the crowd. Even with the erratic movements surrounding him, he moved lithely, with the grace of a cat—unlike herself. She stepped on her partner's foot, ignoring his yelp, as a petite redhead that looked like a younger version of Mrs. Davis stopped Christopher. The woman wore a white, low-cut, diaphanous gown and had her hair piled on top of her head in tousled disarray. A silver ribbon threaded through it.

Gabby frowned trying to figure out who she was supposed to be. A hooker perhaps, she thought cattily.

Her partner, tall and well-built with a head full of white hair, followed her gaze and enlightened her. "Miss Davis has informed everyone *ad nauseam* that she is Venus rising from the waves. Did you happen to notice that the tip of her gown is tinged blue? If not she'll be glad to point it out to you," he told her grinning.

"You know Ms. Davis?" She craned her neck to get a better look at the lovely young woman.

"Known the family for donkey's years." His eyes twinkled mischievously. "Know she has every intention of bringing young Saint to heel."

They watched the attractive couple. Sherry had her hand on Christopher's arm, holding it close to her scantily clad bosom. She gazed up at him adoringly.

Romeo looked Gabby over appreciatively. "I'd say she has pretty stiff competition. I must say, I'm very impressed with his latest acquisition."

The muscles in Gabby's jaw jumped as she clenched them. "I am no one's acquisition."

The aging Romeo drew her closer. "I'm glad to hear it."

She looked straight into his eyes and trod on his instep. "And I'm not on the auction block either."

Romeo yelped then slackened his hold. An engaging smile lit his face.

"Can't blame a man for trying."

Having made her point, she smiled back. With the rules established, they both settled in to enjoy the dance.

Romeo fell silent as he glanced past Gabby. When he whirled her around, she followed his gaze. Curious, she looked in the direction he'd been staring, but didn't see anything. She raised her eyebrows.

He answered her unspoken question. "A beautiful young Asian woman was watching Christopher as intently as you and Miss Davis. When she noticed me observing her, she melted away." He shrugged and changed the subject.

Gabby and Romeo clapped politely as the music ended.

A wildly painted young man, with long black, spiky hair, stepped forward to claim her for the next dance.

Romeo bowed and handed her over.

As the band played a swing number, her partner whirled her around in crazy gyrations.

The dancing continued.

Her feet ached. She might not be the belle of the ball but she was damn close. Before a dance finished someone else would be asking for her hand.

Mr. Mertz, the aging Romeo, managed a dance at every opportunity. A witty conversationalist, he talked continuously. While they danced, he gave her irreverent tidbits of anyone they chanced to encounter.

One older gentleman had an even thicker, more beautiful, head of silver hair than her partner did.

"Hair transplant," Mertz said.

"I can see that."

Mertz threw back his head and laughed.

Christopher who was dancing a few feet away, with Sherry, a bored expression on his face, looked over and frowned. He hadn't approached her since their dance at the beginning of the evening.

A handsome young king asked for the next dance as the music stopped then started back up. She gritted her teeth and smiled when he stepped on her sore toes then jumped as an ear splitting clang sounded. "What's that?"

The musicians stopped playing and the dancers began walking off the floor.

"That's the dinner bell. Must be midnight. Would you care…"

Before he could finish Mertz had elbowed his way between them. "May I take you to dinner?"

She looked around. Christopher walked towards her hindered by Sherry clinging to his sleeve. He caught Gabby's eye and shrugged helplessly.

Mertz winked at him then offered Gabby his arm.

As she took it, Christopher shot him a look that would have wilted a lesser man.

Mertz just grinned.

To Christopher's intense disgust a half-dozen young men trailed Ms. Bell into the dining room.

Dragging Sherry, he elbowed his way between the young men, following Ms. Bell and her Romeo. "Shall we make it a foursome?"

Mertz looked over his shoulder at Ms. Bell's entourage. "Better get a larger table."

"Quite," Christopher said in a clipped voice.

The impromptu group, consisting of the two women and ten men, sat down at a large round table, covered with crisp, white table linen and a lovely floral centerpiece made of lilies and roses.

Christopher introduced the two women, his face stoic.

"So, Miss Dell, where are you from?" Sherry asked sipping her champagne.

A chorus of voices rose to correct her.

"That's Bell, Miss Favis," Ms. Bell said crisply.

Christopher's lips twitched and he began to cough. Since he'd sat down next to her, she reached over and gave him a slap on the back hard enough to send him reeling.

"Thank you," he said dryly.

She smiled sweetly. "The pleasure was all mine."

"I'm sure of it."

Sherry regained the floor, "And where did you say you were from, Miss…"

"Bell. And I'm from Springfield, Illinois, home of Abraham Lincoln." She gave a false bright smile.

"Oh, yes. The heretic that destroyed our beloved South."

"Only if you are into bondage. Are you Ms. Favis?"

And so the rest of the meal went.

Finally, Christopher threw down his linen napkin, stood up and held out his hand to Gabriella. "Come," he commanded.

"I haven't finish eating," she protested around a mouthful of shrimp.

"Gabriella," he said softly.

With a sigh, she put down her fork and stood up. "It's been amusing everyone."

Several of the men looked at Christopher mutinously but Christopher's reputation preceded him. No one that knew him deliberately crossed him.

Sherry laid a hand on his arm to detain him, her mouth pouting up at him, though her eyes were coldly furious. "But, Christopher, have you forgotten? You asked me for the next dance."

"Did I now, love?" he drawled in a bored voice. "I remember it differently, but I would never dream of contradicting a lady." He looked around. "Gentlemen, entertain Miss Davis."

To a man, they would have preferred entertaining the Nordic beauty, but trust Saint to save her for himself. They nodded with a singular lack of enthusiasm. Christopher and Gabby strolled back in the direction of the ballroom. Several others had the same idea. The room filled quickly.

People in elaborate costumes moved about in a kaleidoscope of color. Diamonds and other glittering gems accentuated their costumes.

Christopher firmly tucked her hand under his arm. "So, Ms. Bell, are you enjoying yourself?"

"Quite a shindig." She leaned closer. "I know who you are," she breathed in his ear. "And if one precious stone disappears tonight, I'll tell the world."

He heaved a weary sigh as he drew her into his arms for a waltz. "You do enjoy the melodramatic don't you, Ms.

Bell? Care to tell me what you're talking about?"

For a moment, Gabby said nothing as her body moved in perfect rhythm with Christopher's. The music and the heat from his hand stole insidiously through her, leaving every nerve in her body tingling.

She looked up at him. Her brain turned to mush.

He fell silent. If she didn't know better, she'd swear he was as disoriented as she was.

A scream brought her up short, ripping through the sensual spell.

"My jewels! Someone stole my jewels!" A heavyset matron dressed rather unbecomingly as Marie Antoinette clutched at her throat.

Gabby jerked herself out of Christopher's arms. "Damn you. I know you're The Tiger's accomplice. Who's your accomplice?"

Luckily, the commotion around them drowned her words from everyone except Christopher.

He started toward Marie Antoinette, but Gabby grabbed his arm and dug in her heels. "I'm not going to let anyone pass those jewels to you."

He stopped and stared down at her, his face hard. "Let me go before I strike you."

Her stomach tightened. She had no doubts that he meant it.

She swallowed, but held on determinedly.

With a lightning-like move, he disengaged himself, then reached out and grabbed her arms and gave her a rough shake. "Now listen, you little fool, and listen well. Even if what you are saying is true, and it's not, I would hardly foul my own nest. And I'm no one's accomplice. I work alone. Do you understand? Now stay put. I want to see if I can find the thief before he gets away."

The hands on her arm tightened painfully. She struggled then looked at his face and stilled.

He stared at the entryway, his body rigid.

The ballroom floor was sunken. Anyone entering or leaving was clearly visible.

She followed his gaze. The most beautiful oriental she had ever seen stood silhouetted in the doorway, dressed in a tight-fitting red dress and carrying a glittering red handbag. The woman wore a red silk half-mask. Staring straight at him, she blew Christopher a kiss then disappeared.

Christopher dropped Gabby's arms and started after her.

With a vague notion of following him, Gabby headed toward the entryway. While she was still trying to push through the people mulling around her, Christopher ran lightly up the steps to the doorway and disappeared.

She stopped frustrated. She'd never catch him now. With a shrug she turned and made her way toward the woman still clasping her throat. Maybe Marie Antoinette had gotten a visual of her assailant.

Chapter Thirteen

Christopher moved quickly through the crowd, but not quickly enough. He reached the verandah and looked around...Lai gone. He'd lost precious seconds staring, stunned, from the ballroom floor.

"My car," he snapped at the nearest valet as he ran down the terrace steps.

The valet stiffened at his tone but he didn't have time for niceties.

Something in his face must have relayed urgency. The man hurried off, returning moments later.

Christopher tossed him a twenty, jumped in the car and threw it in first. With a roar of its powerful engine, the car tore down the drive.

Black filled the sky, the only thing lighting the road the car's headlights and a handful of stars. As a gray cloud drifted over the moon, he leaned forward, squinting. The white lines of the road blurred as he pressed the pedal to the floor.

He flipped on his brights. The low hum of the engine reminded him of the well-modulated chatter of another party several years ago.

Musicians played a sedate waltz and sparkling chandeliers glittered overhead. Men in tuxedoes and women in fabulous jewels and colorful designer gowns glided across the dance floor, as he stared across the room at the most beautiful woman he'd ever seen. She wore black satin that fit her sleek body like a glove and made every woman in the room pale by comparison.

He was attending an embassy ball in India. His aunt and uncle had sent him abroad as a graduation present. Fascinated, he'd watched her the entire evening. In fact, he

116

was the only one who saw her lift a diamond bracelet from a gray-haired woman's bejeweled wrist.

Instead of reporting it, he'd shadowed her when she left the ball, trailing her through the opulence of Calcutta to its back streets where the smell of decay and refuse had filled his nostrils, reminding him of the boy he'd once been. Following her to a ratty building that looked ready to fall in on itself, he'd fought his way past two of her back alley henchmen and finally gained admittance to a huge apartment as opulent on the inside as it was decrepit on the outside.

Once inside, he took one look into Lai's mysterious black eyes, smelled her sultry perfume and was lost.

She seduced him to buy his silence.

But the woman with the cunning of a fox and the cold calculation of a man had not counted on her body betraying her. Even at twenty-two, he knew his effect on women and Lai had been no exception. They fell into an affair so hot it threatened to ignite India.

Enamored and impressionable, thinking with his dick instead of his head, he became one of her select group of followers.

She taught him her arts and he in turn became one of her most apt pupils. He became a jewel thief so agile and quick, he'd earned the nickname of The Tiger. Nor was he lacking in ferocity.

Four years his senior, Lai was the most powerful woman in India's underworld. Seldom seen in public, she was an enigma, cloaked in mystery. Her dark mystique fascinated him. The only thing he knew about her past was that she'd been brutally abused and carried the scars on her back to prove it.

He stayed with her three years.

Eventually, he grew weary of Lai's incessant slavish demands. The flames of passion that consumed him, like any fire, burned out. After having known Aunt Tam's warmth and compassion he could no longer deal with Lai's twisted idea of love.

When the fire died and reason returned he'd gone home, the only one who'd ever walked away from Lai and lived. Maybe Lai knew that even she would have problems killing The Tiger.

With backing from his uncle, he'd bought into a small import-export shop. The store had done surprisingly well. He left the tiresome details of running it to his partner, a man in his mid-sixties.

Few people in his social strata even knew about the shop. It pleased his quirky nature to let them think him a dilettante, plus it further separated him from The Tiger.

He traveled extensively looking for rare objects for the store. No one connected the occasional disappearance of fine jewelry with Christopher Saint's buying trips.

His mind snapped back to the present as he came up on a blue compact traveling about sixty miles an hour. He jerked the wheel, whipped over the white and yellow broken line then back into the right lane of traffic.

Leaning forward, he saw the red glow of Lai's taillights traveling fast ahead and stamped down on the accelerator.

* * * * *

With her escort gone, Gabby rode home with Tamara, the judge and Sherry. That had been a treat.

Gabby and Tamara stood on the white planked verandah, waving, as Judge Hermodson's limo pulled away from the curb, the light from the street lamp glistening on the roof of the car.

As the car drove away, they heaved a simultaneous sigh of relief. Tamara unlocked the door. "Thank goodness, this night is finally over. I don't know if I could have stood any more excitement."

They stepped into the foyer. "Why, Beatrice what are you doing up?"

The maid sat on a red velvet-covered antique bench waiting for them, Ned on the floor beside her, his plumy tail waving. Jericho came strolling in from the living room. He had no doubt left a liberal amount of fur on the expensive sofa, Gabby thought with a silent sigh.

"Beatrice dear, you should have gone to bed," Tamara scolded.

Beatrice stood up. "You know I never turn in until I know you are tucked up right and tight." The maid glanced over her shoulder as she said it.

Gabby studied the maid. Beatrice was clasping and unclasping her hands. "Is everything all right?"

The maid spoke in a hushed whisper. "I think someone was in the house. A little after midnight, Ned started to bark. First he headed for the study then the solarium. He knows how to push open that swinging door that leads into the solarium. I went to the kitchen, picked up the rolling pin and followed him. When I got there, I heard him growl. I swear it raised the hairs on the back of my neck.

"I heard a rustling, moving away and heading back toward the door to the house. Then Ned went tearing through the house and back into the study.

When I got there, the window was open. Ned must have jumped through it 'cause I could hear him barking outside. He came trotting back when I called him. If someone was out there, he got clean away."

"Did you call the police?" the policeman's daughter asked.

Beatrice shrugged helplessly. "I didn't think they'd believe me. The security system never went on."

Gabby and Tamara looked at each other and frowned. Whoever had broken in was no amateur. The security system was state-of-the-art.

"Let's take a look at the solarium." Tamara set a brisk pace, with Gabby and Beatrice on her heels.

Gabby's mind raced. The solarium was attached to the house. The globe was in the solarium. If someone was after the globe, they'd have to break into the house to get it.

When they got to the solarium, Tamara threw several switches, flooding the room with light. By unspoken agreement the women headed for the globe.

The green crystal stood in solitary splendor, untouched. Gabby walked up to it and looked around. There were, of course, no footprints. But she couldn't shake the nagging feeling that someone had been there.

"It looks like you were right, Beatrice my dear. Ms. Bell, look at this."

Gabby turned and walked toward Tamara, who stood beside a banana tree. She held a broken leaf in her hand.

"It could have been Ned," Gabby said.

Tamara shook her head. "Too high. And look." Tamara pointed toward a honeysuckle vine bent backward. It was a little higher than Tamara's shoulder, too tall to have been done by the dog.

"Isn't it rather strange we were being broken into at about the same time Mrs. Beaue's diamonds were being stolen?" Tamara mused aloud.

Heavy, exotic scents hung in the warm, moist air. The Chocolate-Scented Daisies rustled causing all three women to start. Jericho came strolling out. Beatrice emitted a nervous laugh.

Gabby bent down to pet him as he wrapped himself around her legs. Jealous, Ned butted against her.

Tamara turned toward the dog and patted his thick soft fur. "Beatrice, do you think tomorrow you can round up a large soup bone for our hero?"

"You bet, Miz. James."

The women tramped out of the solarium, Tamara switching off the lights behind them.

"You'd best tell Master Christopher about this when he gets in Miz. James."

Tamara smiled but remained noncommittal. As Beatrice walked away, she exchanged looks with Gabby.

We are thinking the same thing. Christopher will want the globe locked up and we'll no longer have access to it. Gabby forced herself to say. "Perhaps, you should tell him."

"I'll sleep on it. By the way, why don't you write up a little piece about the excitement at the ball? Throw in some of those tidbits Mertz was feeding you and I'm sure you'd have a juicy item for the society column, unless you object to that sort of thing on principal."

"If it would advance my career, I'd write for a gossip magazine." She smiled at Tamara. "I've a feeling you'd make a pretty darn good newswoman yourself, or a sleuth."

Tamara laughed. "If you are going to do a write-up, I know the owner of our city newspaper, dear. Shall I make a phone call tomorrow morning? Or perhaps tonight?"

"No. Not that I don't appreciate it, but I want to make it on my own. I'm quite good you know."

Tamara laughed. "I never doubted it. And I admire your determination."

The steamy heat of the conservatory dropped away as they stepped into the cool hallway.

Tamara paused at the bottom of the stairs. "I'm going to bed, dear. Feel free to use my study and computer. Turn in whenever you're ready." Unexpectedly, she reached up and placed a feather light kiss on Gabby's cheek. "Sleep well."

Gabby's heart turned to pudding.

The older woman ascended the staircase, her skirt making soft whispering sounds as it undulated against her legs.

Too keyed up to sleep, she walked to Tamara's study and sat down at the computer. She stared at the closed window the intruder had escaped out of. Why would one woman steal an emerald and diamond necklace at the same time someone was trying to steal the globe? Surely, other women weren't seeing Christopher Saint's face in her ball!

Tomorrow she'd talk to Tamara without actually admitting she'd seen his face in the globe. She wasn't ready to acknowledge that particular phenomenon. It would be tricky but she was sure she could pull it off. In the meantime, there was the article to write. The ball and the theft were news.

If there had been a reporter there who would have already gotten the scoop Tamara would have told her. Never mind it was a masked ball. Miz. James, as Beatrice called her, knew everything. It was a sweeping statement but by now Gabby was a believer. Tamara was an amazingly canny woman.

Sitting at the computer, Gabby organized her thoughts and began to type. Her fingers flew over the keyboard, racing neck and neck with the ideas swirling in her head. She didn't have enough proof to accuse Christopher publicly. Nor could she break bread with his aunt while trying to crucify her nephew.

It didn't make any sense. No, the jewel theft had been a diversion to steal the globe. And she wasn't about to mention that either! Instead, she described Mrs. Beaue's ashen face and gave a glittering description of the necklace. Following Tamara's advice, she threw in some juicy gossip about the other revelers who'd attended the party.

She leaned back in her chair and smiled with satisfaction. *Done.* Picking up a copy of the paper lying on the desk, she looked at bylines then went online. Being a reporter that hadn't made a name for herself, she'd discovered the only way to get people to listen was to get pushy, even if it was two in the morning. She started calling numbers 'til she finally bullied someone into giving her the home number of the editor-in-chief.

She dialed and got an answering machine. Unfazed, Gabby began reading her column over the phone.

Halfway through, a brusque male voice picked up. "I've had the police scanner on. Whoever you are, your story checks out. E-mail me what you've got," he barked into the phone then gave her his email address. "If it's any good, I'll print it. Include your byline, name, address and phone number," he finished and slammed down the phone.

She held the phone away from her ear, looked at it then in a daze placed it in the cradle.

"Yes!" She slid out of her chair and danced around the study, waving her arms in the air. "Yes, yes, yes, yes, yes!"

She bent over the desk, attached her story to an E-mail and hit the send button then stared at the screen for twenty minutes, but no new messages popped up. No response showed on the screen. She went into properties that read received and opened. Well that was that.

She glanced down. She'd forgotten to change clothes. A wave of exhaustion washed over her. She pushed away from the desk, left the room and trudged upstairs. The animals close behind.

Carefully, she removed her tiara and laid it on the nightstand. She ran her fingers through her hair then shook it out, the long blonde strands tumbling over her shoulders.

With a huge yawn, she shrugged out of her dress, threw it over the bedpost and crawled into bed, asleep almost instantly.

Jericho jumped on the bed and curled up on the pillow

beside her. Ned whined at the unfairness of cats being allowed on furniture then went to the foot of the bed and lay down.

Chapter Fourteen

Christopher jammed his foot on the pedal and the Jag leaped forward. The odometer needle approached one hundred and still he didn't gain on the car ahead.

Luckily, there were few vehicles on the road at this time of night.

He frowned. Where was Lai going? She had turned away from New Orleans nearly twenty minutes ago, taking several side roads, but like a compass needle the nose of her car always pointed south.

The taillights ahead of him swerved to the right. He cursed under his breath and gripped the wheel. He'd be lucky if he didn't fly past the turn. He swung to his right and onto a narrow lane. His tires screamed like a cougar as he took the turn on two wheels.

"Damn you, Lai," he muttered as he hit a particularly large pothole. As he hunched over the wheel, his fingers grazed the car's dashboard. "Hang in there, sweetheart."

The coal-black road didn't even have a white line painted down the middle. There were fields beside and ahead of him, but no buildings.

As Lai's brake lights flashed, he slammed on the brakes. Both cars fishtailed violently. At the speed his car was traveling, he was on her in moments. To avoid smashing into her, he pulled alongside.

Lai's window was open.

Christopher pushed a button and his window slid down. "What the hell are you doing?" he shouted over the wind.

She raised her arm in a blurred movement. Tiny sparks of glistening light came crashing through his window. The necklace landed against the side of his face. One of the diamonds cut his cheek, stinging his skin. He jerked the wheel and went bouncing into a ditch. The car stalled as his tires dug into the narrow channel of dirt, his head hitting the steering wheel before his seatbelt jerked him back. Luckily, the impact wasn't hard enough to set off the air bags.

Lai stuck her hand out the window and waved, as her car shot down the road.

It took him several precious minutes to ease the car out of the ditch and back onto the road. He'd lost sight of her taillights but he continued doggedly on, searching the road as he drove.

A lane appeared on his right. On a hunch, he took it. The road wound upward. He reached the top and braked. The tires screeched and bit into the ground, rocking the car.

Below, light from an airstrip cut through the dark.

Lai was out of her car and running toward the waiting helicopter. Arms reached out to pull her in.

He could hear the whine of the blades as they whipped around. The helicopter lifted off. It hovered a moment then headed straight up into the night sky.

Exhausted, he leaned his head back against the soft leather headrest. He turned the interior light on and pulled a loupe and a high-powered flashlight out of the glove compartment, half-convinced Lai had thrown a paste copy at him.

He studied the necklace, puzzled. It was genuine all right. What in hell was she up to?

* * * * *

Unaware of the drama playing out in the night or perhaps beyond caring, Gabby slept the sleep of the dead. A little after eight, she dragged herself out of bed. A quick shower, made her feel nominally better. She threw on a faded blue tee shirt and shorts and headed for the breakfast room, tucking her wet hair behind her ears as she walked.

Christopher and Tamara were already seated. Tamara

placidly sipped her tea while Christopher, as usual, had his nose stuck in the paper. He lowered it when Gabby walked in, gave a short nod and then returned to his newspaper.

A jagged cut sliced down his cheek and a bump that was purpling nicely stood out on his forehead. Dark circles underscored his eyes.

Nerves flipped in her belly. She slid in a chair across from Tamara and gave her a questioning look.

Tamara shrugged, trying to look noncommittal, but Gabby could see the worry lines between her eyes.

"What the hell happened to you?" Gabby demanded as she poured herself a cup of hot coffee. She bit back an expletive as the steaming liquid sloshed across her hand. She shook it, sending a few drops on the table, blotching the pristine linen tablecloth.

Christopher looked pointedly at her hand. The sneer on his bruised face made him look more rakish than ever. Shaking his paper, he stuck his nose back in it.

She leaned across the table and mashed down the papers. "Well?"

He looked up, his eyes narrowing.

She waited for a scathing comment. Instead his face relaxed and he studied the creamy flesh visible above her small tee with appreciation.

Gabby reddened. "Well?" she repeated.

"Sit. Sit." He motioned her back into her chair.

"She isn't exactly a dog, my dear," Tamara said dryly. Watching the two adversaries, she added with a twinkle in her eye, "My, this is much better than going to the movies."

Gabby flopped down in her chair, deciding to ignore Tamara's comment.

Christopher rolled his eyes.

Gabby enunciated slowly and clearly, "What happened?"

After sipping his coffee, which seemed to revive him

somewhat, he said, "The jewels have been returned to their rightful owner."

Tamara clapped her hands. "My hero."

"Piece of cake." Christopher reached for his coffee again.

"I can see that," Gabby stared pointedly at his battered face. "Who was the woman?"

"How should I know?"

"Yeah right. How did you get them back?"

He sat his cup down and waited so long she didn't think he was going to answer. Finally, he shrugged. "It was the strangest thing. She could have gotten away with them, but instead she threw them at me, like the theft was a diversionary tactic and the necklace wasn't what she was after at all."

Gabby and Tamara looked uneasily at each other, a look Christopher intercepted.

"What's up?" he demanded.

"Have you seen the local section of the paper, dear?" Tamara asked, as she reached for a croissant.

"You're changing the subject, Auntie."

"Actually, I was talking to Gabriella, but you might find it entertaining, as well."

Tamara bit into the warm roll.

Gabby set down the beignet she'd picked up and reached for the paper.

Christopher's eyes narrowed. He held it just out of reach. "Auntie, you are up to something, now what's going on?"

Tamara looked straight at him. "My dear, I don't know a thing about that break-in."

Only Gabby caught the slight emphasis on *that.*

Christopher gave her a disbelieving look but let it go. Without a word, he turned his attention to the paper, the pages rustling as he did so.

Gabby sighed in relief.

"Very enterprising, my dear," Tamara said in her usual calm voice. "However did you get it in the morning's edition?" Before Gabby could respond, she continued, "You clever thing. You have more of a reputation in the news business than you've let on."

"Marie Antoinette Unwillingly Parts With Jewels," Christopher read aloud then fell silent as he perused the rest of the article. When he finished, he carefully folded the paper and laid it beside his plate. "Well, Aunt Tam," he said, though his eyes were on Gabby, "quite an interesting little piece of journalism—witty, acerbic and champion for The Tiger. And I quote, 'though, the thief known as The Tiger only steals the finest jewels from the richest clientele, this reporter feels if The Tiger was enjoying the gala festivities, he was mingling with New Orleans society and not working'."

Tamara brushed it aside as irrelevant. "Interesting, dear, but I preferred the line about a particular Southern belle and Venus that could have passed for twins, with just one or two more eyelifts."

Heat crept into Gabby's cheeks.

To her intense relief, Christopher's unsettling gaze finally moved to Aunt Tam. For just a moment a flicker of amusement crossed his face then he turned his attention back to Gabby.

"My, my you were quite the busy little bee last night."

"Apparently, so were you," she shot back.

He raised his left eyebrow and grinned hatefully. "Think I was out prowling do you?"

She stifled a yawn. "It makes no difference to me what you were doing." Then added spitefully, "Are you sure you didn't get the jewels back by seducing the poor woman who stole them?"

He gave an inelegant snort. "Poor woman?"

"It's really none of my concern." She hitched her nose in the air and held out her hand. "May I see the sports section? Any mention of the Cardinals' Spring Training Camp?"

"No.

"Good writing." He handed her the paper. "But let me give you a little piece of advice. There are some people I wouldn't go out of my way to alienate."

"Are you threatening me?"

He gave a hard laugh. "You've made it abundantly clear my opinion is of no importance to you whatsoever. No. I was referring to the people you pricked in your column. Some people tend to take themselves quite seriously and don't enjoy being made to look foolish."

"Oh, really? You never struck me as the sort to worry about anyone's opinion but your own."

"I can take care of myself."

"So can I."

"You are a pigheaded, opinionated babe in the woods."

"Coffee anyone?" Tamara inquired.

"No!" they both snapped.

Gabby bit into her beignet counting to ten as she chewed.

Christopher threw down the newspaper and without a backward glance, left the table.

Heat flashed behind Gabby's eyes as she shoved the rest of the warm, sugary yeast-pastry into her mouth.

Smiling, Tamara reached over and patted her arm. "Would you like to see my globe, dear?"

Her unpleasant host forgotten, Gabby masticated then swallowed. "Yes, please. Though I must warn you, I still intend to get it back." It would be so much easier if she didn't like Tamara.

Tamara patted her lips with the linen napkin, sat it aside

and stood up.

"Join the crowd," she said rather sarcastically.

Gabby sighed and rose too. Tamara had a good point. Her globe seemed to be unusually popular.

Tamara interrupted her musings. "My dear, when the time is right, I'm sure it will be yours."

Gabby threw her a startled look. "Why do you say that?"

Tamara smiled, but didn't answer, as she walked toward the conservatory, her gown floating around her.

Gabby asked hesitantly, breaking the silence. "Have you ever seen anyone in the crystal ball?"

Tamara smiled at her knowingly. "My late husband. And you?"

As they entered the conservatory, Gabby touched a white orchid, its texture soft and cool. "Yes." She studied the flower then looked up. "Can you tell me why that is? Why doesn't everyone see a face in it? Do you think whoever is trying to steal it sees a face?"

Tamara laughed. "So many questions. No. I don't think anyone else sees a face in the globe. As for the rest, the time isn't right."

"What does that mean?" Gabby threw up her hands, exasperated.

"You aren't ready for the truth."

She gave her an irritated look, but before she could protest, Tamara changed the subject, "Are you going to continue as the mysterious gossip columnist? I noticed you called yourself Miss Smith-Jones."

She grinned. "I'd hate for the talk to cease when I walk in a room just because people are afraid of what I might print."

"That would be awkward," Tamara agreed though her eyes twinkled. She bent and pinched off a spent blossom from its stalk, her forehead wrinkling in thought. "Your style is fresh and has a bite. The more intelligent members of society will be able to put two and two together and get four. But as long as you are under my and Christopher's collective wings, you'll be all right."

Gabby stirred uneasily. "I don't know if I'll be here long enough to write any more articles." Though there certainly was a larger than life story brewing.

"Time will tell, dear. Time will tell. Here we are."

Her head snapped up. They'd neared the back of the conservatory, where the globe stood in solitary splendor. She quivered, her senses centered on the crystal. It drew her, beckoned her. She would do anything, say anything, just to get her hands on it again.

Tamara broke into her thoughts. "My dear, I give you permission to come here and visit the crystal whenever you wish, as long as I have your word you will not take it out of this house."

She opened her mouth, but the words stuck in her throat. Her father's image swam before her saying sternly, "Bells do not tell lies." That little gem she'd learned the hard way when she was ten years old.

"I can't," she said regretfully then her face brightened. "But I will warn you before I take it."

Tamara laughed and stuck out her hand. "Done." She slipped away as Gabby approached the globe.

Gabby sank into the old-fashioned wicker settee on the east side of the crystal and reached out her hands. She touched the globe and closed her eyes as its warmth enclosed her, caressing her like a lover.

She moaned softly. Almost against her will, her eyes opened as the colors churned. Christopher's image began to form. Only this time it was accompanied by his voice. "What the hell are you doing?" He stood behind her scowling.

She dropped her hands. Mortified, heat flooded her face.

132

She couldn't have been more embarrassed if he'd walked in on her and a lover. Sticking her chin in the air, she said angrily, "How dare you watch me you Peeping Tom."

Christopher eyed her with distaste. "I expect this sort of behavior from Aunt Tam, she's a little fey. But you, you're just plain crazy."

She stood up intent on sweeping past him. But as she moved away, his arm shot out and he pulled her hard against him. He may have been disgusted by her wanton reaction to the globe, but he was also aroused.

That was quite evident.

His green eyes glittered like the globe as he stared down at her. Then abruptly, he lowered his head and his lips hard and sensual claimed hers.

Gabby had no intention of responding to his caveman tactics, but she found herself melting against him, weak in the knees, her insides turning liquid.

His lips softened, becoming less demanding, more persuasive. His hands explored her body. His touch light as a butterfly.

Her nerve ends tingled wherever his fingers moved.

"I can't fight you anymore. I want you, Gabriella. I've wanted you since the first moment I saw you in the rain," he whispered against her ear, his breath labored and uneven.

Heat shot through her like sizzling streaks of lightning. Maybe it was the residual effects of the crystal, but she wanted this impossible, arrogant man as much as he wanted her.

Her hand reached down and settled on his fly. "I believe you," and smiled against his lips.

His breath caught in his throat and the hand on her breast tightened. "I'm going to take that to mean you want me too."

His hand moved from her breast to her rib cage. Bending slightly, he placed his other behind her knees then picked her up.

She wasn't a small woman, but she felt light as a feather and fragile in his arms.

He walked toward the banana trees then through them.

Her eyes widened. A small gazebo had been built behind them. What she'd taken to be a rather large trellis for climbing vines was actually the west side of the pavilion.

He smiled a smile that softened his hard features, as he laid her on a wide blue couch. "Uncle Edward liked his creature comforts."

She nodded, too dazed to reply.

His smile turned to a wicked grin, the one that always sent her poor heart thumping. "I didn't think there was any way to shut you up, but it appears I was wrong."

Under normal circumstances, she would have at least given him a set down, if not a slap across his tanned cheek, but blood coursed so hotly through her body, she was barely aware of what he was saying.

"Shut up." She drew his head down to hers.

He kissed her until they were both moaning then drew back. In a hoarse voice, he asked, "Are you sure?"

Sure? Sure of what? She wondered distantly. That she liked him? No. She certainly wasn't sure of that. That she had to have him? *Oh, yes.* Every fiber of her being on fire with an intensity she'd never known before. Not bothering to answer, she pulled him down on top of her.

Chapter Fifteen

Soft, sensuous fabric caressed her skin as Gabby leaned back against blue silk cushions, her eyes closed and her body aglow with the after-wash of pleasure.

Holy cats, she'd never known anything like that. The gratification had been so intense she'd screamed or nearly had 'til Christopher's mouth closed over hers.

The warm, hard arm across her breast shifted.

Still smiling, she opened her eyes to stare into emerald ones only inches away.

Reality came hurtling back as the aftermath of pleasure dissipated. She sat up abruptly, nearly knocking Christopher to the floor. "Oh, my God. What have I done?"

He reached for his pants. "Nearly killed me, I'd say," he drawled. "I've never been with a more demanding woman in my life, except perhaps..." he named an actress that Gabby had always admired.

She drew back and slapped him hard. The sound cracked through the conservatory. A handprint stood out against Christopher's skin. The mark went from red to white, then began to fade. He rubbed his cheek.

"You son of a bitch." She stood up and jerked on her clothes. Her spine stiff, she strode away and didn't look back.

"Damn," Christopher swore softly. He'd been unforgivably rude. Part of it was an instinctive response to the look of sheer horror in her eyes when she had looked at him. But it was more than that. The truth, Miss Gabriella Bell scared the sweet hell out of him. Never in his life had he experienced anything as intense as his body connecting with hers. And his release had been like a lightning bolt.

He'd had women from one end of the continent to the

other. And he'd enjoyed them all. But this time it had been different. This woman had left her mark on him. The possession had not been just on his end. She had possessed him and in some indefinable way had taken a piece of his essence and claimed it for her own.

And he didn't like it. Not one little bit. So he'd fought back the only way he knew.

He'd hit below the belt when she was at her most vulnerable, humiliating her. Daring her to think it was anything but a casual encounter.

He'd apologize, of course. Someplace nice and public where they didn't run any risk of him sweeping her up in his arms and repeating his mistake.

Good God and in Uncle Edward and Aunt Tamara's conservatory! He'd never done that before. He respected Aunt Tam too much to carry on beneath her nose, in her own home!

He sank back on the couch and put his head in his hands and groaned, his hair falling across his fingers. Gabriella Bell was going to be the death of him.

A thought hit him and he straightened as a chill coursed down his spine. He'd forgotten to use the condom he kept in his wallet. Damn it! He couldn't believe it. He never forgot. He prided himself on being a responsible partner.

A ringing issued from his pants pocket. He slid out his cell phone and snapped open the lid still distracted. "Hello."

"Hello, Christopher. It's been a long time." The voice, deceptively soft and seductive, masked the hard heart of a killer, not to mention one of the most notorious thieves in India.

"Not long enough. What do you want, Lai?" Though he had a pretty good idea. His source had told him an oriental woman wanted the globe. Who else could it be?

"Why, darling, that's simple enough. I want you."

"You've had me. Surely, by now you've found fresh blood. Younger, even more corrupt than mine."

A sigh could be heard on the other line. "I've never understood you, Christopher. Together we could have conquered the world. You are cold and ruthless but you've always had one major flaw."

He laughed, his voice harsh and brittle. "Because I draw the line at murder?"

"I prefer to think of it as eliminating the enemy."

He strode restlessly around the gazebo, his thoughts in a furious tangle. "So what about the necklace? Why did you take it and why did you give it back?"

"It was a diversionary tactic that failed."

Alert, he stilled. "What do you mean?"

"If you don't know, I have no intention of telling you."

He frowned. There was a piece to the puzzle that he was missing. "About the necklace..."

"I want you, Christopher," Lai said in a voice that at one time moved him profoundly.

He expulsed air through his nostrils and his lips went thin. "I'm not for sale."

She sighed into the phone. "If I can't have you, I'll settle for the globe."

An edge crept into his voice. "You can't have that either. I found out quite recently you were behind the theft of the globe. Why? Why waste your time and talents on a trinket?" The woman had never seen it. She couldn't possibly know its worth.

He waited but there was only silence on the other end of the phone. "I repeat. Why do you want the globe?"

"I have my reasons."

"You dared send your minions into my home?" Anger rose in his throat and nearly choked him.

"Which time, darling?"

He tensed. He'd wondered about the necklace, why Lai had bothered with it. Now, he knew. His aunt's words at the breakfast table came floating back to him.

"My dear, I don't know a thing about that break-in." Both women had been evasive this morning. Damn them, they had both known.

"I want the globe, darling."

"Why?" Though he thought he knew.

"Because of its power."

The answer took him by surprise. It wasn't what he'd expected. "Come on Lai. You are an intelligent woman. Surely, you don't believe in all that mumbo jumbo?"

"You've been away from India too long. Perhaps, it's time you came home."

"Perhaps, it's time you went home. Why this sudden penchant for the States? You seldom venture out of India."

"Why you, of course, darling. Besides, I've decided I like it this country. I might set up my small community here."

His jaw clenched. Being on the same content with Lai was closer than he liked, but Lai in the States was unthinkable. If meeting her would get rid of her, so be it.

"Where and when do you want to meet?"

"Tomorrow morning." She gave him an address close to Chicago's Chinatown. "You'll bring the globe?"

"We'll talk about the globe when I see you."

"Christopher."

"Yes?"

"Get rid of the elephantine blonde."

His knuckles whitened as he gripped the phone. "You're having my house watched?" His voice was silken.

"No, Christopher. I'm having her watched." She laughed lightly and hung up.

His skin pricked as her laughter curled down his spine

like a snake. Barely aware of the exotic heavy scents hanging in the air, he stared unseeing at the profusion of orchids outside the gazebo. His lips drew back from his teeth and the skin across his cheeks tightened.

"Mess with me and I'll take you down, Lai."

With a jab of his index finger, he keyed a number on his phone.

* * * * *

Christopher strode to his room, threw clothes into a leather suitcase, tossed his toiletry bag into his carry-on and walked out, closing the door behind him.

Jericho tracked him down in the upstairs hall and wound in and out of his legs, hinting for treats. When none were forthcoming, he hissed and stalked away, his dark brown tail straight in the air.

"Likewise, I'm sure," Christopher muttered.

He ran lightly down the curved oak staircase and went in search of Tamara. He found her in the courtyard. Thank God not the solarium.

She sat on a black wrought iron bench in front of the fountain, a pair of gardening gloves in her hand.

He placed one foot on the bench and leaned his arms across his leg. "You didn't tell me someone broke in last night."

"Didn't I, dear? It must have slipped my mind."

His look told her exactly what he thought of that errant piece of nonsense. "I'm going to lock it in the safe."

"No, dear, you are not. The globe is staying right where it is."

He straightened, dropping his foot to the ground. "Aunt Tam, how can you be so bloody stubborn? That toy of yours isn't worth anyone's life."

"My dear, we have an excellent alarm system. No one would try anything while you are in the house. And Ned is a very good watchdog, I might add."

"If the intruder doesn't bribe him with steak," he muttered under his breath.

"What was that, dear?"

He felt it prudent not to repeat the bribe remark. "That's just it. I'm not going to be at home. I'm going to be gone for a few days."

Tamara raised a finely arched eyebrow.

He dropped a light kiss on her forehead. "Business."

She gave him a shrewd look. "This wouldn't have anything to do with our guest would it?"

"Hardly." He gave a light laugh before he turned serious. "Aunt Tam, I want you to get Ms. Bell out of here. And I'd like you to go visit your cousin Esmerelda for a few days." He put his hands on her shoulders.

"You think there will be another attempt made for the globe?"

"Yes."

"Well, I don't intend to go anywhere. And if you want Ms. Bell to leave, I'm afraid you're going to have to tell her yourself."

A hot flush raced up his neck and spread across his face. He ran his hand around his collar his shirt suddenly too tight.

No problem. And if she didn't think he was a bastard before, this would definitely seal his fate. Not that he really cared, he reminded himself hastily. So be it, it would be better than finding her in an alley with that lovely throat slit. Lai was very vindictive.

"Christopher," Tamara said gently, "if we are in danger, it isn't going to go away just because we change localities."

"You may be right, but nonetheless, we need some distance between you and the globe." His jaw tightened and his eyes narrowed. "I can't be in two places at once and this is one trip I must make."

*****

Gabby had stormed upstairs and began packing. She was in the middle of throwing her worn tennies on top of her peach evening gown, when Beatrice came in with a fresh vase of flowers, followed by Ned, his tongue hanging out.

The dog wagged his tail and walked over to his mistress. She patted his fuzzy head absently.

"What are you doing?"

Gabby looked up, but didn't answer. The maid was dressed in her starched black uniform with a gleaming white apron. Gabby suspected Tamara wouldn't care if she ran around in jeans, but Beatrice had a strong sense of propriety.

"Does Miz. James know you're leaving?"

"I will tell her as soon as I'm done packing."

Beatrice sniffed, walked over to the table in front of the window, picked up the vase filled with drooping flowers and sat down the new one. Without turning around, she walked out.

Ned followed her, looking over his shoulder at his mistress as if inviting her to come. His mistress ignored him and kept packing. With a soft whine, he followed Beatrice out.

A knock sounded at the door.

"Come in." Gabby threw in a handful of white undies.

She looked up and saw Christopher standing in the doorway. Heat built behind her eyes, but before she could say anything, he took a quick look at the suitcase. "Good you're packing."

Glancing wildly around, Gabby picked up a shoe to throw at him, but he was already gone.

Temper skittered down her nerve endings, as she snapped the locks of her worn suitcase. *Bastard.* Her chest heaved as she sucked in air.

Tipping back her head she closed her eyes. How could

141

he have lessened what passed between them? With a few cutting words he had turned something beautiful into something casual and sordid. She clenched her hands. And how could she have made love to a man she loathed and despised?

A knock sounded at the door and Tamara stuck her head in. "May I come in?"

Gabby tamped down her anger, though heat still came and went at a hectic pace in her cheeks and behind her eyes.

Tamara walked in and sat on the yellow settee. "Going somewhere, dear?"

"Home." Gabby heaved the suitcase onto the floor with a little more force than necessary.

Tamara handed her an envelope. "By the way, this came in the mail and I forgot to give it to you."

Gabby stuck it into her back pocket.

"Aren't you going to open it?"

She managed not to roll her eyes, a habit she had when she was annoyed and pulled the envelope out. The name of the local newspaper was typed in the left-hand corner. She drew out the check. It was for an amount that made her head spin.

"Really, dear, if you wish to remain anonymous from your readership, you should get a post office box."

Gabby gave her an admiring look. "You have a very devious mind."

"You know Mr. and Mrs. Murckle are having a party tomorrow night. I'm sure there will be lots of lovely tidbits floating around."

Tamara was pouring it on a bit too thick.

Looking around, Gabby spied a pair of white socks and a pair of pink lacy bikinis on the floor. She grabbed them, opened the suitcase and threw them in. She shut it with a snap then looked directly at Tamara. "Why do you want me to stay?"

"Because I believe it's your destiny."

Gabby's eyes widened and she realized her mouth was open. She probably looked like a trout waiting for a fly so she closed it with a snap.

"And if you were leaving because you had a tiff with my nephew, he has already left. So it's really not necessary. Quite a coincidence don't you think?"

Still gripping the check, she stared at the vase of daffodils. What was Christopher up to? Had she frightened him off, or was he off on another heist?

She made a lightning decision. She wasn't going to be the one to leave with her tail between her legs. Besides if he wanted her to leave that was reason enough to stay.

She put the suitcase back on the bed and began to unpack. "I never turn down an invitation to a good party."

Beatrice came in carrying two sprays of roses, one red, one yellow.

Gabby's eyebrows rose. *As if there aren't enough flowers in the room already.*

She handed the yellow spray to Tamara and the red to Gabby. Her name was scrawled across the attached card. Gabby looked at Beatrice questioningly.

"Master Christopher always gives his aunt roses when he leaves."

"But to my knowledge, he's never given them to anyone else." Tamara qualified, "At least not when he's leaving on a trip."

Gabby gave a brief thought to tossing the roses on the floor and stomping up and down on them. Then decided that would be in poor taste in front of Tamara...maybe after she left.

As if on cue, Tamara rose and walked across the room and stepped into the hall.

"Well, dear, I'll see you at dinner." The door swung shut behind her.

Gabby stared at the closed portal. The woman was as subtle as smoke, but she managed to get her way. And every day drew Gabby more, unwillingly, under her spell. How did one go about stealing from someone who had befriended you? Whom you admired and considered a friend?

Since her encounter in the solarium, she wasn't even sure she wanted the blasted thing. The last thing she had any desire to see was Christopher's hateful face. Her chin trembled. It seemed a no win situation.

Her chest heaving, she unpacked determined to forget that wild, ecstatic coupling. *I will not cry.* Unaware of the tears raining down her face until they plopped warm and wet on her hands.

She swiped at her face with her fingertips. "Damn you, Christopher Saint. Damn you."

Chapter Sixteen

Wearing a faded pair of gym shorts and a tee shirt with the arms and bottom cut off, Gabby paced the confines of her room. Without Christopher's disturbing presence, dinner and the ensuing evening had been uneventful.

Stretched out on the bed, all four paws in the air, Jericho snored. Ned lay on the floor, his head between his paws. Gabby heaved herself on the bed, punched up the pillows and lay down on her back.

She grabbed the remote and surfed until she found an old Richard Gere and Julia Roberts movie. About halfway through, her eyes began to close.

She sat up and looked around. An unfamiliar movie was playing. What woke her? Then she heard the low whine that had penetrated her consciousness. She got up and whispered, "What is it, Neddy boy?"

He stood by the door, his fur on end. She reached out to touch him but he ignored her, his attention on the door. She ran to her nightstand and grabbed her bottle of mace then went quietly back to the door. She hesitated a moment then with a jerk, threw it open.

She stood poised in the doorway, her finger on the cap. No one was there. Ned went running down the stairs barking.

Tamara opened her door. "What is it, dear?" she called from down the hall.

"I think someone's in the house. Stay here. If I holler for help, call the police." She ran nimbly down the spiral staircase after Ned.

"Ned, where are you?" She pitched her voice to a whisper. The house was huge, he could be anywhere.

Beatrice came running from her rooms behind the kitchen.

Gabby's face split in a wide grin when she saw her. Beatrice had on a red satin gown that reached from her throat to her feet. A bright red satin cap hid her grizzled curls. In her left hand, she held a wooden rolling pin.

"What's all the commotion about?" she demanded, panting and out of breath.

"I think someone is in the house."

Just then Ned bayed.

"The solarium. Quick." Gabby began to run, Beatrice huffing and puffing behind her.

"The crystal!" She ran harder.

They'd nearly reached it when they heard a huge crash. The security system began emitting a shrill buzz. The police would soon be on their way.

As she reached the solarium, she flipped the switch, flooding it with light.

She glanced quickly toward the back. The ball winked, untouched. Behind it was a yawning hole, where the would-be burglar had exited through the glass. Ned came trotting toward them, a piece of black cloth in his mouth.

"Good boy, Ned." Reaching down and patting him, Gabby gingerly removed the cloth from his mouth. "Our burglar is certainly consistent in his wearing apparel," she observed, holding it at arm's length and studying it.

Beatrice bent to pat Ned, wheezing. "Dog, you is a hero. Again."

Tamara walked in as casually as if she were out for an afternoon stroll. She stopped beside the other two women and arched a winged eyebrow. "Someone is certainly determined to get my globe."

"My globe," Gabby replied automatically.

Tapping a shell-pink fingertip against her chin, Tamara paid her no mind.

Sirens screamed in the distance.

Tamara turned to Beatrice. "You'd better get dressed. I'll go to the door."

"I'll go to the door." Gabby heaved a sigh. "If you know where to get hold of him, you'd better call Christopher."

Tamara nodded. "He wears a pager. The poor dear is going to be dreadfully upset."

"Isn't he just." Gabby knew her tone sounded more spiteful than sympathetic, but couldn't bring herself to care.

Tamara tilted her head to one side and gave her a quizzical look. At that moment, the doorbell rang.

Gabby shrugged her shoulders and headed for the door.

Two of New Orleans finest stood on the veranda, one middle-aged with a paunch above his belt, the other young and eager.

Tamara made a brief appearance but Gabby fielded most of the questions.

It was closing in on three before the uniformed policemen left, dissatisfied with their report. "We'll be sure and let you know if we run across anyone wearing a pair of black pants with a hole torn out of them," the younger one said with heavy sarcasm.

Gabby shut the door behind them, leaning against it.

"Christopher will be in tomorrow," Tamara said from the stairway.

Gabby nodded, too tired to care one way or the other.

Beatrice came out of the solarium, where she had been cleaning up broken glass and taping plastic over the window. "I'm going to bed."

Without a word, the other two women headed for their respective rooms.

The next morning Gabby dragged herself down the steps to the breakfast room.

Dark circles ringed her eyes and she felt a hundred years old. Some people thrived on lack of sleep, she wasn't one of them. Tamara sat at the table looking relaxed and fresh, wearing a wispy yellow dress that reached to her ankles.

Next to her sat Christopher. His head, as usual, buried behind a newspaper.

Tamara looked up and smiled. "Oh, hello, dear."

Sitting down, Gabby nodded and reached for the coffee.

Tamara dabbed at her mouth with a white linen napkin. "Well, I'll just leave you two young things to finish your breakfast."

Looking at her nearly full plate, Gabby protested, "But you haven't finished your breakfast."

"My eyes were apparently bigger than my stomach."

Standing, she leaned over and kissed the top of Christopher's head. "Have a good day, dears." She floated out of the room.

Gabby took a swallow of coffee. The hot liquid roll down the back of her throat and the caffeine kicked in. She straightened her shoulders and prepared for battle.

"Well, well if it's not the premiere playboy of the South. Who were you seducing last night, anyone I know? The lovely oriental perhaps? A blonde in the afternoon, a brunette that night?"

Christopher lowered the paper. His face looked nearly as haggard as her own. "I'm not in the mood, Gabriella."

She tried a different tack. "So why are your friends trying to steal my crystal? What's so special about a ball that reflects nothing but your face?"

That got his attention. He looked at her like she'd grown a second head. "Excuse me?"

It was hardly flattering, she thought annoyed. "You heard me."

"My dear Ms. Bell," he drawled hatefully. "Were you by chance smoking an illegal substance when you saw my face in *my aunt's*," he emphasized, "globe?"

148

She wished the words back the moment they were out. Oh well, she'd wanted to see his reaction, even if the end result was that she looked a monumental fool.

She rose from the table. She hated wasting a perfectly good breakfast, but the alternative was unthinkable. She'd raid the kitchen later.

Christopher's hand shot out. "Wait."

She looked pointedly at it.

He dropped her wrist, stood and came round the table to stand beside her. "I owe you an apology."

Her eyes widened and her heart sank. *Please, oh please, don't say you're sorry.*

"The last time I saw you I behaved boorishly and said some rather crude things. I'm not going to say I'm sorry for the sex. It was a fantastic experience. I just don't want you to read anything into it. I'm not looking for a relationship."

She flushed, but didn't look away. "And don't you read anything into it. Because I wouldn't have you if you came crawling on all fours."

He gave her a satirical smile. "Don't hold your breath on that one."

She looked him up and down. "So far," she emphasized, "you are the best piece I've ever had. But as a human being you suck. And I have no doubt there are other womanizers out there that can match your performance."

She tossed her head. Her hair flew about her face then settled back on her shoulders. Carrying herself like a queen, she stalked out of the room.

He stared after her, uncertain whether to laugh or go after her and shake her 'til her teeth rattled then kiss those pouty lips until they were both weak.

He groaned and hoped she was making up that little conversation stopper about seeing his face in the globe. If not, he was doomed. But that was the second time she'd mentioned it, once in Springfield and now here.

The noose was tightening around his neck.

He had always been a lone wolf. He liked his lifestyle. He was responsible to no one but himself and his Aunt Tam. He had learned at an early age to take care of himself and avoid commitment. Commitment led to love and love could destroy you. Losing his mother had broken his young heart. And when it had finally healed, he'd lost Uncle Edward. Losing Aunt Tam didn't bear thinking about. But there would be no more on his list of emotional casualties. He would make damn sure of that.

No matter, he didn't believe all that hogwash anyway.

* * * * *

Gabby paced the length of her room. She was a reporter and it was time she started acting like one. She'd let a heavy-duty attraction stand between her and a lead that had all the markings of a story to launch her nationally. And she was living in the same house as the man who held the key to the mystery, had bedded him in fact, or he her. But better not go there.

Christopher was a master at hiding his emotions. He could wriggle out of situations and answering her questions like an eel.

But as much as he hated it, he wasn't nearly as immune to her as he would like her to think. A grim smile crossed her lips. Maybe it was time to do a little role-playing. She walked to the French chest of drawers, opened a drawer and drew out her ammo. She held up a skimpy pink top and a pair of white shorts, perfect for muggy New Orleans.

Several minutes later she was ready.

Taking a deep breath, she straightened her shoulders, marched to Christopher's room and knocked.

No reply.

Looking up and down the hall, she slowly turned the knob.

Entering his suite, she could hear water running. Her quarry was in the shower. Making sure she left the door wide open, she sat on the bed and waited.

Fifteen minutes later, Christopher emerged from his bath. His hair wet and slicked back, his face shaven and a black towel knotted around his waist.

It would be black, Gabby thought irrelevantly.

He stopped in his tracks.

She let her gaze rove over him. What pecs! His skin was bronzed from the sun. A light matting of brown hair furred his chest. His shoulders were broad and his waist tapered. No wonder she'd succumbed. The man was drop-dead gorgeous.

Her glance dropped lower. If the front of his towel was anything to go by, he liked what he saw too.

He arched an eyebrow at her.

She swallowed her smirk and smiled. "Since neither of us finished breakfast this morning, I thought you'd like to buy me some coffee and beignets."

"What are you up to, Bell?"

She widened her eyes. "Just trying to be friendly."

"Knock it off. What do you want?" He looked at her, looked at his bed, then back at her again.

She pushed off the bed, walked over to the far wall and studied his sports memorabilia. Apparently, he had played baseball, football and basketball in high school and football in college.

She sensed his gaze on her. Her body responded with heat.

She turned and glanced at him, once again reminded of a cat—not a tame housecat, but a jungle cat. His eyes were alert and he balanced easily on the balls of his feet. Did the kitty intend to pounce and play with his victim or devour it?

She shook her head at her imaginings. "I have questions and you have the answers."

He gave an exaggerated sigh. "What has your fertile little imagination come up with now? Has someone else's face popped into the crystal ball?"

She started a hot reply then swallowed it. He was doing it again, sidetracking her, making her forget the issues. She crossed her arms. "Are you afraid of me?"

"You scare sweet hell out of me."

Her mouth dropped and her eyebrows shot up. Whatever she had expected it wasn't this.

Unexpectedly, he capitulated. "Give me ten minutes to dress. I know a quiet courtyard that serves a fine cup of chicory and warm beignets."

She smiled, her mouth already watering. "I'll wait for you downstairs." Before closing the door she thought she heard him say, "Saint, you are a fool."

Plopping down on an antique settee in the entryway, she thumbed through a local magazine then looked up when he came running lightly down the stairs, dressed in khakis, an olive-colored polo and loafers.

"Ready?"

"Ready," she smiled, putting down the magazine and getting up. *I hope.*

He escorted her to his Jag and held the door open as she climbed in. After she was settled, he shut her door, walked over to the driver's side and got in.

As the car purred to life, he turned the wheel and slid it into the traffic.

Chapter Seventeen

Gabby headed downstairs, humming under her breath. The day and the evening had been unexpectedly fun. Christopher could be quite charming when he chose. And he'd turned it on full blast last night.

They'd sat in a courtyard bathed in sunlight eating beignets, drinking chicory coffee and listening to a jazz band playing across the street. Afterwards, they'd spent the day touring New Orleans and the evening enjoying its night life.

He'd skillfully parried all her questions about the necklace and globe and turned the conversation to safer subjects. When they'd returned home, he'd kissed her lightly on the cheek at her door and turned away, though not before she'd seen his eyes darken as he pressed her hand.

The ring of the doorbell brought her back to the present. She opened the door, thinking to save Beatrice a trip.

Gulping, she stared into stony blue eyes the color of her own. A foot hastily inserted itself into the doorway as she tried to slam the door.

"Gabriella Josephine Bell, open this door immediately," the voice bellowed loud enough to be heard up and down the block.

She reluctantly opened the door. "Hello, Daddy."

Sergeant Bell stepped inside. "What in the name of Mary, Joseph and Jesus are you doing here?" he thundered.

Christopher emerged from the breakfast room carrying a newspaper. Freshly shaved and showered, and looking impossibly sexy, his eyes met Gabby's and his harsh features softened.

He turned to the older man glaring indiscriminately at himself and Gabriella and said in a cold voice, "May I help you?"

"You bet you can, you young whelp," her father said grimly before lunging at him.

The move took Christopher by surprise. He grunted as the ham-like fist made contact with his flat stomach. He wrapped his fingers inside his palm and clipped the older man on the chin.

"Don't you hit my father!" Gabby screamed. Christopher's upraised fist dropped to his side and his jaw went slack with surprise. "Father?"

The older man didn't hesitate. His fist made contact with Christopher's left eye.

Gabby jumped between the two men. She turned on her father. "Stop that this instant!"

"Get out of the way, Gabriella," he growled.

A calm voice came from across the room. "I must concur with Gabriella, I can't have you beating on my nephew, sir, or have my nephew hitting you."

Everyone stopped and turned as Tamara walked across the foyer.

Sergeant Bell bowed instinctively and reached for his nonexistent cap. "Ma'am."

Tamara nodded. "I take it you are our lovely Gabriella's father?"

He bowed over her hand. "That is correct, ma'am."

Tamara went on as if they were being introduced at a ballroom instead of the middle of a brawl. "And have you made the acquaintance of my nephew?"

A storm cloud once more descended over Sergeant Bell's features. "I'll not have my daughter being seduced by a shady character like this one. Gabby get your things, we're going home."

Tamara laid her hand on the sergeant's arm. "Mr. Bell, come into the breakfast room and have a nice cup of tea and we'll try to straighten out this little contretemps."

The sergeant hesitated.

Tamara smiled up at him coquettishly. "I haven't had the pleasure of having breakfast with a gentleman, other than my nephew, since my dear husband died." She began leading him toward the breakfast room.

To Christopher and Gabby's amazement her father went, though he muttered direly, "It will be my pleasure, ma'am. But don't think to change my mind."

Christopher and Gabby stared at one another, bewildered.

"Your eye is swelling."

"Eff my eye," he said inelegantly.

Gabby giggled.

Christopher smiled back. A vase of roses on the white marble end table filled the room with a heady aroma. He plucked one out of the crystal jar and handed it to Gabby.

"You don't have to go back you know. You're over twenty-one."

She stared at him in astonishment. "I thought you would be dancing in the street when I left."

He shrugged then grinned crookedly. "You are a bit of an acquired taste. But seriously, Gabby, I don't know how safe it would be. At least here, I can keep an eye on you. "

"So you finally realize I'm right," she crowed.

He looked at her as if she were demented. "What in sweet hell are you talking about?"

This time it was she who looked at him as if he were the one not hitting on all eight cylinders. "Why the globe of course. If you think I would be in danger, you have obviously realized it is truly mine, because you must know I wouldn't leave without it."

He swore low and quite fluently. "You are not taking that bloody ball."

She opened her mouth to make a heated protest but

before she could get started her esteemed parent walked in, Tamara on his arm.

Her mouth fell open and even Christopher lost a bit of his aplomb. Her father was relaxed and smiling. Forgetting their earlier tiff, Gabby reached over and whispered. "Do you think she gave him drugs?"

He responded out of the corner of his mouth, "Whatever she offered, I believe he accepted."

They both stared at his aunt.

As Sergeant Bell and Tamara came to a halt in front of Gabby and Christopher, the wispy material of the dress Tamara wore settled around her. The dress was much like the one she'd worn the first day they'd met. Only this one was a pale pink and mint green paisley.

"My dear," Tamara said, "I think all things considered it would be best if you went home, at least for the time being."

A sharp stab of pain speared Gabby, though she wasn't sure why. Why should she feel betrayed? After all she had come to remove the woman's globe, no, her globe, she amended hastily.

She glanced at Christopher, who was eyeing his aunt through narrowed eyes as if he wasn't quite certain what she was up to.

But it turned out to be her father who was her undoing. "Honey, I would truly prefer you come home. Ms. Edwards has been telling me about what's been going on and I don't like it one bit. But as she pointed out, you are of age and the decision is ultimately yours." His voice gentle, she could almost feel his solid arms wrap around her.

Taking a deep breath, she stuck her chin in the air. "Fine. But the globe goes with me."

Tamara responded in her placid manner. "The globe is not yours yet, my dear. It stays with me."

Christopher's eyes narrowed and his jaw tightened as he listened to the two of them. He'd had enough. His home had been broken into too many times to mention.

His aunt was hatching some plot. Lai was back in his already tumultuous life wreaking havoc left and right. And now this irritating, magnificent woman who'd effortlessly wrapped silken strands around his heart much like her golden legs around his body, was leaving him, all because of the damn globe.

"Be damned to the both of you. I'm taking that damn crystal and putting it in the vault."

His suspicions flew into overdrive when his aunt said, "You do whatever you think best, dear." His eyebrows soared causing him to wince at the stress put on his rapidly swelling eye.

"Christopher, you really should put something on that eye."

He bit back the retort he had uttered once already this morning.

"For all of you who seem to be having a hearing problem, the globe goes with me," Gabby said loudly and slowly.

Completely ignoring her, Christopher turned to her father. "Please keep a close eye on her. I've never known a woman more prone to getting herself into dangerous situations unless it's my aunt here."

Sergeant Bell gave a clipped nod.

Christopher looked at the man and knew that this time Gabriella's father was in complete sympathy with him.

* * * * *

Gabby sat in her tiny study staring at her computer screen. She had been home two weeks now. The night they'd left, she'd screamed and fought and literally been held back from punching Christopher in his good eye by her father.

Some character named Billy had bundled her, Jericho and Ned on Christopher's private aircraft, *sans* the crystal. Dad had boarded under his own steam.

She missed the globe much as she would a lover's touch. How dare Christopher put her wonderful swirling ball of mist and fire in a cold, dark vault. And how dare Tamara let him.

Finger-combing her hair back from her forehead, she heaved a sigh from deep in her belly. She missed him, the arrogant, self-centered bastard.

She even yearned for the steamy heat of New Orleans. Even if it was a spring day, it felt downright chilly here in the Midwest.

Ned whined and shoved his nose in her hand, his tail wagging. She patted him absently.

Standing up, she walked through the bedroom to the window. She pulled back the white cotton curtain and stared outside. A tiny smile tugged at the corners of her mouth as a dozen or more robins flew into the backyard. Strutting about, their heads bobbed up and down as they looked for worms in grass just beginning to green.

She loved the cheerful birds with their puffed-up orange breasts. It was hard to stay downcast with the jolly chirping creatures hopping self-importantly about the yard.

Besides, even if she hadn't heard from Tamara or Christopher, she had heard from the newspaper. A nice fat check had been forwarded from St. Charles Street.

Apparently, Tamara had taken over her role as Miss Smith-Jones, a.k.a. gossip columnist extraordinaire. Gabby smiled, maybe someone in the household that she felt so much affinity for missed her after all.

* * * * *

In a darkened apartment the phone rang. "Have all the preparations been made?"

An agitated voice responded. "I tell you, I won't do this.

Saint will kill me. I don't know what the girl means to him. Maybe she's his mistress, maybe she's not, but he takes a proprietary interest. He warned me off in no uncertain terms."

The voice on the other end of the phone was soft and mesmerizing. "Poor little man. What are you to do, caught between two tigers? The bigger tiger may cut out your heart and eat you.

But I, I will cut you into small pieces while you are still alive and throw your remains in the alley." Her voice hardened. "Do not fail me."

The phone clicked abruptly.

Chapter Eighteen

Gabby dreamed again. The same dream she'd been having for the past fourteen nights.

Christopher stood on a mountain top, the wind whipping around him, his eyes as green as the globe and as cold. He was searching, but for what? She could see the green glow of the globe on the valley floor far below. Had he misplaced it?

Then the dream changed from the previous ones she'd been having. He looked directly at her, his expression frantic. "Gabriella you are in danger. Get out of there." He began to growl.

No, it wasn't Christopher growling, it was Ned. She felt groggy and heavy-lidded, remnants of deep slumber and the disturbing dream. Or was it the cloying smell of musk and incense overriding the ever-present smell of dog hair?

She fought to open her eyes. From lowered lids, she saw a small slender figure dressed in black approach the bed. Something silver glinted in one hand and in the other she clutched a white cloth.

Ned sprang, eighty pounds of snarling fury bent on protecting his mistress. The thin silver stiletto flew through the air dropping the dog almost on top of his mistress.

The red stain spreading across the still form of her dog knocked the last of the fog from Gabby's brain. She jumped out of bed. "Why you…"

The tiny figure leaped in the air, her heel connecting with the side of Gabby's face. Gabby dropped without a sound. A white chloroformed cloth was placed over her face and held there.

"Was that really necessary?" a man said from the shadows.

"I don't want the cow coming to!" Lai responded.

"I was referring to the dog."

Lai gave a harsh laugh.

Leaky blanched.

"I wouldn't have thought you would have any objections to the death of this particular cur."

"I like dogs," Leaky muttered.

"Toss the ox over your shoulder and let's get out of here."

"Can't."

"What is wrong with you now?" Lai asked irritably then looked up.

Jericho stood between the bed and Leaky, every hair on his body on end, his teeth drawn back, his tail thrashing, crouched, ready to spring.

"Ah," Lai said pleased. "Cats I understand, especially royal ones. But I can't have you interfering in this night's work, little king." Still kneeling beside Gabby, the cloth in her hand, she straightened. "Come to me," she commanded.

"I said I can't," Leaky ground out.

"Not you, fool."

The cat turned on the woman and accepting the challenge, sprang. Jericho's fangs were bared in a silent snarl, catching the full brunt of the chloroform as Lai's arm shot out. Jericho fell, raking Lai's arms with unsheathed claws as he went down. The Siamese fell to the floor with his comrades.

Nursing her arm, where blood pooled in vertical lines through the dark clothing, Lai kicked viciously at the still form of the cat.

Leaky sneered. "I thought you liked cats."

Lai whirled on him. "If you don't want to join the he-devil, throw the cow over your shoulder and let's go."

Obeying, Leaky reached for Gabby and with a grunt

hoisted her on his shoulder, staggering. "Gaud Almighty, she's bigger than I am."

"Let's go," Lai said impatiently, heading for the back door. She opened the door and stood looking at the moonless, black night. The cat scratching her was a bad omen.

The Siamese's claws had scoured deeply into her skin. She, whose spirit was that of a cat. Her reflexes had been a split second too slow. Lai shook off the feeling of foreboding. "Let's go," she hissed impatiently.

As they crept out of the house, the phone began to ring.

* * * * *

On St. Charles Street, Christopher sat straight up in bed, his hands flat on the silky sheets. The dream had been so vivid he would swear it was real. Beads of sweat stood out on his forehead and his lungs worked like bellows. "It was only a dream," he muttered aloud in the dark room.

But instead of the anxiety subsiding, it continued to mount. He picked up the phone. She would of course treat him like the idiot he felt himself to be. But better her scorn than this paralyzing fear.

He punched in the 217 area code and the rest of the numbers. The phone rang. And rang.

Where the hell was she? It was three in the morning in corn capital USA. She was probably in bed with some stud. His hand tightened on the phone then relaxed.

He didn't doubt that she might be screwing someone else, but he would be surprised if she had left the animals overnight. The woman was a fanatic about those fur balls.

Clicking down the receiver, he took a deep breath and dialed information.

"I'd like the number of the Springfield Police Department."

He left a message for Sergeant Bell then strode to his mahogany antique chest of drawers and pulled open the top drawer. He pulled out his work clothes, black jeans and a black turtleneck, and threw them on. He slipped his feet in loafers not bothering with socks.

In less time than he would have thought possible the phone rang. He picked it up and said tersely, "Is she all right?"

The man on the other end of the phone breathed heavily as he fought for control.

"You young whelp. What have you done with her? If so much as a hair on her head is harmed I will personally cut out your heart then tear what's left of your bloody carcass apart and feed it to the buzzards." His voice took on an anguished tone. "What do you want from me? I have no money. What the hell do you want?"

Christopher gripped the phone so tight his hand hurt, but his voice was as unemotional as if he were inquiring about the weather. "Sergeant Bell, tell me exactly what happened."

"As if you don't know, you young bastard!"

"Sergeant Bell, I can't help you if you don't tell me what happened."

"Someone knifed the dog, broke the cat's rib and Gabriella is gone. Is that what you wanted to know, you spawn of Satan? You brought this to her door. Maybe you didn't actually do the deed, but you're responsible. And you'll pay, I promise you."

"Right now, I suggest we stick to the matter at hand. And that's getting your daughter back. After this is over, if you still want your pound of flesh you're welcome to try to collect it." With great restraint, Christopher laid the phone gently back in its cradle instead of slamming it down as he longed to do.

Refusing to give in to the debilitating panic threatening to engulf him, he strode across the bedroom and into his study, opened the top drawer of his desk and removed the fake bottom. Inside lay a black book with phone numbers too hot to leave on his cell phone. He sank into the gray leather chair and began dialing.

Twenty minutes later, Christopher leaned his head back against the top of the chair.

Lai's trail was littered with smoke and mirrors, her usual style. The only thing he knew for certain was that Leaky was not in New Orleans. He couldn't believe the little weasel had been foolhardy enough to help Lai, when he had given him a succinct description of what would happen to him if he did. He smiled grimly. Apparently, Leaky was more afraid of Lai than himself. A mistake, that.

Why hadn't she called? Probably drawing out the agony. Lai excelled in that. He got up abruptly and with a vicious movement threw the phone against the wall. It hit with a satisfying thunk.

Five minutes later his cell phone rang. "Darling." The voice on the other end was low and hypnotic. At one time he'd thought it the most sensual he'd ever known.

"There seems to be something wrong with your phone."

He looked at the cord pulled out of its socket and the ear piece out of its cradle, lying on the floor. "I can't believe you are calling to tell me my phone's out of order. What do you want?"

"Well, darling, I want you and the crystal."

* * * * *

Gabby stiffened as Lai gave her a sly look. Sitting on the floor, her back against a dirty wall, she was trussed up like a Christmas turkey waiting for the hatchet.

Lai hit the speaker button.

Christopher's voice wrapped around her, but instead of comforting her, it pinched at her. "You've already had me."

Gabby, her mouth taped shut, flinched. So this she-devil had known his hard magnificent body, the gentle questing hands and mouth. She wasn't surprised, but she would have preferred not to have had it confirmed.

Christopher continued, "Now why would a savvy business woman like you want a piece of green glass?" Then added almost as an afterthought, "And how does Ms. Bell fit into all this? I'm assuming since she's missing, you have her."

Ms. Bell waited with interest to hear the answer to that one.

"Well, darling..."

She rolled her eyes. One more *darling* and she might gag, not an easy feat when she had a wadded handkerchief stuck in her mouth and wide, silver duct tape holding it in place.

Glancing at Gabby, Lai said, "Let's just say I have a penchant for green glass and since you inexplicably have a penchant for the blonde Amazon here, she will work as a marvelous bargaining chip to expedite the transaction."

Gabby cringed as she heard Christopher's cold words. "Once again, Lai, your imagination outruns your common sense. You of all people should know Ms. Bell is hardly my type."

Lai shot Gabby a look of malicious triumph. "Then you won't mind if I kill her."

An uncontrollable shiver shot down Gabby's spine.

"Of course, I mind! Your lust for bloodletting is what drew us apart in the first place, Lai."

"Then bring me the globe."

"Where and when?"

"Calcutta."

Christopher's voice snapped like a whip over the phone. "I don't think so. It's too easy for a body to disappear in the Hooghly."

The blood drained from Gabby's head and pooled in her

feet. Dumped in a river? This did not sound good at all.

Watching Gabby, Lai gave a cold laugh and switched to Bengali.

"Are you afraid for yourself or for the blonde cow, darling?" Lai inquired in a silk-threaded voice.

Christopher responded in the same tongue. "I thought cows were sacred in your world."

"But you slaughter them in yours, so perhaps it is better if we meet in your world."

Christopher's gut ached and sweat stood out on his forehead as his hand tightened on the receiver. She was toying with him. If Lai had planned to make the trade in Calcutta, she would have never given in so easily.

He bit back words he longed to hurl at her, to tell her if she harmed Gabriella in any way he would make her pay two-fold and the suffering would be long and painful.

Instead, he switched back to English. "I repeat, where and when?"

"The Appalachians."

He blinked, surprised. "Why?"

"Because like the Himalayas, those that choose not to be found can disappear."

"You are absolutely crazy," he said finally.

Lai did not respond. The silence stretched out, forcing him to respond. "Fine, where in the Apps did you have in mind?"

"Mount Mitchell in the Black Mountains, so romantic, don't you agree, darling?"

"Give me an address."

"It's fifty yards off Moonshiner's Road, near the summit. Two trees growing together like Siamese twins mark the entrance. I'm sure you'll find us."

All Christopher could think about was the whistling

winds at six thousand feet, Gabriella tied and helpless with Lai's hand on her back and then a shove. An icy chill coursed through him.

"When?" he asked between clenched teeth.

"It's nearly dawn, shall we say twenty-four hours?"

"I'll be there."

Lai's voice went dangerously soft, "And Christopher, if you want to see Ms. Bell alive, don't disappoint me."

In a voice as soft as Lai's, he replied, "If you so much as harm one hair on her head, I will hunt you down and make you pay, Lai. That's a promise and you know I always keep my promises."

The line went dead.

In a very controlled manner, Christopher shoved the phone into his pants pocket.

A slight rustling sound made him whirl around, his hand on the gun in his other pocket.

Tamara stood in the doorway holding the globe. "I took it out of the vault yesterday."

"I won't even ask you how you knew." He walked toward her.

Tamara shrugged and handed the globe to Christopher. For a moment, warmth radiated through him and then the crystal once again turned cool.

"I give it to you for peace of mind. But you won't need it to trade because by the time you get there Gabriella will be gone."

Christopher threw her a startled look. "What the hell do you mean?"

Tamara shook her head. "I don't know other than she will be gone."

"Where?"

A worry line knit Tamara's brow. "Christopher, I can't answer that. I just know that she is alive and that you will need the globe to find her."

His hands clenched around the ball and it was all he could do not to hurl it against the wall. "This piece of stone has brought us nothing but trouble."

She smiled gently. "Only if you consider Ms. Bell trouble."

He gave her an incredulous look and snorted. "That woman is as much trouble as the damn crystal, if not more. No let me revise that. She's much more."

Tamara patted his arm, her touch as light as a butterfly, then reached up on tiptoe and placed a gentle kiss on his cheek.

He smelled lavender and the heat of her hand seeped into his skin and brought momentary comfort.

"Be careful, Christopher. Your journey is a long one, but in the end you and the one you love will come home safely."

Love? Before he could respond in the negative, Tamara glided silently from the room.

Chapter Nineteen

Gabby watched the oriental uneasily. The woman's smile chilled her. She knew instinctively that her captor would not only kill her but take pleasure in it. Damn Christopher anyhow for getting her into this mess. She had to get out and get out now.

She looked around, but saw nothing to help her.

The floor was a plain pine. The walls scattered with heads of dead animals. She looked at a moose on the opposite wall and winced, hoping she didn't share his fate.

There was a stone fireplace and an upstairs loft.

The air smelled stale, as if the place was rarely used. They must be in a hunting lodge.

She shivered in her faded gray nightshirt, cold and afraid. That woman kept looking at her as if she were a chicken about to lose its head.

Who else was with her? She was sure there was at least one other man, short and scrawny, but strong enough to carry her like a sack of potatoes.

As if on cue, Leaky came in.

"I'm going to get some sleep. Watch her," Lai ordered, heading for the loft. Before starting up the steps, she circled Gabby then placed a well-aimed kick to her ribs. "What he sees in you I'll never know," Lai said as she headed up the stairs.

Gabby winced. Fury overrode pain. *Just wait, bitch.*

Leaky watched Lai ascend the stairs and said in a low tone, "You don't want to tangle with that one."

He averted his face from Gabby's penetrating gaze. Turning, Leaky walked over and sank down on a faded green couch. Minutes later, his head began to nod. He jerked upright once then his head fell to the back of the couch and his eyelids closed.

Frantic, Gabby twisted her hands. She pulled and jerked 'til her hands were raw and her wrists on fire.

She looked around. Damn it! There was nothing to help her. Her legs were asleep and giving her fits as a thousand tiny pricks of pain shot through them. Grimacing, she moved them up and down then tried to twist her feet.

She felt a slight give in the ropes. Heartened, she wiggled again.

The ropes loosened. Whoever tied her hadn't been nearly as concerned about her feet as they had her hands.

Forgetting about the discomfort in her legs and feet she closed her eyes in concentration. She wriggled her feet until the left foot was over the right. Drops of blood, from her raw ankles, trickled and pooled on the floor.

Taking a deep breath, she pulled her left foot up as hard as she could and hit her head against the wall in the process. Her foot flew free.

She glanced at Leaky and sagged in relief. He continued to sleep.

Putting her hands against the wall she pushed against it and stood up. For one brief moment, she feared she'd topple over as her blood pressed against her veins and began to flow back into her legs.

She took a silent step away from the wall.

The loft was in darkness.

Her hands still tied and her mouth taped, she skulked through the tiny galley kitchen toward the door, bumping into dark-paneled cabinets.

Her elbow hit a soda can sitting on the counter. Turning around, she made a desperate grab as it began to roll toward the edge. The can eluded her. It sailed off the counter, flew through the air and plopped on the edge of a braided throw rug. Her heart in her throat, her body went limp with relief.

Pushing out the pent up air in her lungs, she crept to the door. She turned around, grabbed the handle and pulled. The door stuck, swollen shut. She gathered her strength and gave it a sharp jerk.

It swung open with a groan. Not waiting to see if anyone heard, she ran outside.

A black sky pushed at her senses, the stars hidden by the oak and pine surrounding the cabin.

Ignoring the rutted drive, she plunged into the trees. God, she hoped she didn't encounter a bear or a snake. But nothing could be worse than being in that cabin!

A branch slashed across her face as she moved forward, unsure of her direction. The ground beneath her feet sloped sharply.

Reaching out with the back of her hands, she grabbed trees to keep from falling as she slipped and slid downward.

Tears of pain filled her eyes as she stubbed her toe against a rock.

She took another couple of steps then stopped and retraced her steps, feeling for the rock with her bare toes. The sky had lightened enough that she could make out a shadowy something just beyond her feet. She took an experimental step forward and grimaced as her foot came in contact with the sharp edge of the stone.

She sat down among the twigs and dead leaves and felt around with her hands until she found the stone. Leaning it against the tree, she began to saw. Over and over while muscles held at an awkward angle, screamed.

She pulled and felt give in the rope. Using all her strength she sawed the rope back and forth against the rock. Just as the rope snapped, she heard a shout.

Jumping up she began to half-run, half-slide downhill.

The branches caught at her arms and face. Her feet were raw and bleeding, but she paid them no mind. As she ran, she ripped off the tape around her mouth and bit back a howl, then cursed as she lost her footing and went rolling downhill, landing against a tree face first with enough force to bring tears to her eyes. Trembling, she stumbled to her feet.

Voices shouted behind her. They were getting closer!

Go!

The trail grew rockier and the air thinned, the elevation level high enough to make her giddy. Or maybe that was lack of food and water. She shook her head to clear it and leaped forward.

Suddenly, the trees disappeared and she found herself standing on a rocky plateau, the moon moving out of a cloud momentarily silhouetting her.

"There she is," a man's voice called out.

She whirled. There standing about a half mile up the mountain and to her right stood two figures pointing in her direction, Lai and Leaky.

With a gasp, she started to run across the flat rocky surface and stepped off into space.

Behind her, Lai and Leaky scrambled down the mountain slope until they stopped on the precipice that Gabby had gone plunging over. They looked down. A still shadowy figure lay below, her arms flung out and one leg twisted awkwardly under her.

Leaky glanced down at the figure, uneasily. The moon had turned her blonde hair to gold and a rising mist gave it a halo effect around her head. Involuntarily, he crossed himself.

Lai looked at him and laughed scornfully.

"Do you think I should go down and check on her?" he asked nervously.

"Why? If she's not dead she soon will be. Bears and bobcats still roam this mountain. And since we no longer have a bargaining chip, I suggest we leave this hellish place."

"You are a cold woman," he muttered under his breath.

"You would do well to remember it." Pulling a cell phone from her waist, she flipped open the cover. "Land the helicopter immediately."

* * * * *

Christopher guided his plane to the waiting hangar. Cutting the engine, he stepped out at the small airport in Asheville, North Carolina. Not exactly O'Hare but it was well lit and the asphalt was in top condition.

A full moon and a sprinkling of stars helped lighten the sky.

A stocky middle-aged man of medium height opened the passenger door and hopped out. Billy Burke had been working for Christopher for the past three years.

Billy had a head full of thick brown hair that he combed straight back. He was charismatic and talked with a drawl. But the good ole boy routine hid a man nearly as shrewd as Christopher himself and one who knew how to handle himself in a fight.

He strode over to Christopher and said soberly, "I'd feel better if I was going with you, boss."

Christopher had saved Billy's life once and the man had never forgotten.

"I'll be okay. You need to take care of things here." He touched his cell phone briefly. "I'll be in touch."

Christopher reached into the cockpit and pulled out a canvas bag.

A concerned frown furrowed Billy's brow, but he didn't ask questions.

Christopher walked to the SUV that Billy had rented for him. The moon's reflection bounced off its gleaming black hood.

He stepped inside and slung the bag, holding the crystal,

onto the seat before putting the key in and turning the ignition. The big car sprang to life. "I'll be back."

"I'm counting on it, partner."

Christopher put the SUV into reverse, turned around and headed out of the airport.

He drove along the winding mountain road faster than he should have. Dark surrounded him. His window down, the wind whipped about him, moaning softly.

He still had about thirty minutes to get to the cabin. That would put him there well before dawn, which was exactly what he wanted. It would give him time to scout the area.

A prickling sensation crawled up his spine as he caught a glitter of green out of the corner of his eyes. Glancing over he saw the duffel bag lit with a luminous glow.

He turned his attention back to the road just in time to see the big buck standing in the middle of it.

Swerving hard into the left lane, he hit gravel alongside the road and lost control.

The SUV lurched on its side and hung for a moment on two wheels. The bag, holding the crystal, slammed against Christopher's head and knocked him out cold. He lurched forward, deploying the airbags but not before the pouch rolled out of the open window.

With a scream of protest, the SUV tilted then crashed onto its side.

Chapter Twenty

The dog discovered her first. Whining, he pressed his nose against her, his long brown tail wagging.

The man ambled a hundred or so yards behind, leaning on a knurled walking stick. The trail he walked a thin dirt path lined with pine, newly leafed oak and tightly budded rhododendron that blocked his view. "What have you found, boy?"

The dog's only reply a bark. The man pushed forward to stop at the edge of a small clearing littered with pine needles and dead leaves that were turning to loam.

"Oh, my God." A woman in a nightshirt, bunched about her waist, lay on the ground wedged between two saplings.

He hurried forward. Kneeling, he put two fingers against her neck feeling for a pulse.

He frowned. It was faint, almost too faint to detect. He lowered his head until his cheek hovered above her lips. Her wispy breath tickled his face.

Her feet were a bloody mess and one ankle was swollen to twice the size of the other, her entire leg and foot black and blue. When he touched her ribs, she moaned. One or two ribs were either cracked or broken.

He looked up at the ridge twenty or so feet above and frowned. She had clearly fallen. What the hell was she doing out here wandering around in her nightie?

He was middle-aged but in better shape than most men in their twenties. Probably due to the time he spent hiking the Black Mountains.

Scooping her up, he strode back the way he'd come.

* * * * *

Pain brought Gabby back to consciousness. She was in an austere but clean cabin with honey-colored log walls. A tall, middle-aged man, his hair drawn back in a ponytail, sat at a handsome pine table eating.

She sniffed as the smell of fresh coffee, scrambled eggs and ham permeated the tiny cabin, momentarily forgetting her aching body.

A wet tongue slid across her cheek. She gasped then laughed at a big red dog in front of her, his tail wagging from side to side. She winced as a sharp pain shot through her ribs. Cautiously, she touched them and found they were bandaged.

She stuck out her hand to pet the dog and grimaced, her wrist swollen and sore. A neat white bandage was wrapped around it. Holy Toledo, if she had been in a barroom brawl, it had certainly been on the losing end.

Dressed in a man's plaid shirt, she lay on what appeared to be a bed that, when slid under a pine-hewn bolster, served as a couch.

Her eyes returned to the man at the table. Seeing she was awake, he stood up. It was more like unfolding than actually standing up. He seemed to rise unhurriedly in sections, head, torso and then legs. "So you are awake."

"Who are you?"

"John Paul Adams, who are you?"

"I'm...I'm..." Her eyes widened with panic. "I have no idea," she whispered.

His craggy features softened and his eyes filled with concern. "You took quite a bump on the back of your head."

She gingerly touched the goose egg on her skull. "Do you know what happened to me?"

He laughed, a deep rich sound. "You took a tumble down the mountain in your nightie."

She stared at him in disbelief. "I did what?"

He nodded. "I found you lying in a small clearing. Lucky for you, it was littered with pine needles or I doubt if we would be having this conversation."

176

"Where the hell am I?" She winced as she pulled herself into a sitting position.

"You're in the Black Mountains."

Her eyes widened. "I'm in the Dakotas?"

John Paul laughed again.

She didn't know this man from Adam, but she did enjoy his natural, warm laugh.

"That's the Black Hills. You're in North Carolina. Are you familiar with the Black Hills?" He watched her closely.

Her forehead wrinkled. "I know places, just not me."

"You've obviously suffered a trauma. Your memory will come back. Just don't push it."

"We both hope," she muttered.

"How about some breakfast?"

"Please, I'm ravenous. And aspirin if you have it."

"Coming right up. Breakfast with an aspirin chaser."

She stared at the dog. "I have a dog. Is he mine?"

John Paul stopped on his way toward the stove and turned. "No. But if you remember that, the rest will come." He turned and walked back to the stove.

As John Paul scooped fluffy yellow eggs onto a white plate, he glanced up. "What?" He turned back to the stove and lifted a slab of pink ham from a cast-iron skillet.

"It's just strange."

"What is?"

"We don't know each other. Heck, I don't even know who I am and we've been chatting like we're old friends."

He laughed. She smiled as she listened. There it was. That deep rich sound again.

"Is there a Mrs. Adams?" She watched him plunk a couple of pieces of white bread into a plain serviceable toaster, trying not to think of her aches and pains.

"Used to be." He poured her a cup of coffee in a white mug and brought it to her.

177

"Divorced?" She buried her nose in the steaming mug and inhaled.

He walked to the cabinet, opened a door and came back with a bottle of aspirin. He shook a couple into his palm then handed them to her. "You ask more questions than a reporter."

She paused, the mug halfway to her lips.

John Paul shot her a look of dismay. "You aren't a reporter are you?"

Her brow wrinkled and she shook her head. "I don't know.

"Why shouldn't I be?"

"There you go again." He handed her a plate and some flatware. She put the coffee on the bolster and balanced the plate on her lap. "How can I know things, like what eggs are and that I may have a dog and not know me?"

"You got more questions than I got answers." He walked to the table, sat down and began to eat his now cold breakfast.

"Why did you bring me here? Why not just call 911?"

As the aspirin and food kicked in, discomfort receded.

John Paul shoved a forkful of cold eggs into his mouth and made a face. He scraped the rest of the plate into the dog's bowl sitting at his feet on a small braided rug. The dog's long tail waved, a ripple effect that caused his whole hind end to wag.

John Paul patted the dog. "We are hardly in the middle of a cosmopolitan city. I was a medic in the army. I doubt if a doctor would have done anything more for you than I did. It seemed the right thing to do...at the time. I haven't lived with a woman in a long time. I forgot what chatterboxes women are, you especially. If I'd known you were so nosy, I would have left you."

Gabby wasn't listening. An alarm had gone off inside

her head when John Paul mentioned living with a woman.

He glanced at her grinning then caught her expression and his immediately changed. "Oh for God sakes, save me from virgins and hysterical females."

"I can assure you, I'm neither."

"And how would you know that?" he demanded with a reluctant grin. Adding, "You are either a reporter or a romance writer with a vivid imagination. Girl, I'm old enough to be your father."

"Only if you started very, very young," she shot back.

He rolled his eyes again. "That portion of my life is taken care of. Not that it's any business of yours." He continued, with a baffled shake of his head. "I have never shared this much information with someone I've only known, if you can call it that, for an hour. I used to regret not having any children. But an hour spent in your company has made me realize how truly blessed I am." The twinkle in his eyes belied the words.

Her face heated. Once again, she had made a flaming jenny-ass of herself. Once again? Suddenly she was tired, so tired.

Carefully, setting her plate on the bolster, she lay back down. As her eyes closed, the last thing she remembered was the sound of John Paul's soft chuckle. And bacon sizzling in the skillet as, for the second time that morning, he fixed his breakfast.

Chapter Twenty-One

Christopher floated upward toward consciousness. Soft cotton sheets that smelled of lavender lay against his skin. The feel and familiar smell should have brought comfort, but something terrible tugged at his consciousness. *Gabriella! Oh my God, Gabriella.* He opened his eyes and sat up only to discover he had the mother of all headaches.

Gentle hands pushed him back down.

Tamara's face swam into his vision. "Lie back, Christopher dear," adding in her gentle voice, "I'm glad you've decided to join us."

Fighting his swimming head he struggled to sit up.

With a sigh, Tamara plumped the pillows behind him. "That stubborn streak comes directly from your uncle."

He smiled. But the smile quickly vanished. "How did I get here? Billy?"

"Yes. He got worried and went looking for you."

Fear iced his system. "And Gabriella?"

He read the answer in her clear violet eyes.

With a Herculean effort, Christopher overcame the nausea rising in his throat. "I've got to call Billy."

Tamara's clothes rustled lightly as she leaned over him and placed a hand under his chin. "Christopher."

He looked up.

"She's all right."

He gazed into the violet depths that were clear and bottomless as a pool. "How do you know? Did Billy tell you?"

"No, Billy didn't tell me, but I know she's all right. Now lie back down."

He flopped limp against the pillows.

She got up and sat in the straight-back chair beside the

bed, her long wispy peach skirt falling into place around her. "I think it's time you told me what's going on," and settled back to listen.

He gave a long sigh. But the time for subterfuge was over.

Brutally honest, he spared neither himself nor Lai. While he talked, Beatrice slipped in and poured hot lemon tea into delicate china cups for both of them.

Tamara sipped hers daintily never taking her eyes off Christopher.

His grew cold while he talked. When he'd finished, he leaned his head back against the pillows and closed his eyes.

Tamara said musingly, "So you are the famous cat burglar."

"At least you said famous instead of infamous."

"Lai will have to be dealt with."

His eyes flew open.

"Do you think the harsh circumstances of her youth excuse her?"

"No, but I thought you might."

"I understand and I don't blame her for your wrong choices. Neither do I condone what she's done. Not only do I not condone it, I refuse to allow her to threaten my loved ones."

He looked at her curiously. "Does that statement include Gabriella?"

Tamara smiled enigmatically. "What have you done with the money?"

He avoided her eyes. "I really have the devil of a headache, can we discuss this another time?"

"No."

He sighed heavily. "I was afraid of that," adding flippantly, "women, fast cars and parties, what else?"

She continued to watch him, waiting.

"Oh all right, if you must know, I've set up an orphan fund in Calcutta."

She got up and kissed the top of his head. "Now that's my Christopher." Her skirt rustled as she straightened.

He forced himself to sit up, fighting his swimming head. He reached for the phone, sitting by the bed.

"Who are you calling?"

"I've got to get in touch with Billy. And now if you'll excuse me, I have to get dressed. I can't believe I let you sidetrack me. I've got to find Gabriella."

"Of course, Christopher darling, just let me get you some fresh tea and a little something to eat. You don't want to fall flat on your face now do you? I'll just take that cold cup of tea and pour you some fresh."

He blinked trying to focus as she walked into his bathroom with the cold tea. *What was it he needed to do? Oh yes, call Billy.*

As he tried to dial Tamara walked back into the bedroom and poured a fresh cup of tea from the pot sitting on the bedside table. His head pounded so badly the numbers blurred.

The phone slipped from his fingers. *Clumsy.*

Tamara clucked sympathetically. She stuck the cup in his hand and held it with her own. "Here drink this. It will help."

Maybe it would clear his head enough that he could call Billy. He took a swallow. "You said she's all right. Do you know what happened to her?"

"I know only what Billy told me. Do you want me to tell you what I know or do you want to talk to Billy?"

"Both." He sipped the fragrant beverage. It had the tart bite of lemon and something bitter but he drank it, hoping the hot beverage rolling down his throat would revive him. "Tell me."

"All I know is that Billy went to the rendezvous spot and no one was there."

He swallowed the rest of the tea. "And the globe?" His voice sounded hollow, as if it was coming from a tunnel.

"It was gone."

He looked at his aunt blinking. Tamara's form seemed to grow larger, then shrink.

Damn it she'd drugged him, was his last thought before everything went black.

Tamara eased him back into bed. "I'm sorry, dear, but you are in no shape to get up let alone go after Gabriella." She picked up the phone and hit speed dial. "Billy. Get back to North Carolina and see what you can find out." She paused, listening. "He's going to be all right, but he's out cold again. Call me tonight. I don't care how late."

* * * * *

Gabby sat at the pine table her elbows propped up, her fist under her chin, staring mindlessly into space. She wore John Paul's red plaid shirt and a pair of his jeans, with a piece of rope wrapped around her waist to hold them up, and the cuffs rolled up. On her feet, a pair of thick wool socks.

She'd been living in John Paul's cabin for three days now and other than a swollen ankle, sore feet and ribs, and the tiny little detail of a ghastly migraine whenever she focused on her past, felt fine. Names and faces were flitting through her subconscious like butterflies. But like Pandora's Box, she had no doubt that when she lifted the lid of her memory, all manner of problems were going to come rushing out.

And life in this little cabin was simple and pleasant. Like Scarlett O'Hara she'd deal with it tomorrow.

A blast of cool air brought her out of her reverie. John Paul came striding through the door, smelling of fresh air and pine and something else she couldn't identify. The dog named Red pranced beside him. The canine ran to her and stuck his wet nose in her hand.

She patted his silky warm coat, smiling.

John Paul sniffed the air hopefully, much like the setter at her feet. Then his face fell. "I suppose it was too much to ask that you would have lunch fixed."

She gave him a guilty look. "I'm not sure I know how to cook."

He threw his hands in the air and rolled his eyes. "What's to cook? Do you know how to work a can opener?"

She nodded.

"Then how about opening a can of beans or tomato soup and fixing a couple of grilled cheese sandwiches? Can you do that?"

Standing up, she walked to the pantry and began rummaging through it. She pulled out a loaf of bread and a can of soup then paused, the soup in one hand, the bread in the other. "Why should I make it? Why don't you? Are you a male chauvinist?"

He looked at her as if she'd grown a second head. For some reason the look was familiar. "No, I am not a chauvinist but I do believe in every person pulling his or her weight. So far, I can't see that you've done much to earn your keep."

Heat and shame seared her. "You're right of course. I'm sorry."

John Paul gave her a quizzical look as he walked into the kitchen. "Whoever you are, I bet you're a heller."

She grinned. "I don't think I'm going to take that bet. For one thing I couldn't pay you if I lost and for another, you are probably right."

He opened a gleaming white refrigerator and pulled out the cheese slices. "You don't have to do that." Gabby laid the bread and soup on the counter.

"I don't have a problem with pulling my weight." He grinned. "You grill the sandwiches and I'll take care of the soup." He reached for a copper-bottomed pan over the island-stove.

Picking up a dinner knife, Gabby looked around admiringly. "I never knew cabins were loaded with so many up-to-date appliances. This is really a lovely place." She pointed at the pine table, then at the island-stove. "Beautiful wood furniture and modern appliances, I love it.

"What do you do for a living, John Paul?" She opened the bread and slapped cheese between the soft, yeasty slices.

"You might say I'm in distribution, the family business." He poured the soup into the pan and turned on the burner.

"What do you distribute?"

He stirred the soup for a moment before answering. "Adult beverage."

She laughed. "Oh, you mean like a beer distributor? Do you have a couple of Clydesdales hidden out back?"

"Something like that." He smiled. "But enough about me, I can't keep calling you hey you. Have you remembered your name yet?"

Gabby. Gabriella. Tamara. Amy. Names throbbed like a kettle drum in her brain. She winced as the pain came.

He lifted the wooden spoon and tapped it against the pan. Mesmerizing red droplets, the color of diluted blood fell back into the copper-bottomed pot. He turned the heat down then faced her. "You know, girl, every time I ask you your name your forehead wrinkles like corrugated cardboard and you take to your bed with a headache." His voice gentled. "It's been three days. Amnesia seldom lasts that long.

"Whatever's going on with you I can empathize. When I was in the service I felt the need to escape reality on a regular basis."

Gabby rubbed her pounding temples. "And did you? Escape reality?"

"Couldn't. I was a medic. Too many soldiers and friends depended on me." As if trying to shake off black memories his expression lightened and his eyes danced with mischief. "But when I went on leave you might say I did my damnedest to create an alternate reality." He grinned. "I guess, girl, you're just on leave. Just don't stay there too long. I've got a feeling there're people depending on you too."

He went back to stirring the soup.

"John Paul."

"Hm?"

"I'm not a coward by nature." The minute she said it, she knew it to be so.

He grinned. "Never thought you were, girl, you got too much sass. So what shall we call you? How about Sherry?"

A picture of a petite, buxom redhead with a simper on her face skittered through her brain. "Not unless you have a death wish."

She slathered butter on a sandwich and dropped it in the skillet. "How about Tammy?"

He gave her a skeptical look. "You don't look like a Tammy to me."

She started to butter another sandwich then paused as she realized she'd forgotten her headache. "I believe I would like to be called Tamara."

He gave her a keen look. "Tamara. It's very unusual and very pretty. Do you think that's your name?"

She shook her head, perplexed. "No. I don't think so. But, I think maybe someone is named that who I admire. Never mind, it's a stupid idea." She slapped the other sandwich onto the skillet.

"No. I like it. Tamara it is. At least, until we figure out

your real name."

They finished fixing lunch in compatible silence then sat down at the pine table to eat. Gabby was in the process of pulling her sandwich apart and watching the soft yellow mass puddle in her plate when a knock sounded at the door.

John Paul rose immediately. "Get into the bedroom." He removed her plate, utensils and glass and placed them in the sink.

She looked at him questioningly.

"You weren't in very good shape when I found you. I want to make sure no one is trying to finish the job."

She nodded, her stomach tightening and her heart beating a rapid tattoo against her breast.

John Paul waited 'til Tamara or whoever in hell she was slipped into the bedroom and then walked to the door and turned the handle, the brass cool and smooth beneath his hand. The door swung open. Standing in front of him was one of the most beautiful women he had ever seen.

The tiny-framed woman wore a thick red sweater that accented her beautiful skin, designer jeans and hiking boots. A thick red band kept silky black hair that fell to her waist away from her face.

She studied him as intently as he studied her.

"May I help you?"

"I'm looking for a friend of mine, a woman in her mid-twenties, tall, blonde."

"What's her name?"

"Then you have seen her."

"No, sorry, but I thought if I knew who you were talking about, I could make some inquiries."

She tried to see inside the cabin, but he blocked her view with his shoulders.

"May I come in and we can talk about it?"

"I'm sorry, but I'm on my way out."

"I'll make it worth your while."

"Ma'am, I don't need your money."

She gave him a sultry look. "Who said anything about money?"

"Business so bad, you have to go door-to-door now?" he drawled.

She whitened as if she'd been struck. "You may have just made a very deadly mistake."

"I don't care for threats. Perhaps you had better go." He called after her as she wheeled around and began to walk away. "How'd you find this place anyway? I'm not exactly on the beaten path."

Lai ignored him and kept walking. She wasn't about to tell him that it was blind luck or help from the gods. And since she believed in neither except perhaps the old goddess Kali it must be karma.

If the fall hadn't killed Christopher's lover where was she? She'd watched the news for three days. When there was no mention of a dead woman discovered in the mountains she came back to investigate…and found the body gone.

She paid several mountain people a small fortune for any information they could give her on any unusual comings and goings.

The mountain folk were fiercely independent and protective of their own, but selling information about a stranger and a Yankee to boot, was another matter. So it came to her attention that Christopher's hired flunky had been combing the mountainside. Why?

As Lai pondered Gabriella Bell's disappearance, John Paul shut the door. "You can come out now."

"Who was it?" Gabby asked, as she walked out of the

bedroom.

"I have no idea but whoever it was, she wanted you badly."

"Maybe it was a friend or a family member."

"Do you know any beautiful oriental women?"

A shadow of unease passed through Gabby and a grinding jolt of pain hit behind her eyes. "I don't think I want to find out."

"Wise girl. That woman was up to no good." He walked to the kitchen counter and poured them each a fresh cup of coffee. "A friend of mine told me there has been a stranger, a piece down the mountains, asking questions."

"What kind of questions?" As she bent her head over her coffee cup her hair fell forward. She brushed it back and forced herself to ignore the pain that was trying to separate her head from her neck.

"Questions about a blonde-haired woman, an oriental woman and a crystal ball.

"Since most of these mountain folk are God-fearing Christians, they are rather put off by the crystal ball." He grinned.

Gabby thumped down in a kitchen chair, coffee sloshing out of the cup and onto her hand. She hastily set down the cup. The throbbing in her head receded replaced by a ka-thump of pure excitement that pulsed through her at mention of the crystal ball.

"There was a wreck down the mountain a few days ago. In fact, it happened the same night I found you," he mentioned while sipping the fragrant brew. He stated it casually enough, but he watched her intently.

"Do you think there's a connection?"

He shrugged. "More to the point, do you?"

"I have no idea," she said honestly, adding, "but I am intrigued by that crystal ball. Maybe we should go looking for it."

He grinned. "Ah, the slumbering sleuth awakens," he said, unaware just how on target his words were. "I'll look. You stay put."

"Where are you going?"

"Back to where I found you, then to where the car was wrecked."

"Let me come with you."

"No and don't even think about following me."

She gave him a mutinous glare.

"I'll have your word on it."

"Oh, all right," she said sulkily. "I'll stay put."

"I'll leave Red here for company."

"You're leaving him to protect me. No, you take him. He may sniff out something you would miss."

"Do you know how to use a rifle?" He pointed at the gun over the fireplace.

"Point and shoot," she replied, with an airy wave of her hand.

He laughed. "Pretty much, just don't shoot your foot off. And lock the door." He left before Gabby could respond.

* * * * *

She spent the rest of the afternoon limping around the cabin. From the muscle tone of her body, she was an active person. She could empathize with how rescue or shelter cats must feel confined to a cage. It's a wonder they didn't all go crazy. She turned her hand to cleaning the small cabin. That took a little over an hour.

Then she wandered into the bedroom and sat down at the computer on John Paul's desk. The desk looked to be another of John Paul's creations, too beautiful to be anything but handmade. Really the man was too good to be true.

She sat down, pulled up the main screen and typed on as guest. As the screen lit up she smiled. It was nice to know those particular synapses were still sparking, *sans* headaches.

Wandering back to the kitchen, she pulled a can of soda from the fridge, grabbed some cookies from the pantry and trotted back to the computer as happy as a clam.

She was still there when John Paul got home a couple of hours later.

A wet nose followed by a silky russet head pushed itself under her arm and into her lap. She patted the dog and turned around smiling. "Did you know they have wild ponies on Corolla and Ocracoke Island? Do you think we could go some time?"

"Just how long do you plan on sticking around?"

Her face fell.

He smiled at her. "You are welcome for as long as you want."

For the first time, she noticed the canvas bag he held. "Did you find something?"

In response, he opened it and let the green crystal roll on the bed. Without thought she reached over and picked up the ball. It warmed under her fingertips. The colors blurred and a stranger appeared in the swirling mist. He opened his mouth and though no sound emerged she heard his cry, "Gabriella."

The ball dropped from her nerveless fingertips back onto the bed. John Paul caught Gabby just before she slid to the floor in a dead faint.

Someone was shaking her. "Tamara. Tamara." Slowly, her eyes fluttered open. Her heart beat at an accelerated pace and John Paul was leaning over her, his face inches from her own. Light brown stubble sprinkled with gray visible on his chin. His breath smelled of peppermint.

"Thank God. What happened to you?"

She stared at him uncomprehendingly. The cabin was warm. That must be why she felt so sleepy. Suddenly her eyes widened as memory washed over her in cold waves.

Christopher…Lai.

Her pulse jumped in erratic hops. Even though she knew the answer she had to ask. "Did you see it?"

"See what?"

"The face in the globe. He was calling my name only he didn't call me Tamara."

His face as expressionless as a poker player's, he asked, "And what did he call you?"

She swallowed once and then said as calmly as she could, "Gabriella. My name is Gabriella Bell, but my friends call me Gabby. You may call me Gabby." *Friend.*

He cleared his throat. "Well Miss Gabriella Bell so you saw a man in the crystal."

"Where is it? I'll show you." Gabby struggled out of his grip and sat up.

He reached over, his blue work shirt straining across his muscular shoulders and handed it to her.

Grabbing it, she clasped it to her. Its warmth slowed her rapid heartbeat. The colors, beginning to swirl under her fingertips, hypnotized her. Her body relaxed and went limp. Then like an evil genie Christopher's face swam into view. He was no longer calling her name. His eyes were sharp and probing as if he were looking for something or someone.

"There do you see it," she cried, holding it out to John Paul.

He looked at her uneasily.

"Do you?" she repeated.

"No," he answered finally.

"It's all right. I don't think you are meant to." She heaved a sigh from deep in her belly.

"You've had an eventful morning, Gabriella Bell. Why don't you rest." He gently pushed her down.

"I think I'll take you up on that. The headaches are gone but I'm exhausted." She leaned her head back and closed her eyes. "Please call me Gabby."

"Gabby," he repeated.

When he reached for the globe, she clasped it tightly and wrapped around it in a fetal position, closing her eyes.

As her mind spiraled downward toward sleep, she felt the heavy warmth of a quilt being laid over her and thought she heard John Paul whisper to the dog, "Even with no memory, I would have sworn she was as sane as me. Though, there are some who have doubts about me. Well, time will tell."

Footsteps receded down the hall as she fell into the welcome arms of oblivion.

Chapter Twenty-Two

Christopher awoke clearheaded with Beatrice sitting beside his bed. "What are you doing here, Beatrice?"

She clasped her hands together. "The lord be praised. Let me get your aunt." Her joints creaked as she rose and hurried from the room.

Memory flooded back. He threw back the sheet and black plaid coverlet and reached for his pants at the bottom of the bed. Of course, they weren't there.

Christopher padded to his dresser and pulled out a pair of worn jeans. He was in the process of zipping them up when his aunt walked in.

"You drugged me," he accused, fists on hips.

Tamara answered placidly, "Yes, I did. Let's go into your study and talk shall we?"

He grabbed a white tee shirt and pulled it on as they walked.

Her skirt made a whispering sound as she sank down onto the black leather couch.

Christopher sat down on the overstuffed leather chair across from her.

"This had better be good, Aunt Tam."

She looked directly at him. "Christopher, I want that girl back as badly as you do. But to fight that woman you must be strong and have your wits about you. You were in no condition four days ago. I think now you're ready."

He looked at her incredulously. "You kept me drugged for four days?"

"You act as though I had a choice."

"Well, didn't you?" He ran his fingers through his hair, barely restraining himself from clutching it and howling.

"No!" his normally mild-mannered aunt answered

forcefully. "That evil woman has Gabriella. She's not getting you too."

"Aunt..."

She waved her hand to negate whatever he was about to say. "I know you have to go, Christopher. I just want to make sure you come home to me safely."

He got up, pulled Tamara to her feet and swept her up in a bear hug. "Don't worry. I intend to come home and with Gabriella. Now will you tell me what happened?"

She repeated what she had said before about the disappearance of the globe. How Billy had gone to the rendezvous point and no one was there, then how he'd gone back searching for both Gabriella and the globe.

"So we don't even know if she is alive." A giant fist tightened around his heart. He'd experienced it twice. Once when his mother died and then again when Uncle Edward passed.

Tamara reached over and clasped his fingers. His hand engulfed her tiny one and his grasp made her wince. "That is one thing I am sure of, Christopher. She is alive. And don't ask me to explain it. I just know." Adding in a whisper so low, Christopher wasn't even sure he heard her correctly, "I just know that Gabriella will be the next possessor of the green crystal. That her destiny will not allow her to die before it has been passed on."

He fastened on to Gabriella being alive and let the rest go. His aunt was fey. It was her essence, what made her who she was. But if she said Gabriella was alive then Gabriella was alive. The fist clutching his heart loosened, though it didn't completely go away.

"Is she all right?"

"That I can't say, I just know she'll survive."

He leaned over and kissed his aunt's hand then pushed to his feet. "Thank you."

Tamara tilted her head, looking up at him. He smiled. She looked like a quizzical bird.

"Will you at least eat lunch before you go?"

"Go where?" he parried.

"To the mountains to find Gabriella. It doesn't take a crystal ball to figure that out."

He was relieved that she had used the word "find" not "look for".

"Have you talked to Gabriella's father?"

"Yes, the poor man is beside himself. He has put out a Missing Person's Report throughout the country. He was here a few days ago. He is still very suspicious of you. The only thing that kept him from hauling you back to Illinois and putting you in an interrogation room with your hands tied behind your back and a bare light bulb in your eyes was that he saw for himself you were laid up in bed. He is coming back this afternoon, though, so you might want to start packing. I'll order your lunch."

Giving her a speaking look for waiting until now to mention it, he headed toward the door then stopped and turned. "Does he know what happened?"

She nodded her head back and forth in a maybe yes, maybe no sort of way. "Yes and no."

"What did you tell him?" His stomach did a nervous flop.

"I told him you were in a car accident, here."

"He doesn't know she may be in North Carolina."

"I could have made a mistake," she admitted, "but I can't help thinking the poor man would just muddy the waters."

He bent down and kissed the top of her head. "You are a wise woman, Aunt Tam."

Eyes unfocused, she stared into the distance. "Sergeant Bell is a good man. But I don't think it would be in the best interests of Gabriella's protector to have the law skulking around."

He tightened like a bowstring. "Gabriella's protector? What the hell do you mean by that?"

She blinked. "I have no idea. But I'm sure you'll find out."

He stood for a moment, clenching his fists and grinding his teeth before he pivoted and walked out of the study.

She called after him, "Come down to lunch after you've packed. We'll need to get her dog and cat here before she comes back too."

He muttered. Unfortunately, none of his words were repeatable. The cool air circulating in his bedroom turned blue. He threw his clothes in a black leather bag then picked up his cell phone.

"Billy, have you found anything?"

"Boss! It's good to hear from you. Nope, haven't seen hide nor hair of the ball nor of the girl. But I think there's a good ole boy who knows more than he's letting on. It's nothing I can put my finger on. Just the fact that he wasn't all that interested to hear a beautiful blonde might be lost in the mountains.

"Mountain folk are notorious for minding their own business and expecting you to mind yours, but he's still a man. And what man's not going to have his interest piqued about something like that. It certainly wasn't because he had any interest in my fine-looking self," he added, laughing over the phone.

"Well, you just get your fine-looking ass back here along with my plane. Meet me at the airport in two hours. No make that an hour and a half."

"Got our boxers in a wad, do we?"

The phone line went dead.

* * * * *

The plane hovered then dropped, its wheels extended. It coasted to the end of the runway, wide-ribbed treads screaming as they fought the asphalt for purchase, then came to a perfect stop.

"You sure can fly a plane, boss." Billy unstrapped his seat belt.

"Tell me about this mountain man of yours." Christopher shut down the plane.

"Middle-aged, physically fit, good-looking in a rough-hewn sort of way."

"Dirty ole man," Christopher muttered under his breath.

"Say what?" Billy strained to hear. "Did you just call me a dirty ole man?"

"Of course not." Christopher threw open the cockpit door with more force than necessary.

"Well, boss, all I got to say is you ain't yourself. Nor are you much fun. If you want to fire me or try to kick my butt, so be it. Though, considering you're still convalescing, I'm pretty sure I can take you."

"If you don't shut up you'll be finding out."

"You want to tell me what's wrong?" Billy stepped out of the plane.

Christopher sighed. "Not really, just one of Aunt Tam's predictions."

"Say no more. I know Ms. Tamara is fey. Being a bayou boy I recognize that sort of thing."

Christopher snorted.

They left the plane and walked silently to the rental, a black SUV. Billy headed for the driver's seat.

Christopher looked at him, cocking an eyebrow.

"If you don't mind, of course. It might be easier than trying to give you directions. You drive all cars like you're in your sports car in the city and on these mountain roads it doesn't bear thinking about." Billy shuddered.

Christopher grinned.

Billy gave a relieved sigh, opened the door and climbed in.

Christopher did the same. He snapped on his seat belt. "What does this guy do?"

"Of course no one mentions it, but given his location buried in the back of nowhere in the mountains, I'm guessing he's a moonshiner." He slid the key into the ignition and turned it. The SUV sprang to life.

"Say what?" He turned his head sharply and looked at Billy. A breeze from the open window ruffled his hair and teased his scalp. "Have I stepped into some sort of time warp?" he asked only half-joking.

Billy backed the car out and headed out of the airport down a road that twisted and turned, lined with trees and great slabs of gray rock that intermingled along the roadside.

"Boss you've lived most of your life in the South. How can you not know about moonshiners?"

"Well, I knew they made quite a living during prohibition," Christopher replied defensively. "Besides, I limit my illegalities to jewels."

"Before, during and since. It's a very lucrative field. The stills are located in the mountains because of the limestone deposits. And because it's pretty tough for revenuers to find them," he added grinning. "Though, I've heard ALE spends about $560K each year looking."

"Billy, you've become as loquacious as an old woman. Is there any word on Lai?"

"And your memory's about as bad," Billy retorted. "I've told you four times now. No."

The wind blowing through the open window smelled of pine. Christopher drew in a deep breath while looking around appreciatively. It was amazing really. He had traveled the world and knew so little about pockets of his own country.

The mountains were beautiful and actually did look blue in the distance.

But like small sound bites, his mind could only be diverted from the nagging fear for Gabriella for short periods. Most of the time, it gnawed at his gut making him wonder if he was getting an ulcer. And when his stomach wasn't tied in knots, he was so damn angry he could cheerfully strangle her. If she hadn't been so damn stubborn about the damn crystal, this would never have happened. This was all her fault. She was worrying him sick.

He had always prided himself on being able to deal with any situation in a cool, calculating manner. This was totally unlike him. He knew he was being as irrational as a female with PMS, but was helpless to do anything about it.

He sat up straighter in the car, his body absorbing the lush feel of the leather. She was here. He knew it. He sensed it.

Billy glanced at him, but the man wisely remained silent.

They hit a pot hole in the road that even the well maintained shocks of the SUV could not absorb. Christopher barely felt it.

After another twenty minutes or so, Billy pulled off at one of the lookout points.

Christopher came out of his deep abstraction enough to ask, "What are we doing?"

Billy unsnapped his seat belt and cut the motor. "We walk from here." He hopped out of the car, then strode to the back of it and opened the tailgate. He pulled out two backpacks and two walking sticks.

As Christopher approached, Billy tossed him a backpack. "I know there's got to be a road up there somewhere, but I haven't found it yet."

"Where are we going?"

Billy pointed at the pine-lined vista. A light wind blew,

causing the trees around them to rustle and sway. The sky clear except for a few wisps of clouds flirting with the mountain tops. "Up and over."

The blood began to course through Christopher's body. He sniffed the air and stood as still as a pointer. Gabriella was here. "Let's go."

They hiked for over an hour. Billy stopped frequently to give Christopher a rest, but each time Christopher urged him on.

Finally, they broke through to a small clearing. Even though it was cool, both were sweating profusely. Billy reached in his pocket and pulled out a clean linen handkerchief and wiped his brow. Christopher didn't even notice the sweat pouring down his face he was too busy glancing around.

Birds chirped and swooped in the glen. A birdfeeder hung from a nearby branch where cardinals, titmice and a Carolina wren flew in and out. A woodpecker with a shiny red head flew toward the feeder then veered away as he caught sight of the two men.

He absorbed the scene then focused on the well-made cabin. His heart pounding and his breath coming in short sharp gasps, he rushed forward. Somewhere in a very cloudy portion of his mind, he knew he was acting like a fool. The Tiger never rushed into a dangerous situation without coolly weighing the odds and turning them in his favor.

Billy whispered, "Christopher, for God sakes what are you doing? Do you even have a gun?"

He burst through the cabin door, banging it back against the wall and came up short. The smooth bore of a shotgun pointed at his chest went a long way toward lifting the fog wrapped around his brain.

His eyes traveled from the double barrel to the man holding it. The guy standing in front of him was about his height and heavily built with no sign of fat. His graying hair was pulled back in a ponytail and his eyes resembled the cold steel of the shotgun.

"Tell your friend to lay his gun on the stoop and come in."

Christopher called out, "Come in, Billy, and leave the heat on the porch."

Billy walked in, throwing his boss an exasperated look.

He shrugged. He couldn't blame him. If their roles had been reversed, he would have fired Billy's ass on the spot.

Both the moonshiner and Christopher became aware of Gabriella at the same time.

Everyone spoke at once.

"Gabriella, are you all right?"

"Get back in the bedroom."

"It's all right, John Paul. It's the man in the globe."

"Boss, is it Ms. Bell? What the hell is she talking about?"

"Tamara, er, Gabby, do you recognize these two?" The shotgun was still pointed squarely at Christopher, but the man kept his eye on Billy too.

"Tamara?" Both Christopher and Billy spoke at once.

"Gabriella, what the hell is going on here and what are you doing with, with," Christopher gestured toward the mountain man, "him."

She moved forward to stand beside the moonshiner, which angered Christopher no end. "John Paul, you can put the gun down. They aren't here to harm me."

"What rig are you running? Writing a series of local articles on moonshiners?"

Gabby gave him a confused look. "Moonshiners?"

"Didn't your protector tell you what he does for a living?"

It was obvious the man holding the shotgun didn't like

the direction the conversation was going one bit, probably for several reasons.

"Boy, I would suggest you watch your mouth."

"John Paul runs the family business," she said defensively. "He delivers for the local brewery or something."

A grin spread over Billy's face and an involuntarily laugh became a muffled cough as three sets of indignant eyes turned toward him. "Lord, we've fallen from high drama to farce."

John Paul motioned with his shotgun. "Just who the hell are you two?"

Christopher mentally assessed the situation. *So she's aligning herself with the moonshiner is she? Well tough times call for tough measures.* At the moment he could think of only one quick way to get her home without a shootout. Ignoring the gun pointed at him he walked toward Gabriella his eyes burning into hers, yanked her into his arms and kissed her. A kiss that went on and on.

The room faded into the background along with the people in it. The sweetness of her response took his breath away. He was aware of an annoying droning in his ear. It was like being dive-bombed by hummingbirds creating a continual *buzz, buzz, buzz* in the background.

Gabriella was jerked abruptly out of his arms. She stared at him, her swollen lips parted, a dazed expression on her face.

Christopher was able to control his voice and breathing, but not his wildly dilated pupils. He cut his eyes toward John Paul. "Get her things together. I'm taking my fiancée home."

"The hell you say!" John Paul exclaimed.

"Fiancée? What are you talking about?" Indignation and confusion warred on Gabriella's expressive features.

"Congratulations, boss!" Billy reached over to

enthusiastically shake his hand.

Christopher drew his own back, rather quickly. "Are you forgetting we've got a gun pointed at us?"

"Well actually I had," Billy answered, then walked up to John Paul and extended his hand. "Name's Burke, Billy Burke. You got any champagne around here or are we going to have to drink white lightning?"

John Paul shook hands with one hand and held the shotgun on Christopher with the other. "I have no desire to get jumped by this young hothead."

"He's a good man but he's in love." Billy watched in amusement as Christopher swallowed down what was probably a negative response.

Gabriella looked like an oil rig ready to blow. Sure enough she erupted. "Have you lost your collective minds?" She wheeled on Christopher. "Are you out of your mind, which at the moment is my department? We aren't engaged and we aren't getting married."

She shoved past Christopher. John Paul reached an arm to stop her but was hamstrung by Billy enthusiastically shaking his hand and the shotgun. The dog whined at his heels in confusion.

She raced out the door, slamming it shut behind her, Christopher at her heels.

"Gabriella, wait!"

Billy released John Paul's hand then clamped it on his shoulder. "What say we let them work it out? Now, how about some of your home brew?"

"How did you know about me anyhow?" John Paul asked, leaning the shotgun up against the wall.

"I'll tell you mine if you tell me yours."

John Paul grinned. "It's a deal."

Chapter Twenty-Three

Christopher ran down the porch steps after Gabriella, his heels clicking against the wood. "Gabriella, wait."

He had nearly reached her when a bullet whizzed by his ear. "Damn it to hell."

He took a flying dive and knocked Gabriella to the ground with a tackle that would have made his old college football coach proud.

John Paul and Billy, who were in the midst of toasting the engaged couple with a jug, looked at each other and raced for the window.

John Paul opened the window and let off a shot in the direction of the gunfire. The sound blasted through the clearing. "Are they after you or me?" he asked Billy, the gun resting on his shoulder as he scanned the woods behind the clearing.

"I have no idea. Cover me while I get my gun."

John Paul nodded and fired again. Billy yanked open the door and reached for his gun. A bullet whistled by his hand. Grabbing the gun, he drew back indoors and slammed the door.

"Are Christopher and Ms. Bell all right?" Billy cocked his gun as he leaned against the wall.

"So far, but they need to take cover." John Paul watched them for a second. "Looks like they are crawling for that stand of pampas grass just a few feet away from them. It should provide them a little concealment." He fired off a shot that cracked through the underbrush like firecrackers.

Under cover of the volley of gunfire coming from the cabin, Gabby and Christopher slithered toward the tall stands of ornamental grass rustling and swaying as bullets whizzed through their plume-like silvery panicles.

"I guess it's a safe bet to assume your former lover is responsible for our current precarious situation," she wheezed, her voice bitter. "Whatever did you see in that psychopath anyway?"

"That's rather obvious don't you think?"

As they reached it, he pulled her behind it then threw his arms around her protectively. "Keep your head down."

"No problem. I'm going to hug Mother Earth until all firing has ceased.

"Why did you come bursting through the door like the cavalry and call me your fiancée?" Her head shot up and he pushed it back down.

"You tell me." He bent his head and covered her full mouth with his. The gunfire faded in the distance.

Gabby stiffened.

"Don't fight me, Gabriella," he murmured against her lips.

"We're not engaged," she responded, her body softening and molding against him.

"We're not?" The kiss deepened and all thoughts of conflict vanished.

They were out of view of their attackers, but in full view of John Paul and Billy.

John Paul stared slack-jawed with shock. "What the hell is he doing?"

"Seems pretty obvious to me," Billy's voice was dry. He fired a shot at random.

"I'm not sure if it was that knock on the head he took a while back or Ms. Bell but he's definitely losing his edge." He fired another shot. There was a yelp from the bushes.

"Do you know in some circles he is considered to be

quick thinking, cool under fire and a dangerous man to cross."

"Well it's pretty clear what he's thinking with right now." Before Billy realized what he was about, John Paul lifted his rifle in Christopher's direction and fired.

Christopher's hair parted as a bullet whizzed by.

John Paul roared, "Get the hell in here."

Christopher's head came up, his eyes wild. "He's shooting at us." His voice was high in disbelief. "Your boyfriend is shooting at us."

"He's not my boyfriend, you idiot."

"Now that's the Gabriella I know and love." He grabbed her hand and pulled her toward the house. "Keep your head down and zigzag."

As they sprinted for the house, John Paul told Billy, "Cover them."

Billy fired rapidly. Moments later, John Paul was back with what looked like a sawn-off shotgun. He fired in the direction of the gunfire. The sound echoed through the room in a deafening roar.

"Damn," Billy said in awe, as a sapling toppled and a man behind it flew in the air then as if in slow motion fell to the ground and lay still.

John Paul fired again. Three people made a break for the dirt road, one holding his arm, another dragging the man on the ground.

Christopher and Gabby burst through the door, panting. John Paul watched the fleeing figures, took aim then dropped his gun. "One of them is a woman."

"Lai," Christopher said grimly. "Billy give me your gun, I'm going after her."

"Boss, I don't think…"

Christopher grabbed his gun and ran out the door.

John Paul looked at Billy. "Cool under fire, huh?"

"I better go with him."

John Paul grasped above his ankle where a handgun was strapped. "Here you better take this."

"We are definitely going to have to swap stories sometime." Billy opened the door.

"I'm going with you." Gabby took a step forward.

"No you are not. This is their fight," John Paul said.

"Better stay put, Miss." Billy slammed the door behind him.

Gabby yanked it open and went after him.

"Damn it," John Paul followed after Gabby.

They ran after Christopher, who'd cut through the tall pines surrounding the property. Pinecones crunched under their feet as they ran.

A motor started up. "They found my back road. The sons of bitches must be driving a Hummer. That road is almost impenetrable."

They burst through the trees in time to hear the sharp report of exchanged gunfire. The Hummer careened crazily from side to side making a clean shot impossible as Christopher aimed for the tires.

Lai leaned out the window, gun in hand, placing a shot that sent dust spurting around Christopher's feet.

The vehicle disappeared around a bend in the road.

"I can get my car," John Paul said.

Christopher shook his head. "Listen." In the quiet, the whirl of a helicopter could be heard overhead. "There must be an airstrip around here we didn't know about."

"Nope, but there's a level clearing about four miles straight down. If we had a car here we'd stand a chance of catching them, but not if we have to go back to the cottage. Where's your car?"

Christopher shook his head in disgust. "Too far for us to get to."

It was obvious Christopher was still spoiling for a fight. He whirled on John Paul, "Perhaps you'd care to tell me why you parted my hair with a bullet a few minutes ago?"

Before John Paul could respond, Christopher wheeled and with a lightning jab, punched John Paul in the jaw.

John Paul reeled back, inadvertently squeezing the trigger of the sawed-off shotgun he still carried. The gun went off with a loud roar. A sapling several yards away went tumbling to the ground.

John Paul threw down the gun and charged Christopher like a bull, knocking him to the ground. They immediately began to pummel each other.

"Stop it," Gabby screamed.

Billy just stood shaking his head. "Do you know before he met you, he was unflappable."

"Do something."

His eyebrows elevated to his hairline and he shook his head. "My momma didn't raise no fool."

Gabby threw him a disgusted look then began frantically looking around. She spied a thick limb lying on the ground. Grabbing it, she began hitting at both men indiscriminately. Most of the hits fell on John Paul's mammoth shoulders, but he gave no notice.

She had her stick in the air and was bringing it down, when Christopher flipped John Paul, her club coming down squarely on the side of Christopher's face. "Oww!"

John Paul flipped him back. He stood up and pulled Christopher with him. The ludicrousness of the situation got the better of him and he grinned. "You deserve a sound thrashing, but I'll let your fiancée administer it."

Christopher did not grin back.

"Shall we start over? My name is John Paul Adams."

And he stuck out his hand.

Christopher's hand stayed at his side. "If you touched her, old man…"

John Paul grabbed a fistful of Christopher's shirt and hauled him toward him until their faces were only inches apart. It was easy to read Christopher's expression. He was stunned that a man John Paul's age could move so quickly.

Billy shook his head and said to no one in particular, "The boss, always a lightning-fast learner, seems particularly slow today."

John Paul spoke quietly. "Boy, I've just about had it with you. You mind your manners when you are speaking to your betters." Slowly, John Paul released him.

Gabby and Billy watched holding their respective breaths.

Christopher capitulated, though he still eyed John Paul suspiciously. "I appreciate your care of Gabriella, but it's time she came home with me."

"And where might that be?" John Paul's voice was even.

"New Orleans."

"And what makes you think I'm going to turn her over to a hothead like you?"

Christopher gave a heartfelt sigh. "I can't begin to tell you how much I hate bringing this into the conversation." His lips tightened. "Or having to explain myself for that matter. But did I not hear her say she saw me in the globe? Think of it in terms of a passport ID."

John Paul rolled his eyes. "And speaking of ID?"

Christopher pulled his wallet out of his back pocket and showed him his address.

John Paul looked at Billy.

"He's who he says he is, mate."

"IDs can be faked. I need more confirmation than this to hand her over to you."

Gabby straightened her spine and lifted her chin. "Whether I go or stay is up to me."

Everyone ignored her.

Christopher sighed again, "Her father is Sergeant Bell of the Springfield, Illinois PD."

John Paul blanched.

Gabby shrugged and nodded.

A blue jay screamed overhead. She looked up. "I feel the same way," she mumbled.

"All you've got to do is call the police department and they will verify everything I've said, except perhaps about the engagement," he added hastily. "That may be a bit of a surprise."

Gabby lifted her eyebrows, "Ya think?"

Billy wheeled abruptly. His shoulders shook and he made a noise perilously close to a snort. He turned back and said blandly, "Sorry something stuck in my throat."

"Or you could call my Aunt Tamara," Christopher said.

"Perhaps I'll call both. Give me your phone. If it's traced it will come back to you and not me."

Christopher looked at him with grudging respect and shrugged, handing it over.

"Sergeant Bell thinks I'm a lunatic anyway."

John Paul dialed information, listened then punched in the 217 area code and the number then put the phone on speaker. "Do you have a Sergeant Bell that works there?"

The voice on the other end responded, "He isn't here at the moment. May I take a message or would you care to speak to someone else?"

"Does he have a daughter?"

The voice on the other end sharpened the listener alert. "Who's calling?"

"Is his daughter's name Gabriella?"

"Just a minute I'm going to patch you through to him.

Don't hang up."

"Who is this and what do you know about my daughter?" The voice was harsh with strain.

"Sir," John Paul said, his voice gentle, "I may know where your daughter is. Can you describe her for me?"

"Tall, blonde and mouthy."

John Paul grinned. "Sir, your daughter is safe."

"Where is she? Can I speak with her, please?" he pleaded.

John Paul held the phone toward Gabby.

She shook her head and whispered, "I love my dad but I'm just not up to any explanations right now."

"Sir, she isn't available at the moment. Do you know anyone by the name of Tamara?"

"No. Wait, yes I know a Tamara James in New Orleans. Don't try to tell me that sweet creature had anything to do with Gabriella's disappearance. Though that snake of a nephew is another story," he added darkly.

"Where is Gabriella? Where can I get her?"

"Here, I'll let you talk to the snake," and handed the phone to Christopher.

"Serve you right if I give him your address," Christopher muttered, though had no intention of doing so having a healthy respect of distance from the law himself.

Christopher took the phone gingerly. "Sir..."

"You son of a bitch. I knew it. What have you done with my daughter? I'm going to tear you limb from limb then cut your heart out. And if there is anything left of you when I get through, I'm going to throw your sorry ass in jail."

Christopher's face remained stoic. He breathed heavily through his nose, while grinding his teeth.

"We will be in New Orleans tonight, sir, if you care to meet us there," he said when he could finally get a word in edgewise.

He eyed Gabriella. She moved to stand beside John Paul, then much to Christopher's dismay, threw herself in John Paul's arms.

"Thank you for everything."

"You don't have to leave you know."

Christopher watched in disgust. The man had arms like hambones.

She drew in a deep breath and let it out. "Yes I do, though I wouldn't have minded staying on leave a bit longer." She kissed him on the cheek.

"If you need me, just call and I will come. I love you like the daughter I never had, though with your taste in men it might be just as well I didn't have any of my own."

She looked Christopher up and down, raised her eyebrows and drawled, "I understand your concern."

John Paul grinned and gave her a bear hug. "I expect to dance at your wedding."

Before Gabby could reply Christopher interrupted sourly, "Are you planning on providing the beverages as well?"

"I just might, bucko. I just might."

Chapter Twenty-Four

The silver plane climbed straight up into the sky. Night surrounded them. Gabby looked out the window. Gray clouds floated under the plane while stars winked overhead.

Christopher sat beside the pilot and she sat behind him. The stillness in the cockpit was as thick as the clouds outside the plane, her self-appointed fiancé withdrawn.

What the hell was Casanova up to anyway? His behavior was hardly that of a loving fiancé, he was too wary of her. Had this been an elaborate ruse to woo her away from John Paul? The idea that she could have the upper hand in the constant battle of wills waged between them appealed to her.

She leaned forward and crooned, "Lambkins."

He whipped around wide-eyed and the plane dipped as though the pilot had jerked.

She looked at Billy. His shoulders were shaking. He was either laughing or crying she concluded.

"What did you call me that for?"

"What should I call you, lover?"

"Probably pain in the ass," Billy volunteered.

Christopher shot him a cold look, while Gabby giggled.

"Sorry, boss."

"Is that what you called your protector back there?" Christopher's face grim, his jaw clenched.

"No, I called him John Paul. Is that what you want me to call you?"

Billy began to cough.

"If you were a cat, you'd be hacking up fur balls," Christopher told him sourly.

When the coughing subsided and his shoulders quit shaking, Billy tinkered with the lighted panel. "No wonder the boss is so taken with you. You're not only beautiful, but have a sense of humor as well."

Gabby tilted her head toward Billy. "Have we met?"

"Honey, if we had you wouldn't be engaged to the boss."

"Billy." Christopher said no more, but his voice held a warning.

"Sorry, boss, just a natural reaction to a beautiful woman. I'm sure Ms. Bell knows I'm harmless."

"I'm beginning to wonder." Christopher's eyes slid over his pilot then shifted to the window.

Billy shook his head. "I may be just a good ole boy, but I'm nobody's fool and that's what I'd have to be to poach on your reservation."

Christopher laughed reluctantly. "How many metaphors did you just mangle?"

"Excuse me. I'm not some piece of meat dangling in a butcher shop window and I'd appreciate it if you wouldn't talk as if I were."

Her fiancé gave her a lazy look that made her feel faint. She had to stop herself from fanning her face with her hand.

"It would be very easy to respond with a trite cliché but in the interest of self-preservation I'll respond instead to what I want you to call me. *Christopher* works very well. And in the interest of fair play I'll call you," his eyes darkened and his voice took on the rich timbre of malt whiskey, "the most breathtaking woman I've ever laid eyes on."

Their eyes held and locked in the dim light. For some reason, Gabby was having a bit of a problem catching her breath. "Probably the altitude," she told herself as she sank deeper into his gaze.

"And I'll call you the most breathtaking woman I've ever laid eyes on, I've got to remember that." Billy stroked his chin.

Gabby and Christopher grinned at each other, the tension

broken.

"So, lover, when exactly did we get engaged and more to the point why?"

"Karma. Having the crystal is just like an engagement ring in my family." He laughed as he watched her eyes narrow. "You are so easy to get a rise out of…lover."

"You send off mixed signals," she complained.

"And you think you don't?" he shot back. He rubbed his thumb across his chin, making a light rasping sound. "No, I take that back. Most of your signals are pretty straightforward and translate loosely into nailing my hide to the wall." He grinned at her and she grinned back reluctantly.

He cleared his throat. "Do you believe in predestination?"

She blinked. "Are you trying to change the subject?"

"No, but maybe it would be better if I did. What happened to you? How did you end up with that John Paul character?"

"He found me in a ravine."

The change in Christopher frightened her. His eyes went flat and his features tightened all hard planes and angles, the face of the cold-eyed stranger in the globe.

"Lai has a lot to answer for." The lack of expression in his voice further unnerved her.

Gabby couldn't help it, she shivered.

He noticed. His expression changed. His jaw muscles slackened and his eyes lightened. He reached over and grasped her hand, his warm and comforting. "You have nothing to be frightened of Gabriella."

Stiffening her spine, she stuck her chin in the air. "I'm not frightened."

He grinned and released her hand. "That's what I love about you. You may be as obstinate and wrong-headed as a mule, but you've got grit."

She blinked and turned to stare out the window at the kaleidoscope of stars winking in the dark. It might not have been in the most complimentary context but Christopher Saint, her supposed fiancé, had just used the L word.

* * * * *

It was nearing midnight when they arrived home.

As they stepped out of the car, the muggy night air hit them like a blast from a furnace.

Christopher unlocked the door and opened it for her. She crossed the threshold. Her eyes widened and her mouth opened in a silent scream as a huge brown monster came barreling toward her and knocked her to the ground.

Her head hit the black and white marble floor. Stars whirred above her head and little birds chirped. The monster stood over her covering her face with ecstatic slobber. "Ned!" she screamed and threw her arms around him.

She grunted as something stepped under the dog and onto her chest. Bright blue eyes set in the center of a seal-point face stared at her unblinkingly. "Jericho!"

Both animals had shaved spots and bandages. Bitter waves of remorse washed over her. *I didn't even ask about them.*

"Welcome home, dear." Tamara, looking like an elderly fairy in her gossamer-like dress, beamed at her over Ned's shoulder.

"Thanks." Tears threatened as she gazed into a face that had become so dear in such a short period of time.

"How did you get the animals here?" Christopher asked.

"I sprung them from the animal hospital they were recuperating in and had them flown in."

Christopher shoved the animals off and hauled Gabby to her feet.

Animal hospital? Recuperating? The fairy-like creature immediately embraced her. Gabby was engulfed by soft

217

whispery material that smelled of lavender. She closed her eyes and hugged back. "It's good to see you, Tamara."

"How are you, dear?"

"Better by the minute." A huge smile stretched across her face.

Christopher watched her, his expression dazzled. He masked it as soon as he saw her looking at him.

Billy gave a yawn huge enough to unhinge his jaws. "I've got to be going." He turned toward the door.

"Goodbye," Christopher said absently, watching Gabriella.

"Bye all." Billy stepped onto the veranda and pulled the door shut behind him.

Tamara put her arm through Gabby's and drew her into the room. "You've had a terrible ordeal, my dear. And though I don't know the particulars I'm anxious to find out."

Tamara sat down on the cream-colored sofa and drew Gabby down beside her. "Your father is coming. He should be here any minute."

"Well, isn't that just a cap to a perfect evening? I think I'll pour myself a drink."

And matching actions to words Christopher walked to the beautiful Florentine-style bar and poured a Scotch. "Aunt Tam? Gabriella?"

Gabby massaged her temples with her fingertips. The side of her head throbbed and white lights flashed behind her lids, preludes to the migraines that plagued her in North Carolina. "I'll have whatever you are having."

Tamara turned to Christopher, "Just a glass of wine for me, dear," then muttered under her breath, "I hope I don't need anything any stronger."

Tamara studied Christopher. The area around his eye was an unbecoming shade of purple. "What happened to you, Christopher dear?"

"Gabriella hit me."

"If you didn't want to tell me, you could have simply said so." Her voice filled with gentle reproof.

He walked over and handed Tamara a glass of white wine and Gabby a double Scotch.

Gabby looked at the glass and back at him. Her eyebrows soared.

He shrugged. "You said whatever I was having."

She took a sip of the golden liquid. It trailed a warm path straight to her stomach. As she set her glass down and turned to Tamara someone pounded on the door.

Tamara sat her untouched glass on the mahogany coffee table. "I imagine that's your father."

Christopher swallowed the Scotch in one gulp, squared his shoulders and answered the door.

Gabby stood.

She looked at the tall, burly man standing in the doorway. An unexpected rush of love coursed through her. "Daddy." Her voice caught in her throat. She cleared it and tried again. "Daddy."

He shoved Christopher out of his way, hurried toward her and enveloped her in a rib-crushing embrace. He released her and held her at arm's length. Tears stood in his eyes.

"My darling girl, are you all right?"

She could only nod. Her dad was not normally a demonstrative man.

"Where have you been? What happened?"

"Let's sit down, Dad, and I'll tell you all about it."

He didn't budge. "What happened, Gabriella?"

She sighed and rubbed the right side of her temple. *I will not get a migraine.* "I was kidnapped, taken to the mountains in North Carolina, escaped, fell into a ravine and was found by a wonderful human being who took care of me."

The sergeant stared, stunned, his arms dropping to his

side.

He whirled on Christopher and grabbed him by his shirt. "This is all your fault."

Christopher's eyes gleamed a warning. "Take your hands off me."

She pulled at her father's sleeve. "Daddy, let him go."

Ned whined uneasily.

Jericho sat on the floor a safe distance away, his tail wrapped around his body, his head moving from side to side as he watched the two antagonists.

Sergeant Bell spit out through gritted teeth, "You belong behind bars and by God I'm going to see that you get there."

Christopher's jaw clenched and his knuckles whitened. "Get out of this house and don't come back."

"Oh, I'll be back, sonny, and with a warrant."

Tamara floated toward them. "That's enough." She didn't raise her voice. "Shame on both of you. Gabriella has had enough to deal with without watching two adult males act like they are thirteen years old."

Both men subsided, looking ashamed.

"That's better."

She walked to the small bar and poured Scotch into a cut-crystal glass then walked over to the sergeant and handed it to him.

He slammed it back in one swallow then deliberately turned his back on Christopher.

"Tell me about this wonderful human being who rescued you, honey."

"Yeah, tell him about your mountain man and the cozy little cabin you were holed up in." Christopher's lip curled back in a sneer.

"What are you insinuating you young scoundrel?" her father roared. Then he looked down at Gabby his brows drawing down like miniature thunderbolts. "What mountain man?"

"Mr. Bell," Tamara's voice remained calm, "I must ask you to lower your voice by several decibels." She turned to her nephew. "Christopher, don't antagonize him more than you can help."

"If I go make some tea can you two keep from killing each other?" She glanced from one man to the other, then at Gabriella. "Dear, you may feel free to slay anyone you like. Right now I'd say they both deserve it."

"I think I'd like to come with you if you don't mind."

"Of course."

Christopher looked around. "Where's Beatrice?"

"Her back's bothering her. The poor dear took a sleeping pill. Now you two sit down and don't say a word until we return. I look forward to Gabriella's tale and Christopher's. My, I do believe it's going to be a long night." She floated out of the room, the scent of lavender trailing behind her. Gabby followed close behind.

His tongue hanging out, Ned tagged behind Gabby. Jericho gave a long stretch then languidly followed Ned.

Gabby glanced back in time to see Christopher roll his eyes.

* * * * *

The fragrant scent of orange and another spice that Gabby couldn't identify filled her nostrils as Tamara steeped a tea ball into a fine china teapot. Painted red roses decorated the delicate, gold-rimmed porcelain.

Gabby looked around at the spotless kitchen. Gleaming copper-bottomed pots and pans hung from hooks around the island stove. A rooster motif border circled the top of clean white walls. The floor was checkered with white and forest green tile.

Slipping off her sandals, Gabby squished her toes against the cool tiles.

"Would you get the cups out, dear? They're in the corner cupboard. "

Gabby walked to the white cupboard with ivy painted on it and opened the door and got out four cups and saucers that matched the teapot. Before her brain had an opportunity to filter her thoughts she blurted out, "Christopher said having the globe and seeing his face in it was as good as an engagement. Of course, he was just joking."

Then gave a mental groan. *Where the hell had that come from? One sip of Scotch and I'm a babbling fool.*

Tamara laughed, a light tinkling sound, with just a hint of complacency in it. "So you've seen my nephew's face in it, have you?"

"Yes."

"You alluded to it once in the garden, but you seemed reluctant to add a name to the face. Since the globe only acknowledges my family, it had to be Christopher."

Walking over to Gabby, Tamara laid a hand on her cheek. For a moment, Gabby leaned into it feeling the warmth of Tamara's soft palm against her face.

Tamara slowly withdrew her hand, smiling. "I can't think of anyone I'd rather have for my daughter. The globe chose wisely."

Gabby straightened, panicked and began to babble. "I'm sorry, Tamara, we aren't engaged. I don't know what possessed him to say that, besides a sense of humor that's odd at the best of times and I certainly don't know what made me repeat it." Regret that she wasn't marrying the self-centered egotistical man who managed to turn her world upside down stabbed her.

Tamara merely nodded and patted her hand. "Of course, dear."

"Not that we are engaged because we're not but does this mean you relinquish your claim on the globe to me?"

Opening a cabinet door, Tamara pulled out an expensive brand of mixed nuts and placed them on the tea tray along with homemade chocolate chip cookies. "It has been in my family for generations."

Gabby's heart began to pound and her palms sweat. "I'm sorry. I truly am, but it's my globe."

"Yes, dear, I believe it is."

At Tamara's words, the ceramic spoon holder she held slipped through her nerveless fingers and shattered against the tile.

Neither woman seemed to notice.

"You mean it?"

"You are going back to Springfield aren't you?"

Gabby nodded, her voice barely a whisper. "I can't stay here. I need to go home. Dad needs me and I need him. I need to regroup. I need to get away from your nephew. I'm just not up to going rounds with him right now." Tears formed in her eyes and slid down her cheeks.

Tamara stepped around the ceramic shards and gathered Gabby in her arms.

"There, there. It's all right. Everything will be all right. You and the globe will be coming back, sooner than you think."

She lifted her head from the older woman's shoulder and stepped back. A sting in her left foot reminded her of the shattered spoon holder. "I better clean that up." She sniffed, reached for a paper napkin and blew her nose.

"You take out the tea tray and I'll clean this up."

Gabby nodded, wiping her eyes. Then with the agility of a former waitress, heaved the tray above her right shoulder and walked into the living room. The dog and cat trailed behind her hoping for treats.

The large room had a cozy grouping of chairs and a sofa in front of the fireplace. She sat the tray down on the fruitwood coffee table in front of the sofa.

The men came over to join her. She poured them each a cup of tea and covertly watched Christopher. The steam rose from his cup like a small vapor cloud, but he didn't seem to notice the heat, his mind apparently elsewhere.

Why did she feel such a strong pull toward this infuriating man? It was time and past for Tamara to tell her why she was the only one who saw Christopher's face in the globe.

At that moment, he lifted his nose from the teacup and looked into her eyes.

She had the same sense of swirling colors enveloping her as she did when she looked into the globe, drowning in the deep emerald pools of his eyes. And there was a message there, she'd swear to it. What was he trying to tell her?

She was literally lifting her hand toward him, when her father said in a hearty voice, "There you are."

Tamara glided into the room. Gabby's arm dropped to her side. The men stood sipping their tea, the silence strained. Tamara sat down on the couch beside Gabby, leaving the chairs at opposite ends of the sofa for the men. Both slumped down.

"I suppose Gabriella has told you that she is going home with her father for a while." Tamara's bird-like bright eyes darted about.

"Well, of course, she is," Jimmy Bell boomed.

"You can't. I won't allow it." Christopher's chin lifted, command in his face.

Gabby's head snapped up. "You have no say here."

His voice cutting, he banged the cup on the table, stood up abruptly and began to pace. "We're engaged remember?"

"Engaged!" Sergeant Bell roared. "She's not marrying the likes of you, bucko."

Both Christopher and Gabby ignored him.

Fire snapped behind Gabby's eyes. "That was a sham. You just told John Paul that to get me off the mountain." Her lip curled in a sneer.

The cat, the dog, Sergeant Bell and Tamara all swung their heads back and forth as they watched the two protagonists with fascination.

He whirled around to face her. "You just don't get it do you? Didn't Tamara tell you the legend?" Ignoring the hushing motions Tamara was frantically making. "You don't have a choice. I don't have a choice. We are bound together until one of us leaves this earthly vale of tears and even then I'm not so sure we can get rid of each other."

"Bless my soul, what is the boy spouting about?" The sergeant turned to Tamara for enlightenment.

Tamara shook her head, watching her beloved nephew. She whispered, "Dear boy, I don't know whether to hug you or slap you."

Gabby whitened. "You don't want me." Her voice was as low as Tamara's had been.

His eyes warmed to molten lava. "Oh, I want you all right."

"That will be about enough of that talk. You will shut up or I'll shut you up," Sergeant Bell promised grimly, with a look on his face that fairly shouted he'd like nothing better.

Christopher looked abashed and muttered under his breath, "I can't believe I just said that in front of my aunt and your father."

Gabby sat rigid. "I'm afraid that's not enough."

Christopher threw his hands in the air in defeat. "What can I say?"

"That you love her you fool," Tamara and Sergeant Bell spoke in unison then smiled at each other.

Christopher shook his head. "This is turning into a farce."

Sergeant Bell stood up and walked to Gabby. "Honey, I think it's time we went home."

She nodded.

Christopher looked at her. "You are determined to do this then."

"Yes." Her voice was low and dull.

"At least stay until morning."

"I think it's better we go. I've checked the airlines. There will be a flight leaving in three hours. Technically, it is the morning," the sergeant said.

Christopher looked directly at Sergeant Bell. "She will be staying with you, not at her house?"

Gabby's head shot up. Uh-huh. She hadn't seen her little house in way too long.

"Of course."

Christopher watched Gabriella and sighed. He looked at her father. "It's not going to happen. You might as well put police at the house to watch her. She'll find a way." Before Jimmy could respond, Christopher walked out of the room.

Jimmy looked at Tamara. "He's a strange lad."

Tamara smiled. "If you take the time to look deep enough, you will find a good man with a kind heart. Many never see that deep." She looked directly at him, causing him to blush.

"For your sake, I will try," he responded to the unspoken reprimand. "Now, girlie, let's get you packed and go home."

It took Gabby less than an hour to pack. When she came back down, a large duffle bag thrown over one arm and a smaller bag over the other, Billy was waiting in the foyer. "What are you doing here?"

"Christopher called me. I'm flying you back to Springfield. This way you don't have to worry about the animals."

A stab of remorse pricked her. "I never even thought

about that."

"Now you don't have to."

Sergeant Bell and Tamara came walking in from the living room. "Are you ready, darlin'?" her father asked.

She nodded then ran to Tamara and hugged her. "I'll miss you." For a moment she felt her tipsy world right in the woman's soothing embrace.

"It will be all right, dear. I promise."

She smiled, blinking against tears. She stepped back and looked around.

Christopher was not there. She straightened her shoulders. "Let's go."

Billy grabbed her bags. They all trooped out and got in the black SUV.

She placed her hand against the window. Tamara, standing on the lit porch, waved.

Glancing up, she saw a figure silhouetted in the window of Christopher's bedroom.

Billy started the car. As it purred to life, he swung it out into the street.

She watched as the lone figure in the window grew smaller and smaller and finally disappeared.

Christopher walked downstairs. He joined his aunt on the porch. Putting his arm around her, he drew her inside. "At least, you have the globe back."

"I gave it to Gabriella. It's hers now."

"You did what?"

Chapter Twenty-Five

The doorbell rang. Gabby tripped over Ned as he raced her to the door. Since she'd come back from North Carolina, neither Ned nor Jericho let her out of their sights. Gabby couldn't really blame them. She had left them hurt and alone and hadn't returned for…well for a long time.

The buzzer sounded again. Picking herself up, she reached the door mere seconds after Ned. She hesitated before opening the door, all her father's dire warnings ringing in her ears.

The doorbell rang for the third time, an insistent buzz, buzz.

She put the chain on then opened the door the prerequisite inch. A pretty little redhead stood on the porch smiling at her, dressed in clothes worth more than everything in her wardrobe combined.

"Amy!" Unhooking the chain, she ran onto the porch and threw her arms around her friend and squeezed. Even though Amy barely reached her shoulders, comfort streamed through Gabby as she laid her head against her friend's hair.

Amy hugged her back. "Gabby honey, are you going to invite me in or are we going to chat on the porch? I'm baking out here. It must be eighty degrees."

Gabby laughed. "This would be considered nearly winter weather in New Orleans."

"Well, honey, we aren't in New Orleans now are we? Are you going to ask me in or not?"

"Woof. Woof." Ned ran in ecstatic circles around the two women.

"Can I get you something to drink?" Gabby headed toward the tiny kitchen.

"I'll take a beer." Amy followed her to the kitchen.

Gabby opened her old refrigerator. The motor hummed. "Mm, I have soda and iced tea." She stuck her hand inside the cool interior and moved a ketchup bottle. No beer appeared.

A bubbly laugh burst from her friend's lips. "Don't tell me let me guess. Your dad cleaned your refrigerator out for you. Damn, I wouldn't have minded an ice-cold adult beverage."

Gabby gave a wry smile and nodded.

"It pains your dad that you can party with the best of them. Give me a soda then."

Gabby handed her a soda, the can chill against her palm.

Amy caught a long red fingernail under the tab and gave it an expert pop.

Caramel carbonation fizzed to the top. Her friend took a long swallow. "Ah, that's good. Let's go to the living room." She walked into the living room and sank down on the sagging sofa. Gabby trailed behind her.

Gabby plopped to the floor and crossed her legs. Jericho came in and settled in her lap. She stroked the soft rich fur. An appreciative purr rumbled in Jericho's throat.

Amy took another swallow of her drink. "So tell me about the hunk. My date as I recall."

Gabby moved restively from hip to hip, disturbing Jericho, who complained about it. She scratched him behind the ear and he settled back down. "He came to North Carolina to rescue me, whether I needed it or not."

"North Carolina? You'll have to tell me all about it. Remember I introduced you."

"That's one version."

Amy narrowed her eyes, her expression speculative. "Hm." Then winked and gave her a saucy smile. "Did you do the dirty?"

Gabby began to fan herself with her hand, suddenly hot.

Amy was right about the temperature. "Did you?" she shot back.

"No, damn it." Amy sounded so regretful that Gabby burst out laughing. Her friend settled back against the couch. "Tell me what happened. No, no, tell me about the hunk."

"I don't trust him."

"Well, of course not. Anyone with those bedroom eyes and languid glances is dangerous."

"That too but that's not what I mean." She remembered the mountains and the attack. "He's the kind of man who could take care of himself alone in a dark alley."

"Ooh, how romantic."

"Mm." Gabby's voice noncommittal.

Amy patted the couch invitingly. "Come here and tell me all about it."

She took a long breath, then told her best friend everything...except about the green crystal globe and the fact that she'd had the most intense, mind-altering sex that she'd ever had in her life. Some things just weren't meant to be shared, though she'd never hesitated before. When she finished, she got up and walked restlessly around her small living room, Jericho at her heels.

Amy studied her. "So you're engaged to the hunk?"

Gabby whirled, causing Jericho to bump into her leg. "No, I'm not."

"But you would like to be."

"No of course not."

"Because..."

"He's too, too..." She threw her hands in the air, in frustration.

"Sexy," Amy supplied helpfully then began to croon, "He's too sexy."

Gabby laughed. The doorbell interrupted Amy's off-key crooning.

Ned barked.

"Are you expecting company?" Amy tucked a red-gold strand of hair behind her ear.

"No. It's probably Dad or someone selling encyclopedias. At this point I'd rather have the salesman. I love Dad. But he hovers."

She went to answer the door. Ned raced her to it. He stood at the door his tongue hanging out, his tail wagging madly.

"I guess that leaves out the insurance salesman." She sighed then threw open the door. "Hi, Dad." Her eyes widened. "What are you doing here?"

Curious, Amy came ambling out of the living room. "Well." Her voice filled with appreciation.

"Hello, Amy." Christopher stood at the door holding a dozen red roses.

"I guess this is where I say, I was just leaving." Christopher smiled.

Amy looked at her best friend and shook her head. "You are just like a cat, always land on your feet."

Christopher's shoulders shook with silent laughter. He held the screen door open. "Nice to see you again, Amy."

Amy looked him up and down her expression sultry. "The pleasure is all mine, I assure you."

He looked uneasily at Gabby. She rolled her eyes. "You might as well come in."

Amy gave a tinkle of laughter. "Maybe that's my problem. I just haven't been rude enough. Gabby is being pretty vague about whether you've ever done the Texas Two-Step in bed. But if there's any information you'd like to share…" She wiggled her eyebrows and winked at him.

"Amy!" Heat rose in Gabby's face.

He stared down his nose at her, his expression forbidding, "I beg your pardon?"

Unfazed, Amy gurgled. "I'm going. I'm going."

Christopher and Gabby stood looking at each other. Tension tangible as it whirled and snapped to the breaking point. Finally, Gabby made a sweeping motion with her arm.

Christopher stepped through the door.

Ned jumped up, placing his huge paws on Christopher's maroon silk shirt. Jericho wound between his legs leaving liberal amounts of cat hair sprinkled on his black slacks. He pushed the dog down, laughing.

Gabby pointed at the flowers. "Are those for me or the dog?"

"Who do you think?"

"What do you want, Saint?"

He just stood staring at her 'til she began to tap the tip of her fingers against her pants leg and looked around the room not meeting his eyes.

He took a step toward her. She backed up.

"What do I want? Now that's a good question. It's been one I've been asking myself ever since we met." He cocked his head to one side and studied her. He could see the pulse at her throat jump erratically.

He reined in the raw sexual tautness coursing through his body and gave her a lazy smile.

Wary, she watched him.

This time when he stepped forward, instead of stepping back, she took a deep breath and straightened her shoulders.

He took another step forward and murmured against her mouth. "Now that's more like it." In a tumble of red and green the flowers fell at their feet as his lips settled on hers, gentle and seeking. At his first touch her stiff body went limp. His kiss deepened.

"Wow! I think I've been struck by a lightning bolt," she said against his lips.

His eyes flew open, unfocused. "Have you forgotten what it's like between us? I can't, though lord knows I've tried." The last words a whisper against her lips.

Ignoring it she responded, "Perhaps you'd better give me a refresher," and leaned into him.

"Perhaps I should." *Thank you, Jesus*. Things were going much better than he had anticipated.

His lips touched hers and he groaned, remembering the feel of those wonderfully warm pouty lips as they quested over his body. "Care to show me your etchings, pretty mamma?" he murmured against her mouth.

She giggled shakily. "I expected something more original than that. Have women fallen for this line before?"

Instead of responding he moved his lips to her ears and whispered, "Let me gaze into the sapphire night of your eyes and sink into your body's liquid heat, while our limbs entwine. "

"Much better." She slithered out of his embrace and walked backward to the bedroom her eyes holding his. Christopher followed murmuring poetry by a poet with an erotic bend.

She gave him a sultry glance that stopped his heart and boiled his blood.

"Much, much better." She curled her finger in a beckoning gesture.

They reached the bedroom. He put his arms around her and they fell to the bed, rolling. He leaned over her and murmured, "I have no idea whether it's love or madness but you light a fire that consumes me."

Startled, Gabby looked into his intense green eyes.

He wondered if she saw the hunger and the love. Passion ignited as he pressed his body to hers. "Is this what you want Gabriella or am I taking unfair advantage?" It cost him, God it cost him, but he waited barely breathing for her answer.

She pulled his head down. "Let's get back to that entwining thing." Her lips found his and all thought fled, leaving only urgency and need.

* * * * *

Sensing Christopher's gaze, Gabby opened her eyes. For once, the muscles in his face relaxed and the corners of those devastating lips turned up. She breathed in the minty scent of his breath as he spoke. "It's even better than I remembered and my memory was good enough to keep me awake nights."

"I wonder if every time will be like the first time." Her body satiated was languid and heavy.

One arm held her the other was thrown over his head. "Must I point out that as cataclysmic as the first time was, it just keeps getting better? Though if it improves anymore, it'll be the death of me. If I'd been middle-aged my heart would have stopped." He leered and wiggled his eyebrows at her. "Though I find the idea of mouth-to-mouth resuscitation appealing I'm not sure I want you pounding on my chest."

He stretched like a cat. "If you ever give up journalism you could make a fortune as a kept woman."

She picked up a nearby pillow and hit him, but not hard, she didn't have the strength. "I'm not sure if I've been complimented or insulted."

"Trust me it was a compliment."

"Christopher…"

"Yes, love."

"Speaking of which, are we?" Her eyes searched his hooded ones.

He pulled himself up and leaned against the wall. Gabby went tumbling into the pillows.

"You need a headboard. Hmm, maybe not, the wall is nice and cool against my back." He bent down and placed a light kiss on the top of her tousled hair then pulled her up beside him.

"Our relationship can best be described as rocky."

"That doesn't answer my question."

He sighed. "Maybe you should stay in journalism, you're persistent enough."

Fascinated Gabby watched the rise and fall of the two penny-shaped disks on his sleek chest as he breathed. She reached over and pulled a hair.

"Ouch!" Christopher rubbed his stinging skin.

"You were saying?"

"Witch."

"That wasn't it."

He pushed the sheet back, slid out of the bed and began to pace, distracting Gabby. His body was perfect, lean and supple as a cat's. He reminded her of a young Greek god. Did he have any idea of the effect he had on her? She remembered her cries of delight and blushed. Obviously, he did.

He stopped his pacing, looked at her then cleared his throat.

Gabby's head jerked up to his face.

He gave her a slow, sensual grin. "Insatiable hussy."

Maybe she should just let the love thing go and concentrate on the lust thing. Her eyes traveled over him. If his body wasn't ready, it was certainly giving a good imitation.

"Gabriella."

"Hmm?" Then straightened. "Where are you going?"

He didn't answer, just walked out of the room.

"Was it something I said?" Gabby called after him. With a regretful sigh she stepped into her pink cotton thong, then picked up her *Spay/Neuter Your Pet* tee shirt and pulled it over her head. As her head popped up through the cotton neckline she saw Christopher in front of her, holding two glasses of white wine. "You're right. We need to talk."

She shook out her hair and blinked. "Where did you find that?"

He gave her a wicked smile that made her heart do flip-flops. "Having been here on two other occasions, I have been able to ascertain where you hide your stash."

He set the wineglasses on the bedside table, picked up his black silk briefs and slid them on then stepped into his slacks. Holding the fabric with his left hand, he pulled up the zipper with the right.

Gabby's breathing was a tad bit shallow. If he'd brought the wine for an aphrodisiac it wasn't necessary. But if he was getting dressed, he obviously wasn't thinking along the same lines she was. *Too bad.*

She got up and pulled on a pair of faded gray gym shorts, turning in time to see Christopher watching her appreciatively as the thong disappeared from view.

He picked up the wineglasses. "Let's go into the living room."

They walked in and sat on Gabby's old couch. A piece of stuffing stuck out on the side where Jericho sharpened his claws.

She flopped down, the sofa cushions enveloping her. He sat on the arm of the couch and handed Gabby a glass of wine.

She ran her finger around the condensation forming on the glass.

Christopher took a sip of the white liquid. "Maybe to figure out where we are going we'd better look at where we've been."

"Because?"

He ran his fingers through his short hair. "Because I doubt if either of us has been completely honest with the other and not only do we need to figure out what we are going to do about us, we need to figure out what we are going to do about Lai."

She straightened. Her eyes heated and her teeth grinded. "Oh yes your bitch friend who kidnapped me."

"That would be the one. But let's table her for the moment."

She slumped back into the cushions muttering to herself.

He reached over and massaged her shoulder with his long lean fingers. "Don't worry, darling, that score will be settled. Now to get back on track, our story starts at Earth Religions, where you purchased the globe."

A memory of a hard-faced stranger with a ponytail flickered. *Christopher.*

"My former lover had the crystal stolen from my aunt. It was hidden in the shop. Obviously, not well, since you bought it from that effeminate, weak-kneed clerk."

She bit her lips to keep from grinning. Whoever the clerk was, it was apparent Christopher didn't think much of him.

He twirled his glass, watching the golden liquid eddy back and forth. "I stole it back." He grinned. "You came after me and tried to steal it from Aunt Tam. Interesting you should call yourself Tamara."

"Interesting." That was one word for it.

"Yes, well, you moved in at Tamara's invitation. Lai, my former lover, tried again for the crystal and kidnapped you."

"Why?"

"Why come after the stone or why kidnap you?"

"Both."

"To get to me. Lai wants me back."

"How will either get you back?"

Christopher grinned. "You are my fiancée remember?"

"There seems to be some doubt about that. And why steal the crystal?"

He turned serious. "I believe there's a two-fold reason but let's start with have you ever seen anyone in the ball?"

Gabby eyed him warily. "Why do you ask?"

He leaned forward, his posture tense. "Have you, Gabriella? You have said things in the past to lead me to believe you have. And the fact that my aunt gave you the crystal is mind-boggling."

"If you must know I've seen you," she said her voice irritable. "A fact I've mentioned to you before."

"Anyone else? That moonshiner you were living with, perhaps?"

"Why do you insist on talking so rudely about John Paul? And no damn it, yours is the only face I've had the displeasure to see." She gulped down her wine then choked as it went down the wrong way.

Christopher patted her absently on the back, trying to bite back a triumphant smile and failing.

Her eyebrows drew together. "Why are you grinning like a hyena?"

"Did auntie ever tell you the legend?"

"Not exactly." She looked at him warily.

"The globe has been in Tamara's family for generations handed down from mother to daughter and with it a legend. The women of the family can see their true love's face in the globe. Aunt Tamara always swore she saw Uncle Edward's."

"And you believe her?"

"I never did before. But I'm beginning to think, my darling, that our fate is sealed."

Gabby lifted her head in the air. "I make my own destiny."

He nodded. "Understood. Shall I take the globe back when I go?"

"No!"

"But if you don't believe in the legend, why keep it?" His voice sounded very reasonable.

She gritted her teeth. "You can't have it. It's mine!"

"But what about Aunt Tam?" His eyes and voice teased.

A look of regret crossed her face. "I'm sorry." She shook her head, impatient. "We seem to have wandered off course here."

"You noticed." He gave her a wicked grin that turned her heart over.

"Do you love me?"

"About this love thing." Christopher paced the room then stopped and turned toward Gabby, his eyes intense. "I…"

She straightened, feeling she was on the verge of a cliff and she would either go tumbling into a deep, dark abyss or discover she had wings and fly.

He cleared his throat and started over, "I don't know what your…"

Someone knocked at the door.

He swore under his breath. "Gabby…"

The knocking grew more insistent.

She got off the couch and gave an apologetic shrug. "Saved by the bell."

"Who? You or me?"

"I guess it depends on what you had to say." She gazed at his torso and gave a regretful sigh. "You better get your shirt on. If it's Amy, the sight of your bare chest might be too much for her."

He gave a rueful smile then headed toward the bedroom. "We'll talk later. I promise you."

Gabby waited 'til Christopher was out of the room and then opened the door. Her eyes widened in shock. "Daddy!"

He walked in and enveloped her in a bear hug. "Just wanted to make sure my little girl was all right and to see if you'd changed your mind about living with me."

"Dad, we've been over that a million times." She sent a mental message to Christopher to stay in the bedroom.

He apparently didn't receive it, since he came strolling out, buttoning his shirt.

"You," Sergeant Bell roared.

Christopher gave an almost imperceptible jerk but recovered immediately and continued walking into the room. He nodded his head. "Sir."

"I don't know what you are doing here but you can just get your pretty butt out."

Though anger darkened Christopher's eyes, his expression never changed. "Glad you like it but that pretty butt is solely your daughter's, sir."

Gabby put her head in her hands and groaned. Whatever possessed him? Did he have a death wish?

"You get the hell out of this house right now, or by God I'll take you down and throw you in the slammer and bury you under so much paperwork you won't ever get out."

She moved quickly. Before Christopher could respond she laid her hand on his arm. It was taut beneath her fingers. "Just go, please."

Their eyes locked. For a moment, she thought she glimpsed hurt behind the anger, before the sardonic mask he showed to the world was firmly in place.

Ned whined uneasily at his feet.

Without a word, Christopher patted him absently then walked out the door, closing it quietly behind him.

She rounded on her father. "Whatever possessed you to say those things?"

Her father's ruddy complexion became more so. His eyebrows rose. "Me? The nerve of him."

"You pushed him, Dad, and you know it."

"He's nothing but a common thief, Gabriella."

"There is nothing common about Christopher," she retorted, then shook her head at what she was implying. "You don't know that."

"I can smell a rotten apple a mile away and that one's rotten."

Gabby wandered around the room. "Christopher is a complicated human being."

"So was Benedict Arnold and Lee Harvey Oswald or so I'm told."

She heaved a sigh. "So what is he, Dad, a thief, a traitor or a murderer?"

"Gabby, he's a known associate of an international jewel thief."

Her eyes troubled, she looked at her father. "Who?" *As if I don't know.*

"He's called The Tiger."

"All that makes him guilty of is keeping bad company."

"I know in my bones he's a bad one."

She rolled her eyes. "Your bones have been known to be wrong, Dad."

"Don't be impertinent." He grabbed her and gave her a quick hard hug. "Your experience certainly didn't affect that mouth of yours."

She grinned then turned serious. "About Christopher, what do you really have against him?"

"He's a rich, good-for-nothing playboy. He has more money than is good for him and you are probably nothing more than an amusing diversion for him. What you need is a good solid Irish boy. Now take Officer Mahoney…"

"You take him. We've had this conversation before."

He grinned sheepishly. "Well, maybe once or twice."

"So what you really have against Christopher is his money. It intimidates you."

"Is that any way for a good Catholic girl to talk to her father?" He towered over her in a manner most civilians found intimidating. "Like should marry like."

But Gabby was nothing if not her father's daughter.

"That is completely unfair and prejudicial."

"Oh, so you've decided to give up on being a nosy reporter and become an ambulance chasing attorney instead?"

She rolled her eyes. And the man wondered why she wouldn't move back home.

Before she could respond, his pager went off. "All cars in the vicinity of Eighteenth Street, a robbery is in progress."

She sent a prayer of thanks heavenward, opened the door then gave him a peck on the cheek. "You're a pain, but I love you, Daddy."

He hugged her then gave her a quick buss. "And you're my heart's delight." He strode out and hurried to his car.

In the doorway, she waved as he drove away. Then smiled, remembering her childhood.

Her mom had been a teacher. They were the typical middle-class family. Well maybe not typical. They had been very happy. Were all families as happy as hers? She doubted it.

Dad could be a royal pain, but he loved her ferociously. And the poor man was lonely. Mom had died three years ago. Gabby remembered that with clarity.

She'd always been healthy as a horse or so everyone thought. Mom had taught English at the local community college. By the time she found out she had cancer, it was too late to save her. She died just before her forty-eighth birthday.

A fresh wave of grief washed over her. "I miss you, Mom."

Sensing her sadness Ned nudged her hand with his wet nose and Jericho wound through her legs.

Gabby swiped at a tear that coursed down her cheek. "Okay, gang, let's go look at the globe." She had put it back in a bowl in her bedroom.

She walked in the room, reached over and picked up the globe. The orb cool to the touch. Clutching it to her like her firstborn, Gabby sank down on the bed.

Hues of green and blue began to swirl in a familiar pattern. Then fell away.

Christopher's face appeared. Since her fall into the ravine the ball had always shown her the same picture—Christopher with the cold eyes of a stranger. But this time, the picture changed.

Gabby stared. The blood drained from her face. The ball rolled from her nerveless fingers out of her lap and onto the floor.

This time instead of distant and cold, his eyes registered pain and he was covered in blood.

Chapter Twenty-Six

Gabby punched in Christopher's cell number…again. She'd been calling for two days. "Come on, Christopher, pick up." She paced around the apartment. Once again the recorded message came on. "Damn it, Christopher, I know you are there. Please pick up or call me."

She waited five minutes then dialed again.

"What do you want, Gabriella?"

"Why the hell didn't you answer your phone?"

"I have a dozen messages from you all saying urgent and all you can say is why didn't I pick up my phone?"

"Christopher, what would have been the point in you punching out my father or him hauling you off to jail?"

"You followed the path of least resistance, Bell."

Gabby shot back stung, "Well, no one can ever accuse you of that. If there is a way of stirring the pot you do it."

"Stirring the pot? What the hell are you talking about?"

Gabby shook her head. How had a simple thing like a phone call gotten so complex? "Oh never mind. What I called to tell you is that you are in danger."

"From who? Your old man?"

"Yes. No. I don't know."

"Get a grip, Bell. What are you babbling about?"

She could hear irritation in his voice and since when had he started calling her Bell? She took a deep breath and straightened her shoulders. "I saw it in the crystal."

"What?"

She didn't need to see him to know he had just taken the phone away from his ear and was looking at it as if it were an alien from another planet.

"You saw it in the crystal." His voice had the tone people usually reserve for soothing hysterical children or the insane. Gabby had no doubt what category he pigeonholed her in.

"Just what exactly did you see in the globe?"

"You."

"So? I thought you said you had seen me in it before."

"Of course, but this time it was different." Gabby's voice rose. "You were covered in blood."

"Probably from banging my head against the wall."

"Will you please be serious?" Her voice shook.

"You think I'm not? Okay. Okay. So what exactly did you see?"

"I told you. Don't you understand English?"

Heavy breathing sounded over the phone.

"You were shot, maybe knifed. I just don't know but you were in pain."

"Calm down. If I didn't know better, I'd think you actually care."

"Of course I care, you idiot."

"Could have fooled me."

She paced around the room. "What did you expect me to do, Christopher? Stand there and let you duke it out with my father?"

"You asked me to leave."

"The only other option would have been to gag you. What the hell was that 'my pretty butt' comment?"

"You tell me, your dad made it," he shot back.

Gabby heard the car door slam. She could picture his long sleek body lounging against the black Jag. "Are you leaning up against the car?" Her tone was wistful.

"Looking in your crystal ball again," he jeered.

"No, I'm looking in my heart."

"Don't, Gabriella."

"Don't what?"

"Don't play with me."

"I'm not. Damn it, Christopher. We are getting way off course here. I called to tell you to be careful."

"So noted. You have warned me. By the way, if your dad is looking for his wallet I turned it in to his precinct."

Gabby stared at the phone appalled. "You stole my dad's wallet?"

"That's not what I said."

"The officer on duty said he would be very appreciative. Do you think he will be?

"Gabby. Hello. Hello. Gabriella?"

She had a flashback. *A beautiful Asian leaving the party, followed by a shriek. "My necklace has been stolen."*

"I didn't take the damn thing. Get out of my way before I strike you."

"It was a childish thing to do. It was beneath you."

"How would you know whether it was beneath me or not? Okay, I gave in to a stupid impulse. I haven't lifted a wallet in twenty years. But you know it wasn't to steal it. Just to piss him off. And you are right damn it. It was a stupid thing to do. But I was so freaking angry."

She spoke slowly thinking aloud. "At the ball I thought you stole Marie Antoinette's necklace."

"Are we back to playing 'to figure out where we're going we look at where we've been?' Well forget it, we obviously aren't going nowhere," he snarled.

"And my dad thinks you are a thief."

"I told you this is going nowhere."

"And I think you are hiding something from me. Why is that?"

"You're a newspaper reporter or so you claim, figure it out. By the way Tam said to tell you she has been filling in your column for you and having a blast."

The phone went dead.

"Really? Hello, hello." The dial tone sounded in her ear.

"Jerk." What did she see in the man anyway, other than mind-blowing sex, a great body, loads of money, a quick wit and polished manners—when he chose to use them.

And was she or wasn't she engaged? She looked down at her bare left hand. A definite no on that one.

She tapped her chin with an Auburn-Awe colored fingernail. An evil smile played across her lovely features. No reason Mahoney had to know that. She could always pick up a zirconium ring at a pawnshop. Yes indeedy. That should work.

It was a moment before she realized he had sidetracked her completely from what she had seen in the globe. Eel.

Well if he wouldn't take her seriously, she would just have to do something about it herself. Her chin came up and with it her tenacity.

She punched in speed dial on the phone. She would call Aunt Tam and warn her, then make arrangements to return to New Orleans. "Beatrice. How wonderful to talk to you." *I think.*

"No, no, I don't want Christopher. I'd like to speak to Tam. Oh she's not? Would you have her call me back? No need to mention this to Christopher. Thanks. Bye now."

The phone rang again, almost as soon as she hung up. "Christopher? Oh, I'm sorry I thought you were someone else. Ned and Jericho's shots are due tomorrow? Thanks so much for reminding me. Both of them right? Three tomorrow? I'll be there." She hung up the phone. An inexplicable feeling of dread had come over her while she talked to her vet's receptionist. Something about her voice triggered an unpleasant response.

*****

Driving a nondescript gray sedan, Lai pulled onto Gabby's street, stopped two doors down and killed the engine. She looked at her watch. Two-twenty. Ms. Bell should be leaving anytime.

She had come alone. She'd given Leaky and the fool of a proprietor their chance and they'd failed. Now, she would do this job herself and reap all the rewards. No one would share in the riches.

A police car cruised by. Of course, she thought contemptuously, we don't want anything to happen to daddy's little girl.

She pulled down the visor and looked into the mirror. She wore a curly red wig, designer clothes and large sunglasses. From a distance she would pass for the bitch's little friend. She'd carefully watched the comings and goings since the Amazon arrived home, including Christopher's arrival. Her hand tightened on the steering wheel. She took a deep breath and made herself relax.

The Amazon's friend was an inch or two taller than Lai, but no one observing them from a distance would notice.

As she watched the house, Gabriella Bell came out, a cat carrier in one hand, the dog on a leash in the other. She hustled them into the car then pulled out of the drive.

Lai waited another five minutes then picked up an elegant silver striped shopping bag, walked to the house then picked the lock. She'd just opened the door, when Gabby's neighbor came out on his porch.

"Hi Amy."

Lai waved.

"You just missed Gabby. She was taking the dog and cat to the vet."

Lai pointed at her bag, then the door.

"Oh, you've got a present for Gabby, cool."

Lai nodded and slipped inside. She took a quick look around the living room then glided into the bedroom. Her gaze swept the area as she stepped into the room.

There it was, sitting in a bowl on the bookcase. Lai

smiled, triumphant. "Of course, the woman has no imagination." She approached it eagerly, took out a loupe and studied it. Elation coursed through her and her blood rushed. "Just as I thought."

She dug into the shopping bag and pulled out a white square box. Opening it she took out an identical looking globe. She placed it on the bed then walked over to Gabby's green crystal and started to pick it up then bit back a cry.

The moment she touched it, it froze her fingers. With a cry, she drew them back, stiff and cold.

An untidy heap of clothes lay on the floor. She grabbed a faded green tee shirt and gingerly lifted the globe. Even through the tee shirt, it stung her hands.

She carried it quickly to the box, dropped it in then placed the globe she'd purchased for $19.95 in the bowl. Grabbing the box, she shoved it in the bag then walked out of the house.

Hips swaying, she strolled to the sedan, placed the sack in the passenger side and pulled out into the street.

She caught her reflection in the rearview mirror, her glistening taupe lips parted in a smile, jubilation lighting her eyes. It was a perfect plan. The ox would blame Christopher for the theft.

This would drive them apart. She would have him or no one would. But regardless, she had the crystal and would be rich beyond her wildest imaginings.

Chapter Twenty-Seven

Gabby pulled into the parking lot of Caring Paws and cut the engine. As Jericho began to howl, Ned looked at his friend and whined uneasily.

She opened the door to the backseat, pulled the carrier out, set it on the ground and rubbed her arm. "You're gaining weight."

Ned stuck his head out of the car, looked at his surroundings and like a turtle drew his head back in. She tugged on the leash. The turtle wannabe didn't move.

"Good dog. Good Neddy." She pulled harder on the leash.

He didn't budge.

She yanked at the same moment he decided to cooperate and sat down with a thump in the parking lot. Ned licked her face.

Pushing him away, she picked herself up and dusted off her denim shorts. Carrying the screaming cat and pulling the dog she walked in the door.

The receptionist looked up and smiled. Her hair was burgundy and spiked. "Ms. Bell, how nice to see you again."

Gabby smiled back. "Hi, Nellie . "

The receptionist stood up and tugged on her short, hip hugging skirt.

Gabby's smile widened. Same ole Nellie.

"I'm sorry to hear you'll be leaving us. Where exactly are you going?"

Gabby blinked. How did she know about that? "New Orleans."

"Cool."

An assistant in a white lab coat appeared at the door. "Ms. Bell, you can bring them back now."

Gabby nodded and followed her into the examining room.

The vet, a middle-aged woman with long graying hair and a bit overweight, walked in. "How's my boys?"

Ned wagged his tail and Jericho hissed.

Dr. Smith laughed. "Let's start with Ned." She gave him a brief but thorough exam. "He's healing just fine. I hear you are moving." She talked as she worked.

"How did you know that?"

Dr. Smith looked at her in surprise. "Why you told Nellie when you called to make your appointment."

Gabby's gaze sharpened. She was beginning to get one of those feelings and it wasn't a warm fuzzy. "I didn't call to make an appointment."

Dr. Smith paused, syringe in hand. She looked at her briefly then plunged it quickly into Ned. It was over before he knew what happened. "I'm sure that's what she told me."

"Aren't you moving?"

"Not permanently."

Dr. Smith shrugged and pushed back a lock of hair that had escaped her ponytail.

"Maybe Nellie misunderstood."

"Maybe." The skin on the back of Gabby's neck began to crawl. *Something's wrong.*

"Now for Jericho."

Gabby tapped her fingers against the side of her legs, willing the vet to hurry.

As soon as Dr. Smith finished up, Gabby hustled the animals out of the office, not even bothering to interrogate Nellie. There wasn't time. "Put it on my account," she called over her shoulder as she left.

Hurry, hurry, hurry, pounded in her brain.

She went through an intersection on a yellow turning red.

The next light she ran didn't have a glimmer of yellow. At least I looked both ways, Gabby consoled herself, just before she heard the whoop, whoop, whoop of the siren.

Looking in the rearview mirror, her hands tightened on the wheel. "Damn!"

The white squad car followed her home.

A middle-aged black woman, dressed in blue, got out of the car as Gabby pulled Ned out.

"Going to a fire?"

"Sorry, Nancy." Nancy had been with the force for four years.

The officer stood hands on hips. "Girl, you know your daddy would have a fit."

Gabby swallowed her impatience. "I know."

Nancy shook her finger at her. "Don't let it happen again."

"I won't."

Nancy started back toward her car, as Gabby hauled the cat carrier out with her free hand and began to run for the door.

The officer reached her car, put her hand on the door handle then turned. "Do you want me to come in and look around?"

"Please." Gabby reached for her key, nerves shooting through her, making her legs tingle.

Sensing her urgency, Nancy trotted up the walk.

As Gabby started to open the door, Nancy motioned her away. "Stay here." She stepped inside, her gun drawn.

If she hadn't been burdened with the animals Gabby would have followed her in.

As it was she'd be of more aid to Nancy keeping them corralled outside.

She waited in a fever of impatience 'til Nancy opened the door.

252

"No one's here."

Taking the animals inside, her gaze swept the living room as she unsnapped Ned's leash and opened the carrier.

Both animals rushed to the bedroom.

The police woman, who stood in their path, stepped nimbly out of the way. "Why don't you take a look around and see if anything's missing."

Gabby ran to the bedroom. Her gaze flew to the globe sitting in the shadows on the bookcase. Ned stood with his fur on end, growling. Jericho was puffed up to twice his normal size. "Nothing's missing." *But someone's been here.*

"You want to check the rest of the house?"

Gabby laughed. "Nancy, you know I don't have anything worth stealing." *Except maybe a green crystal ball that has very unusual powers.*

"You've had a tough time. Just take it easy." Nancy patted her arm reassuringly.

She closed her eyes, her face burning. Did everyone know about her situation?

Nancy walked out of the bedroom and let herself out of the house.

Standing by the bed, she stared at the globe. *If someone had broken in, they would have taken it. And why this elaborate ruse to get me out of the house if it wasn't to get to the globe?*

Ned stood next to her, stiff-legged. She patted his rump. "I wish you could talk. Someone's been here, haven't they?" He licked her hand and whined.

She cocked her head to one side studying the crystal ball. Its color didn't seem as brilliant, but in the gloom it was hard to tell.

She walked over and touched it. Nothing happened. Her eyes widened and her stomach dropped.

Her joints frozen, her movements robotic, she picked it

up.

Nothing.

Gabby's breath hitched in her throat and the room dipped. *That son of a bitch switched globes on me.*

"Damn you, Christopher, damn you! How could you make love to me then steal from me." Tears of pain and rage rained down her face. She heaved the globe against the wall where it landed with a satisfying *thunk.*

Splotches of heat permeated her cheeks. "You'll be sorry for this, Saint. I promise you."

A small voice in the corner of her mind whispered, *The animals wouldn't have reacted this way to Christopher.* But hurt pride drowned it out.

* * * * *

Christopher sat in the study nursing a Scotch. He should call Gabriella. Enough time had passed for him to calm down and reflect.

Maybe in her own way she was trying to protect him. As mad as he'd been, he probably would have slugged her pain-in-the-ass father and ended up in jail.

He rubbed his forehead. What was it about the woman that caused him to lose all sense? Up until she burst into his life he'd been considered cool and calculating, seldom if ever bested and now he spent half his time going off half-cocked like a kid in high school.

A ruckus in the foyer disrupted his thoughts.

A dog barked.

Surely not. Christopher's mood lightened and he began to smile. Had she come back? He stood, but before he could take a step the door burst open.

She stood in the doorway, the light streaming in, limning her figure—his magnificent Viking queen. A Viking queen dressed in khaki shorts and a lime green tank top that set off her satiny, honey-colored skin to perfection. She looked glorious—and angry. Now what?

She marched in. Ned pushed past her and nearly knocked him over in his eagerness to lick his face.

"Where is it, you son of a bitch. Where is my globe?"

Whatever Christopher had expected it wasn't this. "Don't tell me you've lost it again!"

"You should know you stole it."

They stood glaring at each other in the gloom.

"And just when did I perform this feat? Sometime between making love to you and you showing me the door?" He stared down his nose at her, breathing heavily through it.

Her chin jutted out. "No."

I'm familiar with the angle of that chin. It means she's in mule mode. "So just when did I take it?" He enunciated each word, trying his best to tamp down his anger.

"Yesterday, when I was at the vet's. Someone called and made an appointment in my name. But I'm certainly not telling you anything you don't already know." She flipped her hair out of her face.

"And you say the globe's gone?"

"Let me count the ways. The globe is gone. I no longer have the globe. You stole the globe. That's three. Shall I continue?"

"Zip it, Gabriella." This time his voice sounded more preoccupied than angry and he began to pace. "When did you first notice it was missing?"

"This is ridiculous. You know when it disappeared."

"Humor me."

She sighed loudly. "When I came back from the vet's and touched it."

He stopped pacing, turned and frowned. "Pardon me?"

She stared at him, the beginnings of doubt creeping across her face. "When I came back from the vet's and touched it nothing happened."

"What usually happens?"

"You know."

"Sorry. Actually, I don't. Other than the one time I caught you in what appeared to be a trance of passion while you were holding the globe, I've no idea. Oh yes and that you supposedly see me in it."

Pink crept into Gabby's cheeks. "The way you say it makes it sound disgusting or bizarre."

"Actually, I found it rather titillating," he admitted.

A wave of scarlet washed from her neck up to her hairline.

He watched in amusement then took pity on her. "But we are straying from the point. You think someone substituted an imitation for Aunt Tam's crystal?"

"My crystal," she replied automatically. "And I know it."

"Go get it." Seeing her mutinous expression he added, "Please."

"It's in the car."

"I'll go with you. You drove? Does your father know you're here?"

"Yes and yes. I left a message on his phone."

He raised his eyebrows and quirked his lips. "Chicken."

Her expression sheepish, she shrugged.

When they reached her clunker he cleared his throat but refrained from making aspersions about her form of transportation as he pulled her duffle bag and ancient suitcase out of the car.

"It runs just fine," she said defensively. "Not everyone can drive a pricey sports car you know."

"That's right, only those with well-honed driving skills." He sat the bags down and shut the car door.

"That's not what I meant," she said hotly.

He gave her a lazy grin.

"You are so irritating."

"Really, love? And I try so hard to please." He watched as amusement warred with irritation on her expressive features and was happy to see amusement win out.

"Whatever the reason, I'm glad you're here, Gabriella."

She looked at him then quickly away. Gaze still averted, she reached in the front seat and pulled out a white square box and started to open it. "Here it is."

He gave a quick look around. "Let's take it inside."

As they entered the house, Gabby asked. "Where is everybody?"

"It's Tuesday, Beatrice's day off. And Aunt Tam is in the solarium. How did you get in? I didn't hear the doorbell."

"I walked in. You should start locking your doors."

He laughed, amused. "Maybe I should at that."

Once inside, he pulled a loupe out of his pants pocket.

He took the ball out of the box and studied it in a businesslike manner. "Well, I'll be damned. She did switch it on you." Damn. Lai was good.

"She?"

"It's got to be Lai."

Her lip curled in distaste. "Well you can tell your girlfriend for me, I'm getting my globe back."

"You stay away from that woman."

She said nothing, her expression mutinous.

"I will send you home to your father so fast your head will spin. I'll tell him he needs to throw you in the slammer under armed guard 24/7 and even then you won't be safe. She is a dangerous woman, Gabriella, and don't you ever forget it!"

"I want my globe."

"Did you not hear a word I said?"

"I'm not deaf. Though by the volume you are speaking at one would think so."

He grabbed her arms. "Read my lips. I will get your globe back."

"How?"

"My plan isn't finalized."

"Meaning you don't have one."

"You are the most infuriating woman I have ever known."

"Why, because I don't kowtow to you?"

"Kowtow? Who uses words like kowtow?"

"I do."

"Never mind. Do I have your promise that you will leave the globe to me?"

"No."

His grip on her arms tightened, causing her to wince.

"But I will make a compromise. Whatever we do..."

"We?"

"We," she said firmly. "We do together."

Chapter Twenty-Eight

Lai sank into the seat of a luxury SUV she'd rented to drive to New Orleans. She would've preferred a limo or an airplane but she'd learned long ago to always do the unexpected. She really didn't think the blonde bitch would tumble to the exchange for a while and when she did, she would surely blame Christopher.

But she'd stayed alive by overthinking. Worst case scenario the ox would blame her. She would tell her daddy and daddy would have the airports watched.

No one would expect her to make a twelve-hour trip in the car when she could fly—no one except perhaps Christopher, his mind every bit as canny as hers.

He'd been her best pupil. And he'd given her the most intense sexual gratification she'd ever known. She might not be in love with Christopher Saint but she coveted him as she did fine jewelry and plush surroundings. It was one of the reasons she'd left her native Calcutta.

Pushing the radio button to a New Age station, she swung onto the highway, merging smoothly into traffic between a semi and a white sports car.

She drove straight through, except for an occasional stop for coffee or any other caffeinated drink. She held the big SUV to the speed limit not taking any chances of getting pulled over by the state police.

At the last stop, she wiped off all traces of makeup and put her hair into two ponytails on top of her head. If no one looked into her cunning coffee-colored brown eyes, she'd pass for sixteen.

Dressed in shorts and a tank top, no one looking for Lai, the sophisticated woman of the world, would look twice at this young girl with the boyish figure.

The only problem Lai encountered was two gangly teens who tried to pick her up. But a few well-chosen words about the pimples on their face and their lack of facial hair had quickly caused them to lose interest.

The teens had thrown out a few phrases of their own. But words ran off Lai like water off a duck's back. She'd been called those particular names since she was twelve years old.

Years ago being called a slut and worse had hurt, but now she had the power to crush anyone that spoke against her. Sometimes she did, sometimes she let them live.

Lai turned into the French Quarter and drove carefully down the narrow cobbled streets.

She gave a low bark of laughter. All these weeks, Christopher had searched for her and she had been in New Orleans, almost under his nose. Having the exchange in the mountains had added a layer of smoke. If he looked for her in the States, he would look for her in North Carolina or possibly Chinatown where she had previously sent him on a wild-goose chase.

She pulled in front of an 1830s Creole double cottage and parked the car. The apartment had two bedrooms, a half bath, a master bath with a Jacuzzi and a courtyard in the back surrounded by black wrought iron.

She shared the cottage with a pretty young black girl. No one would expect her to have a roommate, especially a female roommate.

Turning off the car, she grabbed a small burgundy shoulder bag and two gift sacks, one held the globe, the other a trinket for her roommate. The trinket, bought at an expensive jewelry store, sat in a discrete gold sack with pale yellow tissue showing at the top.

It was nearly five in the morning. The streetlights were still on. The black of night had softened to a deep velvety gray.

The decadence and sumptuousness of the city struck a responsive chord within her. As she pulled a key out of her shoulder bag, her fingers touched the cool metal of an ivory-handled ladies' derringer.

Dangling the key, she walked with the lithe movements of a feline up the brick walkway, the air warm but not unbearably so. Coming from Calcutta, the heat didn't bother her.

She unlocked the door and walked in, closing it behind her. "Becka, I'm home."

A slender young black woman with soft latte-colored skin in burgundy lace boxers and a matching chemise came running out of the bedroom, tousled with sleep. She was a full head taller than Suzy as Lai called herself.

She opened her arms wide. "Darling," and kissed Lai full on the mouth.

* * * * *

Gabby stood tapping her toes, her arms crossed.

"There are some places that I'm going that I will not take you. It's not safe."

They stood inside the library where the walls were lined from ceiling to floor with books. Filtered light reflected off the bookcases, the wood glowing with years of loving care.

Christopher and Gabby stood nose to nose. "I knew it. I knew it," she bit out, her teeth snapping with each word. "You took the globe and you are trying to cover it up. You'll take off and I'll never see you or the globe again."

He slid his arm around her and his voice dropped to an intimate level. The heat of his bare arm soaked through her thin cotton tank and sizzled her skin. "And would that bother you, love?"

It took every ounce of willpower Gabby had, but she managed to push his hand away. "It would certainly bother me not to see my globe again."

"I'll tell you what, you can hold Aunt Tam hostage until I return. If I don't come back she's yours."

She stared at his thin aristocratic face then let her eyes slide over his lean whipcord body. He was dressed in his usual fare, a white polo shirt and khaki shorts and wearing leather boaters with no socks. "You just refuse to take this seriously don't you?"

His arms dropped to his side. "Now there, darling, you are wrong. I take it very seriously."

"Prove it. Take me with you."

He sighed heavily. "You have the tenacity of a bulldog and about as much upstairs."

Ned barked.

Christopher ruffled his fur. "No insult meant. I said bulldog." He turned back to Gabby. "You don't even know where I'm going."

Her facial muscles stiffened, no doubt like the canine previously mentioned. "It doesn't matter."

He closed his eyes and moved his lips. She could read them, one, two, three, four. He stopped at eight.

"Of course it matters, Gabriella. There are countries where a woman like you," his eyes turned cool and he looked her up and down in an assessing manner, lingering on her breasts, thighs and hips, "could be bought and sold in a heartbeat."

She shivered. Not so much from his words but the coldness of his face. He looked like a stranger, a terrifying stranger. His body had the tense expectant look of a dangerous predator ready to strike.

She stuck her chin in the air. It had a tendency to wobble and her voice to shake. "You don't scare me."

He looked at her for a long moment, shook his head and gave a short laugh. "Ms. Bell, you are magnificent, even in your wrong-headedness."

She chewed her lip. At least, the coldness she feared had left his body. "I don't care for the wrong-headedness but the magnificent sounds encouraging. Will you take me with you?"

"No."

"Will you tell me where you are going?"

"Do I have your promise not to follow me?"

"No."

Christopher rubbed his chin with his fingers and thumb, his look speculative. "Where does that leave us?"

"You do your investigation, I'll do mine." *Since I'm not completely convinced you don't have the globe.*

He walked to the desk, picked up the phone and dialed.

She gave him a suspicious look. "What are you doing?"

"Is this the police department? I'd like to speak to Sergeant Bell."

She crossed the room in three quick strides, her feet skimming the beautiful oriental carpet. She clicked down the receiver. "All right you win. I won't try to follow you."

"How do I know you'll keep your word?"

"I said so didn't I?"

"You'll have to do better than that, Bell."

She gave him a look of honest bewilderment. "Maybe you should take a leap of faith."

"You don't trust me and I don't trust you. A leap of faith could drop one of us into an abyss."

"We seem to be at a standoff."

"Do you still think I took your globe?"

She studied him. For some reason the answer seemed to matter to him. "You'd do anything for Aunt Tam."

"How do you know that?"

"It's true isn't it?"

He grinned. His features relaxed. "Pretty much."

263

She stuck her chin in the air. "So did you take it?"

He took her hand, the contact warm and comforting. "No, Gabriella, I didn't."

"How do I know that?"

His voice gentled. "How about that leap of faith you were talking about. You're a reporter. What does your gut tell you?"

Their eyes met and held. "That you are telling me the truth. But I don't know if it's my gut or my heart talking." The words slipped out before she could call them back.

He brought her hand to his lips, kissed her palm and closed her fingers around the kiss. "I find that encouraging."

Wary nerves skittered under her skin, but she held onto his kiss.

Suddenly, he wrapped her in his arms. "Marry me, Gabriella. I plight you my troth." Then he whispered poetic words of love and desire.

Her eyes closed and she clung to him limply. "Do you always quote poetry to women?"

"No. Yes. No more lies. With other women I quote it, with you I feel it." His gaze intensified. "You've made my blood run hot since the first moment you tumbled into my arms in the rain outside Earth Religions. We were at odds then and we've been at odds ever since. "

Her skin quivered as he ran his warm fingers up and down her arms. "Maybe we could change that."

His husky voice made her knees weak. She stepped back and began to rub the sluggish throb at her temples. *At least the throbbing doesn't morph into a full-blown migraine these days when I think about the past and him. That's an improvement.*

He loosened his arms but didn't let go.

"I went in and saw the globe." She looked at him and moved away then began to walk around the room. She turned toward him. "I saw your face. It was the cold face of a stranger."

She paced between the fireplace and the window on the far wall.

Ned sat watching her, whining softly.

She turned and whispered. "You stole the globe from me."

He stood very still, watchful. "Yes."

No excuse, no apologies, just a simple yes. She looked at him. "For Tam."

He didn't answer just stood waiting, ever watchful, as if he were trying to follow the complex workings of her mind.

She gave a half laugh, half sob. "Who are you? What are you?"

"You know who I am." His voice even, held a raw quality, his breathing fast and light.

She stopped her pacing and looked at him. "My father thinks you're a thief."

"If what you said the night of the mask ball was anything to go by so do you."

Gabby laughed, a sound without humor. "Don't do that, Christopher."

"I believe I'd rather answer who I am. I'm the adopted son of Tamara and Edward James."

Her head tilted and her hair tickled the top of her breast. "And your parents were who? Tam's or Edward's family? Brother or sister? Is that why you call them aunt and uncle?"

"I have never told this to anyone, but I freely give you the information."

It didn't sound freely to Gabriella. It sounded torn from his soul.

"I have no idea who my parents were. For all I know my mother was a Calcutta harlot." He winced when he said it. "Even if it's true, I shouldn't have said it. It's like a betrayal to her." He fingered his tiger ring. "Even if she left me, I know she loved me."

Gabby felt her heart ache with sympathy. She reached out her hand, but he'd already turned away.

He gave a harsh laugh. "Your father was entirely correct. I was a thief before the age of seven. I lived off the streets and stole to survive."

"Oh, Christopher." *Poor little boy.*

He whirled, his eyes snapping. "Don't pity me. I neither need it or want it." He shrugged visibly notching down the intensity. "That's how the James found me," he continued. "I lifted Aunt Tam's purse, but wasn't fast enough to escape." He gave a rare grin. "Uncle Edward was an excellent athlete."

Gabby blinked as understanding broke through. "You're going to Calcutta."

He didn't answer. It was all the confirmation Gabby needed.

"But why?"

"It began in Calcutta. Maybe the answers lie there. Lai must be stopped once and for all."

She didn't like it. Not one little bit. But her emotions were on overload. She couldn't, wouldn't push him any further.

"Christopher, about the engagement thing…" Her voice trailed off.

He went to her and kissed her lightly on the cheek.

"I think you've had all the emotion you can handle for one day. Think about it while I'm in Calcutta. It will give you some space." He drew her to him and held her lightly in his arms. "I love you, Gabriella, and I've never said that to any other woman except to Aunt Tam and my mother. And I know you love me." She started to object but he laid a finger on her lips. "I'm just not sure whether you know it or not."

"You are awfully sure of yourself."

He shrugged his shoulders. "I've given up fighting my fate. The first time you told me you saw my face in the globe, I thought—well I thought a lot of things, none of them complimentary."

She gave an indignant gasp.

"But somewhere between sightings numbers two and four, I became a believer.

"I always scoffed at the old legends. Never to Tamara's face mind you. I love her too much for that. But I'd never really believed all that nonsense...until now."

"So, it's not that you're in love with me, it's that you believe some stupid superstition." She puffed up like a porcupine, her voice huffy.

He laughed softly in her hair. "Oh, girl, I love you all right. It's pretty self-evident," and pressed her against his arousal.

"That's just desire," she said in a weak voice, her eyes closed and her head thrown back, leaving her neck at an inviting slant.

He pressed his lips against her throat and her pulse quickened. "Just desire?"

Her eyes closed, she nodded.

He ran his fingers through her hair. "Darling temptress, if this was just desire, it would be enough. But I'm afraid it has gone way past that. I'm enamored, besotted, obsessed."

"You are?" She snuggled against him.

"I am."

"You just want my globe."

"You don't have it."

"So I don't. Are you trying to seduce me then?"

"What an enticing thought. Meet me in the gazebo at midnight."

She ran her hands down to his hips and cupped them.

267

"What's wrong with now?"

"Hussy. You must wait for your pleasure."

"Why?" she pouted.

"If Aunt Tam or Beatrice were to walk in, I'd never be able to look them in the eye again."

"If we were engaged, like you told John Paul, I'd be wearing a ring," she replied, her eyes bold, the words out of her mouth before her brain had an opportunity to filter them.

"I thought we were going to wait on this conversation until after I got back from Calcutta."

"Maybe I changed my mind." Her lips parted and her gaze offered promises, promises of ecstasy and languid sexual pleasure.

"Don't look at me like that, my girl, or I'll forget about propriety and take you here and now as if I were a fat sultan and you my favorite, voluptuous harem girl."

"Christopher!" she giggled.

He heaved a pained sigh and pushed her gently away. Raising her hand, he kissed her fingertips. "Until tonight." He walked quickly out of the library where he almost tripped over Jericho, sitting on the other side of the door swishing his tail.

Christopher looked down into unblinking blue eyes surrounded by chocolate-colored fur. "I wondered where you were. Your mistress and mine," he gave the cat a sly smile, "is inside."

In the hall, despite it being her day off, Beatrice was dusting a gleaming mahogany table. Tamara stood beside her studying a picture of an old plantation, with a little boy running down a dirt road.

Christopher gave his aunt a hug and a hearty buss then did the same for Beatrice.

"Gabby is back."

268

"Really, dear? How nice. Did you hear that, Beatrice? Gabriella is back."

"Yes'm I sure did."

Christopher grinned. "You two old fakes. You knew it all along." Whistling he went on his way.

Tamara grabbed Beatrice's hand and squeezed.

"Do you think our boy is finally going to settle down?" Beatrice asked.

Tamara winked. "I predict, before the year is out there will be a bun in the oven."

"Mz. Tamara!"

Chapter Twenty-Nine

Gabby stole down the steps. The old house creaked and the grandfather clock struck midnight.

Making no sound, she let herself into the solarium. The lush smell of vanilla and roses filled the air. She twisted and turned 'til she found the gazebo.

Christopher stood waiting. She knew he would be. Chilled goblets of champagne sat at a small table along with a small blue velvet box.

He handed her a glass of bubbling gold liquid. Her senses heightened, the wet cool condensation of the crystal tickled her fingertips. They drank without taking their eyes off one another. Moonlight filtered in through the glass ceiling.

He took her glass and sat it down then held out his arms. She glided into them and knew she'd come home.

They made love on the blue velvet divan, sweet and tender. As soon as they caught their breath, they made love again, wild and tempestuous.

She lay in his arms, sated and content. He reached for her finger and slipped a ring on. It felt as if it belonged. "I'm leaving in an hour."

She struggled to set up. He pushed her gently back down. "Don't say anything. Don't look at the ring now. If you are wearing it when I come back, I'll know this isn't some fantastic dream. If you aren't..." He shrugged his shoulders in the darkness.

He slipped into his clothes while he talked to her. "Take care of Aunt Tam for me and tell her I'll be back soon." Then he was gone, leaving her alone in the dark.

She fingered the unusual contours of the ring he had slipped on her finger. Smooth and round encircled by stones of a different texture. "I love you, Christopher," she whispered to the night and knew it to be true.

She picked up the fluted crystal that he'd drunk from, drained the remains of the champagne and crept back upstairs.

When she opened her door, she nearly got knocked down by the two detainees. Flipping on the light, she explained to the irate creatures, "I'm afraid you would have turned my romantic rendezvous into a farce. I've never met anyone at midnight before."

She hugged herself. It had been so romantic. Like a magnet, her gaze went to her ring. Her eyes widened and she sank to the floor only to have her face covered with wet doggy kisses.

"Oh Christopher." She stared at the ring. Tears formed at the corner of her eyes and slid down her cheeks. "Hidden beneath that sneering exterior beats the heart of a romantic."

A perfect round emerald of at least five carats, sat in a bed of diamonds, the ring, a miniature of the globe. He had done this for her.

Jericho jumped to the desk top and batted at the desk phone, knocking the handle off its base. The phone made an angry buzzing sound. Jericho stared at it, his tail twitching.

"Bad cat." Her voice carried no conviction. As she laid the handle back in its cradle she noticed the message light blinking.

She hit intercom then the play button. Walking toward the bed, she paused as Christopher's voice came over the speaker. "And now, my witch, you shall have your crystal ball wherever you go."

"Fool." But found it impossible to bite back her smile of pure happiness.

On an impulse she walked back to the phone, picked it up and dialed. It rang once and was immediately picked up.

"Bell, here."

"Daddy…"

The voice on the other end sharpened. She could picture her father sitting up in bed, his gray streaked hair tousled. "Gabriella! Are you all right?"

She pulled her hair back from her face. "I'm wonderful, Daddy. I wanted you to be the first to know. Christopher and I are getting married."

"Gabriella Josephine Bell, I absolutely forbid it," his voice roared across the phone line.

She sank into the chair by the little white French desk. "Daddy, please, be happy for me."

"Gabby," her father sounded desperate, "he's an associate of one of the biggest jewel thieves in the country."

That was one teeny, tiny thing she'd managed not to think about, used the migraines in fact to keep that particular thought at bay. *Cat burglar. Jewel thief. The Tiger.* "Christopher," she whispered, unaware she'd spoken. She held the phone with both hands to keep from dropping it.

"He's involved somehow. I don't know how. But he's involved. And I intend to prove it."

She closed her eyes and rubbed her forehead, fighting back the pain that burned like hot coals behind her eyes. Her father was fanatical when it came to solving crimes.

"You are talking about the man I love."

"Don't say that."

"Goodnight, Dad."

"Gabby…"

She sat the phone in the cradle, walked to the bed, flopped down and stared up at the textured white ceiling. She would have to find out what she could about Christopher before her father did.

She couldn't afford a private eye but she could do the next best thing.

She jumped out of bed. She'd contact Louie.

About a year ago, she'd done a ride along with her dad. He'd received a call about an illegal dog ring, but by the time they got there the ring had been warned and the perpetrators had cleared out, leaving behind an old golden retriever in bad shape.

She took it to the vet, paid its bills and put up flyers all over town. The dog, of course, had been stolen and used to bait the pit bulls and other fighting dogs the ring used.

One day a seedy-looking man with shifty eyes showed up on her porch to claim his dog. The man saw the dog and his eyes filled with tears. He got down on his knees and spread open his arms. The dog flew into them.

From that moment a cautious association—friendship would be too strong a word—developed between Gabby and Louie. Louie made his living in *sales* as he called his fencing job. He was mortified when he discovered who Gabby's father was. He and Sergeant Bell went way back. The sergeant ran him in on a regular basis.

But Louie and Nugget, as he called his retriever, always reminded Gabby that love sprouted in the most unlikely places.

Louie had become an excellent source of information for her...when he was in town. He had to leave regularly, one step ahead of the law.

She wondered if he had returned. She didn't think she had seen him since Christopher entered her life. She rubbed her throbbing temples, clicked on the bedside lamp with its soft lighting and walked over and flipped off the bright overhead.

Picking up her phone, she called his office, as he referred to the green-painted, tin warehouse he worked out of. Louie had a cell phone, but that was information she wasn't privileged to.

On the third ring, Louie picked up. "Louie's warehouse, our special of the week is TVs."

"Got you working third shift now, Louie?"

"Hey, Blondie, how you doing? Nugget come say hi to Blondie."

She grinned as she heard a "woof-woof" in the background.

"So what's shakin'? Haven't talked to you in a long time."

"Been on vacation, Louie?"

"Yeah, went up North. It was getting a little hot in town if you know what I mean," then laughed uproariously at his joke. "How's your old man? Be sure and give him my regards."

"Will do." They both knew that was a blatant lie. She might not be a well-known reporter but she was savvy enough not to endanger her sources. "And you be sure and say hello to Big Nick for me."

"Of course."

They both knew that was another falsehood. It was rumored Big Nick had mafia connections and would frown upon Louie, whom he occasionally did business with, having an acquaintance with the press, even if the reporter was as small-time as Gabby.

"So what can I do for you, kid?"

"Louie, have you ever heard of..." A banging sounded in the background, making Gabby wince.

"Hey, it looks like I've got customers. I'll call you back."

"I'm not at home. Call me on my cell. You have *my* cell number."

Louie laughed good-naturedly. "All in good time kid. All in good time." The receiver clicked.

She plopped on the bed and closed her eyes. The next

thing she knew, someone was covering her face in wet kisses and a phone was ringing on the TV. She reached for the remote to click it off. A particularly slurpy kissed landed on her lips. She grimaced and opened her eyes. "Ned get down," and pushed him away.

He stood grinning at her, his plumy tail waving. The phone stopped ringing. "Damn it." Sitting up, she winced and grabbed her head, the migraine while not full force still with her.

She dialed Louie's number. He picked up immediately. "Louie's warehouse."

"It's me." She lay on the bed on her back, wisps of her hair sticking to her cheek.

"Make it snappy. I've got some guys coming back for a hundred TVs in twenty minutes."

"Louie you really shouldn't tell me about that."

"Tell you what? That I'm selling TVs that I bought from an electronics company? I'm just a small business man trying to turn an honest dollar."

She rolled her eyes and cut to the chase. "Have you ever heard of The Tiger?"

There was no answer on the other end of the phone.

"Louie? Louie? Are you there?"

"If I had, it would be more than my life is worth to talk about it."

"Okay, Louie," she soothed. "How about this, we'll do a word association okay?"

"I'm listening."

"If I say jewels does a large zoo animal come to mind?" They had played this version of reporter charades before.

"Yes."

"Does this large animal roam in any particular zoo?"

"Zoos are all over the world. But I hear they originated in Calcutta. Zoo animals are smart, quick and deadly, and known for their ornamentation."

Calcutta? She was having trouble focusing. "Ornamentation? A zoo animal?"

"What, haven't you ever heard of a tiger eye? And that's all I'm saying Blondie, except watch yourself."

"Thanks, Louie, you too."

She trudged to the window and stared out at the velvety night. The globed lamp posts threw a soft yellow glow over the large garden courtyard surrounded by wrought iron fencing below her window. Ignoring the AC she opened the window and listened to the soothing sounds of the fountain in the garden.

She took a deep breath and closed her eyes. She opened them and looked down at the brilliant emerald glittering on her finger. Christopher wore a very unusual ring on his right hand, a silver tiger with emerald eyes.

There had been signs, hints, but she'd never made the connection. What had he told her, that Aunt Tam and Uncle Edward had found him in Calcutta picking pockets? Oh, how she wished he hadn't. Wished she hadn't insisted on knowing where he was going.

Her original theory was correct. Christopher was a thief. He wasn't acquainted with The Tiger. He was The Tiger. And while it was one thing to have a thief for an acquaintance, it was another to consider marrying one especially when one had a father just dying to send him up river.

Chapter Thirty

She trailed down the beautiful old spiral staircase, her hand resting on the satin-smooth wooden rail. A wall-mounted crystal sconce bathed the stairs in soft light.

Reaching the bottom, she went straight to the den and poured herself a glass of white wine from the refrigerator hidden behind the desk.

She took her glass and sank into an overstuffed chair. As she sipped, memory flooded back, her globe, the shop, Christopher stealing it back, her pursuit of Christopher.

The mellow white liquid slid down her throat. She grimaced. She may have not been quite so quick to give pursuit if she knew she'd been chasing the premier cat burglar not only in the country but of all Europe. And she sure as hell wouldn't have become engaged to him.

She started to slip off the ring, but couldn't quite bring herself to do it, as she remembered his face as he talked about the little boy that stole to survive. No one else knew about that and now she knew why.

She started to sip her wine and realized the glass was empty. She got up and walked to the fridge and brought the bottle back with her.

She watched the clear liquid cascade into the glass then took another swallow. A scratching at the door alerted her that she was not alone. Weaving only slightly, she got up and opened the door. Jericho followed by Ned came rushing in. At least, Ned rushed. Jericho made a more dignified entrance, weaving in and out of her legs.

"Damn it, he doesn't need to be stealing anymore. He's not that starving little boy."

She walked back as best she could with Jericho making a nuisance of himself and plunked into the chair.

Her headache forgotten she continued to ponder the situation until the bottle was empty.

Jericho hopped up on Gabby's lap, circled several times then plopped down and went to sleep. Ned looked at the cat, whined, and lay down on Gabby's feet. He licked a red lacquered toe and then fell asleep.

The empty bottle dangling from her index finger, Gabby snoozed too.

And that's how Tamara found them early in the morning when she opened the den door.

She smiled as she took in the scene of dissipation. Ned saw her first. He lifted his head from Gabriella's feet, his tail beating furiously from side to side. He got up and came over to be petted.

"Let's hope your mistress doesn't have a drinking problem," she whispered as she patted the fuzzy head.

"Woof."

"I didn't really think so."

Jericho opened one blue eye, then the other. He got up and stretched, hoisting his tail in the air, then jumped to the floor and came over, demanding to be fed. The movement caused Gabby to drop her left hand to her side. Her hand sparkled like a meteor moving through the sky.

Tamara's eyes widened and she tiptoed over to Gabby, trying to stay on her feet as the animals adhered themselves to her legs as she walked.

Her pale pink, floor-length dress whispered as she bent beside Gabby and studied the ring. Her eyes sparkled with unshed tears. *Oh Christopher, my dear boy, you must love this young woman very much.*

She hurried out to find Beatrice then had to grab the door as Jericho sped in front of her and skidded to a halt when Ned stopped in front of him and sniffed the air.

278

They all sniffed, then as one followed the smell of coffee, bacon, eggs and beignets to the kitchen.

Beatrice stood at the gleaming silver topped stove.

"Beatrice, come quickly."

The maid whirled around as fast as someone carrying an extra thirty pounds around her girth could. "Is something wrong, Miz. James?"

"No. On the contrary. Come on."

Beatrice slid two cast iron skillets to the back burners and turned off the stove. She wiped her hands on her immaculate white apron.

"Oh, Beatrice, do come on." Tamara danced from one foot to the other all but wringing her hands.

The foursome trooped back down the hall. Pictures of relatives that went back farther than the Civil War lined the hall. One particular gentleman with white hair and a handlebar mustache looked at them disdainfully.

"What is it, Miz. James?"

"You'll see."

Tamara opened the door. The animals pushed past her. Beatrice was more considerate but still right on her heels. The first thing Beatrice saw was the empty wine bottle. "Does that child have a drinking problem?"

"Let's hope not because I believe she is shortly to join the family." She pointed to Gabby's left hand.

Beatrice clapped her hands over her mouth. "Lawks a mighty." She went over for a closer look.

Gabby sniffed. Her nose must still be inebriated. She was getting two succinct aromas blending together, bacon and lavender. Now if it was bacon and eggs or lavender and chamomile that would make more sense. She opened her left eye a fraction of an inch then hastily closed it. Two gargoyles were bent over her. No, that couldn't be right.

She blinked and this time opened both eyes. Her vision cleared. No, not gargoyles, Beatrice and Tamara. "Good morning," she croaked. They took a hasty step back. She must have a nasty case of morning mouth.

Why were they beaming at her? Or were they crying? It was hard to tell. She looked around still a bit fuzzy. Where was she? She saw the wine bottle resting against the marble fireplace and memory flooded back. "Oh, my God."

She sat up and Tamara hugged her. "Oh, my dear child. I'm so happy." The filmy material of Tamara's dress whispered against her ear. And she smelled, ah, *lavender*.

Beatrice bent down and wrapped huge coffee-colored arms around her, pressing her face against a huge starchy bosom. *Bacon*. "I'm real happy for you, Miss Gabriella."

Oh dear. She struggled up from the chair and the arms trying to embrace her then abruptly sat back down, grabbing her head. "Coffee. And aspirin. I need coffee and aspirin." Unfortunately, she couldn't blame the pounding in her head on a migraine.

"I'll get it, Miss Gabriella."

"I can get it, Beatrice. Just give me a moment." Gabby came from a blue-collar, middle-class family and was proud of it. And acutely uncomfortable being waited on.

"Nonsense. I'll be back in two shakes of a lamb's tail."

"Thank you."

Both Gabby and Tamara watched Beatrice leave the room with the dignity of an old ship, whose white sails were billowed outward to catch the wind.

Tamara squeezed Gabby's hand. Next to Gabby's, it was childlike in size. "I couldn't be happier, dear." She sank gracefully into the burgundy leather couch to the right of Gabby's chair. "Where's Christopher?"

"I believe in Calcutta." She watched Tamara closely for her reaction.

A frown flitted across Tam's features then was gone. "So when is the big day?"

Gabby squirmed in her chair, her head pounding. She really needed that coffee. "Please, don't jump to conclusions."

Tamara looked pointedly at the ring, but remained silent.

As the silence stretched, Gabby felt compelled to break it. "That is to say, we haven't set a date."

Tamara tilted her head, a look of rapt attention on her face.

This woman would be perfect for the good cop/bad cop routine. It was all Gabby could do not to spill her guts. Just as she started to open her mouth, Beatrice came into the room carrying a silver carafe of coffee, cream and sugar dishes, two porcelain flowered cups on a silver tray and a bottle of aspirin. The woman tilted from side to side as she walked. Besides being overweight, Beatrice had varicose veins.

She sat the tray down and beamed at Gabby.

Gabby grimaced back. Obviously, being Christopher's intended placed her on a whole new strata as far as Beatrice was concerned.

The maid poured coffee and handed a cup to Tamara and one to Gabby.

Gabby buried her nose in the steaming liquid. Ah chicory, New Orleans' staple. She looked hopefully around for the beignets.

Beatrice correctly interrupted the glance. "I'll be serving them at breakfast, dear."

Oh yes, her status had definitely been elevated.

Tamara said in that absentminded way of hers, "We'll be there in just a moment, if you want to place everything on the table. And feel free to join us, Bee."

Beatrice's eyes widened, offense written on every line of her well-padded body. "As if I ever would do that."

Tamara gave a long-suffering sigh. "Bee, this isn't Tara, I'm not Scarlett O'Hara and the War Between the States ended a long, long time ago. Besides you know you hail from free men and women. New Orleans never was caught up in that disgusting slavery issue like the rest of the South. Well some were but there were a lot of free people of color that roamed the streets before the war." She threw up her hands, "Why am I even discussing this. You know you're family, Bee, albeit the working portion, but family nonetheless."

Without any trace of the accent she normally donned like a cloak, Beatrice responded, "I know that Ms. Tamara. It's why I'd never leave you." Then she winked. "That and the ungodly amount of money you pay me." Having got in the last word she walked out of the den, closing the door behind her.

Tamara shook her head. "She's as stubborn as a mule, that one, but I love her dearly."

Gabby smiled. "It's obvious she reciprocates those emotions ten-fold."

While Gabby added sugar and cream to her coffee, Tamara leaned back against the couch. "Now, dear, suppose you tell me what's wrong?"

Gabby stirred her coffee until a liquid whirlwind formed in the center of the cup.

"What do you mean?"

Tamara waited.

Gabby took a gulp of the sweet chicory and nearly scalded herself. She waved her hand rapidly back and forth in front of her mouth.

"I suggest sipping it next time, dear."

Gabby sighed. "How well do you know Christopher?"

Tamara's dainty silver eyebrows rose. "Well enough."

"Define well enough."

Tamara smiled. "Spoken like a reporter. I know he is no

angel. I know if he were to do something that you or I wouldn't approve of, he would have a good reason for it."

Gabby went fishing. "Such as Calcutta?"

Tamara paused in the act of topping off her coffee. "What did he tell you about Calcutta?"

"That you found him on the streets there as a child."

Dark fragrant liquid poured into the cup as Tamara gracefully tipped the pot. "To my knowledge he has never told a living soul about his origins. Why I don't know. It's certainly nothing that Edward or I was ever ashamed of. But Christopher has always been protective of his and our privacy.

"No one besides Beatrice knows about Calcutta and now you." Tamara didn't actually come out and say it, she didn't have to. Gabby understood. Guard the secret. Keep it to yourself.

"But that is only partially what I meant. Christopher is no saint," she smiled at her words, "but he is honorable. Whatever he does there is a reason for."

"Whatever his reason it's wrong." Gabby waved her arms encompassing the room. "He surely doesn't need the money. He's your heir isn't he?"

"Of course."

"Then why steal?"

"Maybe that's a question you should ask Christopher." She added sugar and cream to her chicory then sipped daintily.

Gabby stared for a moment at the cup in the older lady's hand. It was much like Tamara, delicate and timeless. The pale red roses painted on porcelain so fine you could almost see through it.

She hadn't denied it. Or maybe she was thinking of the globe. Gabby brought her wandering mind back to the matter at hand. "You may be sure I shall. Anyway, it doesn't

283

matter." Tiny frown lines formed between Gabby's brows.

"There's no excuse for a man to steal, especially a rich man."

Tamara nodded her head in approval. "Spoken like a policeman's daughter. I would expect no less."

Gabby gave a conscious start. *What a hypocrite I am. I couldn't care less about Louie's dubious business dealings. To me he's a source. But the fact that Christopher is the premier cat burglar on the continent appalls me.*

"Loxley."

Gabby blinked. Whatever Tamara had said, she'd missed all but the tail end of it.

"I'm sorry, what did you say?"

"I said have you never heard the story of Robin of Loxley?"

Gabby stared at her as if she'd grown a second head. "Are you comparing Christopher to Robin Hood?"

Tamara smiled in a noncommittal manner and sipped her chicory.

Gabby stood up, ignoring her thumping head as best she could. She walked to the door.

Tamara's bell-like voice drifted across the room, causing her to pause with her hand on the door. "So, Gabriella Bell, will you tame The Tiger or will you be eaten by him?"

For once all traces of the fluttery, absentminded, little old lady were gone. The violet eyes were shrewd as they searched Gabby's.

"I don't know." She fled.

The Crystal by Sandra Cox

Chapter Thirty-One

A handsome Bengal walked down one of the less reputable streets in Calcutta. He wore the traditional white *dhoti*, a rectangular piece of cloth wrapped in a complex manner about the waist and legs and a *kurta*, a loose shirt that fell below his knees. The color of his skin was a lovely mahogany in startling contrast to perfect white teeth. His jet-black hair gleamed like a raven's wing.

The smell of decay from rotting garbage mixed with the smell of engine fumes. Shouts and honks could be heard above the transistorized sounds of a sitar. The street darkened as dusk fell.

A beautiful young woman dressed in a red sari beckoned invitingly from an open doorway. A transparent red veil covered her hair and mouth. She looked to be no more than fifteen but her liquid brown eyes were old beyond her years.

Her keeper, a middle-aged Indian dressed in chinos and a silk shirt sat in the shadows drinking a canned cola.

Christopher stopped directly in front of her so her keeper could not see what passed between them. He handed her a twenty rupee banknote. "For your keeper." He nodded toward the man in the corner. He pulled out a one hundred rupee banknote. "For you." He tucked it into her palm. Even though the night was unusually warm, her hand was ice-cold.

She smiled, but her eyes were wary. "And what must I do to earn this?"

"I just need information. Is Lai back in Calcutta?"

The girl gave him a startled look. "Not that I've heard. But you might try Aamir. Just continue 'til the street ends and a new begins three times over."

"Thank you, sister, does Aamir have a last name?"

The sari made a soft rustling sounds as she shrugged her

lovely shoulders. "I think Dey."

"And yours, sister?"

"Ahsan."

"Ah, beautiful."

She bit her lips together. "My parents planned to sell me from birth. I am but a girl child, not highly valued by my father."

Out of the corner of his eye, he saw her keeper approach, apparently impatient with the length of time the transaction took.

"Hide your money. Tell him I lost my way and asked for directions to Belvedere Road." The sari rustled again as she slid the banknote inside it. He placed his hands on his forehead and nodded, preparing to leave. The long sleeves of his *kurta* fell back.

It was then she saw the ring. Her eyes widened. "Help me, Tiger. I beg."

The man came closer.

Christopher watched his approach. His eyes alert. "There is a small, select orphanage on the outside of town called the Shardul."

She nodded. "The Tiger Orphanage."

"You know of it?"

"Who doesn't that lives in the pits of hell?"

"I have spent time in hell myself, sister. Go to it. I will let them know to expect you."

She grabbed his hand and kissed it. "I will serve you always."

"Serve your people."

He disappeared into the gathering gloom of night and stood in the shadows.

The man raised his arm to strike the young girl who had just lost a paying customer.

She said something and handed him the twenty rupee

note. The man laughed.

Christopher grinned. He was a long way from Belvedere Road. The proprietor was no doubt laughing at his stupidity in wandering so far from it. The girl would be okay.

He walked with long, unhurried strides, sidestepping a cow walking down the sidewalk. He crossed three streets. Aamir's turf should be straight ahead.

At the corner a man leaned against a lamppost smoking. He wore baggy white pants and a light blue *kurta*.

Christopher approached him. He spoke Hindi. "I wish to see Aamir."

The man looked him over in an insolent fashion. "And why do you wish to see Aamir, pretty boy?"

Christopher smiled lazily. A smile that did not reach his eyes and made people that knew him tremble. In a flash, he grabbed the man by his throat. The other hand held a thin stiletto, with emeralds winking on the hilt, that he pressed against the man's cheek. The blunderer's cigarette dropped from his fingers sending a shower of orange embers to the ground where one by one they winked out.

"Son of a rat, must I repeat my question?" The sleeves of Christopher's *kurta* fell back revealing his ring.

His victim's pupils dilated with fear. "I meant no disrespect, *Shardul*, I did not know. No one knows The Tiger is in Calcutta. And you are said to have a hundred disguises. How could a poor, uneducated man such as myself recognize the great *Shardul*?" he whined.

"Well now that you do, little rat, take me to your leader."

It took only a moment for the man to reach his decision. He whispered, "Aamir might not be pleased but he will let me live. I have no desire to become tiger meat tonight." He gasped out, his face purpling, "I live but to serve you, oh great *Shardul*."

Christopher let him go.

The man gulped in air and loosened the *kurta* still tangled around his neck. "Please follow me." He hurried down the street and a few minutes later came to a halt in front of an unassuming brick building. Next to the door were steps leading to a basement with an outside door. The man took the steps. Christopher followed.

He opened the door to a darkened café. A young man played a sitar, while a veiled woman draped in sheer rainbow fabric danced.

The man led him to a table deep in shadows in the corner. He bowed in front of a stranger with a pock-marked face. A woman wearing a long, fitted black dress sat beside him.

"Aamir?" Christopher looked down at the occupants of the table.

Aamir looked at his trembling employee and then at the stranger who stood before him. He motioned the woman and the man away. "To whom do I have the pleasure of speaking?"

Christopher pulled out a chair. "May I join you?"

Aamir motioned with his palm. "Of course and you are?"

"Sometimes one is safer not knowing names."

Aamir nodded.

Christopher pulled out a one hundred rupee banknote and laid it on the table.

"What may I do for you?"

"Where is Lai?"

Aamir tensed. "To tell you would be more than my life is worth."

Christopher leaned forward and said softly. "Can you swim?"

Aamir's hand tightened on his glass of wine. "A strange question."

"Can you swim without hands in the Hooghly?"

A fine bead of perspiration dotted Aamir's forehead. He looked into Christopher's eyes then stared like a rabbit paralyzed by a snake as Christopher slowly brought his hand up from under the table. The emerald in the tiger's eye glittered. In the gloom, the silver tiger on the ring looked ready to pounce. "Aiee, I am caught between a cobra and a tiger."

The sitar wailed an eerie sensual lament in the background. "I haven't seen her in a long time. Rumor is she is in America."

"Where in America?"

"I don't know."

Christopher smiled, a smile that bared his teeth and didn't reach his eyes. "Maybe we should step outside and enjoy the evening."

"I really don't know." Aamir's eyes darted about nervously. "But I have a friend, who has a friend. I may be able to find out."

"Don't fail me."

Aamir drew back his hand as if to reach under the table.

Like lightning Christopher's hand came down atop his, pushing it against the smooth hard wood of the table.

Aamir's body relaxed, though his eyes remained alert. "I am not foolish enough to try to bring down a tiger."

Christopher removed his hands and shifted slightly to the left where he could see the rest of the café and Aamir. "I trust your friends are wise as well."

"My friends are sheep. But I need not remind you that the café has a thousand eyes and ears."

"Can you find out what I asked?"

"If it is the gods' will."

Christopher's robe rustled as he leaned forward. "You have twenty-four hours. I will return at midnight tomorrow night. If the gods' will coincides with mine you will become a rich man. If not I would suggest cleansing your soul before you begin your journey to meet them." His voice low, his face expressionless, his eyes held a menace impossible to ignore. "I will return tomorrow night at midnight."

Aamir's features tightened. "Is that wise?"

"You tell me, O son of a jackal."

"I will be here. If it is the gods' will that I be bitten by the snake then I will accept it."

"A wise choice."

Christopher turned and wound through the tables. As he neared the stage the dancer's movements became more languid and erotic. He ignored the blatant invitation and the feel of her gaze on him as he left the café.

* * * * *

The next evening at midnight an old man shuffled into the underground café. He wore a turban and his once white robe was now gray. Leaning on a sleek wooden staff, he hobbled to Aamir's table.

Aamir sipped a cup of tea whose light teasing fragrance was muted in the heavy smell of incense. He set the white cup on the table and looked up. "Go away, old man, if you value your life."

"One can learn much wisdom from those who have lived long upon this earth."

Aamir's breath rushed out in a hiss. "You! I was told The Tiger changes identity as easily as his clothes. In future, I will be careful what women I pick up." Adding hastily, "I mean no disrespect."

Christopher lowered himself into the chair. "Does this mean you have information for me and will live to pick up women?"

Aamir was not a coward. Nor was he a fool. "The..."

Christopher motioned for him to come closer. He raised

his voice. "I am old and hard of hearing please speak directly into my ear."

A man sitting at another table glanced curiously in his direction then returned to watching a sitar player on stage.

Aamir breathed into his ear, "I pray I live to see the dawn. Your package is in New Orleans."

Not so much as by a glance or a stiffening of his body did Christopher show his alarm. "Thank you, good sir. Perhaps you could spare a few coins for a cup of tea."

Aamir reached beneath the long folds of the *kurta* for some small rupees. When he handed them over, his fingers rubbed against several smooth-- surfaced bills. He nodded his thanks.

"Go now."

Christopher sat staring at his tea, to all appearances a befuddled old man lost in memory. His mind raced, Lai in New Orleans. Why? Why hadn't she taken the crystal and flown back to India? Because she knew it would be the first place he would look or because she wanted to punish him for rejecting her?

His knuckles whitened as his hand tightened around the cup. He knew what form of punishment Lai's revenge would take, Gabriella. Cold beads of sweat formed on his forehead.

He brought the tea to his lips, inhaling its bracing fragrance, but didn't drink it. The Tiger was nothing if not cautious. There was one last thing he had to do before he left India and that would have to wait 'til the morning, this morning as it was already past midnight.

Leaning on his cane, he rose stiffly to his feet then placed a gnarled hand on his back, as if it pained him.

He shuffled to the door and stopped to examine his cane. A small mirror embedded in the smooth wood showed two men had stood up moments after he had. The mirror winked in the candlelight.

He walked outside and turned down a dark alley. Smells of rotting food and cow dung assailed him as he stepped deep into the shadows and waited.

The two men stopped in front of the alley. They looked up and down the street, illuminated by the lamplight. Both wore modified white *kurtas* and jeans. Neither was as tall as Christopher. They walked with a confident swagger, men who knew how to protect themselves. "Where do you think the old fool went?" The man had the raspy voice of a smoker and spoke Bengali. He was an inch or two shorter than his companion.

"Maybe into the alley to relieve himself. By the odor, I wouldn't be surprised."

They passed Christopher, flattened against a wooden building, its paint peeling. He waited until they nearly reached its end then glided silently after them, a deadly cat on the prowl.

He straightened, all signs of the old man gone. He held the cane horizontally, one hand wrapped around the handle, the other near the smooth surfaced end. "Are you looking for me, O sons of jackals?" He spoke in Bengali.

Both men whirled around. The shorter of the two visibly started. They looked at each other uneasily. One whispered to the other, "It is the same old man, but different somehow. He is taller with none of the visible signs of frailty that he'd shown before."

Christopher twirled the staff in his right hand then began to toss it back and forth. His lip curled. "What's the matter, dogs, afraid of a harmless old man?"

They rushed him.

He stepped forward to meet them, staff raised.

They came at him from each side. In a whirling motion that was almost too fast to see, he hit the shorter man in the head. The cane made a cracking sound as it came in contact with the man's forehead. His legs crumbled and he dropped silently to the ground.

The other reached in his *kurta* for a knife, but before he could throw it, Christopher pulled on the handle of the cane. The long blade gleamed in the dark. He skewered the hand of the man holding the knife.

The assailant screamed in pain.

"Be still before half your hand is sliced off," Christopher commanded.

The man tried to draw his hand away.

Christopher made a small movement with the blade.

The man immediately stopped. "Please," he whimpered.

"Who do you work for?"

"Lai." The man's face contorted with pain. He might die a slow death if she found out his betrayal but he faced the certainty of losing his hand if not. Loyalty between thieves was a myth.

"Where is Lai?"

"She's out of the country." Blood seeped from the sword in deep dark blobs and dropped at his feet.

So Aamir had told the truth. "Why were you following me?"

The man trembled like a leaf. He wasn't far from passing out from pain and shock. "We were keeping an eye on Aamir. He talked to a stranger last night. Then you showed up tonight and looked like easy pickings."

Christopher's white teeth gleamed against his dark face in an unpleasant smile. He withdrew the sword in a swift motion then wiped his blade on the unconscious assailant lying at his feet.

"Who are you?" the man whispered cradling his bleeding hand against his body.

As Christopher sheathed his sword in its cylindrical nest the long sleeve of his *kurta* fell away from his hand. The tiger snarled from the ring and the emerald eye gleamed as if enraged.

"Aiee," the man wailed and dropped to his knees. "I meant no offense, Tiger. Never in a million years would I have tried to harm you."

"As if you could." Christopher's lip curled in a sneer of disdain. "If I hear you have attacked anyone else too frail and helpless to defend himself I will come back and cut out your heart. Do you hear me, dog?"

The man's head bowed. "I hear and will obey."

"Then take your friend of a beetle and go before I change my mind and kill you both."

"But I'm injured and he is unconscious."

Christopher grabbed the handle of the cane. Before he could draw it out of its scabbard, the man bound to his feet, grabbed his companion's shoulder with his good hand and began to drag him out of the alley, the man's head bobbing unheeded against the ground.

Like a wraith, Christopher disappeared into the shadows.

Chapter Thirty-Two

Christopher stopped in front of a two-story pink house with a white wrought iron fence. On the gate was a white sign that read Shardul Orphanage, which loosely translated into Tiger Orphanage. Greenery and lush white flowers circled the building.

A young girl sat on a swing, pushing it back and forth with her feet. Opening the gate, he walked up the stepping stone sidewalk. The girl got off the swing. It continued its back and forth motion then came to a stop.

He wouldn't have recognized her if he hadn't looked into her eyes. They were old beyond her years, possibly beyond his.

She stopped in front of him, picked up his hand that bore the tiger ring and kissed it. "Thank you."

He quickly drew it back. "There is no need of that."

"But there is. You saved my life."

"Then use it to help others. Have you decided what you wish to be?" He wanted to ask how old she was but was afraid of the answer.

"A teacher."

He nodded. "Good. India can certainly use you. You will go to school. America, if need be, then return and help the good Father that runs Shardul."

"With pleasure." She smiled, a smile that momentarily lifted the sadness from her face.

He sighed as he walked up the steps. The need was so great and the orphanage so small. He refused to touch Aunt Tam's money for this particular passion of his. It would drain her dry. Besides, Tam and Edward had sponsored their own orphan.

Before he could ring the doorbell, the door flew open. A

295

burly, red-haired man stood in front of it. He threw his arms around Christopher. "It's good to see you, my friend."

"Hello, Greg." Christopher returned the embrace then stepped back. The two men studied each other.

Christopher and Greg had met in college. They became fast friends and kept in touch after graduation.

Greg, in an accelerated learning program, had graduated early and joined the priesthood, but had stayed only a few months, disenchanted with the wave of sexual misconduct that swept through the diocese.

When he left the church, Christopher came to him and told him of the plight of the orphans in India and Greg found his calling. He ran the orphanage and Christopher supplied the money.

Even though Greg was a very religious man, he was also savvy and firmly believed in the adage "Don't ask. Don't tell." He kept abreast of current events and it hadn't taken him long to connect the dots. Fabulous jewels disappeared and money for the orphanage appeared.

He rather thought of himself as Friar Tuck to Christopher's Robin Hood. Of course, he didn't share this particular parable with his partner, who would either snort in disgust or laugh himself silly. Christopher did not see the good in himself that Greg did. But Lai was no Maid Marian and he'd offered up a fervent prayer of thanksgiving when Christopher returned to the States.

"Come in. Come in. Would you like tea or something stronger?"

Christopher's eyebrows shot up. "It's only nine o'clock in the morning."

Greg slapped his head and laughed. "So it is. I attended a birthing last night."

They strolled into a well-lit, sunny kitchen.

"Animal or human?"

Greg stifled a yawn. "Human. It's tough going. I lectured on sanitation and to keep the flies away from the baby, but I'm not sure it did any good."

"You're dealing with hundreds of years of superstition." Christopher pulled out a chair from the table.

"Tell me about it. How about coffee instead?" Without waiting for a reply he poured two cups from the coffee maker. He handed Christopher a cup before he sat down with a weary sigh.

Christopher lifted the cup to his lips. The bracing fragrance teased his senses. Even though the kitchen was warm, he enjoyed the feel of the hot liquid rolling down his throat. "How is Heresh doing?" When there was no response, Christopher looked up.

"Greg?"

Greg sat at the table with his eyes closed. His head jerked. "Hm?"

"How is Heresh doing?"

"Graduated from medical school with honors."

Heresh had come to them in his late teens and had already had a smattering of schooling. He was brilliant and soaked up knowledge like a sponge. Accelerated classes had allowed him to graduate early.

"Simi?" She was another whose thankfulness for a second chance had pushed her to finish early.

"She'll be graduating this summer with honors. Both will be coming home to practice."

"And the little one out front says she wants to be a teacher."

Greg nodded.

"Take special care of her, Greg. She's seen and done things no child should ever be exposed to."

"Haven't they all?"

"Yes. Yes, they have. But it's worse for the girls." The muscles in his face stiffened. He uncrossed his legs and leaned forward. "Which makes what I'm about to say that much harder."

Greg set down his cup and watched Christopher, waiting.

"I'm getting married."

Greg jumped up from the table, sending his chair across the floor. He reached over and pumped Christopher's hand. "Chris, this is wonderful news. Boy, she must be something to have brought the elusive Saint to heel. Or should I say Saint to church," and laughed at his witticism. "Get it Saint to church, on your wedding day."

Christopher rolled his eyes. Greg's sense of humor was an acquired taste.

Greg sobered. "So what's wrong?"

He grimaced and circled his hands around his coffee cup. "Let's just say I don't see my intended being particularly excited about the manner I raise money for my favorite charity." It was as close as Christopher had ever come to admitting he was The Tiger.

"I plan on turning all my attention to the import-export shop that I'm a silent partner in. Max has been talking about retirement and it's time I learned the ins and outs of running the place. But it will take years to bring it to the point where it can support this." He waved his hand around the kitchen.

Greg made a dismissive gesture as he hitched up his pants and sat back down.

"God will provide."

Christopher snorted. He got up and prowled around the room. "I appreciate your faith but don't talk like a fool."

Greg watched his friend pace. "It's time and past. You've been lucky. Damn lucky. Some of the countries that you have worked out of don't exactly have prisons that equal the Ritz."

Christopher paused in his pacing. "How do we take care of them, Greg? If I had to, I guess I could go to Aunt Tam…" He grimaced, finding the idea distasteful in the extreme.

Greg rubbed the back of his neck. "Sit down, Christopher. I'm getting a crick in my neck." When Christopher didn't immediately comply he motioned with his hand. "Sit. Sit."

Christopher pulled out his chair and sat back down, staring out the window at the growth of bamboo in the backyard garden.

"How many orphans have come through these doors in the past five years?"

Christopher shrugged. "Twenty, twenty-five."

"Thirty-five."

Christopher arched an eyebrow. "Really?"

"Really."

"Half of them were young adults when you pulled them off the streets, some are in college in the States. The ones you placed as apprentices have already learned trades and are working. Every one of them owes their existence to you and they know it. The ones that work send money regularly to help the orphanage.

"I never told you about it because I knew you'd find another orphan or two or three to use it on, but I knew this day would come. I've been putting away a portion of the money you've sent us all along. We will be okay. All our students want to help others as you helped them. We've talked about it a lot. They are willing to pay their dues, to sponsor the new orphans as they come through these doors."

He reached over and clapped his friend on the back. "We are going to be okay, Chris. The miracle is that you managed to keep this place from Lai the years you were together and since. Now tell me about your bride."

Christopher leaned back, tipping his chair. "She terrifies me."

Greg's brown eyes sparkled. He chuckled. "I've got to meet this woman. Tell me more."

"She's tall and blonde in a Nordic queen sort of way." A reminiscent smile touched his face. It was one of those smiles that men and women have when they are thinking of particularly great sex. He looked at Greg. "She's an independent reporter and her dad's a policeman who hates my guts."

Greg's eyebrows soared as he straightened in his chair. "Have you completely lost your mind?"

He sighed. "I'm afraid so, right along with my heart."

"Pardon my lack of finesse but I've never known your dick to rule your head before."

He laughed. "I'm afraid I have no choice. She saw me in Aunt Tam's crystal ball."

"I may need something stronger than coffee. Would you care to explain?"

"Sometime, when I have a couple of hours to spare, I'll tell you the story. But right now, I've got to go. I should've already been heading back to the States but I wanted to let you know about our young friend. Though, it appears she beat me here." He gave a light chuckle. "And of course I wanted to see how you were doing."

The chair scraped against the wooden floor as Christopher rose and pushed away from the table.

He clasped Greg's hand in a firm grip. "If you need me call." He loved this man like a brother.

Greg nodded returning the pressure. "And give my regards to the bride."

"Will you come to the wedding?"

"You know I will. When?"

"I'll let you know."

* * * * *

Gabby sat in the study staring at the blank computer screen. The cursor blinked in place, waiting to move across the page.

She had looked through her computer files and found research she had started on crystals and stones. The file intrigued her, especially considering her own special crystal.

Glancing at her ring, she wondered what the oriental witch had done with her globe. She turned her hand back and forth. The emerald sitting amidst the glittering diamonds shimmered in the light. It was very similar in shade to the crystal.

The globe was an anomaly. If anyone had told her about it, she would have laughed herself sick. But she now knew its power and missed it like a lover's touch.

And speaking of which...where in hell was Christopher?

She sighed, feeling torn. Part of her wanted him back with an intensity that terrified her, part of her was glad he was gone. It bought her time. What was she going to do when he came back?

Why did he do it? Why did he steal? Lord knows he didn't need the money. Was he just a bored bad boy? Whatever his reasons, she couldn't, wouldn't marry a thief.

She made a half-hearted attempt to take the ring off. But just like the other dozen or so times she tried, it wouldn't slip over her knuckle. It rested resplendent on her finger like a nightingale nesting on eggs.

Trying to push Christopher to the back of her mind, she glanced again at the blank screen. Getting her thoughts in order she began to type.

Through the ages crystals have been synonymous with energy and energy fields, availing mankind with the ability to tap into the natural world around them. Many believe the quartz crystals beneath the earth's surface help keep the earth's magnetic field in balance.

Gabby hit her stride, the keys flying as she watched the words appear as if by magic on the screen. Totally engrossed it took a minute or two for the gong of the doorbell echoing through the house to register.

She tried to ignore it. Maybe, just maybe, she could figure out what made her globe tick.

The doorbell shrilled again. With a sigh, she stretched and got up. Her feet sank into the plush carpet as she padded to the door. Where was everybody? Shopping?

She nodded. Yup. Tamara had said something about shopping.

She made it to the door seconds before Ned and Jericho arrived. Ned's tail wagged madly from side to side, as if to say, "Oh boy, company." Jericho plopped his fanny squarely in front of the door and stared at it.

She nudged Ned out of the way and walked around Jericho to stick her eye to the peep hole. A well-dressed young Indian stood at the door.

She opened it, but left the latch on the hook. "Yes?"

The young man nodded politely. About four inches shorter than Gabby, he had short black hair and wore a conservative dark suit. "I'm here to see Mr. Saint."

"Is he expecting you?"

He cleared his throat, his eyes shifted.

Gabby lifted her nose and literally sniffed the air. Her journalistic instincts began to quiver. She unlatched the door and gave him her most charming smile. "I'm sorry. I don't believe I caught your name."

He extended his hand. "Joshi. My name is Heresh Joshi. My friends call me Henry."

Gabby placed her arm through his and drew him inside. "Won't you come in, Henry."

She led him into the sitting room and closed the door, shutting the animals out. The last thing she saw before the door closed was two offended blue eyes.

The sitting room was a cozy little spot with old-fashioned roses papered on the wall. Two over-stuffed, cream-colored love seats faced each other and an antique coffee table sat between them. Ecru lace curtains were bunched at the windows, their folds falling in a graceful arc to the floor.

Henry studied the room. "This is nice."

She glanced around the familiar enclosure. "It is isn't it? Would you like something to drink, tea perhaps?"

"Yes, thank you."

"Make yourself at home." Forgetting the dog and cat, she opened the door and nearly got knocked down as they raced into the room and rushed forward to sniff Henry.

She threw up her hands. "I'm sorry."

He laughed. "It's okay. I like animals."

"It's a good thing." She left the room, the critters entertaining their visitor with tales of their derring-do. At least that's what it sounded like to her experienced ears.

She looked back over her shoulder and saw him petting and talking to both creatures. Her mouth muscles went up as she headed for the kitchen.

She filled a small silver platter with a pitcher of tea, two crystal glasses, and a bowl of mixed nuts then sprinkled fresh mint leaves on the golden-red beverage.

"Hope he likes it sweet." She sent a brief prayer spiraling toward heaven that her own teeth didn't decay and fall out.

In the Midwest, one made tea and added sweetener. In the South, the sugar bowl was emptied into the steaming brew, where it dissolved into a liquid confection designed to elevate blood sugar the moment it slid down one's throat.

She started toward the door, then backpedaled and grabbed treats out of the kitty and doggy jar sitting on the kitchen counter, placed a couple on the tray and pushed through the swinging doors.

When she reached the sitting room, Jericho was perched on the arm of the love seat next to Henry and Ned was at his feet, his plumy tail thumping.

Jericho saw her, sniffed and tail in the air raced to her. Ned followed.

"Fickle." She laughed and threw both animals a treat. She sat down across from Henry, poured each of them a glass of tea then sank back against the cushions. "Hope you like it sweet."

"Oh, yes."

She took a sip, the subtle fragrance of mint tickling her senses. "So, Henry, what did you want to see Christopher about?"

He looked at her, his thin features solemn. "To thank him."

She stared at him for a long moment. "Would you care to explain?"

His back ramrod straight he said with simple dignity, "I'm from the orphanage."

She blinked several times then opened her mouth to speak but nothing came out. She cleared her throat and tried again. "I'm sorry, I don't understand."

"I know Mr. Saint is very secretive about us. I don't know why. I always thought perhaps so many people would beg for his help that he would have to turn them away and that would bother him."

He glanced around. "I assumed he was very rich." Then hastened to add, "All this, while being very, very nice, is hardly the home of a billionaire, which we always thought Mr. Saint must be to help as he's done."

Gabby closed her eyes and shook her head. "I still don't understand."

He tried again. "I'm from the orphanage that he and Father Greg run. Father isn't actually a priest anymore but we call him that."

Gabby's head spun. Could this possibly be what Tamara was talking about when she eluded to Robin Hood?

She leaned forward. "I don't know anything about the orphanage but I'd like to."

"It's been in existence for several years. The two of them have helped an amazing number of us. They've taken those of us living on the streets in, given us a place to live and an education. Most of us get our degrees in the States, which I know has cost him a small fortune. In return, all that is asked of us is that we go back to India and help those less fortunate than ourselves." He gave a heavy sigh. "There are thousands."

Gabby leaned back against the sofa. She felt like she'd just been run over by a Mack truck. Who would have thought that there were such unplumbed depths to Christopher Saint?

"I've probably said more than I should. We haven't exactly been sworn to secrecy but we have been told not to ever discuss it outside of the orphanage." Henry looked uncomfortable. His Adam's apple bobbed and he ran a finger inside his collar.

She leaned forward. "I'm very glad you told me. It explains a great many things about him that I didn't understand." *Like why he's a thief.*

Her heart lightened. Giddy happiness assailed her. She wanted to giggle, to dance. Her fiancé was a thief, a premier thief.

Henry stood up. "I had better be going. Would you give him my regards? I leave for India tomorrow."

She held out her hand. "Of course I will."

He took it in a firm grasp, his palm warm.

"Thank you, Henry."

He nodded. She showed him to the door, the critters trailing along behind. After he'd left, she shut it and leaned against it, still smiling. She looked down at the cat and dog watching her. "I must be losing my mind. My fiancé is a thief and I'm actually happy."

Ned woofed and wagged his tail.

No, that wasn't right. She was happy because there was a very good reason for what he did. Not one that would stand up in a court of law mind you. But nonetheless he was hardly doing it to line the coffers.

She blinked as the door thumped against her back. Gabby took a step forward, turned and opened the door thinking Henry was back.

Tamara and Beatrice came tumbling in. For several minutes pandemonium reigned as Gabby tried to pick the two older women up off the floor and Ned and Jericho did their level best to lick their faces.

Once she had the ladies more or less on their feet, Gabby announced, "I had a visitor. Guess who? No you'll never guess. Henry. Did you know Christopher has an orphanage?" Gabby danced around them.

"Yes, dear." Tamara held a sack of bright red tomatoes that had somehow survived their precipitous entry.

"You did? Of course, you did."

Beatrice walked toward the kitchen carrying a bag of shiny red-green apples. They'd been to the farmer's market.

Gabby reached for the bag. "Let me take that for you." She slid the paper strap on her arm and followed Beatrice to the kitchen. "Would you like some iced tea?"

"I'd love some. I'm parched." Tamara took off a wide-brimmed straw hat, that framed her face and had a mint-green ribbon hanging down the back, and fanned herself.

They all trooped into the kitchen. Gabby got glasses out of the oak cabinet while Beatrice put away the fresh fruits and vegetables.

After she filled the glasses with ice, she poured the beverage over the ice and put a mint leaf into each glass. She served the older women then sat down and sipped her own tea.

Tamara watched her, a small satisfied smile on her lovely ageless features. "I know a darling little boutique that has the most beautiful wedding gowns. Would you like to go?"

Gabby smiled. "That would be lovely."

"Say tomorrow morning?"

"Tomorrow morning," Gabby confirmed.

Chapter Thirty-Three

Gabby and Tamara got up early to head for a courtyard café that served chicory and beignets, before their grueling hours of shopping.

Gabby sipped her savory brew while watching a fat gray pigeon work the tables, gobbling down the crumbs the customers threw him.

She sighed in contentment. The wrought iron black fence kept the world at bay while allowing them to watch it go by. Red hibiscus and purple crepe myrtle draped the courtyard. Greedy as the pigeon, she stuffed half a sugar-coated beignet in her mouth.

Tamara sipped her chicory. She set her cup down. "He can't continue you know."

Her mouth full, Gabby nodded vigorously. She swallowed the sweet treat and wiped the sugar off her mouth with the back of her hand. "I know."

Heat flared behind her eyes and determination coursed through her. "He'll stop if I have to use the last breath in my body to convince him."

Tamara daintily patted crumbs off her mouth. "Knowing Christopher, I can't believe he intends to continue with this after he's married."

"He damn well better not," she muttered under her breath.

"What did you say, dear?"

"Oh, nothing."

She sipped her coffee. As she set her cup down, the words tumbled out. "Do you think I'll ever see my globe again? Your globe," she corrected.

"No dear. You are right, it's yours. And yes, I do think so. In fact, I know so. The globe will find a way home."

Gabby gave her a skeptical look. "I hope you are right. Are you ready to go?"

Tamara nodded and stood up. She tossed her remaining beignet to the pigeon.

Gabby held on to hers determined to share it with one of the thinner birds that lurked on the fringes of the pigeon's territory.

In the French Quarter, the ladies walked several blocks to the boutique, gazing in store windows, watching the tourists and generally enjoying their outing.

Tamara stopped in front of an elegant little shop. A mauve colored sign with gold lettering proclaimed Dianna's Boutique.

She opened the door and Gabby followed her in. A chime tinkled as the door opened announcing their arrival. A large white cat got up from the white satin chair it was setting in, stretched and yawned.

One of the most beautiful women Gabby had ever seen stepped from behind the counter.

Passersby gawked through the storefront window.

"Ms. Tamara, it is so good to see you. It's been too long."

The women shook hands.

The dark-haired woman tilted her head. "And what brings you to my bridal shop? Are you looking for an ensemble for the Beauer's wedding perhaps?" She glanced at Gabby out of the corner of her eye, but her main attention focused on Mrs. James.

Tamara drew Gabby forward. "We're here to buy a wedding dress for Christopher's bride."

The shopkeeper's eyes widened and she looked ready to faint. "Your nephew is getting married?"

Gabby wasn't sure if she liked this woman or not.

"Dianna, let me introduce you to Christopher's fiancée,

Gabriella Bell."

Dianna took Gabby's hand and squeezed it firmly. "I'm so happy to meet you."

"Gabby dear, this is Ms. Dianna Blanchard."

"I am so thrilled you've chosen my shop for your wedding gown. Now what did you have in mind?"

"Well, I…"

"Why don't you sit down and I'll show you what we have."

Dianna led them to two white satin chairs next to the cat.

An associate of Dianna's came out balancing a silver platter with two steaming cups of chicory topped with whipped cream and two bottles of water. Gabby glanced at Tamara and bit back a groan.

She gingerly accepted the aromatic brew and gave a sickly smile of thanks. She sat it down on the antique table at her elbow and reached for the water, uncapped it and drank.

The cool clear liquid slid down her throat. She glanced over to see Tamara sedately drinking her chicory. Gabby grinned. She loved that woman.

At that moment, Dianna and three shop attendants walked out their arms full of rustling white gowns.

Tamara and Gabby looked at the beautiful full-skirted gown encrusted with pearls and shook their heads.

The next was a slinky little number covered in sequins.

"That would look good on you, dear." Tamara patted at the whipped cream clinging to her upper lip with a tissue.

"It's not me."

"Perhaps something a bit more simple," Tamara suggested.

Dianna arched a brow and motioned a redheaded shop attendant forward, a silk gown strung across her arm.

Tamara leaned over and whispered to Gabby. "Oh, dear, I should have never used the term simple. I've probably offended her."

Gabby bit down on her lip to keep from giggling. She was a bit overwhelmed in this classy, high-priced boutique. She shopped end of season, off the clearance racks, at the local department stores.

The attendant glided forward and held it up. It was a simple off-the-shoulder white silk.

"You would look absolutely breathtaking. Why not try it on." Not waiting for a reply, Dianna took the dress and headed for a dressing room, discreetly placed down the hall.

Gabby trailed obediently behind, sinking into the luxurious white carpet with each step, hoping she wasn't tracking dirt on the immaculate floor covering.

The maroon silk dressing room curtain rustled as Dianna pulled it back and placed the dress carefully inside. The room was spacious, wide enough for Dianna, Gabby and the dress.

Gabby waited for Dianna to step out.

"You will need help with the dress."

"If it doesn't bother you, it doesn't bother me," Gabby muttered under her breath, pulling a red tank top over her head.

"Did you say something, Ms. Bell?"

"Oh just commenting on...Never mind it was nothing important."

She slid out of the long white muslin skirt she wore and stood in her plain white cotton bra, briefs and sandals.

Dianna nodded. "You have an excellent body. It will be a pleasure dressing you."

She opened the curtain stepped out and snapped her fingers. Another attendant came hurrying forward, handed her something and left.

Gabby shook her head. *You need to be a mind reader to work here.* Then she took a closer look at what Dianna held in each hand. "Candy dishes made from play dough."

Dianna gave a brief laugh. "So droll, Ms. Bell." She held out her hands. "Put them on."

Rolling her eyes, Gabby unhooked her bra and plopped on the silicone, self-adhesive cups.

Dianna pulled the white silk dress over Gabby's head, zipped the back then opened the curtain so she could step out.

She looked at herself in the three-way mirror. An elegant woman she didn't recognize stared back at her.

"My dear, you look breathtaking. Why don't you show Mrs. James?"

Gabby walked out to Tamara, the silk rustling with each step.

Tamara smiled at her.

Sadness flickered over Tamara's face as she admired the gown then quickly disappeared. *She's thinking of Dilly.* Impulsively she held out her hand. "I want to carry yellow daffodils."

Tamara understood immediately. She took Gabby's hand and squeezed it. Her eyes glittered like amethyst pools. One lone tear spilled out and trailed down her petal soft cheek. "My dear, that may be the kindest thing anyone has ever done for me. And I've had a lot of kindnesses come my way over the years."

She wiped the tear away then smiled at Gabby. "So do you like the dress, dear?"

Gabby hedged. "What do you think?"

"I think you look absolutely stunning. But to be quite truthful, I don't recognize our dear Gabriella in it."

Gabby gave a relieved sigh. "Me either. I'm afraid this top would fall down, leaving me exposed with nothing but silicone pasties."

Tamara burst out laughing.

Dianna waited at a discreet distance.

Gabby shook her head.

Dianna clapped her hands and another clerk came hurrying forward, a gown in her arms.

They walked back to the dressing room, Gabby, Dianna and another clerk, this one a pretty oriental. Gabby grimaced wryly. I feel like the pied piper.

Dianna opened the curtain. Gabby stepped through and turned around. Dianna unzipped her dress. The gown fell in a white pool of silk at her feet.

Gabby stared in fascination at her silicone, self-adhered pasties.

"Hold up your arms."

She obeyed and another dress slid over her head.

Dianna spun her around and zipped her up. The woman barely reached Gabby's shoulders with heels on.

She flinched as Dianna zipped the tight-fitting dress, taking a small piece of skin with it. Lord, she hoped she didn't bleed on it.

She looked in the mirror. This one had a street length straight silk skirt and bodice. A draping of chiffon covered her shoulders and trailed down her back to end at the hem of her dress. A light row of sequins edged the chiffon. The chiffon plunged to a V between her breasts. Gabby raised her eyebrows. *What would Daddy think of this getup?*

She almost giggled.

Dianna threw back the curtain and Gabby glided out. The skirt was too tight to take her usual long strides.

Gabby and Tamara both looked at each other and shook their heads. "Do we have a date yet? Just in case this process takes longer than I supposed?"

She shrugged helplessly. "He doesn't even know I'm going to marry him. I'll let him pick the date."

"That's a mistake, my dear. It's well-intentioned but a mistake nonetheless. You leave it to Christopher and you'll find yourself before Judge Hermodson the next day."

313

Gabby laughed. "I see your point."

Dianna joined them. "Well ladies?"

"No. They are beautiful. But I'm just a simple sort of girl. I need something a shade less elegant."

Dianna shook her head. "That's too bad. You wear them like a queen."

Her facial muscles loosened and her lips tipped up. Christopher had called her his Nordic queen as they lay in each other's arms after their tempestuous lovemaking.

And speaking of her fiancé, why hadn't she heard from him?

A brief image of Christopher dripping blood as he had the last time she'd seen him in the globe surfaced in her mind. She shook her head to clear it.

Tamara leaned forward. "Are you all right, dear?"

Gabby drudged up a smile. "I'm fine." No need to share that grisly image with Tamara. Besides, with or without the globe, she would know if something was wrong. And she fully intended to make sure that image never became a reality.

Dianna stood studying her, tapping her finger against her lips. Her eyes lit. "I have it!" She turned and walked briskly to the back.

When she came back a moment later, a gown the color of old ivory filled her arms.

Even before she saw the gown's design, Gabby knew it was hers.

Dianna held it up for her inspection.

Gabby and Tamara looked at each other and smiled.

Dianna, Gabby and the clerk hurried to the dressing room, as much as one can hurry in a tight-fitting dress.

Dianna helped Gabby out of the gown. She caught it before it quite hit the floor.

Gabby fidgeted her impatience mounting.

Dianna and the clerk exchanged gowns. Gabby closed her eyes as the cool silk dropped over her head. The store owner zipped the back and straightened the shoulders.

She opened her eyes, looked in the mirror and smiled. The gown was a simple shirtwaist with a fitted skirt that had a built-in train. Rows of silk-covered buttons ran from a high-necked collar to the waist. Antique lace three inches wide graced the cuffs, the neck, ran beside the buttons and trimmed the train. *Perfect.*

Dianna smiled in satisfaction. "You like it?"

"Very much." She studied her reflection. She looked truly beautiful and it was her in the mirror not some sophisticated Barbie doll.

Dianna opened the curtain and motioned her forward. "Shall we?"

She walked out of the dressing room and stopped in front of Tamara. "What do you think?"

Her head tilted on one side, Tamara studied the gown. "I think you look absolutely beautiful. It's perfect. What do think?"

"I want it."

Tamara sighed in relief. "Now that we've made that decision, we need to look at headdresses and shoes."

She looked up at her future daughter-in-law's face and her gaze sharpened. "What is it, dear?"

Gabby's feeling of euphoria dissipated like mist rolling off a river. In its place was an inimical feeling so strong, she could feel the hair on the back of her neck curl.

She looked around. Two young women stood on the sidewalk watching her through the picture window. One a pretty African-American, the other an oriental with her hair pulled back in a ponytail.

Her gaze swept over them and moved on. While her eyes traveled around the shop her subconscious prodded her. What was it about the oriental woman that bothered her?

She glanced back. Their eyes locked. Hatred sparked from glittering orbs and washed over her. Lai!

"Call the police!" yelled the policeman's daughter.

Lai grabbed the arm of the woman she was with and disappeared into the crowd.

Gabby bolted for the door.

"No, no. You can't wear that gown outside." Dianna flung herself at Gabby's knees with a tackle that would have made The Saints proud. Both went tumbling to the ground.

"She's getting away," Gabby howled, pounding on the carpet in frustration. When she finally untangled herself from Dianna's death grasp and stumbled to her feet, she found the door blocked by the three clerks. "Call the police!"

She hurried to the dressing room, with Dianna in hot pursuit. Dianna got her out of the gown in record time. "Do you want this gown?"

"Yes," she panted while throwing on her shirt and skirt, not bothering with her old bra. "Put the pasties on my tab," she called over her shoulder as she ran out.

Tamara was on her feet, poised for anything.

"It's Lai." Gabby ran past her and out the door.

She looked left and right. Lai was nowhere in sight. She hesitated then headed right, weaving in and out of the crowds.

Nothing.

Had she turned in the wrong direction? She'd gone several blocks with no sign of Lai. She scoured the crowd in front of her.

Something cold and hard pressed against her spine then moved to her side as she stumbled to a stop.

"Keep walking, cow."

Damn it!

"Suzy, what are you doing?" the black woman wailed,

spying the gun.

"Shut up, Rebecca," Lai warned.

None of them saw the taxi following them down the street.

Chapter Thirty-Four

While the fracas that would be known for years to come as the Wedding Boutique Brawl, and published as such in the society columns, was going on Tamara kept her head and instead of calling the police called a taxi, having a good idea what was coming.

Gabriella was a wonderful girl but impulsive. Tamara had no doubt Gabriella would take off in hot pursuit and she would be left to follow as best she could. Either that or stay and completely miss the action.

When Gabby bolted out the door, Tamara was right behind her. Only as Gabby tore down the street, Tamara jumped into a waiting cab.

"Follow that tall blonde, but be discreet," she directed. As the taxi pulled out from the curb, Tamara pulled her cell phone out of her beaded purple purse. She punched the button next to Christopher's name and then the send signal.

The phone rang three times then connected her to voice mail. "Drat the boy," she muttered under her breath. Then aloud, "Christopher, listen carefully…"

As Tamara frantically tried to reach Christopher Gabby listened in disbelief to the bizarre conversation between Lai and her lover.

Becka sobbed loudly as they walked down the street. It wasn't a pretty sight. Her face looked blotchy and she hiccupped.

Apparently, Lai didn't think so either. "Be quiet, Becka. Reach in my purse and get my credit card. Go buy yourself a trinket."

Becka continued to wail. "I knew there had been others and you said I was the first."

Gabby had just never learned to keep her big mouth shut. "Honey, neither one of you has the equipment that does it for me."

Lai grabbed her arm and squeezed, pressing dagger-like, red-lacquered nails into Gabby's arm. Gabby yelped.

Passersby stared.

"Shut up," Lai hissed. "Becka, you know I love you above all others. You've seen the scars on my back. This is the person who put them there."

"Really?" Becka's voice came out in a hiss. "Then I don't care what you do to her."

"That's my angel. Now go buy yourself a little trinket." Lai's eyes never left Gabby.

Walking beside her, she kept the gun firmly wedged against Gabby's ribs, her arm over it so it wasn't visible.

Becka helped herself to a credit card from Lai's small Asian-designed bag as they walked.

"You deserve whatever you get," Becka said to Gabby. She ran her hand lightly down Lai's arm then turned and headed back toward the shops.

"Not too bright is she?"

Lai jabbed her with the gun. "Shut up, cow."

Gabby'd had enough. Too stunned to do anything but acquiesce when Lai had put a gun in her back she had followed Lai's commands.

"I'm pretty sick of that cow routine." She whirled and grabbed for the gun.

Then she yelled at the top of her lungs, "Police. Help. Police!"

Lai grabbed Gabby's finger and pushed it back, nearly dropping Gabby with pain.

"Be quiet," she hissed.

People looked at them uneasily. A couple of men slowed, but all they saw was a tall blonde and young woman half her size that looked to be in her teens. They shrugged and walked on. All except one middle-aged lady who walked beside them, eyeing the oriental suspiciously.

Lai grabbed her cell phone in her free hand and punched in 911, her long red nails clicking against the buttons. "Please patch me through to Officer Daniels."

"Officer Daniels, I'm on St. Peter's Street, could you meet us here? There's a taxi cab that's been following us for the past several blocks. It looks suspicious. You're just a block away? Thank you."

The woman, reassured, patted Gabby's arm. "You'll be okay now, dear," and crossed the street without a backward glance.

"Wait!" But the lady had already disappeared into the crowd. Gabby glanced back and saw the taxi. Her heart sank as the sunlight caught a sheen of silver hair in the backseat. Tamara.

Lai prodded her with the gun. "Keep walking."

Gabby weighed her odds. If she acted quickly, Tamara stood a chance of getting away. She spun on her heel, her fist clenched.

Lai's reflexes were quicksilver.

Gabby's fist hit air. A siren sounded in the distance. "Settle down, blondie, I'm not interested in your boyfriend," Lai said loudly for the benefit of the onlookers.

"The hell you're not." She swung again and again missed.

The cab inched forward. Tamara had the door open as they pulled alongside.

"Get in, Gabby, get in."

She took a step toward the cab and found herself face down on the pavement as Lai stuck out a dainty, well-shod foot and snagged her then made a grab for Tamara, who scooted further back in the cab.

She raised her head, dazed. Blood dripped from her chin. "Go, Tamara, go. Corrupt cop coming."

A car driving on the wrong side of the street, blowing its horn, kept the taxi driver diverted from the proceedings on the street.

Before she could say more, Lai kneeled beside her. "Are you okay?" she asked with patent false concern, just before she pinched a nerve in the back of Gabby's neck that severed Gabby and consciousness.

Hovering over Gabby's limp body, her black eyes filled with malevolence, Lai's gaze locked with Tamara's.

Tamara slammed the door shut. "Step on it," she told the driver crisply. *Corrupt cop? Lai had a policeman on her payroll!*

"Lady, there ain't no stepping on it in the French Quarter." Nonetheless the cab moved forward. Tamara's head stayed craned backward.

They turned the corner. "Stop."

The cabby stopped, grumbling. "Make up your mind, lady."

Tamara opened her tiny beaded purse and handed him a fifty dollar bill.

He turned in his seat. "I don't have change for this."

"Keep it."

He looked at her suspiciously. "What do I have to do?"

"If I'm not mistaken, a police car will come by here any minute. Get its license number and if you can, follow it and get the address of where it's going. If you do that I'll give you an extra hundred."

She pulled out a pen and scrawled her cell phone number on the back of a receipt.

Not waiting for a reply she jumped out of the cab.

A horse-drawn carriage sat across the street, facing in

the direction they'd just come from. She ran across the road and jumped in. "Head for St. Louis Street and turn left toward Dianna's Boutique," she directed.

As the horse clip-clopped onto the street Tamara glanced back. The cabbie had done a U-turn and waited at the front of the street. Seeing Tamara, he touched his forehead with his index finger then pointed it at her. She nodded.

They approached a gathering crowd that was forming around Gabby and Lai.

Tamara picked up a dark blue blanket that lay on the seat for cool evenings and threw it over her head.

An occasional car horn sounded and a blues singer sang on the corner as they went a few yards past the crowd surrounding Lai and Gabriella. "Stop here."

The driver checked the horse. Swishing his tail against the flies, the huge dappled gray halted, just as a police car pulled up in front of the crowd.

A young black man in a blue police uniform got out of the car and began dispersing the gawkers. The sun glittered off the badge on his chest.

As Tamara watched, the policeman and the Asian hauled Gabby into the police car and pulled away from the curb.

A moment later, the taxi swung out behind it. Tamara leaned forward and hissed. "Follow that police car." *Don't worry, Christopher, I'll take care of your bride, but please pick up your phone.*

The man turned around. His eyebrows shot up to his hairline. "Lady you've got to be kidding."

Gabby handed him a fifty dollar bill.

He looked at it dubiously.

"That's in addition to whatever your normal fee is. Please, do your best."

The man turned the horse around barely missing a pedestrian jaywalking in the street. He slapped the reins against the horse's rump and clicked his tongue. "Giddy up, Dobbin."

Dobbin broke into a lumbering trot. "Come on, Dobbin, let's move it."

Dobbin picked up his pace, his huge hooves clip-clopping in a faster rhythm than he was used to.

"Ma'am, he's getting away." The liveried driver had gotten into the spirit of things.

Tamara leaned back against the squabs. The heat from the hot leather seats seeped through her light blouse. "Just do the best you can."

She could see the police car and the taxi, two blocks up.

Half a block ahead, pedestrians streamed out into the street. The driver pulled on his reins. He swore inventively under his breath then stood up trying to get a better view. "They just turned right," he shouted.

"Did a taxi turn right also?"

He paused for a moment then replied. "Yes. Yes it did."

"Then we're all right."

Just then her cell phone rang. "Where are you?" Tamara listened and nodded.

"Good job, James, is it?" She had looked at the name plate on the dash of the taxi. "Keep me posted."

Except for a few stragglers, the street cleared. Like spawning salmon swimming upstream, the crowd had surged across the thoroughfare. The driver clucked and Dobbin stepped out, scattering the remaining pedestrians. Several upright digits pointed in their general direction.

"What have those pigs done?" There was obviously no love lost between the driver and the police. "Confiscated your dope?"

Tamara's shoulders shook. "Worse, my daughter-in-law." She threw off the hot blanket.

He clucked sympathetically. "Works nights does she?"

She choked. "Uh, something like that."

"My old lady turned a few tricks before we hooked up. A body's got to eat."

Her mind turned inward as she remembered a dirty little boy running desperately down the back streets of Calcutta, her purse clasp in his grimy little hand.

"Yes, a body does," she answered softly.

* * * * *

The subject of Tamara's reminiscence walked toward his car parked outside the terminal, a black duffle bag thrown over his shoulder. It was muggy and hot. Beads of sweat stood out on his forehead. The sounds of jets roaring to life, car horns honking and racing motors filled the terminal.

He pulled out his cell phone and checked for messages. It had gone off just as the stewardess had requested all phones be turned off.

Two were from Aunt Tam. He reached the Jag, threw his bag on the front seat then slid into the car and played them back. When he heard Tamara's message heat scalded him, followed by fear so icy it froze his heart.

Throwing the car in gear, he roared out of the terminal. The car in front of him slowed for a stop sign. He wheeled around it, nearly crunching an approaching truck.

He jerked the wheel to the right and pulled sharply back in his lane, a bare inch in front of the bumper of the car he'd just passed.

He threw the car into a higher gear and went screaming down the road.

Tamara's message was terse and extremely confusing. Gabriella had been kidnapped by a young oriental woman with a possible black female accomplice and most definitely someone on the police force.

That part he'd understood. When he'd started doubting his senses was when she'd told him she was parked a block away in a horse-drawn carriage and that a cab driver had staked out the apartment where Gabriella had been taken.

If he wasn't so damn scared, it would be downright funny. But he was scared, petrified in fact, the sweat on his brow clammy and cold. If Lai touched Gabriella, he'd kill her. He was going to have to kill her anyway. If he didn't, she would never stop until she'd killed Gabriella. The woman had no heart, only the cold calculating brain of a cobra.

With one hand on the wheel, his eyes moved back and forth between the road and the phone as he punched Tamara's number and hit the send button. Green overhead signs flashed by.

Tamara picked up immediately. "Christopher?"

"Aunt Tam, what the hell is going on?"

"Well dear, it's been a rather eventful morning. One moment Gabriella was trying on a wedding dress. She looked very beautiful, by the way."

"Trying on a wedding dress?" For one all too brief moment, joy pumped through him right along with blood and oxygen.

"Yes, dear, then she saw Lai, got out of the dress in record time and took off after her."

"Damn it! Has she no sense of self-preservation or just no sense at all?"

"Try to calm down, dear."

"I'm calm. Please go on." Christopher passed an SUV then swerved back in the right lane.

"I knew I couldn't keep up with her so I hired a cabby to follow them. Excellent fellow, the cabbie."

The car in front of Christopher slowed putting on its brake lights.

"Well the bottom line is Lai turned the tables on Gabby and she apparently has enough clout to have someone on the police force working for her. They dragged her into a police car. And I do mean dragged. I think she was unconscious."

His jaw muscles tightened and he white-knuckled the wheel. "Do you have any idea where they took her?"

"I'm waiting down the block from the apartment now."

"Bless you. Give me an address." He listened carefully. "I'll be there in fifteen minutes."

"It may take a bit longer, Christopher. You won't be able to help Gabriella wrapped around a telephone pole."

"Don't worry Aunt Tam. I love you. Did I hear you say you were in a horse-drawn buggy? For God's sake, be careful."

He ended the signal and threw the phone on the passenger seat. His eyes never leaving the busy road, he reached in his glove compartment and pulled out a thin stiletto in a calfskin case and pushed it into his sock then with both hands on the wheel, roared down the freeway.

* * * * *

Gabby regained consciousness in stages. The first thing that surfaced at a conscious level was discomfort.

Slumped forward, her hair fell over her face. Her arms were stretched at an awkward angle behind her. And she had the mother of all headaches.

Squinting, hoping not to make the pounding in her head worse, she opened her eyes.

What she saw made her forget all about her head.

On a marble pedestal, not three yards away, sat her globe. She tugged her arms, trying to reach for it, but her hands were bound.

Even from a distance the globe recognized her. It began to churn. Her headache vanished and a feeling of calm settled over her.

A gargoyle face popped into view. She shook her hair out of her eyes. "Hello, Lai."

Lai gave a nasty smile. "You know me? That is good.

326

It's always good to know the person who has the power of your life or death in her hands don't you think?"

"I think you give yourself too much credit."

Lai's hand lashed out.

Gabby's head snapped back. Blood pooled on her stinging cheek.

Anger rushed through her system like boiling oil. "What don't you untie my hands and try that again."

Lai laughed an ugly brittle sound. "Do you really think that would do you any good?"

"We can find out."

"Maybe we can at that, but first there is something I want you to witness."

Lai walked out of the room and returned a moment later with a hammer.

A shudder shook her and she scooted toward the door. *This is not good.*

Lai raised the hammer over her head and with all her might brought it down on the globe.

Gabby howled in protest.

The force of the blow was so great that the hammer went flying out of Lai's hand.

Gabby cowered as the hammer landed against the wall a foot from her head, punching a hole in the drywall.

She looked at Lai with new respect. Who would have thought such a tiny thing could be so strong?

Then her eyes flew to the globe. She smiled like a proud mama. It hadn't even chipped it. The force however had cracked the pedestal.

Lai shot her a venomous look as she retrieved the hammer.

For once she kept her mouth shut.

Lai rubbed her arm.

I hope it hurts like a son of a bitch. The thought gave her much satisfaction.

Lai swung again.

"Keep your damn hammer off my globe!"

"Shut up unless you want me to substitute your head."

Once again, the hammer flew out of her hands. Gabby didn't duck quickly enough. The corner of the claw grazed her beneath her right eye.

She screamed bloody murder.

"Shut up, bitch."

"Watch who you are calling a bitch, bitch."

Lai started toward her then stopped at the cracking sound that came from the center of the room. Both women watched in fascinated horror as the marble pedestal split in two perfect halves and fell to the floor, the globe rolling unharmed onto the carpet.

Lai lifted it over her head and threw it on the floor in sheer frustration. "Why won't it break?"

"Why would you want to break it?"

"You stupid fool, playing your weak little woman's games with the globe," Lai sneered, her voice brittle. "Don't you realize what's in the center of your precious ball?"

"Uh, Christopher's image?"

The answer earned her an angry slap.

Stupid, stupid, stupid. Why oh, why can't I keep my mouth shut. Her face was going to be more colorful than a neon sign in Vegas before this was over.

Lai picked up the ball. Beads of perspiration stood out on her sculpted white brow.

She shoved it in Gabby's face. "Take a good look."

Gabby's eyes traveled from Lai's heated countenance to the globe. She frowned in concentration. "The center is darker."

Lai gave a snort that did not fit the delicate features the unladylike sound came from. "There's an emerald larger than my fist imbedded in the center and it seems I have a problem getting to it."

"Wow," was all Gabby could think to say, but it was a sincere "wow". *An emerald? Who would have thought?*

"I just don't have the right tools," Lai muttered feverishly.

"Maybe dynamite?" Gabby responded with a polite expression of inquiry on her face.

"Your turn will come," Lai promised before walking out of the room.

She returned a moment later carrying a gray metal toolbox, knelt on the floor, flipped the lock and pulled out a chisel, mallet and a set of clamps. Securing the globe between the clamps, Lai took the chisel and mallet and set to work.

The room was silent except for the sound of Gabby's tortured breathing and the tap, tap, tap of the chisel against the globe.

Gabby bit down on her lip 'til she drew blood.

Nothing happened.

"Aiee!" Lai threw back her head and screamed her frustration.

The hair on the back of Gabby's neck rose. The woman was out of control.

Lai threw down the mallet and chisel, her face contorted with rage.

"The globe will have to wait. Rest assured the emerald will be mine. But in the meantime, I think it's time to deal with you. And when I get through with you, I guarantee Christopher won't find you attractive."

I really, really don't like the sound of this.

Once more she glided from the room.

Scratch. Scratch.

Gabby turned toward the door.

Christopher stood in the shadow, one finger on his lips. In the other hand, a thin tool he'd used to jimmy the lock.

She closed her eyes in relief. She'd never been so happy to see anyone in her whole life.

Lai slithered back into the room. She carried what looked like a perfume bottle. Her eyes were so dilated they looked black.

"I have been saving this for a special occasion. Do you know what's in this vial?"

Gabby could only shake her head, mesmerized as if staring at a cobra doing a slow dance before it struck as Lai waved the bottle back and forth in a sensual movement, slowly pulling out the stopper.

"I do, Lai." Christopher stepped between the two women.

The stopper dropped to the floor.

"You!" Her breath came out in a hiss. "How did you find me?"

He took another step forward. "Oh come now, Lai. Do you really think you can keep secrets from me?"

Lai held the bottle in front of her like a lighted torch. "Stay back. I meant it for your whore, but I would have no problem ruining your pretty face."

"The only whore in this room is you." He glanced at the vial then back at Lai. "I see you are up to your old tricks. If memory serves that was what caused us to part company. I would have thought by now you would have outgrown your need to star as the villain in a cheap B movie. You always were overly dramatic."

His expression bored, he watched her. Only his eyes betrayed his alertness. The back of his hands rested on his hips. With his fingers, he motioned Gabby toward the door.

"You always were too soft." Lai's lip curled in a sneer.

"And you were always a heartless bitch."

"One that is going to take great satisfaction in marring that handsome face. I was going to kill you, but I think I'll let you live. And when I'm through with you, I'll let you watch me kill your cow of a fiancée, if you can see anything." Her eyes glittered with hatred. Smoke rose from the vial, the acid inside hissing like a snake.

For just one moment she looked at him with real regret, anguish shining out of her beautiful brown eyes. "I loved you. I thought you loved me. Together we could have ruled the world."

"You have to have a heart to love someone. Yours withered and died a long time ago."

As she raised her arm, he crouched.

"Hello, anyone home?"

Startled, Lai glanced at the door where Aunt Tam stood.

Faster than a panther, Christopher pulled the stiletto from its sheath in his sock and threw it. It buried itself in Lai's arm.

Her hand jerked and the acid flew in her face.

She screamed in anguish.

The floor smoked and holes dotted the carpet as droplets of the deadly chemical rained around Lai.

Christopher flinched. He started forward. "I'll get you to the hospital, Lai."

She backed away from him still screaming. "You have killed me."

He reached out his hand. "Lai."

She kept backing away screaming. "I curse you and your children and your children's children." She pulled the stiletto out of her arm, causing the blood to flow like a river down her arm and drip to the floor, the bright scarlet blotches mingling with the turquoise oriental carpet.

He leaped toward her but before he could reach her she buried the stiletto in her own heart.

As her last breath slipped away, he murmured, "Go in peace and begin your next cycle of life free of the scars that twisted your heart." With two fingers, he touched his forehead then his heart.

Gently, he laid Lai on the floor, walked to the couch, picked up a blue silk afghan and placed it over her mutilated form.

He straightened then turned toward Tamara and Gabriella. Tam was untying Gabriella's hands.

Gabriella moved them and winced.

"Gabriella?"

She looked at him her face expressionless, distant.

An almost physical wave of pain washed over him. What the hell had he expected?

Tremors of reaction shook Gabby's body.

"Get her home, Aunt Tam. I'll take care of things here."

Tamara nodded.

"Thanks." Fatigue roughened his voice. He gave her a quick smile. Gabriella had already turned away.

Tamara paused at the door. "Should I call the judge?" She was really asking whether Christopher Saint or The Tiger was going to deal with this.

Christopher sighed. "Yes, you better call him."

* * * * *

Several hours later, he pulled in front of Aunt Tam's. Cutting the ignition, he leaned his head against the headrest of the car and let his body relax and his mind drift back over the last few hours.

Things could have been a lot worse. The judge showed a sharpness and acumen that had stunned Christopher.

After he told him what happened, the judge had summed it up neatly, "You've got two eyewitnesses that will swear it was self-defense so you've got nothing to worry about. It will be a nine-day wonder, but I'll keep the lid on the newspapers as much as possible. This is New Orleans after all. The city's seen far worse."

The hardest part had been when Lai's lover came in. Thank God the body had been removed. Becka had been inconsolable. If she'd seen what the acid had done to her lover's face…He shuddered then gave a wry smile. When she found out Lai had no family and there would be no one coming forward to claim her sizeable fortune, it would go a long way toward assuaging her hurt.

Of course the courts would get a lot of Lai's money, but knowing Lai as he did, he was sure there was a fortune in diamonds, currency and pictures strewn around the apartment that would keep Becka in comfort for the rest of her life.

Christopher got slowly out of the car. His bones creaked. It wouldn't surprise him to look in the mirror and find his hair gray. He felt a hundred years old.

Reaching over, he picked up the crystal that sat in the seat beside him.

Who would have thought this seemingly harmless globe would have been a catalyst for so much destruction. No. The globe couldn't be blamed for that. Man, or in this case woman, had brought it all on herself.

He trudged down the cobblestone walk toward the house. Looking up, he saw Aunt Tam waiting at the door. She hugged him briefly, globe and all. "Everything all right?"

He nodded. "I could use a drink."

"Why don't you take the globe on out to the solarium and I'll have one ready for you when you get back."

Giving a mental groan, he nodded.

He walked through the house and out the back door into the solarium. Lush exotic scents assailed him. The sun had not quite set and the red and purple hues painted a beautiful backdrop to the verdant greenery around him.

He sat the ball in its holder, turned around and saw her.

She sat on the bench watching him. He took a step toward her and she stood up. When he reached for her she stepped back.

"You changed your shirt."

He nodded. "In the car, before I left."

"When you stepped away from Lai, you were covered in her blood just as the crystal prophesied. Only I thought it was your blood that would be shed."

His lips lifted at the corners. "I'm very glad it wasn't."

"You loved her." Her voice and eyes were flat, the normal glitter in her sapphire orbs extinguished.

He looked at her face and shook his head. His Nordic queen had taken a bit of a beating. One eye had puffed up and four scratches stood out vividly on her cheek from Lai's talon-like nails.

He reached a finger toward her cheek, but she turned her head.

"At one time, I was…"

Pain flashed in her eyes and she bit down hard on her lip.

He continued, "Enamored and very much in lust. But no, I've never loved her. What finished us for good and all was when I found out she'd thrown acid in a young woman's face for looking at me. Whatever desire I felt for her shriveled and died at that moment and never returned. I had despaired of ever finding a love like that of Aunt Tam and Uncle James. And then I met you.

"I've only loved, and will love, one woman in my lifetime and that's you."

A trace of color crept into her cheeks.

He reached over and took her left hand. It lay limp in his, but she didn't pull it away. That was all the encouragement he needed.

He touched the emerald on her finger. "I see you are

wearing my ring." He ran his fingers lightly back and forth over hers, his smile intimate. "And I have it on very good authority you've been shopping for wedding dresses."

He leaned toward her. "I would very much like to think this means you've decided to marry me.

"I know I'm no bargain, but I promise you I'll make you happy." His warm hands pressed against her cool ones.

Gabby's heart began a rhythmic thud against her chest. What woman could possibly resist this man, who was as sexy as sin, and loved her? But she had to. There were a few more things that had to be worked out for their future's sake.

"I believe Christopher Saint could do just that, but what's to become of The Tiger?"

He slid his arms around her. "Figured that out did you? I knew it was just a matter of time."

She could have sworn there was pride in his voice.

"Determined to make an honest man of me are you?"

She arched her brows, but held her silence.

He drew her hand to his lips and kissed it. "Dear one, The Tiger knew his days were numbered when he met you. I have no doubt who will be the tigress of our pride."

She maintained her silence.

He gave a small laugh of surrender. "Other than the crystal, I haven't stolen a thing since I met you." He gave a devilish grin that made his green eyes sparkle more than the stone on the pedestal or the one on her finger.

It caused her poor heart to miss a beat. "Except perhaps my heart."

The words were almost inaudible and if Christopher hadn't had impeccable hearing he would have missed them.

Encouraged, he continued, "I have a nice little import-export shop on the waterfront. And front used to be the proper term, but lately I've been building up my business." He turned serious. "We won't ever be rich. I have an obligation."

She placed a finger on his lips and looked him in the eyes. "I know."

He kissed it. "Woman, leave me some secrets."

She gave him a look as old and mysterious as time.

He had no idea what she was thinking but it made him uneasy.

Then it was her turn to be serious. "What about the curse Lai placed on us?"

"Let's hope your green ball will protect us."

You believe the legend then?"

"I believe it." His voice was flat. Then he visibly shook himself like a dog coming out of water. "So don't keep me waiting, what's it to be? Will you marry me?"

Her carnal smile promised all sorts of wondrous delights. Christopher forgot to breathe. She threw her arms around him, drew his head down and sealed her troth.

Epilogue

The wedding made the society and the gossip columns. Tamara, who had taken to writing the gossip column like a duck to water, had written a commentary.

The bride, beautiful as a Nordic queen, was given away by her father, Police Sergeant Bell from Springfield, IL.

She did not mention that after a quiet little chat that involved Christopher's life as an orphan she had a feeling that the unyielding policeman might be willing to bend a bit with his new son-in-law.

Accompanying the stalwart father was Ms. Agnes Brown, dispatcher for the Springfield Police Department.

The bride's maid of honor, Miss Amy Cooper, wore a pastel pink designer gown.

Billy Baker was the best man. From the way the best man and maid of honor were seen dancing together, this reporter can't help wondering if another wedding will be in the offing.

Father Greg Fields flew in from India.

Mr. John Paul Adams of North Carolina was in attendance, bringing to the reception vintage refreshment that made the guests quite merry.

Also in attendance was Mr. James Smith, who works for the local taxi company.

The couple left for a romantic evening tour of the city in Mr. Mike Reese's horse-drawn carriage with complimentary roses and champagne.

What she didn't mention was that, during the carriage ride, the dear girl had handed her boy his groom's gift, a piece of paper he never expected to see, his mother's birth certificate. How she'd found it...well that was another story. Suffice it to say her new daughter-in-law had all the makings of a top-notch reporter.

All in all one of the most memorable weddings this city has seen in years.

Other Books by the Author

Nonfiction
Flower Gardens and More
Power Stones

Time-travel Romance
Sundial

Young Adult Series
 Mutants:
Love, Lattes, and Mutants
Love, Lattes, and Danger
Love, Lattes, and Angel
Hunter:
Vampire Island
Moon Watchers
Vampire Bay
Cats of Catarau:
Shardai
Akasha
Makita

Young Adult
Sunset
Minder
Odin Cats
Ghost For Sale

Romantic Suspense
Queen of Diamonds

Anthologies
A Matter of Taste
Parallels: Felix Was Here

Author Note:
If you enjoyed *The Crystal,* please consider leaving a review.

I can be found at:
https://twitter.com/Sandra_Cox
https://facebook.com/SandraCox.Author/
http://tinyurl.com/zj7pbgt

The Crystal by Sandra Cox

Made in the USA
San Bernardino, CA
15 January 2017